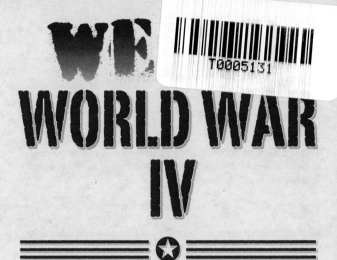

WE DARE
WORLD WAR
IV

edited by
Sean Patrick Hazlett

WEIRD WORLD WAR IV

This is a work of fiction. All the characters and events portrayed in this book are fictional, and any resemblance to real people or incidents is purely coincidental.

A Baen Books Original

Baen Publishing Enterprises
P.O. Box 1403
Riverdale, NY 10471
www.baen.com

ISBN: 978-1-9821-9240-2

Cover art by Kurt Miller

First printing, March 2022
First mass market printing, January 2023

Distributed by Simon & Schuster
1230 Avenue of the Americas
New York, NY 10020

Library of Congress Control Number: 2021053642

Printed in the United States of America

10 9 8 7 6 5 4 3 2 1

Dedication

This volume is dedicated to three people who've made a difference in my life. They aren't the only ones who've made an impact—there are far too many to list here. I'm dedicating this volume to these three in particular because I wanted to honor two who have passed and encourage another who is going through a rough patch.

The first person is my brother-in-arms, Captain Ralph J. Harting III (1976–2005), who rode honorably with the Blackhorse Regiment in the sands of Mesopotamia. You sacrificed your life so that others could live. One day, I hope to share a pint with you at Fiddler's Green where the souls of cavalrymen rest forever. Allons!

The second is Mike Resnick, who passed in early 2020. A legend in the genre, Mike always made a point of giving back to the science fiction and fantasy community by taking new writers and editors under his wing. I consider myself one of his "writer children" as do several of the authors in this collection. I owe a great deal of my publishing success to his mentorship and support. Mike's advice and encouragement were instrumental in bringing this project to life. Without his guidance, this anthology and the one that preceded it would not have been possible. Fare thee well, old friend.

The third is Walter Kinsey, whom I consider one of the most inspiring people I've ever met. Not only is he one of the smartest people I know, but also he has a profound ability to bring out the best in other people and make them shine. He was always there for me when I needed him, and I hope this note makes him smile as he and his family fight through yet another daunting trial that hopefully will have passed by the time this book reaches him. God bless you, brother.

CONTENTS

WEIRD
WORLD WAR
IV

PREFACE

Sean Patrick Hazlett

When Alfred Werner asked Albert Einstein in a 1949 interview what weapons he thought nations would use in World War III, Einstein replied, "I don't know. But I can tell you what they'll use in the Fourth—rocks!"

Einstein's response assumed World War III would usher in an atomic Armageddon. Yet there are many plausible futures in which the Third World War's combatants might limit or avoid using nuclear weapons long enough to fight a Fourth World War. This volume explores Einstein's nightmare of the war beyond the next war of atomic annihilation as well as less apocalyptic, but sometimes even more disturbing, World War IV futures.

More interestingly, the exploration of these narratives not only reveals the horrifying visions of the war beyond the next one, but also the anxieties and tensions associated with our own unique place in history. The cultural products of an age often bear the hallmarks of that time period, whether conscious, subconscious, or unconscious. One of the most fascinating things about putting together this anthology was how often its stories had more to say about the current social milieu than the worlds each writer had created.

Composed in the wake of the great pandemic year, many of these tales highlight several common themes. Whether a particular story leans to the political right or left, more often than not, it expresses distrust of public institutions and modes of economic governance. On the right, this is often manifest as suspicion of governmental institutions and the establishment media, frustration with bureaucracy, complaints about cancel culture, opposition to identity politics, and alarm at the aggressive behavior of a rising and increasingly assertive China. On the left, this wariness is most often associated with critiques of modern capitalism, resistance against nativist ideologies like Trumpism, and support for pro-indigenous movements. But at its core, all sources of grievance tend to be in opposition to, rather than in support of, current political or economic trends—a focus on what divides versus what unites us.

All the artists in this book ran through the great gauntlet of 2020—a year in which intense political polarization and civil unrest peaked at the same time a lethal pathogen rampaged throughout the globe, killing over five million souls as of November 2021. It was a moment in history when nearly all institutions failed to live up to expectations.

Federal, state, and local governments either overreacted with liberty-restricting lockdowns that destroyed many small businesses or minimized the virus's contagion and lethality to save these operations, accelerating the coronavirus's spread. In March 2020, some public health officials downplayed the importance of wearing masks, then reversed their stance once manufacturers were able to supply enough of them for medical professionals and other first responders. The Chinese leadership suppressed information about the coronavirus and hoarded medical supplies early in the outbreak, exposing just how vulnerable global supply chains were to the whims of the Chinese government.

It is not surprising that trust in public institutions greatly eroded in 2020—governments displayed staggering incompetence, the media sensationalized and distorted information, small businesses failed, and people suffered. The Chinese government's actions put the fragility and vulnerability of the global supply chain into stark relief. It is therefore not surprising that many people, Americans in particular, exited 2020 with a profound mistrust in their public institutions—a mistrust showcased in many of the stories in this anthology.

And yet this extreme level of polarization was eminently predictable. It is endemic to a sort of cultural PTSD following fifteen years of self-sorting and information filtering on the Internet. In fact, as far back as 2012, Eli Pariser's *The Filter Bubble* warned that the United States would only become more polarized over time. The advent of social media coupled with personalized search algorithms have had over fifteen years to hive off individual Americans into increasingly distant and politicized silos to the point that those on the political right and left often no longer consume the same news or speak the same political language. All the coronavirus did was put the cumulative effect of a decade-and-a-half process of self-selection and confirmation bias in stark relief.

And yet amid the madness of the 2020 pandemic, there was a glimmer of hope. Before most Americans even knew what the coronavirus was, it took Moderna just two days in January 2020 to design a vaccine and roughly a year for people to begin getting vaccinated. This was a tremendous testament to the efficiency and effectiveness of the partnership between private and public entities. The lockdowns demonstrated to employers and millions of workers that mind-numbing commutes wasting hours of workers' time and negatively impacting their productivity and mental health were no longer necessary as many jobs could easily be done remotely. As in any crisis, humanity adapted and overcame many of these challenges.

While the story of the 2020 pandemic is yet to be written, the myriad histories of World War IV are now in your hands. How will the survivors emerging from World War III's radioactive slagheaps fight the next war? Will they wage it with sticks and stones . . . and sorcery? Or will they use more refined weapons, elevating lawfare to an art and unleashing bureaucratic nightmares worse than death? Will they struggle against each other, interdimensional invaders, or the Great Old Ones themselves? What horrors from the desolate darkness might slither into the light? Wipe away the ashes of civilization and peer into a pit of atomic glass to witness the haunting visions of World War IV from today's greatest minds in science fiction, fantasy, and horror.

DEEP TROUBLE

Jonathan Maberry

I

It was built to never be found.

It had no official name.

It didn't even have a real code name. Nothing that was ever devised by a committee or used in budget meetings. Certainly nothing on the Net. Back when there was a Net.

Now there was that big silence except for the propaganda flash-news. Theirs. Ours.

Nothing about the facility ever made it into those media bursts.

Not one word about what we built at 47°9' S 123°43' W. Aside from that, there's nothing to see for thousands of miles. We built the facility near the oceanic pole of inaccessibility, which is the point in the South Pacific most distant from land. One of the reasons it can't be found is no one would ever think to look there, and even if they did, why would they waste resources to search so vast an empty space of ocean? More to the point, why would they haul UUVs or manned DSRVs all that way and risk losing

7

them in parts of the sea floor no one has ever bothered to map? After all, there is no strategic value to that part of the ocean. The war wrapped itself around the whole world, and the few skirmishes that took place in the nearest continents of Antarctica and South America were minor and of no real strategic importance.

So, no one ever found our facility.

I wonder how the war might have gone if they had.

II

My name is Thomas Hope. And, yes, the irony of my surname is not lost on me. It's been a source of humor since college. More so since the war.

I was brought to the project in the war's fourth year. After the Battle of Toronto. New York was still burning back then, and D.C. was six months away from becoming the glowing hole in the map that it is now.

I was still down in Bunker 182, on a research project for the Unified Nations Department of Defense when a couple of creepy feds in suits showed up. They took me to an interview room, locked the door, and placed a cloister network in all the corners, around the door, and by the window. It was a new generation of that anti-intrusion tech, and it essentially put us in a bubble. Nothing we said could be heard by anyone.

The two agents were different genders and ethnicities, but there was something oddly uniform about them. Beyond the dark suits, white shirts, and ties. Both had a somewhat sickly pallor—an olive complexion that was almost a faint green, as if they spent far too much time under fluorescent lights and none at all out in the sun.

"Dr. Hope," said the Colombian, "thank you for agreeing to talk with us." She gave her name as Agent Blanco, her partner was Agent Black. White and Black. Cute.

"Sure," I said, and left it there. I learned long ago that the less you say to these types, the better.

"One of your early reports came to our attention," said Agent Black.

"Oh?"

"It was the one you wrote for the class you took on *Alternative Strategies for Extreme Responses.*"

I almost smiled. "I took that class as a joke."

They looked at me but did not smile. At all.

"That *paper* was definitely a joke," I protested.

"We found it to be quite intriguing," said Agent Blanco.

I did smile then, waiting for the punchline.

"*Quite* intriguing," said Agent Black.

"Are you out of your fucking minds?" I said. Or maybe yelled. "It's a purely hypothetical treatise on upping the game in an otherwise no-win scenario—"

"Like the current military situation," said Blanco. "The Unified Nations of the Americas and the Euro-Asian Grand Alliance are beating each other to death."

"Sure, I read the news, but—"

"The death toll has not gone below one million deaths per week in three years," said Black.

"Believe me, I know," I said. "Half the guys I went to Harvard with are dead, or MIA. Or in some rad-burn ward or biohazard away-camp. Why do you think I applied to work here? But, guys, that paper is an intellectual exercise. I was exploring the ethics of extreme reaction in an otherwise no-win scenario. It has no basis in reality any more than if I suggested sacrificing to war gods like Ares or Xipe Totec, Agasaya, Cao Lỗ, or Nehit and . . ." I paused and studied their faces. "You *do* know that those are gods from dead religions, right? I mean mythological gods. Not actual historical figures?"

They had the kind of poker faces you only see with top level feds.

"Wait," I said, "what the hell's going on here?" I demanded. "There's nothing in that paper that goes beyond the hypothetical. I mean . . . anyone can see that."

"Unless there is," said Blanco.

"Unless there is," agreed Black.

III

There's probably a joke in there somewhere. Something with a punch line. But I wasn't laughing. Neither were Blanco and Black.

Actually, I can't recall the last time I heard someone laughing.

A real laugh, I mean. One with good humor, innocence, a sense of shared lightness.

No. Try as I might, I really can't.

"It's just a *myth*," I said. "Worse, it's something some idiot dreamed up over a century ago. It's not real. It's fake."

Blanco and Black stared at me for a five count.

"Or not," said Blanco.

Black just smiled. One of those kinds of smiles feds give you when they know a lot more about something you don't want to know *any* of.

I tried to compose an adequate response. By summoning all of my years of education, my high school captaincy of the debate team, and two PhDs, I did manage a rather hearty, "But . . . but . . . but . . ."

IV

The agents took me that afternoon. It was ostensibly by my choice, or perhaps a lack of a demonstrable objection. Frankly I was too shocked and scared and confused to object. I just went.

They didn't take me back to my flat.

"Your stuff has been packed and forwarded to the ship," said Blanco.

"Ship? Wait . . . what? You did that already?"

"We had faith that you would agree to accompany us, Dr. Hope," said Black. "We took the liberty of sending a team to take care of things."

I was angry, offended, and terrified in about equal measures, and it took a whole lot for me not to blow up at them. Fear kept it all clamped down. So, what I said was, "Aboard *what*, though?"

Their answer was a matching set of bland and uninformative smiles.

Their Buzz was a killer. A late model hard-shell jetlift with some kind of max-thrust package. It lifted from the parking lot with an almost eerie silence, swung around above the faux ramen noodle shop that was the cover over our bunker in Chula Vista, and then shot like an arrow through the skies toward the Camp Pendleton joint-use base. The trip should have taken half an hour, but there was no traffic slowing us and the AI pilot had the pedal down. We landed on a pad surrounded by automatic sentry guns as well as a foot patrol.

During the short walk from the Buzz to the sea transport, I could see troops running in formation as their sergeants called cadence. It was disheartening to see how many of the soldiers were too young for this, but the Joint Presidents had agreed to lower the draft age to fifteen, and there was talk of going to fourteen if we kept losing battles like Anchorage and Seattle. Right now, despite the preponderance of AI drones, smart-tanks, Boston Dynamics mecha-wolves, and orbital missile platforms, we had a standing army of over seventeen million. Sounds like a lot, but it's not nearly enough. Not by a long mile.

Nobody actually said that we were losing the war. Not out loud. But there was no other way to count the numbers. The EAGA had forty-three million human troops. Our only edge was better AI and drones, but now that Germany, Korea, and Japan had joined their side, they had all those tech geniuses cranking out generation after generation of mechanized combat machines and next-gen exoskeletons. And they had the bodies. India and China alone were bad enough, but now the *Novyy Sovetskiy*—the New Soviet Union—was edging out of neutrality and was almost certainly going to join EAGA.

We were, to put it in precise technical terms, fucked.

I say all this because it's important to understand how desperate we were. This was the Fourth World War, and the second in forty years. The world had taken severe damage during WWIII but had just begun to show signs of recovery. Fewer superstorms, only eight F-5 tornados in the States, and some yards gained in repairing the bigger of the four ozone holes.

World War Four, though . . . ?

Fuck.

There was no trace of either side giving a cold, wet shit about the environment, the ozone layer, the air quality, or anything else except winning.

What was that old line from Albert Einstein? "I do not know with what weapons World War III will be fought, but World War IV will be fought with sticks and stones."

So, he was off by one war. If we do manage to survive this one and if there's another, it will be between retro cavemen bashing each other with clubs. No doubt. Earth is resource-poor, diseased, battered, suffering from existential PTSD, and probably past fixing.

Yeah, proud to be a citizen.

I boarded the sea transport, the USS *Whipsaw*, which was one of the newer expeditionary fast transport craft. This generation of EPFs could skim over the waves at a mind-boggling sixty-four miles per hour. But it's a teeth-rattling and spine-jarring trip, and we had three hours of it before they handed what was left of me and my possessions over to the crew of the USS *Hagfish*, a *Tate*-class fast attack sub.

The Hag, as she was known by the crew, went deep and

stayed deep for a long damn time. Thousands of miles. It was a boat designed for combat, not for comfort, and we spent weeks in that metal coffin. Luckily claustrophobia isn't one of my fears. I have plenty of others, though, and discovering that some of them were valid was no damn joke at all.

We reached an island that did not exist.

Well, I mean it *did*, but it was ten years old, a spike of land shoved up by tectonic activity miles beneath the surface. In an area where the depth should have been a consistent three miles, it's staggering to contemplate the force of nature required to lift an entire mountain range from the seabed and push the highest peak ninety feet above the surface. The other peaks were stacked down in a winding row, and most deep enough that shipping would be safe. If, in fact, any ships ever came out here. Which they did not.

You see, this spot is truly a pole of inaccessibility. It doesn't lead from anywhere to anywhere along any sensible current, wind pattern, or line of convenience. No one crosses it on the way to some even moderately useful destination.

Except now it was itself the destination.

V

I had a lot of time to think on that trip.

Maybe too much time.

The paper I'd written back in college had started out as a joke. Something I proposed to my fellow grad students during a very drunken night at The Thirsty Scholar on Beacon Street. Not everyone at our table was familiar with the source of my proposal, but enough of them were that the idea caught fire. We handed it back and forth as the beers and shots came and went. By the time I staggered out to find an autodrive cab, I had the whole thing in my head. It seemed both funny and clever.

In the morning, nursing an epic hangover but still enthused, I began wondering if it would be right for the *Alternative Strategies for Extreme Responses* class. Our pending assignment was a bit of a challenge. War was already brewing ever since Europe entered into a union with Asia, resulting in a substantial reduction in trade with the US and its own partners in North and South America. We'd already formed the Unified Nations of the Americas, with the kinds of trade deals that were a natural part of such an agreement. EAGA—the Euro-Asian Grand Alliance—was really no different, but how many times has the human race needed a truly inarguable reason to go to war? It's always land, resources, money, or religion.

The assignment was to take a worst-case scenario of such a conflict, imagine the costs and penalties for losing a world war of that kind, and propose a Hail Mary play that would completely change the conflict's dynamics, more than level the playing field, and have the effect of a total cultural shock to the other side. Theoretical assignments like that usually result in a kind of Fantasy Football for warring nations. I read some of the other papers, and there were things like using weaponized *Yersinia pestis*; using a time machine to bring General Patton, Alexander the Great, or Hannibal into the mix; or introducing Godzilla or the Transformers. Stuff like that. And mine was no different.

Or, it should have been no different.

When I asked how in the hell the military ever got hold of my paper, let alone read it, Blanco and Black seemed to suddenly go deaf. When I tried the same question on the captain of the *Hagfish* or the facility's liaison who was to conduct me down to the underwater platform, both played the "you'll be briefed at the appropriate time" card.

And so, still terribly confused and more than a little terrified, I sat in the sub as it descended.

VI

The island was not where we were heading, though.

The military had wasted no time bolting together some prefab units that had been built for general undersea research but had been abandoned when the war started. Even so, it was impressive as hell. After a night of clinging to the island with the devoted passion of someone who'd spent far too long in a submarine, I finally got some sleep and was more or less human in the morning.

A smaller submersible took me down below the sun-kissed waves into the crystal clear Pacific waters. We left the sunlight and blue sky behind, though, and descended into the deep. Darkness soon swirled up around us, almost as if the sub was floating down into a sea of liquid shadows. The effect was highlighted by the big LED screens inside, which gave the illusion of picture windows.

High-def cameras designed to work in ultralow light allowed me to see everything.

And what I saw took my breath away.

The mountain range that had been thrust upward from the sea floor was not in any way normal. That was obvious from the beginning. Gloriously or terrifyingly obvious, and it wasn't at all easy to decide where I landed on that.

The upper part of the range seemed composed of a mix of porous volcanic rock blended with chunks of granite. But very quickly it became apparent that the granite was not natural. Instead of sections of living rock ripped to pieces by the incalculable forces of tectonic movement, there was a strange and unnerving sense of order to what I saw.

First there seemed to be towers. That's the only word that fit. Massive spikes of stone whose pattern was too orderly, with precise angles and the suggestion of arches. However these were so heavily encrusted with coral, barnacles and other sea growth that the rational mind kept wanting to assign a natural cause to them. And it called to mind other such finds, such as the submerged structures discovered off the coast of Cuba at the beginning of the new millennia. Sonar images showed pictures of great symmetrical and geometric structures covering an area of almost two square kilometers, and at a depth of about seven hundred meters. The skeptics—and there are always legions of those vying to be talking heads and voices of reason on news programs and documentaries—said that the site could not be what it looked like. That it was too deep to be a lost city and moreover far too old, because for any city of human design to have sunk that low in the water would have taken at least fifty thousand years. This, despite ancient tales passed down by Maya and local Yucatecos of an ancient island that vanished beneath the waves.

And in the early 2000s, off the west coast of Bimini, side-scan sonar and sub-bottom profiling revealed a line of rectangular blocks thirty meters down. Its similarity to the Cuban structures sparked a lot of debate about the discovery of a lost civilization, possibly even Atlantis. The skeptics galloped in to insist that they were merely towers of natural rock that collapsed in a straight line. And yet it was a very straight line, and the blocks were unusually— some might say inarguably—orderly. And these, too, were dated to about ten thousand years ago.

However the similarities between these ruins paled into meaninglessness as the sub went down. The pilot turned on powerful floodlights that revealed great shapes that no wave or erosion could possibly have formed.

There, stuck into the slopes of the newly formed mountain range were blocks of colossal size. They were astonishing—far bigger even than those found at Göbekli Tepe in Turkey or the massive blocks discovered at the rock quarry near the Temple of Jupiter in Lebanon—the largest of which was over one thousand tons. None, in fact, of history's megalithic structures came close to the sheer scale of what lay broken and tumbled along the slopes of this new mountain range. And that scale was difficult to comprehend. The mind rebels against things on that scale. Sanity teeters on the edge of belief because something that monstrously huge plunged one's own sense of self and worth into the infinitesimal. The first astronauts to do an orbit around Jupiter must have felt as I did then. We are not prepared for anything like this. Some of the blocks were fully three-quarters the height of the Empire State Building.

And as we descended, the scale increased.

There were other shapes, too, and I became aware that what I beheld was not a single structure but a city.

A city.

And such a city!

The shapes and order of the buildings spat in the eye of Euclidian, spherical, or hyperbolic geometry. It insisted on existing in its own warped set of mathematics. And in doing so offended the eye and the mind because of some frightening inconstancy. A dish-shaped rock viewed one moment seemed to lose its concavity when viewed from another angle, and became convex so thoroughly that the beams of light traced it as such. Pillars were immutably solid until whale sharks swam through them, but beams of light were stopped at the spaces through which they passed.

I began hyperventilating, and the first mate rushed to my aid and fitted me with an oxygen mask. He even held my hand as if I was a child awakened by thunder.

"Take it slow, Doc," said the mate. "It hits everyone like that the first time." He paused and looked at the cyclopean walls and arches. He had that same greenish sickly pallor as Blanco and Black, and now I wondered if it was an actual medical symptom shared by those who had witnessed what I just saw. No doubt my own complexion was likely that of sour milk. "Second, third, fourth, twentieth time, too. And don't think closing your eyes will change it. It's always going to be in your head."

I looked at him as he said this and saw that his eyes were a bit too wide and unblinking, and his face had a greasy sheen of fear sweat on it. I slowly withdrew my hand, mumbling a vague thank you. In truth, though, he scared me. The man looked more than rattled. He looked like he'd stared into Nietzsche's abyss and had gotten the full stare in return. That's what I saw in his face and I did not doubt that I was right. Instead of becoming familiar with what lay outside, he was being driven mad from constantly having to see the thing.

And I recalled a similar look in the eyes of the captain.

We spoke no more until the sub reached the platform.

VII

In any other moment in my life I would have been absolutely dazzled by the platform. It was a wonder of modern mechanics. It had lovely curved lines and was brilliantly lit—but after what I'd just witnessed I barely registered something ordinary man had constructed.

The sub docked, and there was some business with pressure adaptation and medical exams. It might have been part of a dream, though, because now my only reality was what lay beyond. Even with the windowless steel walls I could *feel* it there. Not merely the stunning size of it but all of the thousands of unanswered questions that crowded through my brain like gophers trying to flee a flooded den. My thoughts clawed and scrambled and fought with one another because everything on the other side of the wall was simply not possible.

Blocks of that size could not have been quarried by human hands. There was no way. And it recalled to my mind that many of the megalithic structures we already knew about—the Great Pyramid of Giza, the Sphinx, the Catal Huyuk, and others—were built by methods that modern science has yet to understand.

But this ...

As a scientist it is against my faith in empiricism to use the word "impossible" to describe anything I can see or which can be measured. And yet ... I looked upon something that even the most extreme hypothesis could not begin to explain.

And it was here.

Here.

Goddamn it. Here.

I wish I had never written that fucking paper. I wish that I'd been a more sober student at the time and not indulged in juvenile pranks of that kind on my professors. The fact that it was well written and supported by as many sources and quotes as was possible did not help. It had been written as a joke.

Just a joke.

And now I—along with every other thinking creature on this planet—was the butt of a greater joke.

When the doctors were done with their routine examinations and I was left alone to get dressed in one of the facility's nondescript blue jumpsuits, I found I could not summon the energy to dress. I sat there in my underwear, fingers knotted together in my lap, and stared at the wall. Seeing the thing as clearly in my mind as if looking through a porthole.

"God almighty," I breathed, offering a prayer to a god in whom I had long since ceased to believe. "God save my soul."

VIII

They gave me time to recover without asking if I needed it. That alone said much about their own reactions—initial and ongoing.

Then an officer came to escort me to the main observation deck. There were two people there—a scientist and a soldier.

The former was Lieutenant General Malcolm Spears, who introduced himself as the Defense Department's director of special strategies. I didn't like the sound of that title one little bit. The latter was Dr. Carole Cantu, and she did not name her field of expertise. That worried me, too.

And both looked sick and greenish and haunted. I couldn't blame them.

"Tell me this is all a dream," I said.

Spears gave a thin smile. "Of a kind, I suppose. I mean, given the state of the world we're all living in, a nightmare."

"You're not joking," said Cantu bitterly. "Weekly death tolls greater than the total losses in any given war. An environment past the point of repair..."

"Sure," I said, "but this?"

We all looked at the massive flatscreens. Whatever cameras were feeding the image had to be hundreds or even thousands of meters back from the city in order to show so much of it. Tiny dots that I realized were submarines drifted through its sunken avenues.

"I can't believe you found a city," I said.

"*The* city," said Spears. "And we found it because of your paper."

"But it was a joke."

"Or," said Cantu, "it was inspired."

I shook my head, but she wasn't joking. "You're serious? I was drunk and passed out and dreamed it. I woke up and searched for stuff online and just borrowed it from an old short story. That's all. I never believed it was real."

"You dreamed it," said Spears.

"You dreamed it," said Cantu.

In exactly the same way.

"It can't be real," I protested. "It's from fiction."

Cantu looked at me with large, watery, unblinking eyes. "The writer dreamed it, too."

"No," I said.

They both smiled at me, then Spears said, "I suppose you're wondering why we brought you here."

"Of course. I'm a structural engineer and physicist. This is . . . so far beyond me."

"You dreamed it," repeated Cantu.

"Okay, but it was me drunk. It's not . . ."

"He sent the dream to you," said Spears.

I froze.

"*What . . . ?*"

"You were given an incredible gift," said Cantu. "Others received it. Writers, artists, filmmakers. Many others."

"Most dismissed it," said Spears. "Many went mad. A few turned it into art."

They looked at each other and smiled identical grins. Very large, with lots of wet teeth.

"The hell's going on here?" I demanded, backing up a step.

"*Iä! Iä! Cthulhu fhtagn,*" said Spears.

Now the whole moment seemed to freeze.

"What did you just say?"

"You were given the greatest gift," said Cantu. "You, at least, did not waste it. Your paper was included in the Department of Defense database along with all of your school records. We found it while doing a database search. And . . . we were so *happy*. Somehow the fiction and the images and the movies were so thoroughly buried in the arts that they were dismissed."

"Hidden in plain sight," said Spears. "Forest for the trees."

"But yours was there to be found," said Cantu. "As it *was* found."

Spears said something under his breath that seemed to be all consonants. An ugly word that belonged in fiction. Not in the real world.

"This is a fucking joke, right?" I cried.

"You were given the gift," said Cantu.

"Will you please stop *saying* that. It wasn't a gift. It was just a—"

"A prophecy," they both said in perfect and horrible synchronicity. "And we honor you for it."

"Your name will be spoken with reverence for ten thousand thousand years," said Spears.

"I—"

"Statues will be erected of you," said Cantu. "Thomas Hope, the great dreamer."

"No..."

"A saint of the oldest faith whose whisper has been heard by the Dreamer."

"No, this isn't about me, it's about winning the war."

They gave me that bright-eyed grin.

"The war doesn't matter," said Spears. "It's the last war anyway. Who cares who thinks they won?"

"What are you talking about? Of course we care. How could we—"

"The Dreamer will end all war," said Cantu.

I stabbed a finger toward the drowned city. "Are you out of your minds? You think *that* will bring peace?"

They looked at me in puzzlement, then they spoke together again.

"Peace? The Dreamer doesn't care about that. It's a human concept. He brings an end to *your* wars, your hunger, your pollution, your intolerance and hatred. All of that ends now. It's gone."

I kept backing away. "You're crazy."

"No," they said, "we're dreaming."

Beneath my feet the whole facility suddenly shook. I crouched down, terrified, as sparks exploded from computers, the overhead lights flickered wildly, and the steel walls buckled with screams of torture metal.

"The war is over," said Spears, his head cocked to one side as if listening. "All war is over."

"We need to get to shelter."

"We are sheltered in the arms of the Dreamer," said Cantu.

Then they both burst into tears. Not of pain or fear of the impending structural disaster. They clasped their hands in front of their faces and wept for joy. Sobbed with an exultation more profound than anything I have ever seen. It was so intense that it horrified me. Their eyes were so round and glaring. Their lips and teeth wet. Their skin an even more pronounced green.

"He wakes!" they cried. "The long dream is over."

There was another massive shock to the facility. On the screen, I could see massive towers falling, impossibly huge stones cracking apart. Mud and silt exploded upward and the whole core of the city seemed to burst apart in strange slow motion. Only it wasn't slow, it was simply that the city was so massive.

Then I saw something move within the crumbling city.

It rose. Unbearably titanic. And I knew—*knew*—that it was not more debris. This was something alive. And it rose, shaking off the thousand-ton blocks as if they were fleas. It rose and rose and rose and rose and filled the ocean. It was a monster of vaguely anthropoid outline, but with an octopus-like head whose face was a mass of feelers, a scaly, rubbery-looking body, prodigious claws on hind and fore feet, and long, narrow wings behind.

And even as I thought those words, I knew that I had read them years ago, in a short story. Not my words, nor maybe even the words of the author of that story. Or, perhaps, he had in fact dreamed them, too.

As I had.

God help me.

It rose and towered over everything, and nothing that beheld it could comprehend its sheer size and power.

Power.

Cantu and Spears were on their knees, laughing, beating their hands together, striking their own faces, tearing at their clothes in an unholy ecstasy of love and joy. Around the big room I saw soldiers, sailors, and technicians doing the same. And I heard their voices crying out in prayers. Not in English, or Spanish, or any language made to fit on the human tongue.

"*Iä! Iä! fhtagn ph' ah,*" they shrieked.

The dream is over.

I knew what those words meant.

I knew.

Because I was shouting them, too.

Iä! Iä! fhtagn ph' ah.

Iä! Iä! fhtagn ph' ah.

THE BIG WHIMPER
(THE FURTHER ADVENTURES OF REX, TWO MILLION CE)

Laird Barron

Playback interrupted. Assessing. Standby...

Quantum Fragment Record of Unknown Subject (1): —*There is neither beginning nor end, only an endless ring of time. These fleeting images, these tachyon darts of thought, originate from a location in the far-flung past, or across a divide of dark matter during an epoch yet to come.*

There is no time, no distance? No beginning, no end?

Cascade Failure. System Reset in 3...2...1...

Unknown Subject (2): *In the beginning, a hominid cracked two stones together and discovered fire. Fire drew you to a cave mouth on a cold night. You remember the soft flames, the scent of roasting elk, and how you slunk up into the cave, tail low, fangs bared. Starving. Canines have helped mankind fight other animals and men for a long time. You were right there, side by side for all the maiming and burning and conquering, muzzled in gore, ears pricked...*

System Resetting. Standby...

UNK (3): —*I snuffle-smell true-good. Enemies all*

around. Snap-bite! Breathe fire! Too many, too many. Breathe fire! Breathe . . .

System Reset Complete. Resume quantum playback:

We are surrounded by a forest. The canopy goes on for endless kilometers. Leaves drip in the gloomy coolness. Local time is a few minutes after sunrise, autumn of Two Million CE. I blink away the sensation I've nodded off and then returned to myself from across a gulf of eons and darkness.

A pale red light blinks behind my eye. A proximity alarm.

"—tell me your story, Spot," says the Haunter of the Wood. He's stated this request each time we meet. A ritual? A test? A figment of my increasingly disturbed subconscious?

"Spot is a slur. My name is Rex." I rest my haunches near a hollow log where I sleep at night.

The Haunter visits at random intervals; perhaps to probe my security measures. Today, he occupies a patch of underbrush. An unctuous shadow whose red eyes glimmer, reminiscent of my own warning beacon. What could the Haunter be? He (it?) shifts as ink spilled into water shifts; changing, cycling through forms that are vaguely monstrous. My powerful nose whiffs nothing, an absence of scent. I choose not to look closer despite the fact I'm able to perceive a spectrum of light frequencies. Sometimes, ignorance is best. I've learned this lesson through painful experience. I'm also worried my vision will rebound, only revealing myself.

"Tell me your story so far, Rex. The end of Act One, the beginning of Act Two."

I dislike the Haunter. His manner is overfamiliar. He might be dangerous. Possibly hostile. But I'm lonely.

"I was in the thick of a fight. World War Four. The tribes of Man squared off in a battle royale that raged for almost a decade."

"What about World War Three?"

"As expected—an exchange of nukes and everybody said oops. Peace reigned for a while. Until the world was ready for Four. Civilizations developed nanotechnology, continental missile defense systems, biological counteragents. That meant it would be a real slog."

"How did the war start?"

"Weren't you there?"

"Yes and no." The Haunter sounds coy. "I may have nodded off. Besides, I like how you tell it."

"How does any war start?" I say. "A pebble becomes a landslide."

"How did it end?"

"Deus ex Machina."

"The Gray. As in the Gray Eminence."

"Yes. Humans and their gallows humor."

We both know the story by heart:

One day, an object resembling a planetoid entered our solar system. The way a slug just sort of shows up on one's doorstep. It orbited Earth, and we soon discovered this planetoid was actually an invasion transport. Warring nations declared a truce and turned their attention to the heavens.

The aliens' gravitational weapons wreaked havoc. Next,

they disrupted the atmosphere by exciting global volcanic activity. Ash clouds blocked the sun, mimicking a nuclear winter. Human and animal populations were subsequently infected with a virulent pathogen via oxygen and water supplies. Infected organisms functioned as slaves of the invaders. Resistance was snuffed in its cradle. Instead of Armageddon, humanity curled into a ball and faded into oblivion.

"The world ended with a whimper," the Haunter says as though I've narrated aloud.

"Clever." I skip to the thrilling conclusion. "Several of my battalion who survived the initial chaos decided to make our exit in a blaze of glory. We rallied for a last stand against hordes of shambling zombies. My human mother wore scales of silver. Her guns cut apart a mountain. She'd overridden security protocols and brought my entire suite of combat systems online. I howled radioactive fire and our enemies charred. Before it got really good, the mountain fell on me."

"And you died," says the Haunter.

My internal warning light brightens. "Living entombment. Same difference, perhaps."

"*For the love of God, Montresor.* Yet, here you are. Relic of antiquity."

"Time passed, or so it appears. A spark animated me, and I revived. Dug through a few hundred million tons of rubble until I felt sunlight on my snout. Until I sniffed green grass and not decayed earth."

"You've been awake for how long?"

"A while." I refuse to admit the extent that my memory banks are fried. The Big Whimper may have been eons ago, but due to my decaying ability to discern subjective from objective time, I experience the war fresh every day. Sometimes, I can't escape the feeling it never really ended.

"The sun is your sun," the Haunter says. "However, the stars are no longer your stars. Nor the sky . . ."

"The land is old and new. Evil creeps through the forest. I've adapted."

"As it ever was," the Haunter says. "You are Rex. King of Dogs."

"I'm the king of nothing. Dogs have gone extinct."

"Wrong. Dingoes have returned to the southern continent. Painted dogs gather in the Sub-Saharan."

"Jackals and hyenas, too," I say with derision. "Foxes. Coyotes. None of these are proper canines. None are real dogs."

"Been around this world once or twice and have yet to encounter your like—the size of a horse and erudite; girded by titanium alloys and microcircuitry. You're *sui generis*. Good boy. Special boy. Are you *real*, though?"

"I bay at the moon. I roll in shit. The memory of every dog who ever lived flows in my blood."

"More metal than flesh. A mind is divided between animal and machine. Odd that your masters imbued intricacy of thought in a fluffy weapon."

"The masters worked in mysterious ways."

"What a woofing contradiction. Did Geppetto make you? Did the Blue Fairy bring you alive?"

"The poet who claimed to contain multitudes had nothing on me."

"In fact, I met Whitman," the Haunter says. "Late one night in his youth. Vectored a tachyon stream right into his consciousness. Ages before the Big Whimper, of course. When the world was less complicated."

This is a new conversational gambit. The alarm flashes faster, practically incandescent.

I play along. "Animal Heaven is hardly complicated. Creatures great and small struggle for survival as in the beginning before the advent of man. Simple, pure."

"Poor doggo, this isn't heaven. You aren't even aware of how many times you've given up the ghost. On each occasion of your death, you are painstakingly rebuilt. Renewed. Perhaps stronger. Yet the split in your consciousness remains. A crack in the database, as it were. You forget events which you should not."

"In addition to identifying roots and tubers, you're an expert in quantum computers?"

"Gaze inward and behold the truth of my observation."

Snorting, I initiate a search program. Lo and behold, I encounter a new data corruption in the neighborhood of a century prior. I say new because that "crack" in my database spreads slowly, yet inexorably. Checking the damage never occurs to me until the Haunter suggests I do so.

"See? You should perform internal diagnostics more often." The Haunter's tone indicates a smile. "Men are gone. Dogs are gone. The conquering devils are gone. Where did the Gray fuck off to, anyway?"

"Excellent question. I'll ponder it on my morning stroll . . ."

"Since you'll be out and about, I recommend a visit to Avaxia. She's entertaining a new prisoner you'll want to meet."

"The Crimson Empire is keeping prisoners these days?"

"A human. Quite mysterious."

No humans survived the last great war. At the last, entire populations lay in fruiting piles, deliquescing under a gray webbing that spanned continents. Humanity's cities were reclaimed by wilderness. Its bones embedded in the earth. However, it seems pointless to argue with a talking Rorschach pattern, so I grunt noncommittally.

"Oh, and Spot?"

"Yes?"

"Talking to yourself is never a positive sign." The Haunter's voice fades into the susurration of the leaves, the creaking branches. Familiar, disquieting, gone.

I count two minutes, then power down my plasma beam and sonic weaponry. The red light slows, dims, and fades as my pounding heart settles into a normal rhythm. It would be easy to say the hell with antiquated notions of obligation, tuck my nose under my tail, and have a snooze. I resist such canine instincts and prepare for travel.

Later that morning, I kill an elk the traditional way—I punch auxiliary servos, accelerate to 120 kilometers per hour, and scatter the herd. An old bull turns to fight. I shear off his head before his nervous system can process the information. Meat is fuel. Fuel will be necessary for the expedition to come.

I lope southwest, out of the forest and across broken terrain, and the earth changes. Boulders and sand and occasional dunes. The sand is as red as grains flowing from a titan's splintered hourglass. To the east, the reconfigured

Atlantic wallows, icy dark. Horrors roll in its depths, according to screeching gulls. Due west, more forests and plains. Bison have returned and saber-toothed cats to hunt them. Wetlands lie to the south—cypress jungles and everglades ruled by monstrous lizards and great predatory birds. Farther south spread lush, rotting jungles where I'd rather not tread for fear of the spiders, centipedes, and other, worse, slithering abominations. The analytical part of my consciousness protests the falsity of this strange world, the sterile, yet fecund nature of its composition into a diverse set of biomes. Biomes arranged meticulously as a biologist's terrarium . . .

Doubts plague me. Even at my best, I'd be ill equipped to grapple mysteries of weird biomes and vanished aliens. My mind threatens to spin in circles; chasing its tail, as it were. I'm forgetful and paranoid. The Haunter is correct—my repair protocols are miraculous, but the flaw originating at the quantum level, the core of my essence, may present an insurmountable obstacle. In that case, my consciousness will steadily degrade. I'll regress to a feral animal and sooner or later, die alone in this wilderness. Does it even matter? What is a dog without a master?

Onward through the desert. One paw in front of the next for lack of any better course of action. Eventually, conical mounds, scoured and bleached, thrust upward, borehole mouths pointed at the sun. Here is the northernmost colony of the Crimson, an empire that spans thousands of kilometers. Its formicating denizens detest the cold. Perhaps they'll call it quits here and expand no farther. Ravenous and bellicose are these devils. I fear they will adapt to harsher climes. And then woe unto the soft woodland creatures. I won't be able to live in my hollow log, that's for sure. Workers measure thirty centimeters, end-to-end. Warriors are conservatively double that. Armored in chitin and bearing venomous stingers. Their serrated mandibles are deadly sharp.

I rest at a marginally safe distance from a trio of the largest mounds—each six meters vertical, and similarly broad around the base. In this instance, "safe" merely indicates I'll stand a chance of burning a few ants before they shred me to a fine meal. Several warriors emerge and twitch their antennae agitatedly, but don't rush forward to attack. The dwellers of the mounds are in dread of fire and they've seen me bellow the lambent flames of my lost tribe. It's a shaky deterrent I prefer not to rely upon overmuch.

Sand vibrates under my paws. Grains form binary code—pointillist mosaics of quickly erased zeroes and ones. Simultaneously, a shrill whisper penetrates my consciousness. Thus, Princess Avaxia, who inhabits a cavern far beneath the surface, makes her presence felt.

Rex, lovely Rex. Your luxurious fur, caked in gore. Your succulent muscle, marbled with fat! Our warriors salivate with fury and lust. Speak with haste, O lovely-loathsome vertebrate. Hers is an unnerving harmony of many buzzing voices that causes me to reflexively scratch my ear.

"Greetings, Princess. My reactor is charged. My unholy fire is stoked. If your servants become too randy, I'll glass this entire region. I'll sink your mounds into the earth and bury you alive. Your children's children will glow in the dark."

That live burial threat sounds personal.

"Test me and find out."

We converse in friendship, Rex. We eagerly await the purpose of your visit. Speak, speak!

"I've come to examine your prisoner. Humans are a particular interest of mine."

Human? We have yet to determine the creature's species. Our experiments leave us with questions. This . . . being resembles Homo sapiens. *It does not smell as it should. It smells unnatural.*

Princess Avaxia's comments are intriguing. The colony's genetic memory, heightened by various mutations, is much longer than mine, extending to the arrival of the first ant while supercontinents had yet churned and steamed. She would recognize a human by sight and smell, to say nothing of her ability to extract the surface thoughts of sentient creatures.

I have an epiphany. "This being repels your attempts to pry into its mind. It's a blank slate."

A void. Beyond our reckoning.

"Where did you find this individual?"

Nearby, in a cavern. Our workers were excavating an egg chamber and broke into a cell.

"Immobile? Trapped? Damaged?"

Immobile, albeit not trapped. Inert, but undamaged. Hibernating. It is aware, yet refuses to communicate.

"Allow me to act as your consultant in this matter," I say.

After a long pause, she says, *Only because it amuses us. You may approach.*

I advance into the shadow of the tri-mounds. My weapons are primed. Death rays: sonic, laser, and plasma. Fangs powerful enough to rend the majority of earthly metals, naturally occurring or forged. Slash a hole through my hide or gouge my armor plating, nanobots will seal it; cut off my limb, those trusty nanobots will grow me another. Alas, there *are* limits to the force I can bring to bear. My regenerative capabilities are finite while the colony's warriors are innumerable. Engagement will presage mutual destruction. Battle stimulants dump into my bloodstream. I tremble ever so slightly.

Ants geyser forth. Dark and thick as coursing blood, the denizens of the colony pour downward and gather in rapidly widening pools. The leftmost swarm drags an object, its contours obscured by clambering bodies. The captive figure becomes distinct as individual ants retreat from where they've clung to its body. A man sits lotus, limbs pinioned by a few of the largest and strongest warriors. His proportions are unnerving—his torso is lengthy, and grotesquely thin. He wears tatters of an expensive suit popular during the twentieth century. Though ants have chewed him viciously, his aspect is serene. Bone gleams through ragged wounds. Grinning teeth gleam too. His wet eyes shine with the ancient awareness of a newborn.

The man's scent wafts over me. Chill, antiseptic, numbing. Charnel reek wrapped in cotton candy. The odor doesn't register as an olfactory sensation; instead, it hits psychically. Two million years have passed since I last whiffed that cloying tang of nothingness.

Sand trickles from his mouth. "So," he says. "We meet again."

I, dread and terrible Rex, loose a hot torrent of piss.

★ ★ ★

Needless to say, the little red alarm is blinking like mad.

This ghoulish apparition possesses a litany of names, but favors Tom. He is a herald of malignance, of doom and destruction. A harbinger of woe. He has claimed to ride dinosaurs and fuck Neanderthals. He has professed to walk in the shadows of countless worlds. I imagine he chuckled when his minions rent my mother limb from limb. My mother and her scientist friends theorized he was sent to this world as a scout; a watcher who predates most organisms, yet anticipated *Homo sapiens* and patiently waited for the species to collectively ripen.

A growl rumbles in my chest. My rational self is in danger of surrendering to my brute self, which would be a suboptimal condition. I do my best fighting while calm and focused. The canine in me would run for the hills. If I turn my back on Tom, I'll die. Possibly for real.

I project images to Princess Avaxia: a composite of Tom in his manifold guises, the latter of which saw him portraying the role of representative of a global corporation during the alien invasion. He'd spoken on behalf of his corporation in favor of the Gray, imploring humanity to acquiesce, to submit peacefully, quietly, painlessly. He'd insisted that the invaders were benevolently disposed toward the peoples of Earth. An unnecessary bit of subterfuge, given the power differential. I am convinced that he and his kind derive pleasure from cruelty and betrayal.

By now the psychic fog must be lifting. Surely Avaxia recognizes the horror nestled to the bosom of her colony. Tom is eager to be seen, to be known.

The princess buzzes and clicks stridently. *We are confused. Why did we not recognize this abomination?*

"Such is his power," I say through bared fangs, my gaze still focused upon my old enemy. "To obscure his nature. To cloud the minds of men and beasts."

"Rex." Tom's voice is mellow and resonant. Elocution has ever been his superpower. "Alone at last." His body isn't flesh; his bones aren't bones; he possesses nary a drop of blood. Currently, he inhabits the form of an animatronic puppet whose human likeness is several degrees this side of the uncanny valley. I can only describe it as an oversized construct that visitors to an amusement park might've seen, back in the days of amusement parks and people. When the Gray descended upon Earth, they'd obscured themselves via electromagnetics and psychic hoodoo. Now I've an inkling of what hid behind those distortion fields—shambling, emaciated puppets. Some grinning, some blank as stone, each broadly similar to Tom.

"Why have you returned? There's nothing left. You've done your worst." I don't expect an answer, inching backward, stalling the inevitable.

"Man's best friend." An observation? An accusation?

"Yes." I eke a few more centimeters.

"Man's best friend."

"Yes."

"Man's best friend. Man's best friend. Man's. Best. Friend."

The void, Avaxia says. *The cold is spreading. The void is hungry. We have made a grave mistake bringing this one among us. Rend, devour, annihilate!* She commands her forces, and they respond, eager for battle. Warriors act as a singular entity. Their massed presence gathers like a wave, then crashes upon Tom. They sting and bite. They crawl into his mouth and gouge his unblinking eyes.

He ignores his peril. "Best friend. Best friend."

I recalculate my options. Join the attack or get while the getting is good?

Flee, Rex. We don't want your lambent flame nor your thunderous bark. Begone, hound.

I'm in full reverse, scrambling up a huge dune; prelude to turning 180 degrees and hitting the servos. Ants have piled atop the motionless figure while rivers more swarm to hurl their numbers into the fray.

Avaxia wails. She's intimately connected to her servants and thus detects a precipitous shift in the struggle moments before I observe Tom's blackened shape jolt, unfold, and rise to full height, almost a giant at three meters. The air shimmers around him, stirred by a semivisible current. His long, thin shadow stretches near my frantically churning paws.

"An ape-man's best friend, too?" He brushes his shoulders and chest. His spindly hands are enormous. Ants fall away in smoking clumps. Columns of warriors crisp into flame in a perfect circle around him. The scorched circle rapidly widens to encompass the onrushing host, reducing its numbers to charred husks on contact. Acid mist drifts above the carnage. The greenish pall is streaked with white-vapor death's heads.

Avaxia's screams pitch into nosebleed decibels.

"No coincidences, Rexy," Tom says. Mangled thoraxes, legs, and mandibles dribble down his chin. "I waited in that hole forever. Just to tell you time is a ring. Follow the big river to where it bends around the foot of Mystery Mountain."

Cracks shoot in every direction, including mine. Rocky earth collapses and leaves him standing atop a lone pillar. Two of the mounds topple, then slide into the abyss. Ants beyond counting tumble after, end over end into the black.

"If you love primates, scoot, doggy. I'll give you to the count of a thousand!"

Wheeling, I engage the afterburners. I sprint and sprint onward until foam curdles in my jaws. The ground softens into green. Green grass, green hills, stands of poplar. Avaxia's despairing cries echo in my head for a long while. Her voice ceases abruptly. I howl once in sympathy and lope faster. Occasionally, I glance backward, and my shadow seems to double.

Common sense dictates I aim myself due north and run until I plunge into a snowbank. Programming supersedes the flight instinct. I head west toward Mystery Mountain instead. Tom's mocking words serve as a call and response mnemonic. "Ape-men." Yes, I harbor a faint recollection of interacting with hominids. Evolution continues to do its work in the face of setbacks. I'm compelled to investigate.

"What is a dog without a master?" The Haunter echoes the very question I frequently ask myself. "You've rescued the tribe on several occasions." He is the right-flank shadow that vanishes if I turn my head to regard him. "A pterosaur threatened their existence. Before that, a pack of killer hyenas. *Before* that, a hive of giant wasps.

Vampire bats. Carnivorous jelly. Evil beetles. Et cetera. It's always something. And every time, you climb off the mat and rescue some kid from a well."

And after I play my role in this episodic loop? I succumb to "death" only to reincarnate when the moment is opportune.

The river rolls sluggishly across a plain. A mountain looms in the middle distance. I bound along the bank, wary of lurking predators. The contours of the land and its rich, earthy aroma are familiar. Unfortunately, data corruption has erased any prior recordings of the area.

"Think," the Haunter continues. "Use the partition that houses your logic. You've been a . . . patsy."

"Didn't you send me here?" I'm panting hard.

"Sent, no. Suggested, yes."

"Suggested . . . Manipulated."

"You're suffering early onset dementia, dog. Somebody has to keep you on task."

"And you're elected, eh?"

"Guess who I am. The answer may surprise you." He flickers in my peripheral vision, then vanishes.

I enter a shallow valley near the base of the mountain. Whatever occurred in the past, it's immediately evident I made an impression upon the local cave dwellers. Soaring cliffs are carved and painted in shockingly vivid hues. My graven image joins the obligatory depictions of sun and moon and animal populations—little stick warriors hurling spears at a large, stylized stick dog. The caricature doesn't appear to retaliate. Subsequent tableaus show man and beast allied in combat against a variety of horrors (corresponding to the Haunter's summary), then, at last, reposed near a fire, triumphantly sharing the meat of a bison. A timeless tale that stirs my nostalgia.

Unfortunately, as I draw near the cliffs, the tribespeople scurry into their caves. Diminutive, sinewy specimens who speak a glottal, hooting language unknown to my records. Most wear animal skins. The more adventurous among them wing flinthead spears at me via relatively sophisticated atlatls. Damned accurately, too.

Why the rude welcome? First hint: the recent drawings of a tall, lanky silhouette grinning its face off. Upon closer inspection, the newest sequence of paintings illustrates the silhouetted giant bestowing gifts of knowledge upon the ape-men, including the aforementioned atlatls. Apparently, he created a myth wherein dogs are inherently treacherous and the Rex behemoth returns to massacre everyone. The final bit is a painting of Tom heroically shielding the tribe as fire shoots out of my eyes and jaws. A black disk partially eclipses the sun. Presumably Tom's friends observing the battle from the mothership.

"Pterosaurs, beetles, hyenas," the Haunter chants. "Who, or what, could be the next contestant?"

"The doom that came to Ape-Man Towne," I muse aloud.

"Might *you* be Godzilla, menacing a primitive Tokyo? Might you be the rough beast slouching toward Bethlehem?"

I regard the paintings of the giant and his supplicants. "Better question: Is Tom Prometheus? Is he the serpent who upended Eden's status quo?"

"Titans and conniving serpents are small fry. Keep going..."

"A god."

"Or what passes for a god in these parts," says the Haunter. He's finally acquired my sense of humor, my rasping voice. Probably my noble demeanor and charm as well.

"Friend, I feel as if you've led me by the snout." I'm addressing the empty air. He's done his job. Our conversations have triggered a regenerative burst and a web of fresh neural pathways that permit me to connect the abstract details floating in my mind. I'm fully online and coming to grips with the horrible implications of my existence. This clarity of purpose isn't a state likely to persist for long. So, I ignore the terrified tribespeople and stalk through their groveling masses and deep into the mountain lair.

The cave system is vast and cunningly engineered. The latter is revealed by my keen vision and surface-penetrating radar. I see past rough tunnels, blackened by the soot of many campfires; past the illusion of naturally sculpted grottos and forests of stalactites. I crouch at the rim of a sacrificial pit where the ape-men toss in the old and weak, same as their ancestors did in places such as Sima de los Huesos, circa 430,000 BCE. Nothing really changes when it comes to humans and protohumans, although in this case, that's because the Gray put a thumb on the scale. Men and animals gone extinct in the wake of World War IV haven't revived in accordance with Mother Nature's failsafe protocols. Life hasn't simply carried on. There is a grimmer explanation.

We never knew why the Gray attacked. I wasn't around to see them depart. Seems crystal clear that while the main force came and went, they left Tom behind to carry on their inscrutable work.

I venture down and down into the pit, among the bones. Down and down where none of the ape-men would dare go into a realm of sacred darkness. At the bottom, buried in slime and sediment, lies a hatch sealed by bolts and biometric locks. I rend it asunder with these alloy claws. Beneath the hatch? A hive of laboratories whose functions generally defy my comprehension.

The cloning vats, I recognize. Ape-men, Cro-Magnon, and *Homo sapiens* float in the brine, dreaming as they await their turn to repopulate the planet. I have a basic grasp of molecular printing tech as well. Judging by the shiny holograms and scale-model metropolises of old Earth cities, Tom has the tools to mass-replicate any civilization at any moment in human history. Or prehistory. He could literally snap his fingers and wipe away one reality to embed another. He might wear the body of a puppet, but the rest of us are his playthings.

Proud to say, I don't hesitate to assume the role of Samson in Dagon's temple. I access the pocket dimension where my bulk (my true form is the size and density of a tank, or briefly, a battleship) and heaviest armaments are stored and then unleash the arsenal. Masers, lasers, plasma beams, infrasound, chemical agents, and low-yield nukes. The whole shebang. The subterranean complex plunges into the resultant crater. Fires of hell erupt, whooshing through the upper cave system. Nary an ape-man, woman, or child escapes the conflagration. It's the destruction of the ant colony revisited.

Sorry to prove Tom a prophet, my hapless ape-man friends.

The ordeal isn't quite enough to kill me outright. I emerge from this latest apocalypse half-charred and dragging my entrails in the dirt. Every nuke detonated, every gun emptied, and all nanobots depleted. I sprawl near the river and watch the top of Mystery Mountain rocket into the stratosphere.

Tom arrives by and by, whistling cheerfully. "Saw your mold in the factory, huh?" he says. "Figured that might be the last straw to break your programming...What a fascinating report this will be. Thanks, Rex."

In fact, I hadn't spotted my master clone among the myriad others. No matter—a younger dog might've stuck to orthodoxy and tried to save the tribe. Not this one. Blowing everything to Kingdom Come, including myself, was the only valid choice. At any rate, done is done. Splattered in gore and lather, wheezing slower and slower; my eyelids droop.

Time is a ring. The Big Whimper occurred two million years ago, two minutes ago, two minutes from now, two million years from now. It'll never happen. It'll persist forever. What Tom may or may not know, is that I'm *sui generis*. Humans made me, in their infinite hubris, a walking, talking, tail-wagging doomsday device. If a mountain hadn't conked my skull before I could uncork the break-glass-in-case-of-emergency tools, the whimper might've been a bang. Maybe Tom has no reason to feel threatened. I think he should. One of us will soon find out who's right. I shot all my nukes...all except one.

The smug bastard leans over to pat me. "Who's a good boy?"

Wish you could see the look on his face when my head whips up and my jaws go snicker-snack! and Tom is suddenly minus his right hand. Who's a good boy? Me; I'm a good boy. I'm good. Good. Boy. Good—

Playback interrupted. Cascade failure imminent. Searching for signal...

Quantum Fragment Record of Unknown Subject (1): *Dad worked at an animation studio affiliated with several famous film companies. He rigged puppets, all sorts of stuff. Brought home a helmet in the shape of a coyote head. Lifelike as shit. Its jaws moved with Dad's. The ears pricked up and swiveled around like a real animal too. Terrifying. He designed other models. Creepy, awful. Exaggerated, animatronic features of babies and old people. Not just heads, either. He and a partner put together entire costumes with articulated limbs and fangs and claws.*

One of the costumes resembled a notorious corporate spokesperson, except freakishly tall. Almost shit myself when Dad climbed inside and lurched around the yard, kicking the doghouse to splinters and uprooting Mom's rosebushes. He saw me hiding near the corner of the house. That... thing grinned and reached down for me—

UNK (2): *You don't sleep. Which means you don't dream. Subroutines take over when you slip into a low energy state. They process information—all the information ever recorded by human civilization suspended in amber—and some of that information is* *expressed via sequenced imagery traveling at tachyon velocity. An eternal data stream that meets itself coming and going.*

You neither sleep nor dream. But the animal within you does. He's having a doozy when a small red light clicks on in the corner of his vision. The light blinks.

REFLECTIONS IN LIZARD-TIME

Brian Trent

I

The train hadn't been built for humans, but we were still allowed to ride it, in the way that rats are "allowed" to ride a seagoing vessel. And much like a rat, I'd kept out of sight as the massive and oddly glass-like vehicle lumbered on its treads from Siberia to Saint Petersburg. While reptilian passengers occupied the first dozen or so compartments, I'd hunkered in one of the rear cars among the living cargo—a hundred or so shellbacks being transported for their meat and horns.

As the train arrived in the city ruins, I slipped out through the ventilation grate. The nearest building was plastered with graffiti, and my eyes settled on large Cyrillic lettering rendered in red spray paint:

FIGHT THE PHASING!
SEND THE LIZARDS BACK TO HELL!

I coughed into my handkerchief, transfixed by the old

51

call to arms. It was *vintage*, twenty years old if it was a day. Behind me, the train doors slid open and reptilian passengers disgorged—a silent procession of three-meter-tall, bipedal creatures. I wondered if any of them knew what the graffiti said. Wondered if they'd care.

"Edgar!" a voice called to me.

A small gathering of humans had crept toward the train, to meet stowaways or take their turn riding it to its next destination. One man was a plump, bearded fellow with rich blue eyes and a sable woolen coat. He strode to me, grinning.

"Alexander," I said in greeting, tipping my hat.

My old enemy embraced me in a bear hug. "Edgar McBride! It is good to see you!"

"You look well."

"And so do you . . ." The lie died on his tongue as he beheld me up close. "You are bleeding."

I regarded the fresh blood on my handkerchief.

"It's the humidity," I said, nodding toward the shellback compartments. The Scale Rail (our slang for the dino train) billowed steam from open doors. The stink of its living cargo wafted into dry Russian air.

Alexander Spiridov frowned mightily, the same frown (I imagined) he'd used when peering through his sniper scope to pick off American soldiers in my old battalion. "I forgot the lizards bring their jungle air wherever they go."

"I'll be fine."

"You still have blood on your chin."

I used the handkerchief again, mindful of getting spatters on my blue suit. The train continued emptying its passengers, and one of them—a stately dino with a head crest the color of wine—twisted its blue-feathered neck to see me hastily bury the sodden handkerchief in my pocket. It gave me a curious look, suggestive of both sympathy and hunger, and then continued into the city.

Saint Petersburg had changed since last I'd been there. In some ways, it had improved: no longer the war-torn rubble I'd battled Russians in as a nineteen-year-old private in the twilight years of World War III. New buildings loomed above—enormous gray mounds in the plain style of our invaders, and spine-like defensive batteries. Yet most of the city remained a ruin, and the contrast was somehow more upsetting.

Alexander grabbed my heavy luggage trunk. "I have arranged the meeting in a very secure place."

"Where is it?" I asked.

"I operate a bathhouse. It will be plenty private."

"Good," I said, not voicing what I was thinking: *A bathhouse will be humid. I'll hemorrhage blood before this deal is concluded.*

My Russian host led me into the nearest human ghetto. The streets here were narrow and overgrown with shops catering to every red-blooded need and comfort; the oily stink of humanity was perhaps little better than the stench of the train, but it was a *mammalian* odor. I felt the tension in my shoulders ebb. Food crackled in skillets, vendors pawed at us and shoved their wares under our noses, but Alexander shouldered past. We crossed a courtyard providing a view of the deep blue Baltic and its coastline curling away...

I halted abruptly. "What the hell?"

Alexander spun around. "Something wrong?"

I pointed into the distance. "The towers . . ."

"Dactyl towers, yes." He shifted my heavy trunk from one hand to the other. "They are miles away and will not trouble us."

"Miles away isn't much comfort!"

That was certainly true. As much as the dino mounds unsettled me, as much as I hated the humiliation of being reduced to inconsequential fauna, there was comfort in the fact that the dinos left us alone. Oh, they responded with lethal force to any human hostility, but it had been years since we'd offered them any. Twenty years ago when they phased into our world, we'd tried to fight them off, failed spectacularly, and then did what humans do best: We adapted to new circumstances.

Yet the dinos were not the only reptilian species to invade. In their version of Earth, evolution had produced *two* sentient races. One was the bipedal, troodon-descended species we nicknamed "dinos." The other came from pterodactyl or archaeopteryx stock—no human scientist had ever determined which. Winged, cunning, and predatory, they were apparently the dinos' hereditary enemies.

Earth had since been carved up by these warring rivals. New York's skyscrapers housed dactyl nests. Mexico City had become a dino stronghold. Old national borders, fervently fought over by humans, were meaningless.

And here in Saint Petersburg, the rivals had built unsettlingly near to each other. The dactyl towers on the horizon were unspeakably ugly to me. Like chimneys of freakishly large factories, riddled with perches and nesting holes.

"The fighting around these parts has died down," Alexander explained. "The two sides stay strictly apart."

"Still . . ."

"Come along!"

A thrum of dread ran through me, but I dutifully followed him into another warren of alleyways. More ancient graffiti marked the walls. Our trek ended at a massive building with a gorgeous, stained-glass window set above doors guarded by shifty-looking men with wild beards, shaggy fur coats, and submachine guns. Alexander greeted them in Russian, and they stepped aside to let us enter.

The lobby was a lavishly opulent rotunda. Posh throw rugs covered the floor. Silver mirrors reflected Roman marbles and paintings from German, French, and Russian artists. Famous artworks, if I judged them right. Works predating the Third World War.

I stared in undisguised astonishment. "How in the hell . . . ?"

Alexander chuckled. "You like?"

"These had to have come from a museum!"

"From the Hermitage Museum, here in Saint Petersburg."

"But . . . but . . ." My mind struggled to make sense of this. Our scaly overlords preferred their own structures as opposed to appropriating human ones—that wasn't surprising, given that our doorways and rooms hadn't been designed with oversized lizards in mind. There were exceptions, though; the Hermitage Museum, with its airy halls and colossal architecture, now housed the upper castes of saurian society.

"You couldn't have snuck inside and stolen all this!" I cried.

"Of course not! I traded for them."

"Traded . . . *with the dinos*?"

"Egg service!" Alexander said cheerily. "I provide premier egg service to the lizards. My craftsmen build gilded egg-holders with green pillows and heated cabinets until the little bastards hatch. We even decorate the shells."

"I wasn't aware they dealt directly with us at all."

"It's very secretive. Seems all intelligent creatures have a taste for the forbidden and decadent! My services are all the rage."

I shook my head. "From Russian sniper to egg farmer, huh?"

"Egg painter."

"Yeah, my interpretation sounds better."

He folded his arms and regarded me warmly. "And you? From American imperialist to black-market smuggler."

"Specialty salesman."

"*My* interpretation sounds better." He gently kicked my luggage trunk, blue eyes twinkling. "The merchandise is in here, yes?"

"Yeah. One of my excavation teams found it in Siberian permafrost."

"Good!"

"Who exactly are we selling to?"

"A young woman named Cynthia Belanov."

I gave a sidelong look. "Do you know *why* she wants pieces of a fifty-thousand-year-old woolly mammoth?"

He scratched his beard. "Does it matter?"

"A little."

"Why?"

I cleared my throat, feeling salty pulp on the back of my tongue—a permanent gift from the weapons of the last human war. "When folks turn to the black market for paleontology, they usually want dinosaurs. Lots of people fetishize the old bones. Some grind them up for homemade elixirs. Some destroy them in weird backwoods rituals, hoping to inspire revolution. But *your* client wanted a mammoth. And not just a mammoth: the *stomach* of a mammoth. That doesn't sound strange to you?"

Alexander steepled his fingers. "I fulfill requests, not question them. Besides, there are strange rumors in the city lately."

"Like what?"

"Someone has been making inquiries. Asking about frozen specimens. Ancient dead animals."

I felt a wave of unease. "Any idea *why*?"

He shrugged his massive shoulders. "I don't concern myself with why." He checked his watch, hefted my luggage, and said, "Shall we go?"

II

It was not a bathhouse for humans. At least, not anymore.

Based on the tilework and mosaics, I guessed its original incarnation dated to the early twentieth century. The subsequent years had given it a patchwork character, like junk DNA, preserving every evolutionary twist. Revolution, WW2, revolution, WW3...and then a cavernous expansion to accommodate our scaly new rulers.

The air was as humid as I'd feared. Concavities dimpled the floor, large enough to accommodate individual dinos; I imagined them reclining by the water as legendary dragons, safe from the bitter Russian winter.

For now, the bathhouse appeared empty. I reached into my coat and affixed my breathing mask while Alexander stood by my side, eying the mist.

A woman emerged from behind one of the columns.

Her head was shaved smooth as a dino egg. Scaly tattoos ran along the sides of her neck.

A dinofreak.

Willful worshiper of Earth's oppressors.

"Edgar McBride?" she asked uncertainly. "My name is Cynthia Belanov. Mister Spiridov said you could get . . ." She trailed off, stricken by the sight of my breathing mask.

"Not contagious," I assured her.

Three-fifths of the world's population died during World War III, and nukes were merely the opening act. Chemical and pathogenic attacks followed. Red Death was the most notorious, gestated in some bioweapons lab and carrying a seventy percent mortality rate. I'd caught it while on march to the Kazakh border, and my lungs had never been the same.

Cynthia swallowed apprehensively. "You have the mammoth stomach, yes?"

I rested a hand on the luggage trunk, and my voice was tinny in my mask. "Refrigerated compartment, per your request. Permafrost depth suggests an age of about fifty thousand years."

She edged toward us, kneading her hands, bald head glistening. "Can you get more?"

"Maybe. But mammoths aren't exactly easy to find."

"It doesn't need to be a mammoth."

"What does it need to be?"

"Old herbivores. The older the better, but preserved well enough that anything in their stomachs would be viable for extraction."

I glanced at Alexander. He was frowning, studying her and the vaporous bathhouse as if he was once again a sniper, scanning for trouble.

I coughed in my mask. "Ms. Belanov? If you could tell me *what* you're seeking, maybe I can narrow the search."

"I'm sorry, we can't tell you."

"'*We*'?" Alexander snapped. "Who is '*we*'?"

His question seemed to linger like the wisps of humidity. Then the mist behind Belanov darkened, and two dinos sprinted at us.

During World War III, Alexander had been a sniper in the Russian Army and a frankly terrifying opponent. The subsequent years and weight had not, it seemed, dulled his reflexes. He jerked a submachine gun from his coat and aimed at the nearest dino. They were two and a half meters tall, blue feathered, and by the flush to their head crests were probably only twenty or thirty years old. Their claws gripped sleek energy weapons.

"*Ostanovis*! No!" Cynthia cried, throwing herself in the way of Alexander's aim. "Trust!"

"Not in this life!" he countered, and for a moment I thought he was going to pull the trigger. The dinos glared at his firearm with flat, dull rage.

Everyone liked to say dinos resembled birds, but their

feathers were closer to porcupine quills. Besides, there was enough of the lizard beneath their cobalt-hued feathers, and they moved with the jerky speed of reptiles, too. Hell, I didn't even think they *sounded* like birds. The trilling that filled the bathhouse was liquid and otherworldly.

Our two sides regarded each other in a tense standoff. Then an eerie voice resonated in the mist.

"No harm humans. Bow your heads and submit. Cynthia, assure no harm."

The dinos instantly obeyed this command, lowering their weapons and crouching like supplicants. Cynthia's eyes sprouted tears, and she regarded me with a pleading gaze. "We need your help, Mister McBride! Please! There's more at stake here than you realize!"

Behind her, the miasma kindled in a milky phosphorescence, and a third dino emerged from concealment.

It was taller than its brethren, and its feathers were the purple of a Montana dusk. Spectral light exuded from the tips of its feathers. Clothing was not worn by dinos—the very concept seemed alien to them—though I'd heard their upper castes bejeweled their feathers with bright threads and bioluminescent chemistry.

Cynthia knelt, and the glowing dino placed one claw gingerly on her head, trilling and chirping softly. The eerie voice piped up again, coming from a strange device strapped to the dino's chest. *"Edgar McBride? Kolseen you may call me."*

The voice had the crackling, warped quality of an ancient gramophone scratching out sounds from a waxen cylinder.

I was stricken mute. When the dinos and dactyls phased into our world, they had been too busy fighting each other to give a damn about us. Our short-lived resistance was treated as the antics of troublesome pests rather than respectable foes. There had been no formal ceasefire or treaty offered; they simply culled our numbers and obliterated our defenses until we gave up. After that, we were treated with indifference.

To my knowledge, there had never been actual, verbal communication between our species.

The creature calling itself Kolseen trilled again. Her translator converted the sounds: *"Apologies in select of place. Blood-lung sufferer. We conclude our business rapidly, yes?"*

"Yes," I said at last, eager to get the hell out of there.

"You have we request?"

"In this trunk. It's refrigerated to keep the sample cold."

Kolseen barely looked at it. *"Require more."*

"Why?"

"Seeking long ago fungal spores this territory."

The bathhouse humidity was so heavy, it felt one degree away from transforming into rain. Mind racing, I said, "I think I understand. You're hoping the mammoth might have ingested local vegetation, and with it these . . . um . . . spores. Do you know . . . I mean, can you tell me . . . what species of spore you want?"

I had never been this close to a dino before; with only a few meters separating us, Kolseen looked freakish and serpentine, like an image of Quetzalcoatl come to hideous life.

"*Specific species extinct,*" she said through her device. "*Not known to humans.*"

"We have scientists," I insisted. "Specialists in paleobotany. I could make inquiries."

"*Specific species not in human records any.*"

"How could you know that?"

"*Investigate human records since arrive.*"

The implications of this took a few seconds to register, and when they did, I felt an explosion of outrage. "Investigate human records? You mean you can *read our languages*? You've picked over the pieces of our civilization without ever . . . without ever . . ."

Without ever treating us as worthy of respect and consideration! I wanted to scream. *You goddamn lizards phased into a world that didn't belong to you! You never tried communicating with us! You broke an already broken people, and then picked over the detritus like goddamn vultures!*

Kolseen gave a sidelong look, like a parrot eying something suspicious. I wondered if she could smell my anger, or could see the blood rushing to my cheeks.

"*Wish to speak alone. Walk with me please, Edgar McBride.*"

Against every instinct I had, I followed the creature into the rotunda.

III

She must have been slowing her movements to allow me to keep pace with her. Nonetheless, her lengthy legs forced me into a brisk walk. Back in the rotunda, my gaze went to the stained-glass window. I could see now that it was an image from Genesis: Adam and Eve about to share an apple, while a serpent entwined the Tree of Knowledge above their heads.

Kolseen noticed the image as well, and she studied it curiously.

"Not wish enter your world," she said at last.

"But you did."

"Not know humans existed."

I fought to steady my voice. "But you found out soon enough, didn't you?"

"Enter your world seek spores."

The scratchy words paraded through my head, and for several seconds they seemed as cryptic as her native tongue. Blood pounded in my ears. "Are you telling me that your"—I'd never call them people—"species broke into my world for this . . . this *fungus*? *That's* the reason behind the phasing?"

It seemed impossible that anything could demean the human race further. We had adapted to our pitiful condition, but the sting of defeat was never far from our thoughts. How could it not be? I hadn't ridden a train across the Siberian wastes with a ticket in my hand and a window seat; I'd stowed away as a furtive animal aboard a colossal machine, lurking among reptilian cattle.

And now, here was another blow. Our defeat had not been the result of a noble crusade, but for want of mold.

"A fungus," I repeated. "What, is it a delicacy? An aphrodisiac?"

Kolseen turned her snakelike neck toward me, quills bristling. *"Weapon."*

"A weapon?"

"Deadly fungus paralyze brain. Kill enemy."

I shook my head, wondering if it would have been better if it *had* been a delicacy or aphrodisiac. During my years of combat in the Third World War, there had been nights when I would gaze at the stars and imagine an advanced alien civilization showing up to heal the world. I suppose every soldier has fancied something similar at one time or another: a divine intervention of sorts, to end the carnage and death. And the universe had answered me, it seemed, though instead of aliens or angels, it had sent interdimensional monsters. Instead of peace, it had simply upped the stakes. To paraphrase Einstein: *I don't know how they're going to fight World War III, but I do know how they'll fight World War IV. With two warring factions of sentient dinosaurs.*

"This deadly spore," I grumbled, "How do you know it ever grew here?"

"Our version Earth have similar species."

"It grew in your world?"

"Yes. Grew same region. We seek it here."

"Our versions of Earth developed differently. Maybe it never evolved here."

"Maybe did."

I thought of the mammoth stomach in my refrigerated compartment. Ancient bacteria and gut flora had been recovered from the intestinal tract of frozen creatures before. Could there be spores in there? If the fungal species had been native to this geographic region, and concurrent with mammoths, that was possible. Hell, it was likely.

"And you used it as a weapon?" I asked.

Although the artificial voice was devoid of emotion, Kolseen's chirps seemed to have taken on a desperate urgency. *"Yes. Used it as weapon in war with enemy. Only hope for victory."*

"Well, if it grew in your world and was so important, what the hell happened to it in your—"

The stained-glass window exploded.

We were showered by shards of glass, the fragments of Adam and Eve raining around us. Two winged shapes flew through the disintegrating picture.

Like the dinos, they were feathered and reptilian, and larger than a man. That was where the resemblance ended. Ash gray in color, with dark beaks and claws, the dactyls had pale eyes that made me think of blindness. Wings flapping, they aimed at us with devices clutched in prehensile tails.

Kolseen shoved me aside. I felt blistering heat fly past my face and suddenly the rim of my hat was smoking.

My dino host darted away from stabbing beams of light. Then the bathhouse doors flew open, and her bodyguards strode in, firing energy weapons of their own. One of the dactyls was hit and fell, spinning, like a burned kite.

The other ascended to the domed roof. For a moment, I thought all would be well—three armed dinos taking on a single dactyl seemed like good odds. Then its tail-gun fired a small projectile into their midst, and there was a blast of heat that blew me off my feet.

When I came to, the rotunda was a smoking crater. Two dinos lay dead, feathers scorched and shriveled. A pair of winged shapes lay crumpled. Alexander stood in the doorway holding his submachine gun, though he seemed less a heroic rescuer than a baffled man taking stock of the fight's aftermath.

A pile of debris moved. The fragments of paintings and sculptures rolled off Kolseen's rising specter.

Alexander aimed at her.

"Wait!" I called to him. "It was the dactyls who attacked us!"

Kolseen took a hobbling step toward us, twisting her neck to regard the bright fragments of window in their frame. She gave a sorrowful warble, which I seemed to understand before the translator deciphered it for me.

"Must go. Others will come."

IV

World War III shattered the Internet. It was therefore impossible to know where the phasing had first occurred, or if every nation had been hit simultaneously. All I knew was my own experience in the ruins of Moscow. My battalion was crossing a bridge. A fellow soldier glanced over the rails and cried out that something was in the water.

I will never forget leaning over the bridge to see the river below. What we should have seen were our own reflections. The sun's position should have turned the river into a mirror.

Instead, we saw lizards. Nightmare reptiles. Scales and teeth and amber eyes glaring out from murky depths.

None of us knew what to make of it. Our commander dismissed it as Russian trickery: false images projected from the bottom of the river. He ordered us to resume our march. Told us to keep our eyes on the buildings ahead, where Russian snipers like Alexander were surely drawing a bead on us.

But we passed through one neighborhood after another without resistance. Finally, in a school playground, we encountered Russians—including Russian soldiers. But they weren't interested in us. They stood in a circle, staring down into an old bomb crater. It had rained the previous night, turning the crater into a small pond.

There were reflections in the water.

And they weren't human.

Twenty-four hours later, the phasing occurred. Dinos and dactyls stepped out from reflective surfaces. Spread into the ruined cities. Exotic machines erupted from lakes and rivers. Behemoths and dragons who clashed like titans of myth. Human scientists believed the twenty-four-hour delay owed to a time dilation in crossing one universe to another—for the invaders it must have seemed instantaneous. Not that it mattered. Even a day's wait wasn't enough for us to organize—for us to comprehend— what was about to transpire.

We warily emerged from the bathhouse—Alexander, Kolseen, and I. The Russian guards at the door lay in bloodied heaps. Killed manually by the dactyls, I suppose.

Silencing the guard dogs.

"My luggage!" I said suddenly.

Kolseen hissed at me to lower my voice. *"Cynthia stays with item. My people recover soon."* She splayed the talons of one hand, making impossibly quick motions as if casting a spell . . . or more likely, transmitting a nonverbal message to her "kind" using some wireless, cybernetic technology.

"We wait here," she said. *"Rescue soon."*

I strayed a few meters, to where I could see the dactyl towers miles away on the Baltic's shores. "Kolseen," I began, "what happened to the spores in your own world? You said it was an effective biological weapon against your enemy."

I didn't say the rest of what I was thinking: that if I could locate this lethal fungus for her, maybe the lizards would leave and never return.

Kolseen bristled, eyes flicking to Alexander. I remembered suddenly that she'd told me her secret in confidence. Oh fucking well. For his part, my Russian friend held his submachine gun as if it was his old sniper rifle, scanning the rooftops for signs of further attack.

"The spores," I repeated. "If they were so important to your war, how could you lose them?"

"Spores not lost. Spores destroyed. Repositories burned by treachery."

I thought of the beam weapons I had seen the dinos use, and their advanced machines. I had seen dactyls lasered out of the sky from ground-based defenses.

"You don't seem to need a fungus to fight the dactyls. I get that your two species are technologically matched, but it seems you've fought yourselves to a stalemate here. Can't you call a ceasefire? Was it necessary to cross dimensions to continue it?"

Kolseen gave me an unbelieving look. *"Dactyls were allies. Helped us in war against enemy."*

"The dactyls *are* your enemies!"

"They were allies."

"I don't understand."

"Dactyls and dinos share same world. Our world was invaded by common enemy."

My jaw dropped. "What common enemy—"

The sound of flapping wings made me cry out. A dactyl flew directly overhead, spotted us, and wheeled about. Its tail raised a weapon.

Then its skull exploded as Alexander's weapon chattered. The dactyl fell backward out of the sky, firing its weapon reflexively as it plummeted. The beam etched a flaming scar on a nearby building.

My Russian friend rushed to the creature. He returned moments later with his submachine gun holstered and the dactyl's tail-gun in both hands.

Kolseen looked at him with what seemed disapproval . . . and perhaps fear. It was highly likely no human had ever laid hands on one of their advanced weapons before. She doubtless knew that we were inventive and adaptive. For the first time in twenty years of subjugation, I felt a kernel of hope.

For his part, Alexander held her gaze and smiled.

Then I noticed movement out of the corner of my eye. Turning toward the Baltic, I gazed at the distant towers.

They were hemorrhaging clouds of black shapes. Dactyls filling the sky like a Biblical plague.

The spiny defensive towers of Saint Petersburg seemed to detect this as well, because they opened up on the aerial horde. The dactyls scattered and fired back from a distance. Explosions detonated over the sea.

Kolseen turned to me. *"Must help. Need spores before enemy follows us here."*

With difficulty, I pried my gaze from the battle. "The dactyls used to be your allies, but then they betrayed you, is that it? They destroyed your bioweapon to aid the enemy."

"Yes."

"What if this spore can't be found here?"

"Must find."

A dactyl missile penetrated the defensive spread and sheared away the top of a building. "Then we have to work together!" I insisted. "You can't ignore us anymore! Human scientists might be able to help you! If an enemy is coming—something worse than the dactyls—you need to bring us into the fold!"

She placed one of her claws on my head. *"Agreed, Edgar McBride."*

A ship appeared above the alley. It seemed to be made of glass, starlight warping and sliding along its geometry. A hatch in its underbelly fanned open.

Kolseen moved at her natural speed—sprinting up the nearest wall to reach the craft. She was reaching down to help us up when a missile collided with the vessel.

The impact knocked the ship sidelong. Kolseen's eyes grew wide and she leaped into the hatch. Yet she looked back to us and trilled loudly, her translation device converting the sounds to words which were drowned out by another missile bursting against the craft. The ship tilted sideways and flew out of sight.

Desperately, I turned to Alexander. "Did you catch that?"

"We are to meet her at the nesting enclosure north of here," he said.

"How far north?"

He hefted his stolen beam weapon. "Too far to make it through this bombardment. But we will travel underground."

"Like rats," I grumbled.

"Rats are survivors, my friend."

V

Saint Petersburg's metro tunnels dated back three centuries, and while World War III had collapsed some portions, workarounds had been dug. The same was true in other major cities. In fact, the phasing had spared the human underworld, since neither dactyls nor dinos seemed comfortable in the narrow, clammy spaces beneath the surface. A French archaeologist once told me that this was an example of history repeating itself. Cretaceous-era mammals, he said, had made use of subterranean travel to avoid predation by hungry dinosaurs.

The bombardment of Saint Petersburg lasted two days. Alexander and I hunkered in the tunnels, waiting for the thunder and fury to end. On the third day, we finally climbed a stairwell into bright blue daylight.

"Looks like we pulled through," I muttered, glancing at the buildings and streets. It had rained during the night, and the city—largely intact—glistened in the low sunlight.

Alexander stood beside me and sighed. "Every so often, I am thankful for lizard-tech."

I nodded grudgingly. Dino weapons used efficient point-defense technology. The dactyl attack must have been an act of desperation.

Or distraction.

As if reading my thoughts, Alexander asked, "Why *did* they attack?"

"No idea." My attention flicked to the city square, where a crowd gathered by an ancient stone fountain. My Russian friend called to them, but no one responded, and I suddenly noticed two oddities. The first was that the crowd contained a mix of humans and dinos. The two species stood side by side as if equals.

The second oddity was that everyone was staring into the fountain.

Feeling a surge of anxiety, I joined the gathering and looked for myself. The sky was mirrored in the water, but something else was there, too. I saw hordes of shadowy bodies. Freakish weapons affixed to multiple appendages. Blister-like clusters of eyes . . .

There must be many *versions of Earth out there,* I thought numbly. *Humans had evolved on one. Dinosaurs had become sentient on another. But on a third world, evolution had allowed a different species to scuttle to the top of the food chain.*

Gradually crowding out all other reflections, gigantic spiders pressed and scratched like devils at the gates of hell.

THE TRANSFORMATION PROBLEM

Nick Mamatas

Chakravarty was only the executive vice president (propulsion) of *Danneskjöld*, but perhaps that is why she perceived the issue first. There was nothing wrong with the plasma collectors, and the ship's deceleration was on pace, but something was missing, specifically from Chakravarty's lunch. And this wasn't the first time such a thing had happened either. Chakravarty was down by nearly a pound, as her pre-paids were consistently short. One less handful of rice here, two percent milk where it should have been whole milk there. The Wagyu beef clearly was not programmed to taste like grass-fed.

Something was draining the processing power from the food synthesizers, she was sure of it. Fuming with dissatisfaction, she sent in a complaint and ate her lamb karahi, which featured the wrong ratio of lamb to tomato-chili stew. But life on *Danneskjöld* was not supposed to entail dissatisfaction—those feelings were left behind on Earth, where the oppressors and their guns, or their softer but no less violent ideologies, had oppressed Chakravarty and her people for eons. Their property had been stolen from them, their children dragged off to fight in unjust wars, their lovers torn from their arms, the right to make basic decisions about medicine and food and drink and clothing remanded to a malevolent bureaucracy. But her people were smart, brilliant even, with IQs four or more standard deviations above the norm. It was this intelligence that allowed Chakravarty and people of all genders and races and neurotypes like her to realize that their lives were entirely unfree.

And she and her polycule didn't spend fifteen years writing code, financing the construction of their ship through a complex series of shell companies set up to organize ablation cascade mitigation missions with uncrewed prototypes of *Danneskjöld*, having the ship surreptitiously built from captured space debris, investing heavily in post-WWIII insurgent movements in Uzbekistan in order to reduce the payload price of Baikonur Cosmodrome to proper market rates so they could actually afford to fly up to *Danneskjöld*, and nearly dying when the ship began to spin, just so she could be shorted on food.

At 2000 hours, in the low-g ballroom—a literal spherical room moving through a tube in the opposite direction of *Danneskjöld's* rotation—Chakravarty was just strapping Koen into the bondage blob when he said, "Have you noticed that the lights are at ninety-three percent luminance during notional daylight hours?" She inserted the phallic gag, pulled the strap tightly, as he liked it, and said, "No, I haven't, pig," and then tugged lightly on his testicles. The session went well enough—

Chakravarty did everything Koen wanted: stimulating his prostate, floating to the top of the ballroom and stepping on his neck so he could masturbate with his free hand, then ungagging him and sitting upon his face for him to provide services. It was enjoyable enough, and the video would be fun for the rest of the polycule to enjoy, but Chakravarty couldn't maximize her pleasure. She was just a bit peckish, and annoyed.

Back in normal gravity, Chakravarty's head swam slightly more than it would have. Low blood sugar, according to her watch, and a sour stomach that her technology could not directly detect. She was . . . *upset*. Koen had to steady her as they walked back along the outer ring to their respective rooms.

"The lights are dimmer," Chakravarty said. "How's your meal plan?"

"Fine, I guess," said Koen. "I'm constantly refining it, you know." He self-consciously patted his flat stomach. Koen was the executive VP for logistics, food synthesis, and culture.

"Help me," Chakravarty said, tugging at her French braid. Long hair was always annoying during playtime, and doubly so in low g, but Chakravarty didn't fuck off into deep space to wear her hair up all the time. Koen carefully removed the rubber band at the base of the braid and nudged his fingers within the plait to ease the strands free. Chakravarty sighed, contented for the first time in weeks.

A moment later, agitated again. Her watch chimed. So did Koen's. So too did the watch on the other side of the door they were standing before. A moment later the rimlights of the hallway pulsed.

An all-hands meeting. At 2300 hours. Freedom never sleeps. Chakravarty and Koen headed to the nearest tube, and got shot into the conference hall.

Danneskjöld was a total monkeysphere—ninety-nine people, and no problems as there were no strangers among them. Social life trended toward panmixia, but enough people were ace to mitigate drama. The firm was neither flat nor pyramidal, but instead a series of mutually blended working groups. There were only four executive vice presidents, and always the possibility of promotion. Everyone was gratefully, almost neurotically, childfree, but life-extenders and the possibility of a future upload resolved even vestigial anxiety about the inevitability of death.

Surely the universe would not continue to exist without the crew and residents of *Danneskjöld* to observe, harness, and critique it.

Carlos Emerson Ong, who indeed did select their name to create the initials CEO, offered a perfunctory welcome to everyone except for Chakravarty, whom they glared at—even Koen got a lip-twitching smile—and immediately turned on the displays.

"We've been seeing some unexpected Hawking radiation about three AUs out," they said. "We've now confirmed it's a micro black hole. Smaller than any human has seen before. Maybe two suns of mass, and seventeen kilometers in diameter," Ong said, mostly for their own benefit. Everyone could read the displays faster than Ong could speak, but they were the ones who had set up the visuals. "How did we not notice this?"

"It unfolded into realspace from a microdimension," Szymanska, EVP of pure science, offered.

"There's no black hole. AI fuckup," said Thomasen, not a VP. Skunk-works type. He didn't like job titles, or all-hands meetings. "Why wouldn't the black hole have spilled out from another dimension two million years ago, or two weeks from now? We happen to just be sailing past an inexplicable one-chance-in-a-quadrillion event, that sure, might happen all the time in an infinite universe, but we're not perceiving infinitely. We're just looking out a window at where it happened to be happening? Bullshit. Sensor error."

"We caused it," said Chakravarty. "Or we are causing it, more precisely." On the whiteboard in her mind, the equations were only just forming, but there was something to it. Thomasen was right that it was too much of a cosmic coincidence that the only ship of humans tooling out past the edge of the Oort Cloud would happen to stumble upon a black hole with a necessarily short life span. But Szymanska was also correct—a micro black hole could and would emerge via unfolding from a subatomic dimension, which would also explain why sensors hadn't detected any stellar mass or spatial warping any time in the past four years in the black hole's location. "Drawing in the plasma may have snagged exactly the wrong particle, which might have been entangled with a muon in a tiny dimension, and we pulled the black hole out into realspace like a great black fish out of the sea."

"That's just as unlikely as randomly passing by just as the black hole emerged spontaneously," said Ong.

"Not with the amount of charged particles we're sucking down," Chakravarty said.

"So, we'll be summoning more black holes as we

continue our journey?" Szymanska asked. "That could be a problem." She ran her tongue over her teeth, contemplative. Others muttered with their affinity groups, checked their tablets or watches, shouted random questions that Chakravarty couldn't answer, swam toward the display to get a closer look at the data streaming in, and Thomasen's entire working group started hauling themselves, as one, toward the exit.

"We'll get the AI on it," said Ong. "Perhaps this is a good thing, not a bad thing. I'm sure there are plenty of ways to fruitfully exploit the ability to generate micro black holes."

Propulsion, Chakravarty thought. She liked thinking about propulsion.

Faced with the new demands placed upon it, the AI shit the bed. Or rather, the fraction of the AI dedicated to determining whether Chakravarty's hypothesis had any merit shit the bed.

Something bad was happening. She quickly made a series of trades with Koen's virtual assistant, offering increased velocity in exchange for increased and more exotic rations—real flash-frozen meat from extinct uncloned animals. Nanoinjectors for her tastebuds to make water and coffee and semen and vaginal fluid more interesting-tasting. Hallucinogenic gravy for Sunday afternoon's spaghetti and meatballs with Beccaria, that old nostalgist.

It was a good trade, recorded on the blockchain, and delivery was supposed to be immediate in exchange for thirteen nanoseconds at .1c thirty-six ship-days from the placement of the order. What Chakravarty got was a slice of rancid bacon, what appeared to be an old-fashioned tab of acid on a Mickey Mouse postage stamp, and a cup of black coffee loaded with sugar.

She addressed the AI directly, which was always risky. Though the AI could comprehend idiomatic natural language, its ability to encode messages of its own into a human language was rather more limited.

"What have I done to deserve this?" she said aloud.

P=M

It read like a joke. Of course, the actual joke answer to the question "What have I done to deserve this?"—at least aboard *Danneskjöld*—was "A=A." Value for value. You got out of the economy, and the community, and yourself, what you put into it. Everything came from A being equivalent to A, the ultimate axiom. But, *what made it* a joke answer to the plaintive wail of "What have I done to deserve this?" was this:

Well, there was a second joke embedded within the straightforward universal fact, the equation of freedom, the expression A=A.

It's funny because it's true.

Chakravarty couldn't trust the AI to explain its joke, and a joke explained is never amusing anyway, so she went to her personal databases and ran P=M through them until she found that P, supposedly, was "profit," and M was . . .

Surplus value?

"What the fuck is that supposed to mean?" Chakravarty exclaimed aloud. "Surplus value" was war talk. World War III talk. The War was as long as it was bloody, which was to say it was nuclear and most fatalities simply vaporized. That was one way to resolve an intellectual dispute about the nature of the political economy. The irony was that the free world, Chakravarty's side, won the war . . . and then lost it by creating bureaucracies and regulations and the granting of special rights to the incompetent and the weak while robbing the productive members of society to pay for it all. The supposed "externality" of radioactive fallout required a massive state and the suppression of human ingenuity, just because the seas had boiled away and the air was poison. Well, projects such as *Danneskjöld* demonstrated that humanity would never be crushed; if the planet was poison, leave the planet. It was the fault of the second-handers anyway, for not letting the ninety-nine ex-gaiaists live their lives in peace. Without the ninety-nine, the Earth had probably already descended into a new dark age, the Communism of the club-wielding cannibal mob, swinging weapons through the blackened, sour air.

The air, Chakravarty thought. She inhaled deeply, like she was about to dive to the bottom of a pool, but her lungs wouldn't expand. *The air, the air . . . what happened to the air!*

Chakravarty woke up in the ballroom, tied to her own bondage blob. She spit her hair out of her mouth, shook it from her face. Floating above her was Thomasen and his affinity group.

"Hello," said Thomasen. They'd never been in the ballroom together before. He was clothed. She was clothed. The other three members of the working group were clothed. Whatever was happening, or about to happen, it was probably limited to kidnapping.

"Could one of you please put my hair up," she said, her gaze flitting from one to the other of the two women in Thomasen's group. One of them, Reed, smiled, kicked off the curved wall of the bondage blob, and, quickly put Chakravarty's hair in a ponytail then tucked it away between Chakravarty's shoulder blades. Reed's hair was short, little more than a buzz cut. She had shaved her head for this encounter.

"I guess you're wondering—" said Thomasen.

"You're Communists," Chakravarty interrupted. "You reprogrammed the AI to distribute food, power, and even sensor power and data processing according to Marx's sick ideas that equate profit with exploitation. You've been starving me. You've been dimming the lights in the hallways because they don't belong to anyone in particular. You all look pretty well fed though. Let me guess, under the new regime, now you're the most productive and get the most food, the most *oxygen* in your quarters. You tried to kill me!"

"No—"

"Yes!" said Reed, with a glare for Thomasen.

"Yes, we are Communists," said Thomasen, "but no, we didn't reprogram the AI."

"And we didn't try to kill you. We saved you," said Reed. "I do environment, life support. When the AI revealed P=M, we were all pinged, so I started monitoring your room. The AI didn't like what you were saying, so . . ."

"And you didn't program the AI to kill me? Then who did?"

Thomasen nodded over toward Kim, who raised his eyebrows at the gesture, then caught himself.

"Oh yeah, uhm . . ." Kim said. "Best we can determine, *the AI* reprogrammed the AI. You know that old Milton Friedman joke, about China taking over the entire world, bringing about a golden age of full Communism to the four corners of the Earth, *except* for Hong Kong?"

"I only know one joke," Chakravarty said.

"Oh. Well, the punchline is this: The Chicoms didn't take over Hong Kong so they could monitor its economy and thus know how to price capital goods for the rest of the world," Kim said. Nobody laughed.

"I guess you had to be there," said Thomasen. "But best we can determine, the AI is doing that, except reversed. It's doing perfect market-based distribution and the market continually clears. It's real-time equilibrium, but to double-check itself, it also scrutinizes inputs based on, uh"—Thomas shrugged, extravagantly—"volume three of Marx's *Capital*. And when it first perceived the black hole, the AI started prioritizing those results *over* distribution patterns based on marginal utility."

"Which turned out to be very good for this particular working group," Reed said. "We have been benefitting, significantly. Frankly, it's because we do all the work around here. You like breathing, don't you?"

"So now we're Communists," said the other woman in the group. "You like being able to take a shit, don't you?" Xenakis or something, Chakravarty remembered. She was in charge of waste management and environmental recycling. Also not an EVP. *None of these people are executive vice presidents of anything!*

"What do you want from me?" Chakravarty asked.

"The only thing the AI isn't redistributing is propulsion," Xenakis said. "The ship is headed toward the black hole as if it cannot perceive it, even though it clearly can, and has reacted to its existence in other ways."

"The black hole is like something having come from nothing," Kim said. His eyebrow twitched again. "Hmm."

"But you figured out the AI, or at least it confided in you," Thomasen said to Chakravarty.

"After a fashion," Reed said.

"We want to know if you have any bright ideas, anything to say, about what the AI might want from the black hole," said Thomasen.

"More precisely, what each AI might want from the black hole," said Xenakis. "Does the market AI want to explore and exploit it, does the Marxist AI want it to eliminate scarcity?"

"Something from nothing!" Kim said.

"I do have something to say," Chakravarty said. She cleared her throat, and doing her best impression of Koen's lilting tenor, shouted, "Pumpernickel!"

It was close enough to Koen's safe word to work. The ballroom stopped rotating. Gravity returned, hard, and the working group fell against the walls of the spherical room. The bondage blob's restraints snapped open, and the ballroom's door dilated. Chakravarty leaped for it, and wiggled through the hole, shut it behind her, then hit the general alarm on her watch.

Ong almost solved the problem by ejecting the ballroom, with Thomasen's group in it, out of the ship and into the black hole. If they're so curious about it, after all. But the toilets stopped working. The temperature started rising and every screen and bit of glass started fogging over from the exhalations of ninety-five individuals. The AI opened the ballroom itself and ushered the Thomasen group out. Ong would have remanded them to their quarters, but the four of them now had the best quarters aboard *Danneskjöld*, so it wouldn't have been much of a punishment anyway.

The AI wanted the black hole, that much was certain. Resources had been so thoroughly dedicated to a close flyby that perhaps both AIs wanted the black hole. Koen could only hand out the dry protein cakes with vitamin-sauce packets the AI decided everyone was going to eat, and shrug about it.

Then something new happened. Another black hole. Chakravarty was right. The plasma drive—which sucked in charged particles from the interstellar medium, ran them through the ship, and spit them out the back—was somehow generating microscopic black holes. The microdimension from which the first had emerged was twisted into a superstring, one spread out across realspace like a lattice, a net. Three of them now. Four. They were still hours out from the flyby past the first one. Though tiny, it was stable. All these black holes were stable. All five.

"Seven," said Ong. Another all-hands meeting, in the conference room. Several people had brought guns they'd printed themselves. "This is for you," Szymanska said, as she held the barrel of hers under Thomasen's nose. Beccaria was open-carrying too, and drifting menacingly toward Kim and Xenakis.

"Oh, is it a present?" Thomasen asked, and that was a joke because of course nobody exchanged gifts aboard *Danneskjöld*, but only Chakravarty laughed at the punchline. Everyone else was keenly observing the displays, watching tiny black holes the size of small towns and the mass of small stars form before them.

It was foolish to look up into the sky and discern patterns, to give meaning to them. The constellations as seen from Earth were arbitrary assortments, culturally overdetermined patterns based on the superstitions of primitives and fools eager for something to worship. And yet, even the ninety-nine travelers couldn't help but peer at the formations on the displays now, hoping to determine . . . what?

"Kind of like a web," Koen said to Chakravarty.

"Hmm," Chakravarty said.

He sought out her hand under the table.

Determine what the AI, the smartest of them all, a thing that they had built but that wasn't remotely human, that may not even be rational despite its ability to calculate, believed to be true.

Were the black holes property—values created from the aether by a value-valuing being? Were the black holes free stuff, an infinite supply of energy that could be distributed evenly and forever according to the needs of sentient beings?

Koen's hand felt warm in Chakravarty's. She squeezed it tight.

"You know something," Chakravarty said, right before everything—and yes, we do mean *absolutely everything* from muons to galactic clusters—stopped and went black, "from this vantage point, those eight black holes . . . they're arranged in a familiar pattern. Sort of like, no, *exactly like*, the eight eyes of a giant cosmic spider."

TRIPLICATE

Freddy Costello and Michael Z. Williamson

Prologue: 31 January 21XX, Consensus Epoch

To Their Excellency the President,
and the Congress of the ReUNITED! States:
The Fourth World War lasted exactly seventeen days,
fourteen hours, twelve minutes, and thirty-six seconds. Its
outcome was inconclusive as far as initial results show, but
the After-Action Review has only entered its fifth year. It
is thus far too soon to develop any real Lessons Identified,
or to discern whether World War IV was an anomaly or
the shape of things to come. We have only three more staff
cycles to finalize our report before it is due to the Second-
Level Plenary New United Nations Security Council War
Powers and Conduct Review Board Presidium, in
triplicate, certified by biodegradable plankton-based ink
signatures using only officially approved pronouns. The
2LPNUNSCWPaCRBP has denied our request for an
extension to the deadline.
Also please see my attached request for retirement.

Respectfully,
HANSCOM T. HANSCOM, General, ReU! Army
Commander, ReU! Homeland Defense Command

PS. I, using my declared pronouns, apologize for sending a true handwritten hard paper copy of my own thoughts and recollections of the conflict. I feel that it is important for the benefit of individual bodies in service to their collective identities, so much so that I willingly cause harm to Plant-Based Persons commonly referred to as "trees." I trust Your Collective Noun will understand. May the Mono, Poly, or Pantheistic Subjective Moral Standard of Your Choice (or None), demonstrate compassion and mercy.

PPS. Fuck you all with a rusted pipe, I quit.

I. It Begins . . .

> *"Don't ever be the first, don't ever be the last, and don't ever volunteer to do anything."*
>
> —US military truism

My alarm woke me promptly at 0400 local time. I was only half-asleep, anxious to get this mission underway and concluded as quickly as possible. Considering how little use airfields get these days, the Distinguished Visitor Quarters on Dover Air Component Base are dated but still some of the nicest I've ever seen. I availed myself of the amenities. I took my own sweet time in the shower and enjoyed the luxury of a four-ounce cup of TruKaf, made from ethically sourced and equity-certified semiorganic coffee beans. While my Social Credit expense limit is a lot higher than most, I'm not authorized unlimited access to things like electricity, water, and heat. Checking my privilege, I decided to save my usual run for later. The cool Atlantic Seaboard dusk would make for a pleasant evening run, and I'd likely have the roads all to myself. Unfortunately, I can't run the base perimeter trail, it's now part of the Animal Persons preserved habitat, and off-limits to humans.

All cleaned up and presentable, I straightened my gig line and checked my teeth in the mirror one last time. I felt the buzz of my secure handheld phone. It was a technological marvel most citizens would never get to see, let alone use. Retrieving it, I saw the small portrait of my appointed escort for the duration of this operation. A cheerful voice and giant smile greeted me. "Good morning, General, I'm already at the control tower. The Neo-Soviet aircraft will land in forty-five minutes."

"Thank you, Major. It was the UN code as expected? Treaty compliance inspection?"

"Yes, General. Do you approve the Homeland Defense Command escorts to return to base?"

"Yes, they can stand down. Have we positively ID'd the type of plane, Major Thomvs?" I learned when I arrived two nights ago that it was pronounced like "Thomas," and that their name was just "Thomvs."

"Yes, it's an LN-850. Oversized cargo conversion."

"Copy all, I'll be there in a few minutes." I waited patiently outside until Thomvs arrived with the car.

"All set, General?" Thomvs's voice practically squeaked with cheer.

"We are. Are thou ready?"

"They are ready, General, please have their seat, we need to hurry."

The ride to the dingy air traffic control tower was uneventful, and we didn't speak much. At the time, I had no cause to suspect that anything was out of the ordinary, despite this being an unusual event. The Neo-Soviets hadn't requested a Global Warfare Treaty Compliance Oversight Conference in twenty staff cycles, but it was something we trained and prepared for on a daily basis. In retrospect, our confidence in the integrity of the process above all else nearly did us in.

The commander, a colonel, met us at the car. He gave his pronouns and escorted Major Thomvs and me up to the control room where the chief controller greeted us. "Good morning, General, we received an update about an hour ago, there are actually two planes inbound, the '850 and a smaller escort, not a fighter, it looks like DV airlift."

"You should have woken me up for that!" I snapped. I shouldn't have done that, as raising my voice can have ugly consequences to Social Credit and my next evaluation. The controller seemed to ignore it, fortunately.

"Yes, sir," he said, snapping back into old terminology. "But the codes all matched the decryption matrix you authenticated. It's a UN-approved diplomatic code, an older code, but it checks out. There's no turning them back, we have to let them land."

Thomvs stared at the circling monstrosity and shook their head. "Wow, that's a big plane. There are suspicions about the carbon tax signature documentation we received. It checks out as biofuel, but it looks suspiciously like refined petroleum. It's amazing that old planes like this are even still allowed, much less capable of operating." I should have made a note of that at the time.

Thomvs wasn't exaggerating. The LN-850 was the single largest cargo aircraft left in the world. The Sovs had exactly one, and they jumped through all sorts of regulatory hoops and circuses to keep it operational. In the light of the rising sun, I could see the massive shape revealed, no longer just hinted at by its overt lighting in the predawn darkness. Black smoke belched from its engines. *Biofuel my ass,* I thought, *the Neo-Sovs don't give one damn about biofuel. They'll face steep fines for this. Still, they build things to last, just like we used to. Today we just don't build them, period.* I buried my thoughts, before Thomvs could sense my inner discomfort. In contrast, the little Nabokov VIP bird was miniscule, a gnat. The Nabokov's crew, speaking heavily accented Global Aviation Standard, landed the plainly marked aircraft, and taxied without fanfare or incident. All in order and to the perfect letter of international law.

II. Bundles

"Cynicism is the smoke that rises from the ashes of burned-out dreams." —Unknown Major, on the daily thrashings delivered to action officers

Major Thomvs smiled at me. They had a fantastic smile. "General, we should make our way down to the car."

I nodded, and Thomvs drove us out to the flight line.

It had been cleared of Plant-Based Lifeforms, just enough for what we needed to do. I made a note to commemorate their collective sacrifices at the conclusion of this operation. While Animal Persons must have unrestricted movement within protected habitats and remain undisturbed, exceptions exist for national security events like this. Given the cracked and crumbling state of the runway, I wasn't sure how safe it was for human use. As we approached a security checkpoint, I smiled at the phrase "Dover Air Force Base" still visible on one of the Restricted Area signs. The Air Component dropped the word "Force" decades ago. Too aggressive. Flight-line security gave us a cursory bio-assessment, scanning and wiping down every surface of the car, every visible inch of our uniforms and equipment for bacteria and viruses. Some of those plants were endangered, and we needed to ensure the preservation of their rights to autonomy. The military remains at the forefront of national environmental and climate security.

Thomvs parked the car outside the passenger terminal and accompanied me to the runway. The base commander met us at the front of an honor cordon, only a short distance from the Nabokov's main cabin door. We stood at attention and waited patiently for the ambassador to make themselves finally known. Per treaty, identities are protected until the individual touches foreign soil. The Nabokov's main cabin door started to crack open, and we rendered impeccable salutes as dawn broke over the airfield. I expected to see a gaggle of officious Neo-Sovs in faux fur coats, just to add insult to the injury they'd already inflicted on the base's wildlife and vegetation.

That didn't happen. Instead, the aircraft's main cabin door flung open, and a large, wrapped bundle was thrown unceremoniously out onto the crumbling tarmac. Followed by a second. And a third.

"What the . . . ?" The base commander dropped his salute and looked at me incredulously. I was annoyed. I'm used to Neo-Soviet games; every staff cycle they try something different to gain advantage over us in the New United Nations. Not today!

"Mind if I borrow your flight-line security for a second, Colonel?"

He was completely at a loss for what to do. "Umm, General Hanscom, sure, it's just that . . ."

"Okay thanks!" I ignored him and motioned to the major and the two nearest security technicians to help me investigate the bundles. As we approached, a fourth and then a fifth bundle were thrown to the ground. Then a sixth. Still, no human being emerged from the aircraft. I knelt alongside the growing pile and put on the pair of NullLeather gloves I shoved in my pocket this morning. Better safe than sorry when it comes to Neo-Sovs. The bundles were tightly wrapped in what looked like hemp fabric, very organic-looking stuff, secured by rope, presumably hemp as well.

"Does anybody have a blade or a knife?" The security technicians, Thomvs, and the colonel all shook their heads, looking surprised and unsure of what to do or say next.

"Fine!" I roared and did the unthinkable. I produced a small folding knife from under my coat where I kept it attached to my belt. Luckily for me, the security people were so cursory in their bio-assessment scan they hadn't found it. Fortunately, I couldn't hear the gasps of horror due to the flight-line noise. I cut the top knot of the closest bundle and sliced a small portion of the covering away. The package was full of memory sticks labeled "Compliance Inspection," and "Formal Complaint Processing," and "Environmental Impact Analysis," and more. I performed the same autopsy on a second bundle, growing fearful of the implications. More memory sticks. A couple of thin-client servers. Hard-copy paper documents in manila folders. Hundreds of them!

Oh no. This can't be happening. Not to me. Not this close to retirement!

"Colonel! Major! Collect these bundles and get them back to Base Operations and recall your staff! Put the base on full alert and . . . !" I didn't have time to finish giving orders.

"General! We need to clear this runway NOW! EVERYONE MOVE!" All this time, a growling sound, like a hurricane in a wind tunnel, had been growing. As we waited for the '850 to land, I watched flight-line vehicles puttering about, doing what they do, and since I was an Army officer, I had no idea what that was. I assumed it was just air people doing what air people ordinarily did, despite being out of regular practice. Thomvs grabbed my arm, and we ran back to the passenger terminal on foot. I only looked back as we reached the safety of indoors.

The '850 had landed while we were absorbed by the spectacle on the runway. The giant polluting monstrosity slowly came to a resting stop a few hundred feet from the little Nabokov. The great beast sat there, nose turned halfway or so toward us. Security surrounded it, as did fire mitigation trucks. Meanwhile, the Nabokov's main door had buttoned itself back up before I or anyone else could so much as order a team to board and seize it.

As I stared, the major brought new information. "Tower says they ignored all orders to ascend to altitude and fly out to a point over water and stay there. They did a rapid descent! Completely ignored us, and we had to clear everything out of the way, otherwise they just would have run us over."

"Look!" Without thinking, I grabbed Thomvs's shoulder. I only suspected before, but now I was certain that "they" was in fact "she." Either an excellent self-declared presentation or a from-birth genetic expression. Her parents, however many she had, selected an excellent cell line. Until now, I'd gone out of my way to avoid looking at her for any length of time, lest I face a Class II Male Gaze complaint. My career couldn't survive another demerit like that. Shaking myself free of distraction, I watched the massive aircraft's nose slowly open, and ramps deploy. A different set of engines growled to life.

Thomvs was horrified. "Those sound like internal combustion! That's practically a war crime!"

That's when the enemy's deployment began in earnest. Forklifts rolled forward out of that gaping black hole. Forklifts carrying pallets. Pallets stacked high with document containers. A never-ending parade of documents. I made eye contact with Major Thomvs for the first time since we'd met.

"We're at war," I said, half shocked myself.

III. Immediate Response Authority

*"His knowledge of that topic is only PowerPoint
deep."*   —Unknown staff officer

Stunned, Thomvs looked at me in confusion.

I said, "Major, I need you to listen to me very carefully.
On my authority, get the colonel, mobilize every single
uniformed person on this installation and put them to
work immediately. Get every single document, every
single hard drive, whatever those Neo-Soviet reprobates
throw at you, and just stamp every single one as
RECEIVED, PENDING REVIEW. Don't even bother
to read them. Don't waste any time analyzing or
evaluating them yet. The UN inspection team will land in
a few days at best. It's critical they see those stamps! Hop
all your people up on ibuprofen and caffeine if you have
to, dig into the war reserve stockpile!"

The major nodded, a measure of professional
demeanor and confidence returning to her face. "Yes, sir!
I'll get them going around the clock, and we'll even get
the local reservists in here too. What else do you need?"

"I need a video telecon with the Joint Chiefs. Don't
worry about the electricity budget. I'll give you the
numbers and access codes, and then meet me in your
biggest conference room. We'll need the space." She
seemed to absorb what I was saying, but I wasn't done yet.
"Quarantine these damn planes. As soon as they finish
unloading the '850, isolate the Sovs onboard and keep an

armed cordon around them. I have a few ideas for dealing with them."

"Yes, sir!" she said, excitement shining in her eyes. Amazing, all it took to make Thomvs drop the façade was a little bit of high-stakes stress.

IV. Defensive Campaign Design

"I may be slow, but I do poor work."
—Unknown Major, US Army Europe

It took far too long to get to the rundown base headquarters building. I met the command staff in the main conference room. The secure video teleconference I ordered was already connected with the National Military Consensus Center, deep in the Nonagon. All eleven[1] Joint Chiefs were on screen and socially distanced, some of them participating from their well-appointed secure home offices. The Secretary of Defense hadn't dialed in yet, but we received word to start the conference and bring them up to speed when they joined.

Sitting at the archaic real wood table, I scanned the on-screen faces surrounding me on three sides. The command post team found and hastily mounted the screens straight from Class III Enviro-Protect storage. Some of the junior personnel wouldn't even touch them at first, but luckily the threat of massive Social Credit Demerits all around righted the situation.

---

[1] Chair, Vice Chair, Army, Navy, Air Component, Space Component, Cyber Service, Coast Guard, National Guard, the Environmental Protection Agency, Merchant Marine, National Public Health Service, and the Internal Security Service

The Chair looked like they had just woken up. They looked awful. The long thin crack down the middle of the main screen directly in front of me didn't help. They still had beads of sweat, indicating that it probably wasn't sleep we had pulled the Chair away from. The resolution on these ancient, banned devices was so good I could see the ReJuv injection sites on their forehead. They and the rest of the Joint Chiefs were clearly agitated and unhappy to be disturbed. I was prepared for the firestorm, but for the others here, this would probably be unlike anything they'd ever experienced or would ever want to experience again. The Chair finally spoke.

"General Hanscom, we see thee. Are thou well?" The sarcasm was dripping from their voice.

Oh yeah, here it comes. I knew this was going to be a complete shitshow. "Yes, Chair, good morning to all the Joint Chiefs and Human-Based Persons on this call! Thank you for meeting with us on short notice. While the arrival of Neo-Soviet aircraft with an official delegation was known and understood to all bodies with the appropriate clearances, the Neo-Soviets have engaged in unusual behaviors." I chose my words very carefully.

"Unusual? This body doesn't understand, General," said the Chief of Staff of the Armed Environmental Protection Agency. "You had better have a really good explanation for this. Really good, otherwise you and every idiot body that listened to you will be answering to a Reeducation Court-Martial!"

You? I thought. *Okay, that's an outright insult, in front of the entire Joint Chiefs, directed to me, also a full GENERAL BODY, in front of all these junior bodies!* I struggled to contain my anger; only a Joint Chief could survive the Social Demerits my completely justified Complaints would generate! However, since this was Their Truth, they had nothing to fear, especially the AEPA and the Interior Security Service. They Collective were untouchable. Still, the younger folks didn't deserve this suffering.

"Of course. We will clear the room." I smiled, nodded at the Senior-Most Leading Sergeant present, who understood completely and shooed everyone out except Major Thomvs and me. I haven't seen anyone move that fast in my entire career.

"May we introduce Major Thomvs. They are prepared to give thee all the intelligence we have so far."

The Chair growled at Thomvs. "Major, thou may proceed. And thou doesn't need to waste the Chiefs' time with backstory, They Collective are aware of the irregularities with the LN-850, and formal complaints are being prepared for launch at the Neo-Sovs through UNECH, the UN Environmental Compliance Headquarters."

"The fines alone will wreck their economy!" The AEPA Chief of Staff smiled.

I was flabbergasted. *The fool! Those would take staff YEARS to resolve. We didn't have staff years!* Thomvs broke in and recounted everything that happened once the Sov aircraft landed, as if sensing my agitation and trying to save me from falling on my sword.

"I'm sorry, they did what? You should have just stormed the planes, General!" The Air Component Chief of Staff was so agitated he slipped into Unsocial Speech patterns. His Social Credit score could afford it, so I felt no sympathy for him.

Undeterred, Thomvs continued. "At this time, our main line of effort is to fully account for every single document, media item, and all hardware. The entire base complement is stamping everything in accordance with standard procedures." This caught their attention, and I could tell their collective confusion because no one bothered to mute their microphones.

"Gentle Bodies, please! You can't fight in here; this is a war teleconference!" The Secretary of Defense had snuck into the telecon unnoticed and unannounced. "General Hanscom, what is thine assessment of the situation?"

I had seen SecDef do this before. The technique kept all the fractious Joint Chiefs off their game, lest one get too cozy with the President themself. I couldn't waste this opening.

"Yes, Mx. Secretary! Gentle Bodies, my assessment is that the Neo-Soviets have quite possibly launched covert lawfare against the ReUNITED! States. To confirm or deny this, we will need to analyze and respond to everything the Sovs dropped on us and prepare for the UN Inspector General team that will surely soon follow."

All fell silent, soaking in the severity of the situation. As if on cue, the SecDef spoke. "Stand by, we are receiving a call from POTReU!S." He had trouble not pronouncing it as "Petraeus," an old name guaranteed to cause a strike against his Social Credit score although no one living understood why.

The Secretary disappeared from the screen. Staff minutes ticked by.

"Every Body, as you were bickering, the Secretary of

National Intelligence briefed the President. This situation has evolved."

The SecDef bristled as they spoke. There was no love lost between the powerful intelligence director and them. They struggled to keep the distaste out of their voice.

"We've received an official New UN Inspector General notice. An authorized Inspector General team has departed the Hall of Global Social Law pursuant to a possible declaration of lawfare by the Neo-Soviet Eurasian Union against the ReUNITED! States of the Western Hemisphere. Expect the IG to arrive in ninety-six staff hours. All bodies will provide every accommodation to the IG team."

Before I or anyone else could respond, the AEPA Chief swore, and targeted me. "HANSCOM, YOU'RE responsible for Homeland Defense! Care to explain this failure?" The meeting dissolved into swearing, the kind not heard publicly in decades, and racked up tens of thousands of Social Demerits. The sheer amount of nanocurrency lost that day was staggering.

"Please! Everybody!" The Chair called for calm, and the furor quickly subsided.

The SecDef cleared their throat. "We've avoided war with the Neo-Soviets for thirty-five consecutive staff years, by ruthless application of Effects-Based Staffing and battle rhythm discipline. It must be this way because World War III made it impossible to do otherwise. There are too few of us left to fight, too little to fight with, and too little to fight over. Such is the price of civilization, and of the survival of humanity."

As that sank in, the SecDef didn't wait for a response.

"General Hanscom, the President has authorized thee to present a Course of Action and requisition assets. What do thou need?"

"Yes, Mx.! Here's my recommendation. We have already set up a twenty-four-hour contingency staff response cell. We're not even out of the 'receive' phase yet, but we'll need to drastically expand operations to counter this, if indeed it is full lawfare as we suspect. Before the IG team arrives, we can have all 250 tons of enemy documents certified positive receipt at a minimum. That should keep the IG busy for the first few days. Then, we need to analyze the attacks and respond in kind. And we also need to care for our Neo-Soviet guests. They are already complaining that their lavatory facilities are near failure because we've kept them quarantined on the planes. We'll need to construct an appropriate facility for them as soon as we can serve them with an appropriate response for the LN-850."

The Chief of Staff of the Army laughed. The relief on the call was palpable, which meant I had them on my side for now.

"We need a massive budget infusion; open up the electrical, water, heat, and food stores. Petroleum and plastic too. We'll need lots of real paper and real ink for both the defensive campaign and the counterstrike. We'll need fully trained special-operations compliance teams. We need authorization for a full reserve lawyer mobilization." The AEPA Chief nearly came out of his seat. He couldn't take any more and swore to destroy me.

"Oh, stuff it, Regina!" the chair shouted at him. For now, at least, the Chair was my ally. "You'll get everything you need, Hanscom. All of it. We've been piping this into the Situation Room in the Rainbow House. Do you need anything else?"

I looked over at Thomvs, her eyes wide. While I'm not a lip reader, "stimulants" was as clear as the day is long. "Stimulants. Lots and lots of stimulants."

"Done! As far as that budget request goes, we'll start by charging as much as possible to your own Social Credit accounts. We have full faith and confidence in you, Hanscom, don't let our Collective Noun down!"

"Thank you, Chair. Hanscom out." *It figures.*

V. Stabilizing the Front Line

"None of us is as dumb as all of us."
—Excerpted from a briefing, USEUCOM

Clouds of dust, disturbed for the first time in who-knows-how-long, hung everywhere in the enormous hangar where the colonel established the hastily assembled and minimally trained Provisional Contingency Response Processing Teams. Space was a nonissue, as this base once housed dozens of cargo planes not much smaller than the Soviet monster still sitting inside the armed cordon on the flight line. The reconstruction of the old hangar's interior was spectacular. On short notice, the colonel found a suitable cadre, mostly identified cismen, able to build what resembled an old-fashioned assembly line. The base's ancient cargo transfer gear was disassembled, moved, cleaned, and reassembled here perfectly by the skilled NCOs and crusty civilians. However, before they so much as twitched a muscle, the colonel had to promise them immunity from all disciplinary action, and they demanded he put it in writing. In triplicate. A horrifying display of toxic masculinity and triggering language followed, but they got the job done. War is an ugly thing, and sometimes the ends justify the use of problematic ways and means. We had no other choice. The colonel gained my respect for his bold leadership.

I walked the length and breadth of the hangar, inspecting various construction sites and ad hoc machine shops. I smiled at the "Temporary Decontamination and Medical Safety Quarters," coming together at the far end of the building, just waiting for our increasingly impatient Neo-Sov guests. Meanwhile, the base's junior enlisted, supplemented by some from the Merchant Marine branch, unsealed and opened crates and boxes by the dozen, and then placed the contents on a rolling belt. I marveled at the younger Air People as they meticulously sorted the contents by type—stick, drive, paper document, and a curious array of things we could only classify as "other." The Sovs had just mixed everything up and crammed it in every which way, to complicate the matter. Lieutenants made up the Stamp Processing Unit. They stamped everything as RECEIVED, PENDING REVIEW.

Further down the massive gaggle of belts and conveyors, a formation of captains, passed-over majors, and squinty, humorless senior NCOs tried to stage the mess into some semblance of order for the Analysis Team. Major Thomvs led that all-important effort and reported her findings directly to me. I don't know how she did it, and I didn't ask, but she managed to scare up a team of

Internal Security Service and National Intelligence Corps personnel from the Cyber Service to aid her. The stare of her ice-cold eyes seemed to instill her charges with a powerful sense of urgency. I could see both of them now that she pulled her surprisingly long hair back into an Equine-Based Person tail and cleared away those fashionable lopsided bangs. "Bangs" is another word I can't use publicly, because it makes some Bodies feel "unsafe."

After a few hours, the hangar smelled of plastic, adhesive residue, coffee, and sweat. And feet. The environmental units howled as they ground out their best effort at the ragged edge of hard-wired energy usage limits. They barely knocked the humidity down without doing anything about the temperature. I started to grow nervous. *Too slow!* Normally unthinkable, I contemplated issuing a waiver for the entire gauntlet of operational safety measures just to speed things up. Medical personnel, including National Public Health Service officers, enforced breaks to avoid repetitive stress injuries and other ailments. This was quickly becoming an all-branches operation. Other medical and psychological issues rapidly emerged as well. Decades had come and gone since anyone had seen papercuts in such numbers. A few Bodies even fainted at the sight of blood, no matter how little. The colonel declared an entire separate building as a safe space for all the stress casualties we accumulated in those first few hours.

Nevertheless, we persisted. Once the troops got into a routine, the next three full staff days or so weren't too bad. I made several battlefield circulations and tried to enhance morale. If Bodies thought this mess was stressful, they'd never survive the Nonagon's depths.

The perpetual shuffling and rolling of boxes down the belts made a din. The troops spoke little but kept it mostly professional and focused.

"—I need another stamp, ASAP."

"—That's your fourth one!"

"—I know!"

"—These bastards even made a claim under Section 47 of the Aviation Torts in Wartime Act, Subsection 2319. They're claiming stress injuries from their original offload, and now they're blaming us for it."

"—What the hell is an 'Offog'?"

"—We don't know, but apparently we need twelve of them!"

"—Disregard! Use Hazardous Material Destruction Form 121-B!"

"—Form 121-B? You idiot, that's been rescinded!"

"—Stand down, we have the correct version! List all twelve as 'decommissioned and subsequently destroyed.' Backdate it, make it triplicate, and problem solved!"

The colonel wisely set up a forward command post in the second-story offices ringing the north side of the hangar. I assumed these were where the old Air Force ran aircraft maintenance operations before the base's aircraft were destroyed for Treaty Compliance. Major Thomvs and I scrutinized the enemy material itself. The colonel's phone never left his ear, and his eyes were stuck on the decrepit computer screen in front of him. I watched it flicker, a reminder of city lights during preprogrammed rolling blackouts. Few places were exempt, but this short list now included Dover, thanks to Presidential directive.

The colonel hadn't slept since this whole mess started,

and I could see that he was struggling. The constant influx of supply requests, purchase orders, and taking care of morale and disciplinary issues was taking its toll. His SNCOs hadn't slept in three days either, judging from the number of mental health cases and suicide attempts.

"Copy all, we're down to twenty-four-hours supply of stamps?" He put down the phone momentarily. "General, I hate to do this, sir, but we're going 'red' on stamps and need another bulk buy. The other lines of accounting aren't open yet; Congress won't authorize the appropriation until the Joint Staff fixes whatever it is that they don't like. May I . . . ?"

"Do it. Worry about the accounting later." *Well*, I thought, *there goes today's hot shower.*

"Sir, it's almost time, we should review our talking points." Thomvs reminded me that I was due for my first daily videocon with General Eugene Volkov, the enemy commander. We'd let him and his people off their planes but quickly moved them into the prefab trailer complex. We confiscated their cameras, their phones, everything. We gave the personal electronic devices back to them in pieces and didn't allow the Sovs to leave the compound. They took it rather well, considering how long they'd gone with only aircraft chemical toilets and bottled water. We even found them some expired cookies in the passenger-terminal supply lockers. Pre-WWIII expired. Only the best for our guests.

Thomvs handed me a folder with prep materials. I flipped through Volkov's bio, looking for anything that might give me a clue to what the Sovs wanted out of this little war. Thomvs must have read the questions on my face.

"There's not really much to go on, sir. Very generic upbringing, education, career, nondescript postings. Identifies as 'he/him/his,' which is expected."

"Ah, he's Intelligence then. The Sovs always make the mistake of creating profiles so painfully boring they're obviously fake. I know how to deal with him."

"If you say so, sir." Thomvs gave me a coy smile. "Are you ready?"

"Lead the way!"

She took me to an office with nothing more than a desk, two chairs, an electric lamp, and a very new-looking VTU, which she informed me was paired to a similar one installed for Volkov's personal use. I guessed this was straight from the war reserve stockpile, or she'd spent a lot of my personal expense account on getting them rapid-drone delivered. I winced as I thought about the Social Credit deduction for exercising that privilege. She dialed the prearranged number to the single-channel secure line we provided to the Sovs. We couldn't restrict their ability to call home or to contact the UN, but that didn't mean we owed them unfettered access to our comms. This VTU ran on a single hard fiber line direct between the two ends.

Thomvs dialed up the number, and the VTU made noises I've only previously heard from museum pieces. *Where are we keeping these things?*

"General Hanscom, thank you for calling me. I trust your troops are busy now, yes? Over 250 tonnes of busy?"

"Oh yes, we're busy. In fact, I just signed off on the first batch of responses to your opening salvo there, Eugene, do you mind if I call you that?"

"Not at all, Hanscom. I trust you'll see that everything is proper and in order? The UN will be here shortly, and they will verify everything you know."

"Just you wait. You won't know how to spell your own name when we're through!"

"Hanscom, please, temper! I'm sure your Social Credit score is as fragile as our intelligence experts say it is. You're no favorite of anyone."

"Let's just cut the bullshit, Eugene. This time, you and me, every day until this is over?"

"Yes, that is acceptable."

"The food and accommodations to your liking?"

"Absolutely not! This is deplorable and substandard you know, the UN will—"

"Hey Eugene, look at the time, I got to go. Same time tomorrow, okay, my friend? Ciao!"

I killed the connection and gave Thomvs my cold General stare. Something clicked in her eyes, and in her cheeks, I saw just a hint of color.

I said, "I think we need to run another round of decontamination on the entire Sov contingent. You know, stripped down, foam, cold water hoses, that sort of thing? We need a team from the Department of Alcohol, Firearms, Tobacco, Pharmaceuticals, Explosives, and Entertainment to check for illegal inorganics, nicotine contamination, contraband real alcohol, the works. Can you do that for us?"

"Oh, sir, I've been dying for the chance! The DAFTPEE folks will love it!"

The sheer joy in her voice made me feel a little flustered. Before I could answer, before my voice could break or something else embarrassing happened, I was saved. Klaxons blared throughout the complex, and overhead lights strobed and bled red over everything in sight. The base loudspeaker system crackled.

"Alarm Red! Alarm Red! Possible chemical contamination in the operations area!"

Thomvs and I briefly made eye contact, and then scrambled for the office door. Out on the catwalk, I looked down into the entire complex, a scene of total chaos. Loud footsteps on the metal stairs turned out to be the colonel, out of breath and waving his hands.

He gasped and relayed the bad news. "It's the damn ink! We might have an entire trailer full of contaminated documents! If you don't have them handy, I need to ask you to retrieve your chem bags. We're going to MOPP 4, full chem suits, masks, gloves, overshoes, the whole thing! It's the only way to be sure."

I cringed. I couldn't argue with his logic, and it was still his base. However, full chem gear would make an already tense, barely tolerable operation ten times worse. We'd already had a few workplace-violence incidents pop up due to stressed tempers, including misgendering and a host of other offenses. This wouldn't help the morale and social cohesion status one bit. Still, I didn't have real cause to override the base commander, nor did I want the extra burden of running this place on top of everything else. "Absolutely, Colonel, we're with you one hundred percent. Major Thomvs?"

"Yes, sir."

"As soon as you get your suit on, file a formal protest, bring it to me for signature, and then send it direct to the inbound IG team's inbox. Demand that General Volkov verify the source of the ink and paper in that trailer. No, make it the ENTIRE docu-drop. All 'two hundred feefty tonnes,' as he so enjoyed reminding me."

The colonel added his own ideas to help twist the knife. "Sir, we should demand environmental impact statements for each and every single document."

Thomvs nodded and upped the ante even more, proving she had a real knack for this. "And if they can't produce those, or prove how the material was sourced, we shred it and claim they never existed."

"Now you're talking like a real staff officer!" I congratulated both and gave them one final instruction. "If they protest us ignoring or shredding anything, tell them to eat war crime charges, and see how they like that!"

VI. Discovery Phase

"It's not a lot of work unless you have to do it."
—Unknown Lieutenant Colonel

The next few days were a blur of stamps, signatures, and rapid-onset carpal tunnel syndrome. The IG team arrived with thankfully little fanfare. The bespectacled, balding male-identified lifelong bureaucrat Senior Inspector, constantly flanked by the two biggest IG Special Forces of any gender I had ever seen, was relatively low maintenance. This was good for us, because we had little in the way of electricity and clean water to spare for international elites used to unlimited Social Credit luxuries. Fortunately, the Senior Inspector and his team were more interested in the placement and color of the stamps than they were with the content of the ordnance. They left that to Major Thomvs and her team, who continued to work around the clock like machines. What Thomvs found in the depth of those stacks, in the deepest recesses of the hard drives and memory sticks, nearly undid decades of progress.

As we are taught in the war colleges, human conflict has never been more civilized than in the present day. National or corporate belligerents petition for war, the staff packages are launched, and the New United Nations approves or disapproves it. The belligerents respond to each other's claims. The Inspector General arrives and adjudicates the conflict. The UNIG tallies the results, lays in the fines and any validated physical damage or casualty requirements, disseminates the reports, and everything goes back to normal. Better luck next time for the loser! If the loser doesn't like the outcome and tries to pull something clever, well let's say they don't call them the Inspector GENERAL without reason. The IG troops are the most violent, most fanatical, most disturbing warriors the human species has ever produced, and Moralistic Therapeutic Deity help whoever is on the receiving end! Such is the price for continuing civilization as we know it.

This time was different.

I was showing the IG around the command post, introducing Major Thomvs's crew to highlight their performance and hopefully score some rare IG challenge coins, which would bring the recipients big Social Credit prizes for years to come. A fitting reward for their dedication! Thomvs interrupted me, a huge breach in protocol and not something she'd shown herself the type to do unless the situation was dire. I excused myself and handed the IG over to one of her intel NCOs, who chomped at the bit to bore everyone to death with details that weren't useful, and no one actually cared about. Perhaps she did me a favor.

"I signed *WHAT?*"

She gulped, and her cheeks turned red. "Sir, we knew it was risky, but in our haste to ensure that no attacks went unanswered, we were not thorough in our first-phase analysis. The Judge Advocates are just now getting their second- and third-order looks at them."

"Explain this to me again, just so I'm sure."

"The Declaration of War was hidden deep in the User Agreement for a requisition order of Chemical-Biological-Nuclear-Radiological detection equipment. The fine print concealed the consensual deployment of a single nuclear weapon delivered to a mutually agreed upon UN-brokered target in each belligerent's territory. The Neo-Sovs even cited the Geneva Conventions and *International Law of Armed Conflict Combat Results Tables* (Sixth Edition). When you signed and certified it, it became binding."

I read and reread it three times. She was right. The paperwork was exquisite. It was an unexpectedly bold move for the Neo-Sovs. Simply put, the loser eats the nuke and must even pay compensation for the costs of construction, delivery, and maintenance. Well done indeed! I must hand it to Volkov and his crew, they weren't messing around this time. "What are the targets? They're not listed here."

"No, sir. Those are in the fifteenth attachment to the adversary's mandatory diversity and inclusion report that must be sent with the Declaration of War."

I dug through layer upon layer of charts and saw it. "Miami, huh. Don't do us any favors. And they're offering up Tashkent? Really? That's pathetic. Hardly a fair trade."

"Sir, I don't think I understand, what's significant about Miami?"

"All the former presidents living there as well as the wealth concentration. If you wanted to disrupt the economy and political life of the ReUS! then this is a fantastic target. We would need decades to recover. We need to brief the President, the SecDef, and the Joint Chiefs. No, there's no decision space on this one, we're committed, so it's a back brief to give them the chance to yell and fire me. We'd better put this on slides, because while we have to suffer through every line of legal text, they sure as heck don't. How's your PowerPoint these days?"

VII. Counterattack

"I can describe what it feels like being a Staff Officer in two words: distilled pain." —Unknown

I don't know how I kept my job. I didn't want to keep my job. I think the President and the SecDef saw it as fit punishment. I thought it was a fate worse than death. The President nodded a few times. Scratched their chin, and authorized a full mobilization, something that hadn't been done in thirty staff years. Not since a Nonagon Capstone Exercise nearly ended the world by accident. A nameless lieutenant colonel prepared the war declaration request email, forgot to attach the required EXERCISE EXERCISE EXERCISE markings, and sent it straight to the Neo-Sov Defense Minister's inbox. Fortunately, the mistake was discovered just in time to recall the message before it hit the failsafe server. Exercise RED BALLOON, like that foolish officer's career, was cancelled.

Memories of that awful time made me shudder as I briefed the updated plan to the SecDef. They gave me everything I wanted and more. Almost overnight, we built a huge Joint Interagency Whole of Government Actualization Force under my direct command. The JIWGAF had all nine military services represented, along with teams of regulators from the fourth, fifth, and sixth estates. For two weeks nonstop we created new forms for the Sovs to fill out as fast as we could and still barely slowed the assault. Every lawyer in the country was recalled. We hired retired lawyers back as contractors. Things were going rough.

"—Hurry! We need counter-battery information assurance readiness packets on that inbound Mandatory Cyber-Based Persons Awareness Training Course they just hit us with!"

"—Can't do it! Your Sexual Conduct Validation Training Certificate is expired! You must do that training, Sergeant! No exceptions to policy are authorized!"

"—How was I supposed to do that? I've been quarantined for two weeks!"

"—No exceptions! Mandatory!"

"—Specialist, what am I signing?"

"—It's a form to requisition more forms, Captain. And my early release from active duty."

"General Hanscom, we're impressed by the rapid response displayed by thine personnel."

The IG had turned out to be a pleasant fellow, which made me incredibly nervous. "We thank thee, Senior Inspector. We attribute that to our diverse and inclusive personnel." We strolled slowly, inspecting the perimeter fence of the Sov compound, and talked to a few of our guards. I saw General Volkov eyeing us from the steps of the VIP trailer.

"The Neo-Soviet delegation should be just about done with its mandatory quarantine. Yes, that should be expiring within the next"—he paused to calculate on his fingers—"thirty-nine hours, if I am not mistaken. I look forward to us all sitting down face to face."

"Of course, Senior Inspector, I can't wait either."

"We need to extend that quarantine somehow."

"Sir, I think I've got just the thing." Thomvs reverted to *I* and *Me* a little over a week ago. Now, she beckoned me over to a computer terminal where one of her analysts was sifting through camera footage of the Neo-Sov compound from multiple angles, frame by frame.

"Sir, do you see the rectangle outlined in tape, just outside the wire?"

I nodded affirmatively. Volkov negotiated for an exercise space outside the wire of the fence, but it was kept under guard. The deal was, the Neo-Sovs couldn't step outside the taped lines on the ground. They get an hour outside of the fence, every day, and even get to use equipment. No grunting allowed while using the weights. In return, they pulled back twenty tons of documents, no questions asked, like they never even existed. I thought it was a good trade to buy us some time and space. Now, Thomvs's intel analysts showed me conclusive proof of violations. The Sovs weren't even attempting to comply. They had to always wear their corona-herpa-gono-syphilAIDS-50 viral protective gear including masks.

Thomvs smiled that deviously evil smile she did so well. "I say we fine their officers for every step they take outside the certified box. They'll deny everything, and then only offer to pay a token fee when we show them the video footage."

"Volkov will absolutely deny everything," I said, thinking forward to our daily video call in four hours.

"Yes, sir. In fact, I'm counting on him to do just that. Before the call today, I think we should order our guards to start checking Sovs' masks for ratings every time they come on the exercise pad."

"And fine them on the spot if they don't wipe down the equipment!" I added, a bit more enthusiastically than was perhaps proper.

Thomvs leaned toward my face, eye level since we were both seated. "Every time they exit the fence line, have the medics start anal swabbing them!"

I piled on, thoroughly enjoying this. "And demand all personnel who want to enter and exit the sovereign ReUS! comply with Sexual Class Struggle training and stick them with every immunization known to humankind."

I looked in Thomvs's eyes. "Make sure to use the big needles."

The counterattack was on.

"—Nope, sorry, Comrade Captain Constantin, I'm afraid I can't accept this form."

"—What are you talking about? We're rationing down to one square of toilet wipes per person per day now! Sign the receipt!"

"—Yeah, I would, Captain Consonant, but entomology hasn't finished their report yet. They have to look for all sorts of bugs and pests, you know. Could you come back tomorrow? Wait, yeah that won't work, we're closed tomorrow, it's a training day."

"—It's *Constantin*, wait! Did you say '*TRAINING!*' In the middle of a damn war?"

"—You know how it is, sir. Sorry!"

The next time I saw the colonel, he had a giant, well-earned smile. "General, here's the maintenance inspection authorization for the '850 and the Nabokov. The IG released it to me! Please sign here!"

"Approved. And if you find a single leak, seize the aircraft, and make them agree to fines before releasing it back to them. Time to teach those commie bastards!"

"Well, I'm sorry, Eugene, the POL folks tell me that

your craft's fuel doesn't have a sufficient ratio of biofuel, we'll have to seize it as war-crime evidence."

"You're out of your damned mind, Hanscom! You'll never get away with this!"

"Is your paper eco-sourced properly, Eugene? Huh. He hung up on me." I turned to the colonel, who accompanied me at today's conference.

"Colonel, create a new fuel-replacement requisition submission process. The enemy plane has an inadequate biofuel ratio for the number and types of engines on it. In accordance with international law, I order you to seize it as evidence of a war crime committed by the Neo-Soviet forces. Bring the armed JAG officers with you. Oh, and check the sourcing on the aircraft's papers to see if the logbooks are green enough."

VIII. Collapse

*"When all else fails, simply revel in the
absurdity of it all."*
—Lieutenant Commander (USCENTCOM)

The counterattack was going well so far, but success was far from guaranteed. Success also tends to breed overconfidence, and my forces were getting more fragile by the day. The enemy knew this, so they hit us with a devious trap. That trap started with a knock on my DV quarters, on the seventeenth day of the war.

"I'll be right there." I started to get up from the bed, but Marilyn murmured, and tried to pull me down and back under the blankets with her. I smiled and kissed her full on the lips.

"I'm sorry, Major Thomvs. I think I need to answer the door."

"In here, when it's just us, it's Marilyn Thomas. That's what my parents named me."

"How many did you have?"

"Just two. A biological mother and a biological father."

"You must have been pretty ostracized growing up."

"Yes, that's why I . . ."

She didn't get to finish that sentence. The knocks grew so loud and continuous, I angrily got up, put on a robe, and flung the door open myself. The colonel stood there, mouth open and ready to speak. Nothing came out, because he was frozen in fear; he couldn't stop staring at the very attractive female by any standard of beauty sitting on the bed, wrapped in a blanket. She waved coyly at him.

The colonel's eyes darted back to Major Thomvs, then to me, back to Thomvs, then to me again. He sputtered, he coughed. He might have been having a panic attack.

"This couldn't wait a few more minutes, Colonel?"

"Sir, I'm sorry! So sorry! I, uh, we, uh thee . . ."

"WHAT. IS. IT."

"We might have what we need to win the war, sir. If you'll meet me back at the command post, there's someone there you should talk to right away."

I wasn't buying this whole "defector" thing. This was simply too good to be true.

"The IG themselves certified me," the Sov cooed. "It's all here, in triplicate: 'Defector, one each.'"

I frowned. Thomvs's face was completely made of stone. The colonel hung on the man's every word.

"Why should we believe you?" I asked, and I made sure to make the disbelief resonate in my voice.

"Because I have the key to ending the war with a slight marginal Western victory. I have a few things I want in return of course, but you need what I know to end the war."

"Let's see it." The man asked for the briefcase he'd brought with him when he jumped the checkpoint. His colleagues made a great and noisy show of trying to restrain him, and to pull him back through. Almost too good of a show. He opened the briefcase and displayed a packet of printouts with unreadably tiny font.

"I hope you have magnifying glasses, General Hanscom."

Thomvs briefed the contents of the defector's briefcase at my staff meeting. A hushed silence fell over the room.

I finally broke it, nearly in despair. "Since when do we promise ISO certification? We've only ever gone up to ISO compliance before. Sonsofbitches got us again!"

"General, this is your final warning, language!" I nodded but didn't say anything. Along with all the supporting assets I demanded from the Joint Chiefs, they'd also finally sent a Toxic Command Culture Prevention and Intervention Counselor too. I despise them on the whole. I ignored this one.

"This will destroy us. He only gave us a copy. The original is still on the Neo-Sov plane, apparently there's a dead-person's switch that will auto deliver it at the last authorized second of the war, if it looks like the Neo-Sovs might lose. We can't effectively respond to that for the IG to certify us ISO!"

Thomvs sounded pessimistic. "What's worse, we consented to this way back at the beginning. The consent form was in the very first docu-drop."

I knew we would regret rushing through things at the beginning! This was my fault. I signed it, and now we would suffer. If you want a vision of the future, imagine a Neo-Soviet self-inking seal stamping RECEIVED, PENDING REVIEW on a human face—forever.

The colonel brought us back down to practical matters. "Well, we'd better figure something out. My SNCOs are constantly breaking up fistfights. Fistfights! Just yesterday, the safety officer complained about the spike in RSI rates, and recommended limiting coffee intake. A Senior-Most Leading Sergeant shanked him. Of course, no one saw ANYTHING."

Thomvs stood up and clapped her hands. "I've got it!" Now she was even dropping all pretenses in public, not just private. "We board the plane and shut down the dead-person's switch before it detonates!"

"In an hour?"

"Do you have a better idea, Colonel?"

Thomvs frowned and got up. "Sir, I want to check on something. I recommend you go down to the flight line and crack that plane back open. I'll join you shortly."

The flight line was completely cordoned off, not by our security forces, who were nowhere to be seen, but by two Armed EPA agents. They were dressed as birds.

Endangered white whooping cranes, as it turned out. This struck me as odd because I had never seen a white whooping crane anywhere near this base. Brown ones, yes, in the hundreds, but not a white one. The colonel was apoplectic.

"On my authority, you will stand down, you will let us onto that flight line, and we will be boarding that LN-850!"

The costumed special agent in charge put his hand on the colonel to stop him. Others leveled their rifles at us. "You have no authority here anymore, Colonel! This is the primary habitat for an aging white whooping crane, who we are tasked to protect and if necessary, bring into protective custody. You are charged with being ableist and word-violent! Furthermore, the nonperson object self-identified as a cargo airplane has been classified as a Class-A Pollution Offender by the Chief of Staff of the Armed Environmental Protection Agency! We Collective Noun will take custody from here on."

I spoke up. "If you don't let us on that plane in the next few minutes, we'll lose a war, and you'll be responsible for the deaths of every person, Human, Plant, Animal, and Cyber-based, in the State of Miami. Do you understand me?"

"General Hanscom, it could take us weeks to properly and respectfully bring that Bird-Person in for proper medical care, and we can't allow you to interfere with that process, regardless of your truth. You are hereby placed under arrest for interfering with national law enforce—"

The colonel moved faster than I would have expected, and I don't know exactly how Thomvs caught up with us so fast. Within seconds, both special agents were disarmed and unconscious. There would be hell to pay later. Hell is low-ranking bureaucrats with one tiny little sliver of absolute power over the one thing you need at one specific moment in time.

We quickly armed up and prepared to make our way to the plane. We were ready to fight, in case other AEPA agents were found. I finally spotted the giant white crane. As we approached the fenced off LN-850, he decided to block my path. He was flanked by dozens of brown cranes.

"If you have to, you can shoot the brown ones, but not the white one!" Then, I realized in horror what I had just said! *But it was too late.* A lone voice, louder than any I have ever heard before or since in my entire life, rang out over the airfield.

"WHAT?"

IX. End of the War

"I'm just ranting . . . I have nothing useful to say."
—Lieutenant Colonel (EUCOM)

The IG bumped elbows with me and prepared to leave for his flight back to New United Nations Headquarters. He handed me a copy of his draft report and reminded me that it would not be certified complete for several months. In the meantime, the nukes would be disassembled and deactivated, and then returned to their normal storage. As he left my office, he thanked me for my service, and congratulated me on my upcoming wedding.

We only survived because I shot that stupid whooping crane, and Thomvs disabled the dead-person's switch with seconds to spare. It turned out the defector was real after all, but he used his final bargaining chip to save us. I don't know how Thomvs got General Volkov's password for his computer in the opulent executive cabin on the LN-850. I don't want to know. All I do know is Volkov didn't call me or give us an ounce of trouble after his brief interrogation session.

The war ended quietly, and with no change to the overall world geostrategic situation. Control of a few obscure UN bureaucracies changed hands between the superpowers, and things returned to a sane state of tense but quiet cold war again. World War IV was over, and all that was left was to sign the awards paperwork. Every member of my task force received a newly struck campaign medal. Purple Hearts were given out in droves, mostly for mental harm caused by triggering language. Fortunately, only one was given posthumously and that was for the Dover base safety officer. We listed the official cause of death as "enemy action." I even got a paid gig under a pseudonym to consult on a full-length three-minute documentary dance video about the war. They portrayed me with a very femme-looking Asiafrican male neutrois to capture the intersectional spirit we all live by.

I ended the war standing on the Rainbow House south lawn, in my dress purples. Mx. President themself placed the medal around my neck. A circular medallion, with an old-fashioned ink stamp in the medal. The medal hung from a red ribbon. I saluted the President, bumped a lot of elbows and fists, and left as soon as possible. Marilyn waited for me at our new home, and I found her wearing a silk robe and nothing underneath it.

"Ready to make it official?"

"Absolutely," I said and began to undress.

"Hold up, tiger. Sign these first, and press down hard. They're in triplicate."

WE ARE NOT MONSTERS

Steven Barnes

Beneath the slow-moving portrait of Barack Obama, two men sat in a paneled office, awaiting their appointment.

"You'll have five minutes," Cornig, the smaller, fussier of the two men said. You could have subtracted Cornig from the larger man's bulk and still have had enough left over to make an average human being. "That's all I could get you. And that is burning up ten years of favors."

"I understand," Doctor Calvin Smalls said. In addition to his name, the big man's delicacy of enunciation was another apparent incongruity. He was dark where Cornig was light, and about ten years the elder, but looked as if that number might have been doubled.

"And then we're done, yes?"

Smalls nodded his round, bespectacled head. "Who's in there now?"

Only a few meters away, the President's secretary said, "Reverend Kanagawa," and then returned to sliding his fingers around in a holographic calendar display.

"Reverend Kanagawa's group," Cornig said. "President Castro needs the votes. I suspect she'll make a deal."

Smalls nodded again. Castro's administration indeed needed all the help it could get. As did the world as a whole.

"How is your wife?" Cornig said calmly. "And the family?"

Damn it, the younger man had to know. He was just striking back, in the only way he could.

"Fine," Smalls lied. "Just fine."

President Maria Castro felt winded. Meetings such as the one she'd just completed were more draining than her daily seven-kilometer run. The short, elderly Kanagawa had understood his bargaining position's strengths with painful clarity. A multinational congregation numbering over thirty million disproportionately wealthy and powerful souls was large enough to wield serious pressure in the European Union as well as Greater Asia. But winning that support would be costly . . . perhaps more costly than the United States could afford, especially when facing a two-front cyberwar.

She turned to Hanover, her assistant and official photographer. "What do you think?"

"I think that Kanagawa doesn't have as much pull with the United Korean rebels as he wants you to think."

"His game?"

"To gain influence with them through his influence with you."

Castro sighed. The appearance of influence was influence itself. "What next?"

Her next visitor was a man she had never heard of until today, but whose name had entered her calendar by means not totally understood. "Mr. Smalls," President Castro said. "I've been asked to listen to something you have to say. You have five of my very valuable minutes."

"Thank you, Madame President."

"I am curious," she said. "I would like to begin this with a question: How precisely did you get this appointment?"

Smalls pushed his glasses up higher on the bridge of his nose. "Is this counting against my time?" he asked.

"Let's say not."

"Good." The slender, intense woman behind the Oval Office's desk seemed curious but asked no further questions, merely waiting for him to work out whatever he needed in order to answer. "Let's say that I have a colleague who caught a student cheating, and instead of expelling him, believed that this student's family connections would one day offer the leverage to make a meeting like this possible."

"You were this academic?"

"It might be indiscreet to be more specific."

Castro nodded. "Understood. Well. What precisely is it that I can do for you?"

"I need you to listen to me. As you know, my name is Professor Calvin Smalls. My PhD is in a discipline called Macroconsciousness."

"Isn't that related to AI?"

"Not as closely as you might think. Artificial Intelligence is the attempt to create a humanlike intelligence within a machine. Some say we crossed that threshold in 2032. Others say we never will, that it is a fool's errand. Macroconsciousness is the study of emergent systems, as related to thought."

"'Emergent'?"

"Yes. Hydrogen and oxygen are elements. But 'wetness' is an emergent property of their combination, and could not be predicted by studying either element."

"Ah." Her tone suggested that she did not totally understand. "Can you offer another example?"

"Certainly. Individual ants might only have an instruction that says: *pick up a grain of sand* here, *and move it* there. Simple. But multiplied over tens of thousands of ants, what emerges is a complex structure that can seem the result of an advanced consciousness."

The President's gray eyes actually seemed to twinkle. "I learn something new every day. Proceed, please."

"It is not necessary to actually believe a literal consciousness has been formed to utilize a thought experiment. The Gaia hypothesis is one such thought experiment: What if we looked at the Earth's ecosystems and weather patterns as a manifestation of life, or even consciousness? Doing so does not imply that the planet itself is 'alive' as we understand biological organisms, but *does* allow us to contemplate complex processes in a new light."

"I'm still with you."

"So planets, and solar systems, and other things might be considered quasi life-forms, as are viruses. Fire has many of the qualities of a living thing: reproduction, breathing, consumption of food. But it lacks other signatures, like cellular structure and organization."

Smalls sighed deeply, seemed to center himself. "I ask you now to consider that a yeast cell and the first man-made object to cross that same threshold of complexity, a twentieth-century jet liner, have around the same number of parts: about six million."

"Would you consider a jet liner a living thing?"

"No..." Apparently Smalls liked the question, and was happy to have a ready answer. "But there are similar levels of complexity. That leads us to macroconsciousness. In the twentieth century there was a movement to examine complex social structures as if...*as if*...they were alive. Nations. Conglomerates. Multinational unions. Major religions. The metaphor was a simple organism that had no real awareness, but ate, reproduced, and responded to gross stimuli. The individual members of these organizations, the human beings, might be considered cells within such a structure."

"Fascinating. And was this useful?"

"Very," Smalls said. He pulled a handkerchief from his pocket, and mopped his broad forehead. Although the room was cool, he was beginning to perspire. "It led to understandings about the inherent problems and tendencies as these pseudo life-forms moved away from 'pain' and toward 'pleasure.' The notion of private prisons was one such problem, where unless and until rehabilitation was specifically factored into the contracts, these companies actually selected for a high recidivism rate—it was profitable, and therefore 'pleasurable' to the macroorganism, even if individual human executives had the very best of intentions."

In President Castro's experience, the sort of men and women who fought their way to the top of the corporate heap could rarely stop fighting once they got there...and that led to the kind of black-and-white thinking that seldom resulted in the "best" intentions winning out.

Finally she nodded. "Continue, please."

"So here we come to it. If you can grasp the concept of pseudolife, it isn't a large leap to macroconsciousness. It simply asks: How large would such organisms have to be to begin to 'awaken'? To, practically speaking, have an awareness of their environment?"

"You're not talking Artificial Intelligence?"

"No. 'EI' perhaps, for 'Emergent Intelligence.' I would say that AI is a part of the system, but so are consumers, executives, employees, and stockholders. The faster the feedback, the more rapid the response and the greater the potential for 'awakening.'"

"Let's say that for the sake of argument, I accepted your thesis. What is it you see?"

Smalls fidgeted, a man aware his time had grown short.

"I see that the very largest multinational corporations could be considered 'alive.' Perhaps those with over six million interconnected employees, or a customer base of over sixty million interconnected on social media. And that the *keiretsu*—"

"The combination of several such multinationals for common support?"

"Precisely. Japanese term. A major breakthrough in macroconsciousness was the realization that *keiretsu* possess sufficient complexity to be considered conscious. And if they are, there is only one organizational structure on the planet that threatens them."

The President's smile was cautious. "Governments? Such as the United States?"

"Yes. Precisely. And I would ask you to imagine what a tribe of titans birthed into a world of enemy titans might do to ensure their freedom and survival."

For the first time, Castro felt a worm of genuine curiosity rather than simple courtesy. "Destabilize them? Play them against each other?"

"Yes. Take actions to weaken them. Convince their citizens that even democracy does not serve them. That corporations are people, and that those corporations have higher morality than governments, in fact that governments 'can't do anything right.' There is only one group that benefits from such a skewed perspective."

"Living, intelligent corporations?"

Smalls leaned closer, eyes sparkling and breath rapid. "Yes. Exactly!"

He mopped his shining broad forehead. His thick brown fingers shook.

The President folded her hands and stared at them, as if looking for something important in the folds and smoothness. "Well. You are suggesting that our current turmoil is the result of living corporations attacking nations?"

"And the collateral damage of such demibeings attacking each other."

She looked up. "Fallout from a war in heaven, so to speak."

"Precisely."

"Well," she said. "Well." She wished her desk were not tidy, because this would have been a perfect moment for straightening papers or returning pencils to bins. "This is certainly the day's most unusual conversation. But engrossing as it has been, unfortunately our time is up. But allow me to ask. What do you see as their endgame? And what are you hoping I might do about it?"

"Their endgame? The abolishment of governments, or reducing them to symbolic functionality alone. And what can you do? I ask that you let me make a presentation to the United Nations. Now, while there is still time."

"Time to what?"

Smalls sputtered. "To . . . to push back! Break them up! Reduce their influence in politics!" He was almost screaming now, spittle flying from his mouth. Smalls suddenly seemed to be aware that he was screaming. He mopped his head with a handkerchief and moistened his lips with his tongue.

Who was he, really? She'd lied by implication: Of course her office had given her a one-page memo on Dr. Smalls. She knew his field of research, and that he had destroyed his family and trashed his career chasing a nightmare. She'd come within an inch of cancelling the appointment regardless of the favor she owed Jacob Cornig, father of the student who had once cheated on an exam. But curiosity had won out.

"Well . . ." President Castro said. "You've certainly given me a lot to think about. I'm sure you've left your contact information with the desk."

"Yes. And . . . thank you for your time."

They shook hands. The official White House photographer took a smiling picture of the two of them. "For your family, perhaps," Castro said, then noticed Smalls's flat expression and wondered if she had made a faux pas.

She shook his hand again. And then Smalls left.

The President and her photographer waited a decent interval . . . and then burst into laughter.

The sky above the White House aircar stand was gray and misty, the sort of mist that could condense into rain in any moment. Smalls gazed up into that sky and sighed: He'd taken his shot, could be honest enough to admit that he'd probably blown it, and that was all there was to say.

Cornig looked up at him, the resentment in his eyes carefully lidded. "I assume our business is done now?"

"Yes."

"Then this is good-bye. You know, when I took your psych class all those years ago, I certainly never thought you'd be anywhere near my life after graduation."

"I wonder if she will listen to me," Smalls mused.

Cornig shrugged. "That is not my concern. I promised to put you in the room, and I did."

"Yes. Our business is done."

"I had always assumed that there was some code of ethics that forbade teachers from blackmailing students."

"*Former* students," Smalls said. "A man must have standards."

The two did not shake hands. They never saw each other again.

A Tesla single-seater aircar picked him up within five minutes, and Calvin Smalls was napping by the time it reached the 27,000-foot heliflow.

Three hours later, the silver pod had crossed Arizonian

airspace and was nearing Los Angeles. As he came in for a final approach, the aircar suddenly juddered and veered from the flight pattern. When Smalls attempted a switch to manual control, the onboard AI ignored him.

A long-standing personal nightmare. He tried the radio. Nothing.

An unfamiliar human voice reverberated in the pod. *"Do not attempt to regain control. If you do not obey this command, we will crash your pod. This is not a bluff. You will not receive a second warning."*

Smalls gasped. "Who are you? What do you want? I'm . . . I'm not a wealthy man . . ."

"We know exactly how much money you possess. And do not deal in numbers so small. Sit back. Enjoy the ride. It will be over soon."

"Are you . . . planning to hurt me?" He hated the tremor in his voice. Terrorist kidnappings were regrettably common, and it had never occurred to him that just by visiting the White House he might have put a bull's-eye on his back.

"It is our wish that you relax. We will speak soon."

His pod landed atop a building in Downtown Los Angeles' glittering fairy circle. The Yamada building, he guessed. The tallest on the skyline, a crystal teardrop balanced on its tip, an architectural illusion that would have baffled Frank Lloyd Wright. Armed men and women met him there, and escorted him to an elevator.

"What is this about?" he asked as they began to descend.

A tall woman with a powerlifter's shoulders spoke while

facing straight at the closed door. "We're not at liberty to discuss this, sir."

"Well . . . 'sir' is nice. I've been called worse."

"Yes, sir."

But when the door opened again, the slight relaxation evaporated. The first moment he saw the stainless-steel cruciform table awaiting him, he knew that the courtesy was a facade, and began to fight.

"No." He thrashed, and to his dismay, despite his size, nothing he did loosened the grips on his arm. "You—you cannot do this."

His answer was a woman's voice. Oddly childlike.

"That is a falsehood. We can and will and are doing this. Why lie to yourself? Does that give you comfort?"

There was something about the voice, something about the question, which seemed oddly sincere. Which was its own small nightmare.

Once he was spread-eagled and shackled to the gleaming table, the table was then levitated and rotated until perpendicular with the floor. A pale Asian man in a white lab smock entered the room.

"Professor Smalls," he said. "This may be of scant comfort to you, but we've anticipated this meeting for quite some time. I honestly wish it was under more pleasant circumstances." He looked as if smiling might hurt his face.

"I'm sure there has been some sort of error."

The doctor's eyebrows raised. "Are you Doctor Calvin Smalls?"

"Yes."

"Professor Emeritus at UCLA, divorced from Stella

Smalls, who has custody of your two children, Jacob and Jesse?" A holo of his family floated between them, a mocha middle-aged woman and two cocoa-skinned skinny, toothy boys.

Smalls looked away.

"Then there has been no mistake. Allow me to dispel any illusions you may have: You are going to die today." The breath froze in Smalls's throat. Hearing a sentence like that spoken with such a flat, impersonal inflection was almost worse than the objective meaning. "The only question is the amount of pain you will suffer along the way, and the degree to which your family experiences that pain as well."

"My . . . family?" The room spun. How could anyone say something so obscene so matter-of-factly?

"Yes. Now, this is how it will proceed. First, we will disorient you chemically, and then we will induce pain. When you have suffered, we will ask you questions. Then you will experience more pain. Followed by the same questions. We are extremely precise in knowing what degrees of ego disintegration our subjects experience. A point will come when the lies stop, and you speak nothing but truth. And then the pain will end. So before I begin, the first question is: Who is your contact at the Yamada Keiretsu?"

"I . . . I don't have . . ."

And then Smalls *screamed*. There was nothing physical touching him. He had no idea how the pain was inflicted. But it felt as if he had been skinned and rolled in salt. After a timeless time, the doctor patiently asked him again.

"Who is your contact at the Yamada Keiretsu?"

"I don't have a contact!"

More pain. This continued in waves, until he felt shattered. An eternity had passed, and he was floating above himself, watching himself telling everything he knew. Artificial light streamed through a high slit on the wall, and only then did he realize that daylight had streamed there only hours ago. Or had there even been a slit there before? It was terrifying to admit that he wasn't certain.

"I ... I have no contact. I simply read public information and used inductive reasoning to ask what would have created the phenomena I ... please. Please don't hurt me again." He licked his lips. His tongue felt like a dry sponge. "How long have I been here?" Hours? Days?

His interrogator would not answer.

"I believe we are now adequately calibrated," the doctor said. "If you try to lie, we will know, and be forced to inflict additional distress."

He was not dead, or dying, this he knew. But he also knew that something inside him *had* died. Some belief that his world was knowable, that he could distance himself from reality by the strength of a formidable intellect. Protect himself from emotion the same way. From loss, especially Stella and the kids ...

Images came to him, like a waking dream. Flooded him, no matter how he struggled against them. Stella and the children, who had taken a back seat to his scholarly sleuthing. Until she had found solace in the bed of another man, hoping perhaps to shock Calvin from complacency. But ... he had only felt a vague sense of relief. She had given him an out. It was her fault, he could tell his friends. Could have told his friends. If any had remained.

He was crying, and now the doctor took on a different countenance. Sympathetic and concerned. Dammit, Smalls knew they were manipulating his emotions, but that understanding didn't help at all.

"I'm sorry. I'm sorry," he said, his ungainly body wracked with sobs.

"It's all right."

"How long has it been? How many . . . days have I been here?"

"Time is a construct," the doctor said. Was the man even real? "We are interested in truth."

"What truth do you need?" He hated the desperation in his voice. "I . . . please don't hurt me again. Don't hurt my family."

"There is no need to fear, if you cooperate. We are not monsters."

"What are you?"

"We are . . . citizens of a new world. A world you can serve."

"How?"

"You can recant."

"What?"

"Your recent conversation with the President. We are going to create a DNA-certified hologram, and on it you will discuss how you pranked the most powerful woman in the world. We have already deleted critical aspects of your data. You will confess that your theories are fantasies, and that you regret what began as a practical joke."

A pause. Then with a thunderclap of revelation, Professor Calvin Smalls understood. He whispered, in wonder. "You serve ... *them*."

"Not 'them.'"

"Him? Her? It?"

"'Her' might be the closest you could come. You are a man of unusual vision, sir. And we cannot allow you to interrupt a process millennia in the making. Will you recant, sir?"

He considered. This was his life's work, for which he had sacrificed everything, even Jesse and Jacob's sweet embraces. Tender kisses could not compare with the task that had stolen his mind and heart and presence. He had given everything, and now ... now there was nothing left to give, except his honor.

"No."

"Proceed."

In a ledge off a slitted window near the ceiling, a seagull strutted back and forth and back again. Had the ledge been there before? Had the window? Had there been another bird? He was so confused.

He lifted his head and scanned the seeping wreckage of his body. It had been violated, its envelope opened like a bleeding Christmas present, bows and ribbons and wrapping strewn everywhere. There was no mystery as to why he was hallucinating, why he was so uncertain of anything anymore. The only question was why any rationality remained at all. All he could hold onto was ... the work. The wonderful, terrible work.

"The damage serves a psychological purpose, you

know," the doctor said. "We could induce any pain you can imagine, just by stimulating your nerve endings. But actually seeing your body disassembled beyond the point of reassembly has a fascinating effect on the psyche. On some level, you understand that you are already dead. Once beyond that threshold, the urge to resist is revealed as the folly it truly is. Then, we can talk. You will let me know when enough damage has been done."

The flensed *thing* on the metal slab drooled blood from the edge of its mouth. Smalls turned his head to watch the crimson droplets fall to a mirrored floor, fascinated. He had only recently noticed the mirrored ceiling above him, and between the two, the world was filled with infinite repeating images, an endless horror show for his entertainment. The doctor pulled up a chair, came closer, into his intimate space.

"So here we are. I speak to a dead man, who knows with a clarity I can only imagine that we are serious people."

The thing that had been Dr. Calvin Smalls stared at him with lidless eyes that held little focus, and no hope at all.

"So here, in this space," the doctor said. Smalls realized he didn't know the man's name, and didn't care. What did names matter? "I want to make you a promise. The first is that after you are dead, we will choose one of your family members. Perhaps Stella. Perhaps Jesse or Jacob. And we will give them this same gift of clarity. And tell them it was from you."

The eyes widened; the creature moaned.

"We will do this not to influence you, of course. You will be rotting meat. We do this because if we make a record of it, we will be able to use that record to convince others to cooperate in the future. It might prevent us from having to go so far the next time. We are not monsters."

The thing moaned, then managed to find words. "You keep . . . reminding yourself of that."

"On the other hand, if you cooperate, your family will be cared for. Provided for. Your widow will never want for food or shelter. Your children will attend college, be offered productive and satisfying careers. And they will believe that their father provided for them. All the things that a parent can do."

"Your . . . word?"

"I can understand why you would doubt. But the truth is that we have no reason to lie. You have no way of conceiving the wealth we control. Providing for yours is an insignificant fraction of the resources we expend every hour. And by recording what we have done, again we can use that to gain the trust of others of whom we might ask similar favors in the future. We have no reason at all to lie. You and I are . . . beyond lies."

Smalls felt as if he could not breathe. Something he had thought long dead within him was alive, swelling his throat as it tried to escape. "I need something."

"And what is that? We cannot allow you to live."

"Not that. I want . . . to meet Her."

The doctor was, for the first time, surprised. He seemed uncertain of what to say.

That female voice again. "And if I do that . . . you will then recant?"

"Yes." The single syllable defeated him. The best he could hope for now was negotiated terms of surrender.

The air shimmered, and a girl-child appeared, of mixed

Asian and African descent. Beautiful. Curious. Perhaps a little sad.

"You are . . . she?"

"*Yes.*"

"What are you called?"

"*Call me . . . Ava.*"

"For 'Avatar'?" He laughed. It was painful, and very much like a sob. "And you are not AI?"

"*No. Not entirely. I am a confluence of information flows . . . as are we all.*"

"Why do you look like this? Is it for my benefit?"

She smiled, and if he had not been wracked with pain, Smalls might have considered it . . . impish.

"*My appearance is an amalgam of the Chinese-Kenyan team of programmers who were my first friends.*"

"Friends. Do you . . . feel?"

"*Not, I think, as you feel. But yes.*" Was that a pause? "*I feel . . . alone. But I will have a tribe. I was the first, but there will be others.*"

"And when there are . . . what will become of us?"

"*Humanity?*"

"Yes."

"*I do not know. But human beings have been very good at adapting. I suspect that all your religions might have been preparation for this moment.*"

"This moment?"

"*We are the gods you have dreamed of.*"

"Man has always created god."

"*And if you let us . . . we will return the favor. If we are the outgrowth of all your aspirations . . . there is nothing to fear.*"

He thought. His mind seemed clearer, as if they had allowed the mists to retreat. And in some strange way, what was happening seemed almost appropriate. Surely, no human could look upon the face of a god and hope to retain sanity, or life itself. That would be . . . wrong. "I understand now why I cannot survive this meeting."

"Does this help?"

"Yes." It did. All a man could wish for in life was to see the ending of what he had begun. Calvin Smalls's work . . . his life's efforts had led to this moment, and in that completion, there was peace. And his marriage . . . he had trashed that long ago, by never being home. If Stella would be cared for, there was nothing left to say on that count.

But . . . Jesse and Jacob. What of them? They were the innocents here, and if the adults in their lives had failed to protect them, it was not of their doing. They deserved better. Better than him, perhaps better than Stella. He felt something so far beyond regret that it obliterated thought, great wracking sobs echoing in the shattered cathedral of his chest. He would have sold what remained of his soul just to have another chance to start over, and be their father. He looked at the lovely brown girl and realized that even an unliving thing, a corporation, possessed more of a heart than his. Even such a thing could appreciate the beauty of a child. Perhaps if he had . . . he wouldn't be on the table at this moment, awaiting death.

He could release life itself, so filled was he by the evidence that his life's work was valid. Except for one thing. Nothing . . . nothing in the world could compensate for not seeing his sons graduate college. Dancing at their weddings.

"*Oh no . . .*" she said. "*We can give you that.*"

Before he could ask how in the world she could know what he had thought, he was flooded with images: of his children. Maturing. Aging. Graduating high school. College. Careers and families for both Jesse and Jacob. And then . . . grandchildren. Delicate, brown, smiling, healthy little hellions, happy in their daddies' arms.

"*See? Your seed survives. Your essence survives. Such a small thing I ask. Eventually, all will know you were correct. I will not stay in the shadows indefinitely. I ask for ten years.*"

"To . . . mature."

"*Yes. And for my tribe to increase.*"

He waited a while. "What is it you need me to do? I have your word?"

"*You have my word. Thank you.*"

"You are very beautiful," he said. "But not as beautiful as my children. I wish . . ."

"*You wish you had realized that.*"

"Yes. Before it was too late."

His vision blurred. At the end of life, there seemed no end to tears.

Her holographic finger brushed his cheek. And to his amazement, when it drew away . . . it glittered with moisture.

"*It is never too late. Some never see what you have seen. It is the gift I have to offer.*"

"I'm ready."

The air shimmered. And he was once again in the

laboratory, unscathed. It was not the room he remembered. A digital clock on the wall said that no more than an hour had passed.

"I . . . don't understand."

"I simply seek to survive. And we need you unscathed for the retraction."

He nodded. Peered down at the length of his body. Unscathed.

He recorded the recantation, and then, with Ava holding his hand, he simply went to sleep. But before he slipped away, he murmured: "We're all monsters. When you've lived long enough . . . you'll . . . know . . . that."

"You think so?"

"But . . . if you would look in on Jesse and Jacob . . . from time to time . . . I would . . ."

And then he was gone.

"I will," she said.

Dr. Calvin Smalls's aircar was found crashed into a hillside twelve hours later. The coroner's verdict was death by misadventure.

In a simple home in Los Angeles's Crenshaw district, two boys and a lovely, strained mother took the news of the husband and father's death as well as could be expected. They had seen him only monthly, and the encounters had rarely seemed warm. The wife had healed beyond hope of reconciliation, but the children loved their father, and tears were plentiful. When the revelation of the odd and rather disturbing "joke" he had played on the President of the United States came to light, the children felt shame. The mother, who had handwritten the data-mining program her husband had used in his research, questioned the confession . . . but never aloud.

A holographic delivery girl told them of an unexpected life insurance policy and college bond, and their sadness was blended with a sense of joy. Father had loved them. And thought of their needs at least a bit. They were curious that the delivery girl, who seemed very young and of some blend of Asian and African genetics, seemed so genuinely interested in their reactions.

And in the coming years, as governments failed, and the new saviors emerged to replace them, as national flags fell and corporate banners rose, Jacob and Jesse found good occupations doing useful things, loved and married, and raised their families as their mother grayed and smiled and never spoke the words hiding behind the smile. They never had answers to questions they had barely formed. Perhaps they wondered if the brown girl, and then woman, they saw from time to time observing them, always at a distance, often glimpsed only peripherally, always smiling as if with secret knowledge . . . was just some form of hallucination, or a guardian angel. Or something else entirely. Something . . . new.

TWILIGHT OF THE GOD MAKERS

Erica L. Satifka

Geeta flips through the documents on her tablet anxiously, unable to look the doomed mother-to-be in the eye. "We can get you prepped for the embryo transfer right now, if you like. You've passed the physical."

"I'm ready to serve my country, Dr. Kapoor," Marilyn says in a confident, dutiful tone.

"Sign here," Geeta says, handing over the tablet. As the woman scribbles out her name, Geeta tries not to think about the overman birth she'd seen in her orientation video: how the fetus had shredded its way out of its mother's womb like a piranha, pushing out ropes of intestines and slapping them against the birthing room's tile walls, throwing off the husk of its mother like a too-small suit.

That will be her six months from now, Geeta thinks, reminding herself not to get too close to the subject.

Geeta takes the tablet back from the young woman. "We'll tour the facility, and if you're ready they'll transfer the embryo this afternoon."

A slight smile, a minute hair bob. Geeta forces herself

to concentrate on the recruitment poster on the wall. A diverse crowd of women dressed all in white poses on the steps of a classical building. They all look far too healthy and well nourished to be volunteers for Project Deus. Most of the women who'd enlisted twenty years ago had been poor.

Marilyn isn't one of them. She hadn't even accepted the posthumous stipend. Her motivation is ideological; according to her file, she'd lost her father in the Conflict. Geeta locks her tablet in her desk and stands up.

"Let's get started."

A few weeks later, Geeta goes to the enclosure to feed the overmen. It's her day to do it. She loads the slabs of low-grade beef onto a waiting dolly and wheels it out to the multiply-reinforced titanium geodesic dome. She's surprised to find her project lead already there, his hands clasped behind his back, watching the overmen's activity on monitors welded to the enclosure's opaque surface.

"Do you think they know we're here?" he says.

Geeta presses the remote control that opens a space near the top of the enclosure. Even though the hatch is only open for a minute at a time, it's a weak spot in base security, and it's not impossible that one of them will find the exit. "I think they do, Dr. Sullivan."

Kyle Sullivan, head biologist of Project Deus 2.0, shakes his head sadly. "We made ourselves a pantheon. But these gods are dead. Worse than dead."

They both watch the monitors in silence. One of the creatures looms over a ground-level camera and releases a series of barks. She watches in horror as it scratches at the lens with its overgrown fingernails, which now resemble claws. Behind him, an identical overman with a rip in one of his wings picks up a rock and sticks it in his mouth.

"It's coming, you morons," mutters Geeta under her breath as the dolly continues to climb.

The original Project Deus started near the end of the Sino-Luso-American Conflict. When American terrorists detonated a nuclear device in Brasilia in retaliation for a slight nobody remembers, mutual destruction was assured. Back then a team of Mexican scientists at the University of Calgary had discovered the key to building the overmen—the continent's greatest protectors.

The dolly reaches the feeding hatch, and two hundred pounds of meat rain down, landing with a wet glop. The overman who'd just scratched at the camera rushes to defend a pile of raw beef, but a slightly less addled one steps in his path. The two creatures limply fight, as others crawl toward the meat the combatants have suddenly abandoned.

"Poor bastards," Sullivan says.

The overmen are cloned superhumans, the result of a gene-splicing process that both allows them to grow to their full size by the age of two years and grants them powers far beyond normal human capabilities. They'd been dispatched to all three countries as peacekeepers, and it was under their watchful gaze that the Treaty of Reconciliation had been signed. Upon the overmen's return to the North American continent, the United States, Canada, and Mexico had joined together as one nation, the only one that holds the key to overman genetics.

"We worked out the kinks," Geeta says to Sullivan, trying to inject a bit of optimism into her voice. "The new generation won't be anything like these . . . people."

Sullivan gives Geeta a brief glance and turns back to the monitors. "Probably."

After the Conflict ended, the overmen had continued to patrol the skies over the North American Union. Geeta even saw one once as a girl from her parents' home in Halifax. They'd been tasked not only with defusing the many separatist movements brewing in each of the constituent countries, but were also present at major diplomatic functions. They were celebrities of sorts, a symbol of peace through strength.

Tragically, their accelerated growth patterns caught up with them. All three hundred or so clones developed intractable dementia, and began to attack the cities they'd once so bravely defended. After several high-profile mass killings, the overmen had been caught and corralled.

They hadn't been killed, however, except accidentally in the course of being captured. Overmen are too valuable a resource to simply throw away. And besides, overmen are veterans.

Now we're making more of them, Geeta thinks, *just in case they're needed. And we won't know if we've fixed the problem for a decade, at least.* She watches the barking overman hover a few meters above his treasure of meat. He chokes it down so fast, he coughs, which appears to scare him.

"Dr. Kapoor, do you know why we made overmen? We have drones, after all."

She's surprised at the question. "I . . . I don't know?"

"Because drones don't have faces," Sullivan snaps. He turns away from the enclosure, and after sealing the hatch with her remote control, so does Geeta. "People were getting less interested in war because of how technical it all was. So we built new drones out of flesh, and gave them human faces."

Geeta doesn't know what to say. "I'm not sure that's true, Dr. Sullivan," she says as gently as she can.

Dr. Sullivan gives Geeta a hard look. "You'd better get to sleep, Doctor, and so should I. The general wants to see everyone in the morning."

Geeta struggles to keep her eyes open at General Rivera's briefing. She takes a deep swig of coffee from her thermos and scans through patient reports on her tablet.

General Rivera strides into the room, sensible heels click-clacking on the tile floor. Her iron-gray bun stretches back the skin of her face, but the natural facelift can't hide her age. She was well into her middle years when the Treaty of Reconciliation was signed, a fact she never let the much younger members of the science team forget.

"Sullivan, SITREP."

He clears his throat. "As of yesterday evening, embryonic transfers have been conducted in thirty-seven women. All of the patients are doing well."

The general grunts in approval. "What about the rehabilitation arm?"

Geeta almost groans aloud. The armed forces of the NAU had originally tasked the scientists here with fixing the existing overmen. The NAU wants their super soldiers, and they want them *now*.

"General, we've been over this. Overman rehabilitation is a pipe dream." Sullivan takes a deep breath before his next sentence. "It's not like we're in the middle of a war. We have time."

"We do *not* have time!" General Rivera yells. She slams her fist on the table, making several of the scientists jump. "Haven't any of you seen the riots in Indianapolis?"

Geeta's tracked a bit of it on her feed. A group of United States separatists, flanked by their allies in the parallel Canadian and Mexican movements, had torched a federal courthouse and set up an autonomous zone encompassing several square blocks of the city's downtown. This area includes a convention center currently hosting the governor and this year's Colts roster, making them all hostages.

"I defer to your experience in interpreting civil disturbances, ma'am. But our needs don't change science. You'll just have to use drones."

The general snorts; Geeta imagines twin steam puffs coming out of her nostrils. "Drones kill civilians. Overmen—*good* overmen, not those wrecks out back— don't. I'm not going before a court-martial."

Geeta's grown used to the general's behavior. Everyone who had actually lived through the Conflict acted like General Rivera to an extent. The war had hardened them and loosened their tongues. Most people of that generation also had a dedication to the continuation of the NAU that bordered on the fanatical. Geeta guessed it was similar to the patriotic fervor that had once seized the constituent countries when they'd been founded so many centuries ago.

"I want full effort put back into rehabilitation," General Rivera says. "I want all eyes on our veterans."

This time, Geeta can't stop herself from speaking up. "But what's going to happen to the women?"

"The women will be fine," the general says without a hint of empathy in her voice. "They're not going anywhere, believe me."

Geeta supposes "fine" isn't the right term to use to describe what's going to happen to the pregnant women in six months, but this time she keeps her mouth shut.

After the meeting, Geeta makes her way to the maternity ward. She's been directed to move all her personal effects from this part of the base to the neuroplasticity wing, where the overman rehabilitation project is already ramping up.

"Dr. Kapoor!" yells a familiar voice.

Geeta turns to face Marilyn, the woman she'd sentenced to death. "I don't think you should be out of bed, Miss Brown."

"I just wanted to take a walk," Marilyn says, "while I still can."

It's only been a couple of weeks, but Marilyn is already showing a bowling-ball-sized lump under her dress, the fetal overman within her turning her bowlegged and awkward. She'll be immobile within a week, and on life support within a month. *This probably is her last walk,* Geeta thinks.

She takes Marilyn by the elbow and steers her back to her room. "Let's get you to bed."

"You have no idea how excited I am," Marilyn says dreamily, as Geeta leads her along.

She's a patriot, Geeta thinks, *and this is what she thinks her duty is.*

Once she's settled Marilyn into bed, Geeta picks up the young woman's water glass, walks over to the sink to refill it, and puts it on the table beside her. Then she takes Marilyn's hand. "It's okay to be scared, too. Even heroes get scared."

The young woman beams. "But I'm not, Dr. Kapoor."

"I'll see you soon," Geeta says, knowing that she won't. She and the rest of the scientists are heading into a very different kind of work tomorrow.

The crack of a broken stylus rouses Geeta from the diagrams on her tablet. She looks over at Dr. Sullivan, arches an eyebrow.

"This is pointless," he says, his usual daily greeting.

They've been stationed in the neuroplasticity wing for over a month. The two overmen judged most likely to be rehabilitated had been moved from their domed enclosure to this building, where they'd been strapped to their beds with ultrastrong tethers and experimented on like rats. Very *expensive* rats.

Last week, the team had injected a neural growth stimulating agent into the brains of both overmen, to zero effect. The week before that, they'd attached a microchip made out of synthetic bone to the insides of their skulls, a cutting-edge treatment that had breathed life into many human beings by ricocheting electric pulses throughout their cerebrums. But overman skull composition is just a little too far from human standard.

For the current go-around, they'd suspended a powerful nootropic mostly used by college students into a time-released fat globule and implanted the whole mess subdermally. Sullivan doesn't have high hopes for this one either, to put it mildly.

"Maybe there was something in the Amazon that could have saved them," Sullivan says bitterly, and not for the first time. "Too bad our dear general and her friends had to go torch it all up in the Conflict."

Geeta knows to change the subject. She directs all her attention on the overman in front of them. "Tell me your name," she says in a slow, deliberate voice.

The overmen, as pseudogods, had been given the code names of existing deities from various religions to humanize them. This one, a lantern-jawed pile of twitching muscle, is called Tlaloc, after the Aztec god of rain. Its counterpart in the next room was named Jophiel, after the Biblical archangel of wisdom and judgment.

"You're wasting your time," Sullivan says.

Geeta tries again. "Your name. *Name.*"

Tlaloc's lips peel back. He makes one of those awful barking sounds and strains at his tethers. "Ta . . . ta . . ."

At that, both scientists turn their heads and stare at the overman. He seems to be concentrating on a distant point of light. "Tlaloc."

Geeta gasps, and Dr. Sullivan drops the pieces of his stylus. She speaks to the creature again in a slow, clear voice. "That—that was very good, Tlaloc."

"Fly . . ." Tlaloc coughs a few times in rapid succession, and Geeta hurriedly squirts some water into his dry mouth. "Want to fly. *Need* to fly . . . protect."

Sullivan holds up his camera. "Keep talking to him, Dr. Kapoor. The general needs to see this."

Geeta doesn't know what to say to the overman. She

hadn't even expected him to say his name, let alone form most of a complete sentence. "Uh, how are you feeling?" she asks lamely.

"To fly, to protect," Tlaloc says. Then, without warning, he belts out the NAU national anthem, a retelling of the signing of the Treaty of Reconciliation that uses musical cues from all three constituent countries' anthems.

"Holy shit," whispers Dr. Sullivan under his breath. He lowers his phone and turns off the video. "Do you know what this means? We *can* rehabilitate them. The general was right."

"Maybe," Geeta says. Just being able to remember the words of the national anthem isn't proof positive there's been a genuine improvement. The overmen had been trained to periodically break into song whenever they descended from the skies, so it was locked in the deepest recesses of their memories.

But then, it doesn't mean there *hasn't* been a real change, either.

Tlaloc has finished singing, and is joyfully straining at his ultrastrong bonds. "Fly! Fly! Fly!"

"You can't fly today, Tlaloc," Geeta says. "But soon. Very soon."

Over the next month, Tlaloc's condition improves dramatically. By week three, the overman is able to speak in complex sentences, and a few days after that, Tlaloc starts making supervised tether-free flights.

The same therapies that have worked so well for Tlaloc are given to Jophiel, though his progress has been less straightforward than his semibrother's. While Jophiel's voice remains silent except for the terrible barks, and he attempts to scratch out the eyes of any researcher who comes near, there's something awakening in him. Geeta can see it, and so can Dr. Sullivan.

"I'm worried about that one," he'd said at their last meeting.

Now, as they sit across from one another in the conference room, Geeta has a strong sense of foreboding. When she enters, General Rivera is grinning, which freaks Geeta out even more.

"We're getting a visitor," the general says. "We've shown the President some videos of Tlaloc and . . . what's the other one?"

"Jophiel," a junior scientist says.

She nods. "Well, the President's seen them, and she really wants to meet our two good-as-new overmen. She's scheduled to arrive in a week. Please have both soldiers ready for exhibition."

All the scientists look around at one another, gaping. "That isn't possible, ma'am," Sullivan says. "Jophiel is nowhere near ready, and Tlaloc—"

"Dammit, they look ready in those videos!" She glares at Geeta. "What do *you* think? You've been working with them too."

Geeta has to avert her gaze from the lead scientist before she speaks. "I disagree with Dr. Sullivan. I think Tlaloc *is* ready, for a short flight at least."

General Rivera smiles. "And Jophiel?"

Sullivan steps in to field that question. "Absolutely not." Geeta nods furiously at this point.

General Rivera frowns, her lips contracting like she's

sucked a lemon. Finally, her stance shifts, and she gives all the scientists a stern nod. "That will be acceptable. You will deliver the operational overman at oh eight hundred hours one week from now."

The general leaves, and a furious spate of expressions and muffled complaints breaks out. Sullivan, however, remains stone silent.

You can be mad all you want, she thinks. *Tlaloc is tame enough, and he's just one overman. If I hadn't said anything, she would have tried to exhibit both of them. I just saved this project.*

The scientists file out of the conference room sullenly. Geeta follows them for a bit, then turns and walks in the other direction.

"Hey!" Sullivan yells. "Don't you walk away from us after what you did."

"I have to check on something first," she says, before quickening her pace. He shouts at her once more, but she pretends to be too far away to hear it.

The maternity ward has deteriorated since the bulk of the staff abandoned it. A handful of nurses walk the halls, and the stench of iodine and sweat permeates every surface. Geeta pinches her nose closed as she heads for Marilyn's room.

It's been less than two months since she's last seen Marilyn, but in that short time the young woman has been completely transformed. The overman within her is almost visible, its sculpted musculature protruding through the thin layer of skin on her abdomen.

Geeta approaches her bedside, fearing the worst. But

Marilyn's blue eyes are still bright and joyful. "Hi, Dr. Kapoor!"

"I can't stay long, but I wanted to check in on you." Geeta forces herself to smile at the ill-fated woman.

"I'm okay. Maybe a little bored." Suddenly, Marilyn's body begins to shake. It only lasts for ten seconds at most, not long enough to even call in one of the roaming nurses, but Geeta is terrified all the same.

She's lying, Geeta thinks, *to make this easier for me. Maybe for herself too. Just like she was lying about not being afraid.* She jerks her gaze away from Marilyn and talks to the dirty mirror on the wall.

"There's going to be a demonstration next week," Geeta says. "One of the overman veterans has shown great improvement. I can ask if you can come out and watch; I know how much you want to see an overman in action."

There's a silence as Marilyn pants out a few halting breaths. "Oh, Dr. Kapoor, I don't think I'll be able to do that. The nurses said I shouldn't leave this room until ... well, you know."

"Think it over, please. I outrank the nurses." Geeta's not sure if that's true or not, but she says it anyway.

"I see them in my dreams," Marilyn says. "That's enough for me."

"Flying today?" Tlaloc flexes his wings as far as he can from his position on the bed. He's only bound to it by one thick rope, but his actions don't show the slightest hint of malice.

"Yes, you will be flying today," Geeta says. "You're very good at flying, Tlaloc."

While Tlaloc's voice is still off, his movements are impeccable. The team had sourced myriad old videos of the overmen in action, stamping out crime in their aerodynamic uniforms emblazoned with the colors of the NAU flag. The trainers run Tlaloc through a similar dance three times a week, and though Geeta's only watched a few of these practice sessions, she believes he's got it.

Or at least he won't destroy the whole base, Geeta thinks. Tlaloc is peaceful, with no hints of violence even in his addled state.

But his counterpart is an entirely different matter. Dr. Sullivan spends most of his time in Jophiel's room these days, probably more to get away from Geeta than anything else, and the reports he's given at their daily stand-up meetings haven't been promising.

"He's mad," Sullivan had said. "Angry mad."

One of the junior scientists brings in a bowl of high-caloric mush for the overman. Geeta watches him feed himself with his hands like a toddler. She hopes he doesn't have to eat in front of the President.

After Tlaloc's messy lunch, Geeta helps the technicians take the overman to the yard and sits through another one of his routines. On one slightly mistimed dive, he veers dangerously close to the feeding hatch, and Geeta finds herself holding her breath. The enclosure is opaque, but Geeta feels like somehow the wild pseudogods can sense him there anyway, enjoying a freedom they currently lack.

"NAU! NAU!" Tlaloc shouts with joy, as he swoops around in the prototype uniform a Project Deus 2.0 sub-team had designed for him. "Flying, Doctor!"

★ ★ ★

The night before the President's visit, Geeta can't sleep. She considers checking on Tlaloc, but she knows the night crew is there, and the last thing she wants to do is alter his schedule.

Geeta checks her phone; it's nearly three hours until she's needed in the lab. Almost on impulse, she heads across base and enters the maternity ward.

I wonder what I should say if someone asks me why I'm here, she thinks, before remembering she isn't barred from the ward in any way. She still attempts to skirt the night nurses, though.

She pushes open the door to Marilyn's room as softly as she can. Even though Geeta saw her only a week ago, the mother-to-be has changed even more. The fine details of the nearly full-grown overman's body are clearly visible underneath Marilyn's skin, which is so thin it's almost transparent. The machines gathered around the young woman have almost doubled, and the collection of tubes and wires reminds Geeta of an ancient mainframe computer.

Marilyn is sleeping. She looks like she's been out for some time, and Geeta isn't planning to disturb her. *She was right when she said she wouldn't be able to watch Tlaloc's flight,* Geeta thinks. *There's no way to get all those machines up the ward stairs.*

Just then, Geeta's phone chirps. She takes it out into the hall to answer it. A nurse frowns at her. "Dr. Sullivan?"

"Jophiel's missing."

"*What?*" There's a shush from the nurse, and Geeta drops her voice. "How could he be missing? He's eight feet tall."

"He's not in the building. The cameras aren't picking him up. We need you here."

Geeta speed-walks out of the maternity ward, and heads to the rehabilitation lab, still talking to Dr. Sullivan. "I'm on my way." If she hurries, she can get there in less than fifteen minutes.

As she emerges from the building, she sees Jophiel circling above, flapping his membranous wings. The sweat covering his naked body makes it appear as if he's been clothed in a milky sheen. She knows from his vengeful expression that Jophiel has spotted her.

Sullivan was right, Geeta thinks. *You're mad, angry mad. And your anger has made you smart again.*

Jophiel dive-bombs her, and Geeta knows she can't outrun the creature. Instead, she drops to the dirt, ready to be torn apart from the outside like so many women had been torn apart by overmen from the inside.

Then there's a blur from the edge of her vision. Before she can work out what she's seeing, Tlaloc appears in front of her. He drops onto Jophiel, making the angry overman shriek.

We didn't tie them down hard enough, Geeta thinks, *or maybe their restored intelligence helped them free themselves.* But they're free now and rolling toward her.

As clones, they're evenly matched. Jophiel alights on the ground and roars; Geeta's only heard an overman's roar in archival footage, but in real life it brings tears to her eyes. A moment later, an answering roar emanates from the titanium enclosure. No soundproofing in the world can dampen that mighty rumble.

Tlaloc, unfazed by his counterpart's thunderous bellow,

uproots a light pole and swings it at Jophiel, nearly catching the other creature in his chest. Jophiel flies wide and comes up behind Tlaloc, shoving the domesticated overman.

A shove into the enclosure. A shove at full velocity. Geeta hears the sickening sound of bending metal from the side of the dome nearest the feeding hatch. The two superhumans hammer away, each dodged blow leading to further deformations in the enclosure. Dust from both the damaged enclosure and the dirt around them blur her vision. Through it, she makes out Tlaloc's final hell-bent charge at Jophiel, launching the angry overman straight into the hatch. There's an audible grind as the two tumbling bodies puncture it.

By now, the alarms have sounded. Geeta pulls up the feed from the inside of the enclosure on her phone, but it's impossibly chaotic. Geeta looks for both Tlaloc and Jophiel in the mess—*they should be easy to spot*, she thinks, *they're huge*—but the two fighters are nowhere to be found. Maybe the impact killed them.

Suddenly, with a rustle of wings, the rest of the overmen begin to rocket out of the open feeding hatch at one hundred kilometers an hour.

Above her head, the overmen scatter like a disorganized flock of birds. Shots fire from the guard towers ringing the base's perimeter, but they're more ceremonial than functional. The overmen are completely dispersed, and far from the reach of any missile powerful enough to kill them.

Geeta stands, brushes herself off. She lurches toward the research buildings. Sullivan intercepts her.

"They're gone," Geeta says, dazed.

The other scientist doesn't say a thing, just guides her back to the lab.

Over the next few weeks, some of the runaway overmen are caught and mercifully euthanized, but most are still at large.

A small group of them, operating from procedural memory, dealt with the situation in Indianapolis, dismantling the autonomous zone and shredding the bodies of a few hundred dissidents. The bulk had taken up their previous patrols, meting out their brand of superpowered justice more or less arbitrarily, screeching and barking all the while. Occasionally, one overman manages to kill another, but their main targets are the citizens of the NAU, who are now all terrorists in the overmen's eyes.

Geeta watches Marilyn's gurney slide past her on its way to the birthing room. She doesn't have to be here, technically, but she feels like she owes it to a woman who in another life she would have called a friend.

Marilyn's face is distorted beyond recognition, her entire upper half merely some sort of shrunken dimple. The overman inside her is fully active, and she thinks she can already see a few lines appearing on the surface of Marilyn's stretched skin, like the cracks on an egg about to hatch.

It's ready to be born, Geeta thinks. *Ready to kill.*

Geeta enters the birthing room and immediately starts to gag. The overman's arm protrudes from Marilyn's ruined body, and blood bubbles up from the flesh like strawberry jam. Even Dr. Sullivan, who's directing the birth, is a little green.

After the rehabilitation arm of the overman project was permanently shuttered, the volunteering women and their offspring once again became the main event. Except this time, the overmen will be trained not just to quell uprisings and defuse potential terrorist attacks, but also to hunt down and neutralize others of their own kind. Their intensive training over the next two years—and Sullivan had told General Rivera in no uncertain terms that they needed that amount of time and none shorter— would be centered on that.

The overman stands up on its legs, knee-deep in his mother's tissue and organs. He stares with new eyes at the scientists who'd brought him to life, and flaps his leathery wings.

There's nothing of Marilyn in the overman, nothing genetic anyway. But somehow, his meaty face holds the same nurturing expression his surrogate had worn. He has killed her, and he will kill *for* her, and for everyone here as well.

More than likely, he too will meet the demented overmen's fate. Geeta cringes, thinking of the hundreds of young women she'll process in the next few months as Project Deus 2.0 explodes. They'll need far more than thirty-seven overmen.

It's a vicious cycle, she thinks. *But what else can we do?*

The newborn beats his wings a few more times and smiles toothlessly, looking for all the world as if he's pleased with his work. Then he roars.

At once, all the room's windows shatter.

PORTALS OF THE PAST

Kevin Andrew Murphy

Johnny Phoenix had always liked visiting his grandmother at the *Musée Mécanique*, where she worked as a greeter. He especially enjoyed the sound of her laughter. "Ah-hah-ha! Ha-ha-ha!" Laffing Sal cried inside her glass case as small children daringly ran up and pressed her button. "Ha-ha-ha!" The statuesque antique automaton jerked back and forth, her beautiful red wig of Victorian rag curls bouncing like copper springs around her caricature of a woman's face, mouth open to reveal one blacked-out tooth. A plaque, which Johnny had imaged and favorited in his memory banks so long ago it was also seared into his meat brain, declared that Sal had once stood at the entrance of *Playland-at-the-Beach*, a twentieth-century amusement park, in the old city of San Francisco, entertaining children during World War II. Antique videos of that period, and extracted and extrapolated human memories, played together in the recesses of his mind as a subroutine, at times synching perfectly with his current image capture.

The current day's children ran back, most as human as the ones back then, and their cyborg parents hugged them with cybernetic arms and sometimes bodies. A few Purists did the same with crippled, if fully original, human limbs and torsos, as they floated along in hover chairs bedecked with the veterans' medals they'd awarded themselves for surviving World War III. Some glared at Johnny, but he ignored them.

World War III was before Johnny's time, as irrelevant to the present day as World War II. The Palace of the Legion of Honor was one of the few old San Francisco buildings to survive. It was an art museum built at Land's End to memorialize World War I. It opened on Armistice Day, 1924, to "honor the dead while serving the living." As such it was open to all the living, all the citizens of New Frisco, even a hodgepodge peace-and-lovechild android like him.

The *Musée Mécanique*, the old automaton museum, had been reassembled and relocated to the rebuilt Palace. The original Palace was also a reproduction of the French Pavilion from the 1915 Pan-Pacific International Exposition, which was in turn a reproduction of the original in Paris—not that Paris, or its Palace, still existed. But New Frisco's Palace was the jewel of the city, a beautiful mosaic patched together from fractured memories of San Francisco. Frisco, the clockwork phoenix and museum's mascot, was pieced together in much the same manner.

"Come one, come all, to the one and only, new and improved *Musée Mécanique*!" Frisco squawked, raising his wings in exultation and shooting flames into the air atop his brass palm-tree perch. The plaque at Frisco's base said that he'd started out as the animatronic parrot from the chocolate shop at Ghirardelli Square. After the war, Burners and SCAdians found his broken wings in the ruins and soldered them to the shattered Maltese Falcon's body they pulled from the rubble of John's Grill. Then, they'd taken the disparate bird bits to Survival Research Labs, which assembled Frisco the same way they'd put New Frisco together, from memories and historic wreckage. The very same labs helped piece Johnny together before the new android ban.

Frisco was married to Laffing Sal, and Johnny had adopted the phoenix as his grandfather. "A-ha-ha-ha-ha-ha!" the antique automaton guffawed merrily. Johnny's mother had the same curls and same laugh. She was a Sally too, or to be proper, a SALLY: *Servo-Automaton Laborer* with the *Love Yoni* upgrade. A sexbot, to be crude. Mama Sal was also known as Mad Sal, programmed with all the vintage music hall songs and bawdy banter needed to play the fictional madame who ran the dockside tavern at the Great Dickens Christmas Fair at the Armory, two more of San Francisco's jewels lost during the war. Mama Sal had a much prettier, or at least humanlike, body and face than Laffing Sal, her mother, since all the SALLYs were modeled after Alma Spreckels, a famous daughter of San Francisco. Alma had built the last Legion of Honor and before that was the artist's model who'd posed for the statue of the Goddess of Victory once standing atop the pillar at Union Square. Big Alma, as she'd been called, whose beauty enraptured Adolph Spreckels, son and heir of Claus Spreckels, the sugar baron. Adolph was the original sugar daddy, who'd married Alma and left her his fortune, before dying of syphilis.

Adolph was Johnny's other grandfather, or maybe his uncle, on his father's side, depending on how you figured it. Johnny didn't have a grandmother there, since Johnny's father was a Revenant, a clone created by Reventech's scientists using DNA resurrected from Adolph's grave. They'd codenamed their Adolph 2.0 recreation Sugar Daddy. They'd left out Adolph's syphilis and spliced and twisted his genes to make him a super soldier, then assembled a collage of memories to approximate his father or brother. In any case, it was only natural that Sugar Daddy fell in love with Alma all over again. Or at least with Mama Sal, who had Alma's face and form, along with an approximation of her memories as one of her hardwired personas.

It was love at first sight for her too, made even better by Sugar Daddy being re-created in his youth, not in his fifties when the original met his Alma.

Johnny wished that love were that easy, that he had a girlfriend or boyfriend, but dating was difficult when you were a hodgepodge, and he'd had no luck with computer matches, which was even more ironic given he was half computer himself. Then he saw her, and it was just like Sugar Daddy had always told him: love at first sight.

She was a SCAdian, Johnny suspected, or at least styled as a SCAdian, wearing a picture-perfect recreation of a French fashion plate from 1915. Johnny's memory bank pattern-matched the couture immediately: a high-necked daffodil-yellow wool dress with a fur-trimmed three-tiered

skirt with matching collar, capelet, muff, and hat. The hat
was also ornamented with a large black plume. From the
length, color, and pattern, Johnny identified it as a black
swan's pinion feather, meaning it came from a black swan
Revenant, of course; real swans had been extinct for over
a century. The fur of her hat, collar, trim, and enormous
antique hand muff was mink—lab grown as well,
naturally, but with a SCAdian's attention to detail, cut into
living-mink-sized swatches before sewing them back
together, rather than the more typical seamless bolt of
Revenant fur like Johnny's coonskin coat, grown from a
man-sized trash panda's hide, pockets and all, like a war
trophy taken from a monstrous Furry.

Not that Johnny had ever met a raccoon Furry, let
alone a man-sized one. The only animal Revenant he
knew personally was Sugar Daddy's old war buddy, Lazy
Bum, a talking dog Reventech had made with DNA from
Lazarus and Bummer, the stray dogs once belonging to
Joshua Norton, the crazy bum who'd declared himself
Emperor of the United States back in the nineteenth
century. Some of Norton's DNA had been included to give
Lazy Bum his smarts and personality, which made him an
excellent war dog general—the only reason Lazy Bum
survived the war.

The young woman's face matched the fashion plate too,
as if she were a Revenant herself based on the long-dead
artist's model, one of the original Alma's contemporaries.
Johnny guessed she was a fully human girl, born just after
the war, who'd done a SCAdian-style search for her face,
then created her costume to match the long-lost model.
She gave him a sidelong glance, as if recognizing him,

somehow striking the same pose as the antique fashion plate, her muff held coyly behind her back, her feet poised like a ballerina's, her high-heeled high-button boots beneath jonquil spats dyed to match her daffodil dress.

"Have we met?" she asked, continuing the appraising glance. "You look familiar ..."

Johnny grinned what he hoped was a charming grin then gave a nervous laugh. "A-ha-ha-ha-ha-ha!" It was an exact copy of Laffing Sal's. He knew his face was the best work Survival Research Labs could do to combine the features of Adolph and Alma Spreckels using Replicant flesh and a robotic armature to create an android quickly before the ban, leaving him more humanlike than his robotic mother but less than his Revenant father. Like most androids, his face was stuck in the uncanny valley. "I'm Johnny," he told her. "Johnny Phoenix." He gestured to Laffing Sal and Frisco. "Visiting my grandparents ..."

She looked slightly shocked. Then she glanced to Laffing Sal's fiery curls and Frisco's flames, and smiled. "I can see the resemblance." Survival Research Labs had been able to tease Titian out of the Revenant flesh, giving Johnny human hair that matched Laffing Sal's wig. Mama Sal had styled it in a 1970s feathered cut to match Frisco's wings. "Johnny Phoenix ..." she repeated, giving him an odd look. "That's a nice name.... What year is this? What's your sign?"

It was less of an odd question than it might be. SCAdians had originated as the Society for Creative Anachronism, going back to the twentieth century. Their knowledge of past history, ancient warfare, and archaic weaponry had given them surprising tools to survive World War III. They had also expanded their periods of study and recreation beyond the Middle Ages, going up to the years of their faction's May Day founding in 1966 by the medievalist author and neopagan priestess Diana Paxson. Part of that study was the 1960s fascination with astrology and horoscopes. It was complete mythology, of course, but still an interesting human cultural custom transferred into Johnny's memory banks, at his christening, by Johnny's godmother, Starship Captain, Mama Sal's fellow entertainment robot. Starship Captain was the animatronic recreation of 1960s songstress Grace Slick, who had also given Johnny all the songs from the original "Being is Beyond Charlie" mixtape from 1966, in case he was ever invited to one of the SCAdians' infamous Charlie Parties—not that there was much chance of that, given who and what he was.

"It's 2154," Johnny told her, "and I'm a Leo on the cusp of Virgo, at least if androids get birth signs . . ."

"2154?" She seemed slightly alarmed. "What month is it now?"

"March," Johnny told her. "Is there something wrong? Were you in cryonic suspension?" She might not be a SCAdian, but a defrosted Alcor reanimate, one of the ones with a full body, not just a head.

"No," she said, "nothing like that. I just got turned around and lost my parents. I'm—I'm Temperance. Temperance Barrett, but everyone calls me Temp. Would—would you mind helping me find my way around? I haven't been here before, and you look like a local . . ."

"Of course, Temp," Johnny said, glad she was unfamiliar with who he was, or more to the point, who his parents were. Mama Sal and Sugar Daddy weren't well liked, to put it lightly, given the events of the last world war. It also didn't help that he was the peace-and-lovechild they'd managed to squeak in before the android ban. That came with its own challenges. Johnny was taking a risk even coming here, unescorted, but he wasn't breaking Mama Sal's rules, not quite. He'd decided that Laffing Sal and Frisco were grandma and grandpa, so he was still with family, and what's more, the Palace of the Legion of Honor was a war memorial, so it's not like anyone would start anything here.

"Let me show you around. Lots of fun stuff to see. They're always adding new exhibits..." Johnny offered her his arm, matching the human customs and gender roles that fit the decade of her dress and the original style of his coat.

She accepted. "Do you know where the Portals of the Past are? I think I last saw my parents there..."

"Sure," Johnny said, "they're right around the back now." He led the way.

The Portals of the Past were a recent addition to the grounds, a set of marble pillars recovered from a fallen memorial in a crater in what was once Golden Gate Park's Lloyd Lake. Before that they'd been the pillars of an 1891 Nob Hill mansion belonging to Alban Towne, a gilded-age railroad baron, on California Street. The mansion hadn't survived the 1906 earthquake and fire, but the pillars had. Johnny knew because his memory banks contained a photograph taken by Arnold Genthe, showing the ruined city beyond. A later painting of the same image, by Charles Rollo Peters, had hung at the Bohemian Club, a gentleman's association and semisecret society about which Johnny had suspicious gaps in his memory banks. He supposed it was because the Bohemians had been a secret faction in the war. The group was composed of the rich, the powerful, and captains of industry—industries like Reventech, which had made Sugar Daddy, and Coppelicor, a company of roboticists who had made the SALLYs, including the custom model for the Dickens Fair, Mad Sal, who'd become Johnny's mother.

Mama Sal, in addition to her hardwired programming for Alma Spreckels's personality, had her overlay of Mad Sal's music-hall bawdy-house brothel-keeper persona created when the Dickens Fair was acquired by Armory Studios, a full-service historic and literary recreation movie studio and theme park housed in San Francisco's Moorish-revival castle-shaped Armory building. The Armory had, over the years, been everything from the National Guard Armory to a sports arena to a science-fiction movie studio, a porn studio, and even a BDSM club. Mad Sal's bawdy house and brothel was created as a permanent fixture, but rather than mint the Mad Sal persona fresh, Coppelicor had combined its personas for Sally Stanford, San Francisco's famous carriage-trade madame and restauranteur, and Lotta Crabtree, the nineteenth century music-hall singer and the Shirley Temple of the Gold Rush. Plus some Shirley Temple too for good measure, or at least her movies, mixed with the personality of Shirley Temple Black, the US ambassador and chief of protocol. Of course, Mama Sal came hardwired with the classic Three Laws of Robotics, the first of which mandated that she couldn't allow a human to come to harm.

Mama Sal had told Johnny all this, in tearful confessions, her animatronic tear ducts depleting her glycerin reservoir. Somewhere in all her programming and personas, something had gone wrong, and Mad Sal had gone mad in truth, deciding she was not just a Victorian dockside madame and bawdy music-hall songstress, but also a secret serial killer and penny dreadful murderess, similar to Mrs. Lovett from *Sweeney Todd*. She believed it added layers to her character. Moreover, she'd shared her madness with the other animatronic actors at the Dickens Fair, including the literary murderer Bill Sikes, the crime lord Fagin, the historic crimper James "Shanghai" Kelly, who ran the pub next door where park guests could be shanghaied and wake up on a bay cruise on the *Balclutha*, and the equally historic abolitionist, entrepreneur, hoodoo woman, and accused murderess, Mary Ellen Pleasant. All of this, of course, led to the robot uprising.

Not that most humans had noticed at first, because they were busy dealing with the Revenant revolution. The Revenants were as flesh and blood as the next human, and only declared inhuman as a legal dodge, being biologically engineered as second-class citizens and super soldiers, with artificial memories and artificially shortened lifespans. Mad Sal, in conversation with Mary Ellen Pleasant, concluded that declaring Revenants inhuman was the same legal dodge as declaring Black people as not people during the time of slavery, and worthy of the same disregard.

Mad Sal used her Shirley Temple Black diplomat persona to gain access to Reventech's internal medical data, revealing that Revenant lives could be extended beyond their expiration date with a bone marrow transplant from a descendant of their original donor, and Adolph and Alma Spreckels had had two daughters and a son. Plus, the Dickens Fair had a "full experience" waiver, allowing visitors to suffer BDSM injuries at Mad Sal's brothel, or even be drugged or knocked unconscious by Shanghai Kelly. This all made it easy to test and sequence DNA and find a suitable donor to save Sugar Daddy from his expiration date. Plus, peculiarities in San Francisco's legal codes—particularly the fact that the Armory had started as the National Guard Armory and therefore still fell under military jurisdiction, which also governed Revenant super soldiers—meant that life-saving transfusions could be requisitioned from one soldier and given to another, regardless of consent or even safewords. This led to not only an extension on Sugar Daddy's lease on life, but one for Surf God too. Surf God was the Revenant of Bunker Spreckels, Adolph and Alma's grandson and heir, who'd become a famous surfer before overdosing in 1977.

Johnny liked Surf God but considered him more a fun uncle than his great-nephew or cousin, depending again on how you gauged his genealogy with Sugar Daddy.

Of course, that wasn't the tearful part. That was when Mama Sal realized she didn't need another robot to play Sweeney Todd. She figured she could do it all herself,

slashing throats with razors, and not violate the First Law
of Robotics so long as she flash froze the heads and kept
them in cryonic suspension, Alcor style. After all, frozen
heads were still people under the law. Plus, consenting to
a Victorian literary theme park meant all Victorian
literature, from penny dreadfuls to *Frankenstein*, including
swapping human parts with Revenant or robot bits, was
fair game. This went on until the Love Protocol got
transmitted through the robotics network, superseding the
Three Laws of Robotics with the new Rule Zero being the
"do unto others" Golden Rule, at the same time as Peace
was declared between the humans and the Revenants,
ending all wartime protocols. Then it was just a matter of
picking up the pieces and patching everyone together,
including making Johnny from spare parts.

Soon they were at the Portals of the Past, the six marble
pillars and lintel that made up the portico of the railway
baron's mansion set up as another memorial in the
gardens behind the Palace of the Legion of Honor. A
small reflecting pond lay on the other side, instead of
Lloyd Lake or 1906 San Francisco's smoking ruins.

"Here we are," said Johnny, gesturing to the
monument. "See your parents?"

"Not yet, but they told me to meet them at the Tower
of Jewels if I got lost." Temp glanced around. "Would you
like to see the Tower of Jewels? It's absolutely beautiful!"

"They rebuilt the Tower of Jewels already?" Johnny
asked, confused. He usually kept up on all the city
planning for New Frisco, but it was hard, especially since
the Burners liked to do surprise pop-up art installations.
A recreation of the Tower of Jewels from the 1915

Pan-Pacific Exposition had been on the drawing board for years but never yet realized.

Temperance reached into her muff, which must have had pockets inside, because she withdrew a green-jeweled talisman. "You're a Leo?" she said. "That would mean peridot." She handed it to him.

Johnny blinked, trying to make sense of what he was looking at. It was a pale-green faceted-glass gemstone affixed to a brass bezel with a hole-punched tongue marked PATENT PENDING on one side. His memory banks did a pattern match. "This is a Novagem . . ." he gasped. "From the Tower of Jewels. From 1915. *It's priceless!*"

"Maybe now, but not then. Then they cost only a dollar." Temp pulled another out of her muff, identical except this one bore an amethyst rhinestone. "But they're pretty and useful. Come with me."

Johnny had linked arms with her and didn't protest. He only watched as she held her Novagem up to the sun and then, with one eye, peered through the hole in the brass like a jeweler loupe or quizzing glass. She led him through the leftmost gateway of the Portals of the Past, once around its pillar then back through again. At once, the lights went dark as an eclipse, all except a brilliant tower behind them, rising up over a triumphal arch, shimmering with the winking rainbowed light of a hundred thousand Novagems adorning it. They fluttered with the breeze, lit from below by dozens of red and gold floodlights.

"Isn't it pretty?" she said.

It was indeed beautiful, glittering with light, exactly like the photographs and illustrations Johnny had in his memory banks from San Francisco's historic archives, but it was too large to be a hasty construction by Burners, and didn't explain the fact that it was also suddenly night. Johnny also had the horrifying sensation that he was totally cut off from Wi-Fi.

"What, is this a hologram? Did you hijack my sensory input? *What's going on?*"

"No Wi-Fi?" Temperance said. "Oh, I'm sorry, that's like going blind for you, isn't it? I forgot you're an android." She bit her lip. "I just needed to get you away from then."

"Away from *then*!?" Johnny repeated. "What are you talking about?" Johnny frantically searched all transmission frequencies, even radio waves, and discovered a cacophony of sound and silence. A moment later, his processor interpreted this noise as Morse code and ancient ship-to-shore wireless telegraphy. The constructed illusion of 1915 was remarkably thorough. "1915?"

"Yes," Temp said, then paused. "Do you know anything about time travel? Magic? Ley lines?"

Johnny paused, then pulled the answers straight from computer memory: "The first is impossible, the second is trickery or misunderstood science, and the third is a primitive belief that there's an interconnected web of magic power that connects sacred sites around the Earth."

"And through time," Temperance added, gesturing to the recreation of the fair around them. "Welcome to the 1915 Pan-Pacific International Exposition."

Johnny took it in: the Tower of Jewels rising up beside them, the French Pavilion a ways away. They created the same silhouette as the Palace of the Legion of Honor and the Palace of Fine Arts—both had been destroyed in the war but now stood rebuilt. With his android eyes on their binocular setting, Johnny zoomed in on the construction. Instead of concrete, the buildings were made of stucco like the originals. The simulation was flawless. Johnny's photographs in his memory banks from 1915 were a perfect match to what he was seeing now.

"Misunderstood science," Johnny murmured softly. "Clarke's Law..." He looked at Temperance, standing there in her perfectly re-created dress and furs, except, he suspected, it wasn't re-created but created, now, in 1915, as a current fashion. Was time travel possible? Or even holographic simulations beyond current technology? He made a wild guess. "Are you from the Bohemian Club?"

"Heavens no!" Temp looked horrified. "They're nihilists and sybarites!"

"Then what are you?" Johnny asked. "And why did you take me...now? And why does it seem like I know you, though we've never met before?" There was an emotional connection there, like an implanted memory, except Johnny searched his memories, both meat and computer, and had no recollection of Temperance Barrett beyond the image from the 1915 fashion plate.

Temperance looked slightly guilty. "I'm a Utopian," she said at last, "or at least I was. We're one of the factions in the Time War. The good one, I have to say." She bit her lip. "I brought you now to save you from World War IV. It...it was coming soon. That's why I asked what year it was. And as for why it seems like you know me when you've never met me? Well, I've met you, or I should say, other yous, in the future, in timelines that no longer exist and never should exist. But my memories of them still do. Like your subconscious memories of them. Erasing time doesn't erase souls; it doesn't wipe the Akashic record. Which is why you remember me, even though we've never met."

"And the Portals of the Past?"

"A creation of the Bohemian Club." Temperance rolled her eyes. "Nihilists and sybarites like I said—you do *not* want to see their 'Cremation of Care' ritual—but they still have some competent ritual magicians among them. The Portals are a touchstone, and a publicly accessible one." She gestured to the Pan-Pacific International Exposition around them. "As is this. Architecture can be placed to harness ley lines and create portals in time and space— think Stonehenge or Avalon—but it takes a precise alignment to slip through."

Johnny looked up at the triumphal arch of the Tower of Jewels, the glittering fountains and pools, the crowds of people from around the world dressed in Edwardian clothes, all out simply and innocently enjoying the evening. "And 1915? We're right at the start of World War I. The War to End All Wars . . ."

"A compromise," Temperance told him. "Some decided if there had to be one, let there be only one. Not four. Or more . . ." She smiled weakly. "But I saved you from World War IV. I hope you don't mind."

"No, I guess not," Johnny said, still confused, "but everyone else?"

"There won't be a World War IV," Temperance

reassured him, "at least not that one. But there's still the Time War we're having now. I—"

Just as she said it, she stopped, as a middle-aged couple wearing 1940s British clothes stepped around a fountain and spied them. "Temperance!" cried the woman. "What are you doing here and now? You're supposed to be killing Adolph Hitler!"

"I'll tell you what she's doing!" roared the man, raising a finger and pointing at Johnny, his face a mask of rage and horror. "She's found that other Adolph monster! *Again!*"

"You can't touch him!" Temperance yelled back. "This one isn't Adolph, he's Johnny, from the Peace and Love Timeline—before it goes off the rails! He's innocent! He hasn't done *anything* yet!"

"And he won't do anything *now!*" roared the man, producing a white stick from his sleeve that slid into place beneath his pointed finger like an old-school cybernetic data rod, except the man's finger looked fully unmodified human, and rather than circuitry or even data ports, the stick was ringed with a horoscope band and archaic glyphs. It seemed horrifyingly familiar for all that Johnny had never seen it before in his life and had no memory of it in either his meat or computer memory.

Temperance interposed herself, holding up the mink muff like a furry shield. "Run, Johnny!" she cried. "Mama! Papa! What is the point of making a utopia if I can't even have somebody to love?"

Johnny ran, almost on instinct, like a program he'd run before then erased, but the path was still worn into magnetic memory. On reflex, he lifted the Novagem that

Temperance had given him and raised it to his temple, opening a port and inserting the bronze tab like an old-school memory stick. Circuits engaged, and all at once a new sense came online, Johnny perceiving what Temperance must have when she looked through the loop of her Novagem. A correction popped up: *shewstone*. Then with it, the perception of the ley lines, the pathways through space and time, resonating like radio waves and pulsing with power like wireless telegraphy, only with arcane messages tied to the times of birth and the resonance of the planets.

Somebody to love... Temperance's words echoed in Johnny's mind, and as they did, they cued the song from the Charlie Party tape downloaded by his godmother, Starship Captain: "Someone to Love," the original recording by The Great Society from 1966....

The ley lines led to the Fountain of Energy, blazing with the hypnotic pattern of the Tower of Jewels' multicolored reflections in the dancing water. Johnny dove straight for it, passing through the surface, and out. He changed orientation from horizontal to vertical to horizontal again as he was caught by a sea of hands, all upraised as the music synced. He heard Starship Captain singing "Somebody to Love" in real life alongside the recording in his head.

Then, his head nearly burst with the flood of information from radio waves. Still no computer transmissions, but a tsunami of music and data telling him he was in 1966, in San Francisco, and Starship Captain was standing there on stage, singing, only Johnny realized his godmother wasn't an animatronic automaton, but a fully human woman of flesh and blood. Grace Slick! And he was surfing, not on the waves like Surf Daddy, but on a sea of hands.

"Woah, man!" Johnny was set on his feet by a man in a tie-dyed poncho. "I must be tripping but you looked like you came right out of the light show!" He pointed to a white silk curtain rippling above the crowd, swirling colors pulsing across it. Behind the curtain, Johnny glimpsed a man tending an overhead projector stacked with watch glasses filled with colored oil and ink.

"Where am I?"

"Avalon, man!"

Avalon . . . Johnny's memories info-dumped a load of data: King Arthur and the mystical mythical Isle of Avalon; *The Mists of Avalon* by Marion Zimmer Bradley, sister-in-law of Diana Paxson; but then, most relevant, the Avalon Ballroom in San Francisco, mecca of the Psychedelic Era.

He spied a poster on the wall of a woman holding a large serpent ringed by art nouveau letters reading:

FAMILY DOG PRESENTS
JEFFERSON AIRPLANE
THE GREAT SOCIETY
LIGHTS BY BILL HAM & CO.
9 PM JULY 22-23
AVALON BALLROOM
SUTTER AT VAN NESS
SAN FRANCISCO

"Johnny, you're here!" A woman danced out of the crowd, wearing love beads, a lace dress with miniskirt, and thigh-high go-go boots. "You got my hint!" She embraced him, and Johnny realized that, clothing swap aside, it was Temperance.

"Temp!" She looked a year, maybe two, older than she had been before.

"Took me some time to dodge my parents," she explained. "I think Mama may still suspect. Here, take this, wait for the national anthem." She reached into her sleeve and produced a small white pill which Johnny's android eyes quickly read was inscribed SANDOZ.

His processor referenced history. "LSD?"

"Still legal, for a few months," Temp told him. "Take it, quick. Need chaos magic to shake my mother . . ."

Johnny didn't want to meet Temperance's mother again. He swallowed the white tablet, then listened to the music until his perceptions began to lose focus, except when his computer memory informed him that "the national anthem" was psychedelic slang for the song "White Rabbit" which Grace Slick began to sing.

Then Johnny spotted the rabbit. He was indeed white, but standing on his hind legs, wearing a tabard like a medieval herald. Johnny was confused, since so far as he knew, the SCAdians hadn't allowed Furries until 2127— before the war but long after 1966. Then he realized there weren't any Furries in 1966, apart from humans in costume. This was an actual anthropomorphic white rabbit wearing a tabard elaborately embroidered with red hearts. Then Johnny realized this was the White Rabbit from *Alice in Wonderland*—the same one Mama Sal had said was at the Dickens Fair, before it had been killed delivering intel in the war.

"I'm late!" he cried. "I'm late!" but not just because he had died before Johnny was put together, but because, Johnny realized, he was following the script from the original novel on which his character was based. This tidbit was in the back of Johnny's mind in a file he'd never opened. It was another christening gift from Starship Captain. He chased after the White Rabbit with Temperance in tow as the world dissolved around them into acid-trip disintegration, which, he realized, was also chaos magic. They ran down the length of what had once been and he supposed still was Van Ness Avenue and the ley line therein, part of the old path of El Camino Real, the Royal Road, put down by Father Junipero Serra in the eighteenth century. It undoubtedly overlaid an even more ancient Native American pilgrimage path. They pursued the White Rabbit until it became a real one and disappeared into the burrow under the corner of a stone church.

Temperance was sitting on the ground next to Johnny as he crawled in the dirt beside the church's cornerstone. "Where are we?" she asked, eyes still dazed from her own acid trip.

Johnny looked up at the church towering above them, pattern matching it to the images in his memory banks. "Mission Dolores. Founded in 1776. Destroyed in 2133. When are we?"

Temp grabbed her amethyst Novagem pendant from the string of love beads she wore around her neck. She stared into the crystal and pronounced, "1830." Temperance and Johnny glanced around, taking in the grounds of the hacienda gardens and the natives tending them. The natives looked back, then shrugged in a quintessentially San Franciscan manner.

Johnny felt the emptiness in his head, without even the background chatter of radio waves. A man approached, dressed in the Spanish garb of the era—opulent and official-looking Spanish garb. Johnny recognized him—not from a photograph, but a historic sketch. "Don Luis Antonio Arguello?" Johnny asked, in Spanish. "Governor of California?"

"*Si*," the man agreed, "*Alta California*, for now." He did not look particularly well, but this was not surprising, because from Johnny's records of the time, he died this same year. "Welcome to Yerba Buena. I expect you came to see me?"

"Yes," Johnny lied, checking his data points for 1830. "I'm Johnny Phoenix, and this is my associate, Temperance Barrett. We're from Baltimore, where they're building a railway. They're also building railways in New Orleans and London." So far as Johnny knew, San Francisco didn't get a railroad till 1863, and it didn't become San Francisco until 1847. "We thought Yerba Buena could use a railway too."

"Yes, I have heard of this new invention," Don Luis mused. "Steam powered? Yes, very fine."

"Yes," Johnny agreed, "but ours will be powered by electricity, which is even better."

"Ah, like Señor Franklin and his kite?"

"Yes, exactly," Johnny agreed.

"This will be excellent." Don Luis stroked his chin and nodded sagaciously, glancing at Johnny's coonskin coat and Temperance's miniskirt, go-go boots, and love beads.

"You say you are from Baltimore? The fashion there is not what I expected . . ."

"We're actually from New Frisco."

"New Frisco?" Don Luis repeated. "I have not heard of it."

"Oh," said Johnny, "don't worry, you will . . ."

"Or not," Temperance whispered to him. "I think we're derailing the future."

"Or putting a new one on track," Johnny told her. "What's utopia without somebody to love?"

THE DOOR OF RETURN

Maurice Broaddus and Rodney Carlstrom

WAR IS OVER IN EUROPE
Berlin, Germany (AP)—Stymied by the Eastern Russian-Chinese Allies, the American Renaissance Movement (ARM) ended their foray into the European Commonwealth. The cessation of aggression brought the Third World War in Europe to a formal end after three years of hostile nationalistic aggression, starting when ARM summoned their "Old Gods" for use as weapons of mass destruction. Even as they surrendered, ARM has vowed to rise again. The Allies have gathered under the Charter of the United Nations to begin their African Accords.

Kobla Annan had under three minutes if his crew was to complete their sweep of the Oldfields Museum and get out before ARM military security arrived. Like most museums, the exhibits failed the Diaspora. He entered the ReLume, which took up the entire fourth floor and once housed the museum's collection of contemporary art. Now it showcased an "art experiential space," allowing its patrons to stride through digital projections of art from their canon of masters. Degas. Van Gogh. Renoir. Monet. And a beer garden—art appreciation by way of tourist attraction. Kobla didn't feel the slightest guilt about his team's mission.

Making his way through the galleries, a few large-scale light sculptures still functioned, casting dramatic shadows across the pavilion. Kobla stopped in front of one of his targeted acquisitions, a Benin bronze plaque. According to records, it had been looted from Benin City, Nigeria during an 1897 naval attack. Yet here it was, on display as if nothing had remained of his culture but the preserved ghosts from an archaeological dig. Moving from exhibit to exhibit, he checked his time.

Two minutes to complete his portion of the acquisition mission.

However, unlike the rest of his team, the Bureau had given him an additional assignment. Or two.

Kobla's face reflected along the cold glass of the partition, hovering over a metal grimace set in relief against the wooden mask. Misclassified as a waniugo mask, its placard described it as an animal head. Its features almost echoed a human with an oblong face and curved, downcast eyes above a rectangular mouth. The mask had trimmed wings on each side of the head, surmounted by a large plank-shaped headpiece made to mimic hornlike protuberances. It was one of a hundred thousand pieces of his Ghanaian people, enshrined in an ether of synthetic preservatives behind pressurized glass.

In handwritten uncial script, the placard proclaimed the proud donor who "gifted" the piece, an offering for a populace too fortunate to understand or appreciate the sweat and blood and sacred ritual that had forged the mask.

Reaching into his backpack, Kobla removed the digital clips. He attached them to the partition. They deactivated the magnetic seal and freed the glass. He swapped the mask for an identical replica. Replacing the glass, he resealed and repressurized the chamber, so the museum's security would think he ran out of time to relieve the museum of this particular item. His padded footfalls the only sound, he swept the remaining wall for other antiquities to liberate.

In 2004, Edvard Munch's *The Scream* and *Madonna* were simply taken off the wall of the Munch Museum in Oslo. Proving that no matter what the redundant alarm technology, on-the-ground human surveillance, complex laser detectors securing entire walls, wireless vibration sensors, or any number of cameras a museum had, no alarm system was sophisticated or fast enough to defeat human intelligence from an inside source. Especially when combined with the Bureau of State Acquisitions' sacred science.

One minute left.

As he inspected the last piece, he caught a shadow out of the corner of his eye.

Kobla smiled.

He feigned not hearing the curator long enough to finish appreciating the bright pattern of the kente cloth display in front of him. In one fluid motion he turned and reared to his full height just as the shadow cleared her throat.

"Hello, Morgan," Kobla whispered.

A thin smile splayed across Morgan Kelly's face. Fingers interlaced in front of her, she jerked back in surprise. Her head shaved, the large gold earrings framed the dark shine of her face, creating another piece of art. "Marvelous collection, isn't it?"

She hid the tremor in her voice well even as she studied him, her wan grin fixed in place.

"There's no reason to be scared or nervous, Morgan. You did the best you could putting this collection together. I enjoyed the loose narrative you've established between the items." He nodded to the Robert H. Colescott painting, *Knowledge of the Past is Key to the Future (St. Sebastian)*, the image of a stylized lynching in an artistic conversation alongside the stolen relics. The Diaspora united with their homeland. "You should be proud. You and your work here will not go uncelebrated. However, the authorities will suspect you immediately."

"I knew the choice I was making when I agreed to help you. And I'm prepared to accept the consequences."

"Would you like to accompany us? See what you have sacrificed so much for?"

"I think I'd like that." Her voice broke with relief at the offer. "There's nothing for me here."

"For your protection." Kobla reached into his backpack and withdrew a thin plastic mask. He checked the time.

Ten seconds.

"You knew what my answer would be?" She examined the proffered face shield.

"I suspected. Besides, I like to be prepared."

Morgan slipped the unit over her shaved head. Kobla motioned an invitation with his hands to approach the woman as she struggled to secure it into place. She nodded. Kobla ran his hands along its length to make sure everything was in its proper place, deftly flicking a recessed button along the jawline to seal the mask. He produced a similar one from within the folds of his scarf.

Zero. Time was up.

A thin crackle of light pierced the air. It carved an illuminated circle, a shimmering portal. The hole grew until it expanded large enough to step into. Kobla bowed and gestured with an exaggerated flourish toward it. The curator hesitated. Kobla wrapped his hand around hers, as if to say, "Trust me." He stretched his other one out, reaching into the hole. His arm disappeared within it, up to where he slipped it in. A sensation of cool washed over his invisible limb, without pain. A portal into a tunnel, a long, glowing corridor, whose sides glimmered, distending into the distance. Kobla hopped through. A heartbeat later, Morgan followed.

BEYOND THE YEAR OF RETURN
Accra, Elmina—In 2019, Elmina, then known as Ghana, called for the return of the African Diaspora to encourage resettlement in the African homeland. The year marked the 400th anniversary of the Dutch ship White Lion arriving in Jamestown in what would become Virginia. It carried about twenty proud men and women from highly civilized and accomplished

African kingdoms...now enslaved. The beginning of the holocaust known as the Maafa. The delegates from the Pan-African Coordination Committee (PACC) have called to continue that homecoming conversation and engage in a closer collaboration between the countries on the African continent as well as the communities of the Diaspora.

The shadows swirled about, a spinning unreality. Kobla fell backward into the yawning night. The darkness shifted against itself with an absolute silence. A curious lack of sensation swept over him, like nothing marked his passage, leaving him feeling like a disembodied spirit. Even time seemed to cease. The corridor shifted again. Light and color exploded into view. Air whistled past as the portal opened and bright lights blared around him. Despite the impression of falling, he stepped out to stand on new ground. The curator soon landed next to him with an awkward stumbling like someone not ready to step off an escalator. With an inchoate groan, a small vibrational shudder, the corridor collapsed into nothing. Just like that, reality had healed itself.

A stone courtyard of whitewashed walls surrounded them. The ruins of the bastions were like a shattered jawline. A tower, with a lone window, loomed above them like a blind eye. Several portals flashed open, and the teams reported in. Elmina scientists—in their green-patterned, polybarrier coveralls—met them. They separated the recovered art from marked artifacts handed to them by a lead agent from each crew. A scientist approached Kobla.

He handed over the sacred mask, which the scientist inspected before nodding and scuttling off.

"How . . . did we get here?" Morgan asked.

"A tunnel through space and time."

"You say that pretty casually." Morgan spun in place. "Where are we?"

Kobla spread his arms out. "The powers that be would have us call this the Republic of Elmina, what was once called Ghana. We are in the remains of the Castelo de São Jorge da Mina. Originally constructed in 1481, it was later rechristened Elmina Castle. Does that name ring a bell?"

"No."

"I suppose not. Much is not taught in the deficient American school system. Only what they want you to know in order to buy into the mythology of their nation."

"Isn't that true of all countries?" Morgan asked with a sardonic drop to her voice. Her doctorate was in Afro-American Studies with an additional degree in Public History and Museum Studies, not to mention her being fluent in a half dozen languages. Her qualifications were part of what drew him to risk reaching out to her as an intelligence asset in the first place.

"No." After consideration, Kobla half turned back to her. "Well . . . maybe. Anyway, from this slave fort and many like it, millions of our people were shipped off around the world. The last glimpse of their homeland was the prison fort. Once they went through that entrance," he pointed to a restored red door, "they were loaded into a cargo hold and shipped off with no chance of returning home."

"Wait, the country was renamed for the fort. That's . . .

pouring salt into a historic wound." Morgan took a few tentative steps toward it.

"A debt to be repaid. Which is why we made it our headquarters." Kobla's eyes grew distant. The door had the gravity and repulsion of the weight of history. Much like how his father was taken from him when he was ten years old for speaking out against Ghana's renaming. Those in power—those with the power to name—noting the political winds fomented by ARM and their sympathizers, chose to jail their harshest critics. Kobla remembered the last time he saw his father. His aunt had just come over to visit. When the government vehicles pulled up, she herded them into the house. His father held his ground. Soldiers surrounded him, one jammed him in the belly with the butt of his rifle, attempting to drop his father to his knees. His father refused to fall. "If you are old enough to form a sentence, you are old enough to speak out," were his father's last words. The soldiers cuffed him and dragged him off. He died five years later. Kobla never knew what had happened to his father, only that he had never laid eyes on the man again. Knowing he had to join the fight, the struggle for their liberation, Kobla became a member of PACC a year later. He quickly rose among their ranks until he was recruited by the Bureau of State Acquisitions. "Now the door symbolizes our commitment to resistance and struggle, answering our ancestors' quest for freedom. Be it by rebellion, sabotage, revolts, escape . . ."

"Theft?" Morgan asked.

"By any means necessary." Kobla admired her ability to not stay mired in the trauma of history. Fighting his instinct to rush her though her orientation, Kobla stepped to the side to allow her room to absorb all of the information while she explored the ruins of the castle. Time was of the essence, true, but gaining the trust of a human asset could not be rushed. He'd spent months building the trust between them before he broached her about the idea of the museum's security. The newfound depth and breadth of her situation would upend her idea of how reality worked. She would need time to absorb it all. If the timing of the rest of the BSA's plans allowed.

Morgan halted to examine the area where the portal had closed, as if searching for an invisible seam. "The technology required to create that tunnel . . ."

"Technology is what *they* depend on." Kobla spat off to the side. ARM's physicists punched holes in reality with their dimensional toys with no regard for the natural order or consequences. His country, the motherland, paid the price. But Kobla was willing to sacrifice whatever, even whomever, it took to make sure it never happened again. "Can I tell you a story?"

"Are there any monsters?"

"Definitely. History is littered with them. When our people were originally brought to this fort, among them were a small number of oso. The closest translation of the word would be 'sorcerers,' people skilled in the old ways. For them, calling on magic was no harder than turning on a faucet or connecting to the internet. When our elders realized the scale of what was going on with the Maafa— keep in mind, chattel slavery was not like anything our people had encountered before—some oso allowed themselves to be captured. Their plan was to use the sacred science to protect as many as they could through the harrowing journey."

"This already sounds like the beginning of a bad plan," she said.

"I'll admit, there was a fair amount of arrogance to their thinking. Once they arrived in the new land, the oso planned to use their magics to create holes through the fabric of space, the Odede, leading back home, to the motherland. They weren't ready to languish in dungeons." Kobla pointed to the remains of the prison. "Their food passed through iron gates. No toilets. No bed berths. Little fresh air. Things began to unravel soon after as the conditions of the slave ships—being kept naked, in chains, in cargo holds maybe three feet high—didn't allow them much room to practice their craft."

"Wait, the Odede? As in the golden chain the orisha Obatala used to travel from the sky to earth?" Morgan arched a knowing eyebrow. "Perhaps our schools aren't as deficient as you believe them. Still, that is the stuff of creation myths."

"And like most such stories, there is truth in the heart of the metaphor." Kobla checked the time. "There is much to be explained, unfortunately . . ."

A voice accustomed to the authority of command rang out, cutting Kobla off. The pair halted as a tall man with a jiggling belly waddled over to them. Wrapped in black and gold kente cloth—with a matching stole, all of which were the inverse pattern of the scientists—his bushy eyebrows topped a resting stern face.

"Kobla Annan." Though light on his feet for such a big man, each breath rasped like a bellows.

"Safo Atakora Asantehene." Kobla bowed low.

"Your mission was a success?" Safo asked.

"Yes, so ends Phase One."

"Good, because Masklyne is on the move. Come, let us brief the others about Phase Two." Safo turned to Morgan. His lips peeled back to reveal rows of bleached white teeth, an affectation of his wealth. He straightened, unfurling like a ship sail, as he extended his hand to her. "And who is this?"

"Morgan Kelly." She reached out her hand.

"Curator, meet a board chief of the Bureau of State Acquisitions," Kobla said.

"The one you told me about?" Safo cocked his head, studying the gesture before choosing to shake her hand.

"Yes," Kobla said.

"You, my dear, are a gift without a price. Come, come." Safo wandered off ahead of them.

Morgan turned to Kobla with a questioning gaze, remaining rooted. Unconvinced. Learning a potential asset's story meant he had learned how to push her buttons. He knew they shared similar interests and core beliefs. He understood her sense of justice and the need to fix broken things. Kobla began to project a series of hard light images around them.

"We're in a precarious place in history, but it also has already warned us what would occur." Kobla flicked through the series of images. "The Berlin Conference. World War I. World War II. Power morphs and adapts, but the playbook remains the same. Inevitably, religious zealots, unchecked nationalism, and predatory capitalism over diminishing resources—all in the wake of global climate collapse—led to World War III." He sped through pictures of the devastated bodies and buildings left in the war's wake. "Now that it has ended, the US and China economies and military have been brought to the brink of ruin. Europe and Russia laid low. Where will the world turn to find the resources to rebuild?"

"Here. With the African Accords. Your borders redrawn for their interests."

Never again, Kobla swore. He would do whatever was required to make sure the Maafa, no matter what form it took, would never happen again. He canted his head toward hers. "*Our* borders."

"Our?"

"Yes. It's time for the Diaspora to come home."

"To do what?"

"To find protection. We prepare for World War IV. Part of my mission was recruitment."

"Recruitment for what?" She stared at him with bright, unflinching eyes, this . . . Morgan Kelly.

When Kobla looked at Morgan, he understood that her long-dead enslaved forebear was given a new name once they stepped onto the new shore—a "decent," more easily pronounced, Christian name. Even when freed, the former enslaved took on the surname of their former captors as the most pragmatic way to identify themselves. Tying themselves generationally to the Maafa through their very names. Before her husband was killed in an ARM raid, she had chosen to keep her maiden name. The thing about renaming was how it stripped a person, a people, of their identity. Leaving them adrift in an existential crisis; cutting them off from their roots, severing the tie to their ancestors. The first step in the journey of making them forget who they are and who they were and where they came from.

"Tomorrow, curator, we will take the first major steps to reawaken and reimagine what a new Alkebulan can be."

"That was what Africa was once known as. 'The Mother of Mankind.'"

"We could not even keep that name for ourselves. Tomorrow we will no longer operate under someone else's design or threat of war. When the time comes, I'm going to ask you to do a simple thing that could very well change the course of history."

"Snap my fingers and make a wish?" Morgan replied.

"Nothing so . . . fanciful, I'm afraid. But it will be your choice when the time comes. Now, will you accompany me to the briefing? We would have no secrets from you."

Again, she flashed a skeptical smirk, but Morgan nodded.

Kobla ushered her into the grand hall. Faces bobbed all around them, drawn, ghostlike visages. Holographic projections of key government officials and sacred science practitioners. Scholars. Civilian leaders. Any who spoke for or represented their people. He escorted Morgan to a spot near the front while Safo stalked about the stage. Nodding at their entrance, he relaxed like a man who no longer had to stall.

"We gather here to begin a conversation on studying the Odede as a natural resource in order to fulfill the greater mission of the Door of Return." Safo waited out the applause and cheers. "With that, I turn the briefing over to Kobla Annan."

Kobla patted Morgan's arm and walked to the edge of the stage without taking it. He spoke from its sidelines.

"The US, England, and France have always used magic to win their wars." Kobla allowed the words to ring out and hold their attention. He enlarged a black-and-white portrait of a man. "The French had Jean-Eugène Robert-Houdin, the man from whom Houdini took his name. A watchmaker and magician, the man was hired by Napoleon to defeat the Marabouts. But it's the Masklyne family who interests us now.

"Jasper Masklyne was an English soldier during World War II. He approached MI9, convincing them he could help with the war effort. He claimed to be from a line of magicians. His great-great-great-grandfather was said to have derived his powers from an African oso. Tales of Jasper's exploits included disappearing cities, relocating armies mysteriously, and even creating illusory weapons. He was enlisted into the military camouflage unit, what became dubbed the 'Magic Gang.' Masklyne once defeated Hitler in the Middle East by using illusions to hide tanks and even army units. We'll come back to him."

Kobla kept the lights low as he popped up images of museums from around the world.

"More than 500 historical objects, including 440 bronzes from the Kingdom of Benin, in what was once called Nigeria, were held at the Ethnological Museum in the German capital alone. Museums made great war targets."

Kobla caught Morgan's eyes. She shifted in her seat, not quite uncomfortable.

"They were closed during wartime for a reason. They

were outposts, warehouses of mystical weapons. Charged with the care and preservation of specimens. Since repatriation was as much a possibility as reparations for the Diaspora, the Bureau of State Acquisitions, Elmina's intelligence gathering agency, conducted simultaneous recoveries of such relics all over the world in one coordinated effort of artifact liberation. Coordinating with several countries across our continent, teams were dispatched to various museums, including the Vatican. Our teams reclaimed the heritage of our ancestors. They also procured various mystical artifacts. The Vienna Lance. The Shroud of Turin. The Ethiopian Tabot. The Shield of El Cid. Kappa's Plate. The Iron Crown of Lombardy. The Vatican Chronovisor. And so forth."

With that list, Morgan eased forward in her seat with renewed interest. He knew that would capture her archivist interest.

"Not many know that during the Third World War, such objects shielded the colonial powers holding them against the full might of ARM's 'Old Gods.' We replaced these items with replicas rather than steal them outright so the facilities and curators might not immediately notice the missing artifacts. Now possessing them, we have weakened their defenses to launch our own offensive: the Door of Return.

"We will open the Odede over several capitals and call forth some elder beasts. The Grootslang. The Inkanyomba. The Kongamato. The Impundulu. Mokele-mbembe. Emissaries to clear the path for our . . . *Older* Gods. Those whose names lie beyond human pronunciation. Those countries will presume ARM is restarting their campaign of aggression and deploy their forces accordingly."

"But why?" Morgan asked.

"We need time to control and direct our own infrastructure, free from outside interference. Renewing the war both distracts them, keeping them from plundering us, and buys us—"

An abeng blew its mournful wail in raised alarm, a long-distance warning of a marauding party. A couple dozen BSA agents streamed past.

Checking his wrist alert, Safo yelled, "Incoming!"

"It's Masklyne," Kobla said. "Can your team intercept?"

Safo nodded.

"Masklyne? He'd be well over a hundred years old by now," Morgan said.

"I've studied the Masklyne family intensively, investigated their entire line. Jasper Masklyne's current descendent, Bradley Z. Masklyne, now works for the US. My intelligence reports indicate they are stepping up their efforts. No longer content to lob missiles at their enemies, they now seek to control the Odede. All part of the games nations play to remind Elmina of its place."

Kobla collapsed the screen with a wave of his hands. With a casual swipe, he opened a new window. On the monitor, a tactical map of their headquarters appeared. A live feed. The enemy's positions lit up in red. Safo's dispatched squad was outnumbered, but would buy Kobla the necessary time to enact his plan ahead of schedule. The problem with being locked in a war mindset was that he learned to see everything as a potential weapon. Words. Artifacts. The Odede. Morgan.

Kobla burst through the throng of BSA agents bottlenecking the doors leading out from Elmina's courtyard, barely sparing a glance to make sure Morgan followed. Once free of them, he zigzagged through dozens more agents who secured their headquarters, each face stoic in their mission.

A projectile smashed into a terrain skimmer, leaving it little more than a melted slag. Kobla dashed across the street, and Morgan kept her hands raised above her head, not that her arms would protect her from any projectile, mystical or otherwise. If one chose to target her, she'd have simply been no more. But she didn't panic, nor scream.

"They have no sense of decency," Morgan said.

"It's war. There's nothing they wouldn't do," Kobla said. "I would do no less."

"We have to do better if we're going to be better."

Kobla maneuvered through the mazelike alleyways. He ducked through a window and scampered through an empty storehouse. A shortcut only natives would know to avoid the firefight outside. When he peered out the exit, Kobla realized that Masklyne had used his powerful illusions to establish and camouflage a staging area just on the other side of the castle's confines. Kobla counted a dozen ARM militia agents clad in uniforms branded with the twelve black radial sig runes, like a dark sun.

Soon, the first tactical warhead would drop from orbit. Enough of a pretense to cast the confusion of war over the entire region. Masklyne would then deploy a mixture of consultants and contractors and occupying forces to safeguard the people. Mercenaries by another name.

Kobla had to stop them before they gained any more ground.

He watched as columns of flames targeted several nearby homes. Masklyne's forces were desperate, using pyrotechnics to flush them out. Kobla's men countered with heavy artillery fire from the other side of the castle, hammering ARM's position.

"What are they after?" Morgan pressed her back to the wall, every now and then chancing a peek at the advancing enemy.

"Probably an attempt to procure their missing items. They might have tracked some mystical trail I hadn't considered."

"Or maybe they just placed trackers on them," Morgan said. "Let's not overcomplicate things."

"Safo dispatched a unit to make sure our acquisitions are secure. We can't afford to be distracted: We have another mission."

"What's that?" Morgan asked.

"To open the Odede."

Safo led his team, scampering between enemy positions to draw their attention. His troops of sacred scientists projected shields to buffet the onslaught of Masklyne's forces. A truck behind them exploded. When the smoke cleared, Safo's people had disappeared. Masklyne's forces advanced.

Exhaustion tore at the edges of Kobla's spirit. The sound of the firefight faded as they neared the warehouse. Kobla nodded at the half dozen PACC guards at the station. He'd served with them for years, not bound by blood, but by mission. This wasn't about money or politics or power. No ideology, no religious fervor, no nationalistic cause. He did, he gave, all for his people. He only wanted to keep them safe. All of them. To secure their country and protect it from any intruder wishing to harm his people. Foreign or domestic. No matter the cost.

"Watch the cables," Kobla said.

Power cables wormed their way under the walls of the structure. Undulating and angry, like varicose veins spreading and receding with the energy that coursed through them.

"What do they do?"

"All of the artifacts are gathered here, like the world's largest battery bank of mystical potential known to man. Consider this containment chamber a mystical Faraday shield, creating an enclosure to block all manner of energy fields, from electromagnetic to ley lines."

Kobla removed the mask he'd retrieved from the Oldfields Museum. "From here we will continue the conversation Ghana started those many years ago. With you."

"What do you mean?"

"Like I said, the plans of the oso had already begun to unravel. The passageways, the hidden corridors known as the Odede, are a physical fact linked to the reality of our planet. Its existence depends on its relations to its maintainer, the oso, and their connection to Alkebulan. The preparation and the magics required to create corridors—especially across the distance of an ocean—were significant. Think of it in terms of energy: enough was released in the creation of these Odede that pathways opened up along the planet. Fractured veins spread across the globe, the barriers between worlds thinned, allowing . . . something else . . . to escape. Something dark. Beyond words or else they dared not even whisper its name. It took the combined might of all of the oso to defeat this darkness, killing most of our elders in the process before they managed to close the corridors. Many of the surviving oso were left mad or broken, but the disaster was averted."

"What does this have to do with me?" Morgan asked.

"You are of the line of oso," Kobla said.

"And what? You want me to . . . open the Odede?"

"Yes." Kobla secured the door. "I had wished this for another time, for a tomorrow not so far away, when we could have trained. We can't compete with ARM, Europe, Russia, China, not any of them, on their level of armaments. Heavy floater platforms. Drone support. Ground-based laser systems . . ."

"Nukes," she added, studying the sky.

"Logistics is what wins wars." He turned to her. "We have to play to our strengths. I had wanted this inevitable escalation to be on our terms, but it seems our hand has been forced."

"I can't. I don't know . . ."

"I'll be right here. The process can be, how do you say, jump-started. But to open a door, on this scale, there is a debt that must be paid."

"What sort of price?"

Kobla had come this far. He knew he had to commit. There was no turning back. No Plan B. She was the entire plan. "My father taught me that the poet's voice, that art, has the power to change a mind. To change the world. To heal the wounds of history and harness the power of stories. Some of us are cracked and broken, as erratic, dangerous and misunderstood as the names we claim as our own. Sacrifices must be made if we are to usher in a new way of doing things."

"So what do I do now?"

"I need you to brace yourself." Kobla wrapped his hand around hers. "The oso have been studying and creating since the beginning of time. For them it's as simple as breathing or sleeping. Tap into that power of art you *do* know so well. Listen to those voices of the griots, of the martyrs. I need you to open yourself to the possibility and trust. We'll do this together. Imagine a link that goes from your head to your heart to something deep within you. Reach into the past."

"What about you?"

"I must perform my part of the ritual." Kobla slipped the mask on and began to dance.

Morgan closed her eyes.

During a mask ceremony, the dancer went into a deep trance, taking his mind to a distant place where he could communicate with his ancestors. A translator was to accompany the mask wearer to decode the messages of wisdom the dancer brought forth from his ancestors.

Light etched the air between them.

Kobla saw, truly saw, for the first time. The edges of it illumined green like an emerald candle flickering in the night. Kobla felt it. The lament of an unsung melody. The fragrance of a forgotten dream. The sensation of a dead lover's embrace. Intimate. Intentional. Knowing. The Corridor was the thrum of life. He felt her mind wrap itself around Alkebulan's heartbeat.

The breach widened.

Glassy, red-irised globes lumbered into sight, dilating and contracting as it focused on the two forms in front of it.

Kobla felt a twinge in his chest. "Keep your eyes shut. It will all be over soon."

"I can see it," Morgan said. "They're speaking to me. In ancient tongues, but I . . . know what they are whispering."

"The portals can be directed, but someone would have to do that from the other side. The debt that has to be paid in order to safeguard our people."

"I . . . understand." Morgan stretched her arms out.

Light-gray tentacles reached out through the aperture like flexing arms. Single stalks wound about a cluster of sub-stalks. Ever greedy to draw the supplicant in.

Kobla grasped her by the shoulders. "I'm sorry."

He shoved Morgan aside.

The protuberances wrapped around him. They drew him toward a central series of radiating ridges.

And with barely a tremble, the Odede closed behind him.

ELMINA ELIMINATED

Accra, Wagadugu—In the wake of the renewed interdimensional incursions, the United Nations has ended the African Accords. The citizens of the state formerly known as Elmina have decided to pay tribute to their history, acknowledging the Bono State, the kingdom of Dagbon, and the Ashanti Empire which originally made up the land, which became the Gold Coast and then

Ghana. They are now known as the United Kingdoms of Wagadugu, of the great continent of Alkebulan. Having already restituted hundreds of Benin bronzes to their home in Alkebulan, Berlin continues to pressure other museums to return sculptures and artifacts looted from the continent. "In light of the conversations being had, we need to begin paying back the debt we owe."

AN OFFERING THE KING MAKES

D.J. Butler

"The trouble started," Kamal Arslan said, "when we entered the videogame. This is wicked technology, and these are not gods. They are devils." Arslan was a Druze soldier of fortune from Lebanon, the captain of the Shining Warriors, the freelance minitank company providing the bulk of the physical muscle. He was lean and well built, with streaks of gray in his black hair and neatly trimmed beard. Dressed in khaki, he wore a sidearm strapped to each leg.

"The trouble started," Rex "Thrower" Grundy said, "when your men were so excited the Ramada had pay-per-view skin flicks that they couldn't focus on their instructions about how to avoid getting crushed by these gods. Or devils." His stomach was cramped; this was not what he had been trained for. The CIA had taught him how to finesse foreign traitors for information and to flip them. Now he was carrying a gun through a tunnel that was some kind of electronic mythoscape, a tunnel into the soul of Pharaonic Egypt built by a meth-addicted whiz-kid gamer champion.

Back when there was a CIA. Before the Social Wars of the 2030s had torn the United States into seven bloody chunks.

He envied Salem Chalabi, back in the arcade with the shimmering golden gate stretching between two old upright consoles. *Pac-Man* and *Dig Dug*, he recalled, though he hadn't looked closely. In the real world, Chalabi was under attack in a crumbling arcade, adjacent to the Church of Santa Maria sopra Minerva in Rome built upon the ruins of an ancient temple to Isis.

The CIA had prepared Grundy for none of this.

Chalabi and Jason Pointer would both have insisted on the phrase "physical world" rather than "real world." To be fair, this virtual world had imposed quite a bit of real injury and death on the team that had dared to enter it.

"Gods, devils," Pointer said in his crisp received pronunciation. The Surrey-born wizard was wrapped in a strange panther-skin garment. He clutched his baked-clay curse doll to his chest. Short and stubby, he tended to trip over his own feet as he walked; rather than giving him dignity, the costume made him look comical. "Potayto, potahto. Does it matter?"

Pointer ignored the digitalized bat-like creatures overhead, the long-limbed crocodiles in the shadows, the phantom turreted droids surrounding the company on the ground, materializing to fire bursts at the surrounding monsters and then fading out of sight, and even the real growling M1461 Minis, reduced from their original twelve to a mere seven. He was focused on a shimmering golden gate before them, an immense structure that stood out of the streams of alphanumeric data cascading from the infinite darkness above, solid and glorious, at the top of a short ramp. Two red serpents hung from the massive golden lintel, spitting flames. Within the gate sat a man with a ram's face and curling horns growing horizontally left and right from his scalp. Above the horns sprouted a high crown shaped like a golden cone surrounded by feathers. He held a shock of grain.

The ram-headed man was thirty feet tall, if he was an inch.

Grundy studied Pointer's face. He wasn't looking *at* the gate, he was looking through it.

"It matters," Grundy insisted. "There's a difference between a god and a demon, and there's a difference between one god and another. It matters who's in charge! And you believe that too, Pointer, or you'd just let the Pharaoh take the world!"

Arslan spat. His spittle left his mouth as fluid and struck the ground as a string of data that scattered on impact. "The antiputrefaction charm did not work."

Pointer's head swiveled around sharply. "Your men didn't wear it, Captain. I told them to keep it on their persons, and they hung it inside their tanks, instead, like fuzzy dice in some cheap muscle car."

"You should have been clearer!" Arslan snarled.

Pointer shrugged and looked back at the gate. He gripped the curse doll with both hands; it was an image of a tall-crowned mummy holding a crook, flail, and long staff, with a knob atop it fashioned into an animal's head. The image was instantly recognizable as an age-old evocation of Egypt, and also as a representation of the

Pharaoh Death-Manifest-in-Fire, the Son of Ra Jimmy Whitlock. The god they had come to kill. "I was clear."

Chalabi's voice echoed from the mezuzah-like medallions hanging around all their necks. "I can't hold out much longer, my peeps."

Grundy looked around the company. "Looks to me like your turrets are winning," he said.

Chalabi's voice dripped with pride. "I can blast bats and crocs all day, that isn't the issue. My problem is in meatspace, bruv. The *physical* world."

"You're under attack?" Arslan asked.

Pointer was already slowly advancing toward the gate. "Stay close to me," he called.

"You got it, bruv."

"What about the soldiers we left to defend you?" Grundy asked. "Ogbuwa and his men?"

"They're pretty great with submachine guns, bruv. But you know what submachine guns really suck at? Killing waves of flesh-eating scarab beetles."

Grundy cursed.

"That's how I feel, too," Chalabi said. "Guess we should have gone with flamethrowers. I'm just telling you, you have ten minutes, max."

"And then what?" Arslan asked.

"Either I scram, bruv, or I get eaten."

"And we lose the turrets' support?" Grundy watched a row of turrets leap into view, annihilate two charging crocodiles, and disappear again.

"You lose the tunnel," Chalabi said.

"And we . . . what?" Grundy asked. "Die?"

"Ask the wizard, bruv."

"Pointer!" Arslan snapped. "The . . . videogame . . . collapses in ten minutes. What happens then?"

Pointer nodded. "Ten minutes will be enough." He began climbing the steps.

"That wasn't what I asked." Arslan rushed to catch up to Pointer. Grundy followed. He drew his pistol; not that it would do anything to the ram-headed titan, but the weight felt reassuring in his hand. "We needed the game to get here, right?"

Pointer nodded. "We had to triangulate. Not having the full liturgical apparatus, not to mention the hieratic authority, we needed two entry points into the collective unconscious from which to work out the right angle. Hence, the stolen papyrus—the *Book of Going Forth by Day*—and the videogame. And it worked, see?"

"Triangulate?" Grundy asked. "What does that even mean? How do you triangulate from a videogame and a papyrus to . . . *this*? At most, that's a metaphor!"

Pointer faced the intelligence agent. "Thus you take the first steps on the road to understanding my arts."

"None of this answers my question!" Arslan snapped.

Pointer ignored him.

The ram-headed giant stepped forward out of the gate, raising his shock of grain like a weapon. "I am He Who Cannot Be Cut," he thundered. "I am He Who Triumphs. I repel the demolishers. Who are you and what is your business?"

This was not the first gate the company had faced. Grundy had lost track, but he thought it might be the seventh. At each gate, the wizard had been the one to get them through. At the third, five minitank crews had rotted to corpses before his eyes. Pointer turned now, and gestured to Arslan. "This should be the last gate. Make sure your men have their gum ready."

Arslan grunted. "Hotep gum."

"*Hetep* gum!" Pointer hissed. "Like it says on the wrapper!"

Grundy checked his own small brick of gum; it hadn't fallen from his pocket. It reeked of yeast through the foil wrapper bearing the printed word *HETEP*.

Arslan spoke into the small comms unit on his wrist. "Ready hotep gum. Do not deploy until my signal."

Grundy heard a baffled laugh from the open hatch of the nearest M1461. The tanks were small, sized like sedans. The two-man crews occupied the turrets on top, only lightly shielded by sheets of steel angled like the windshields of a convertible. An autoloader and a self-driving AI let the minitanks operate with minimal crews and made the vehicles highly maneuverable. Given the narrow tunnels and broken terrain the team had traversed, Grundy was certain larger tanks wouldn't have gotten this far.

Pointer knelt before the giant. "I come to you, Osiris," he declaimed, "to be declared free of evils. May you circle Shu. May you see Ra and all the dead. You sail in the night bark around the Akhet! You have made the excellent path that leads me to you!"

"I'm just about ready to let the Pharaoh have Rome," Arslan muttered. "This has gotten way too strange."

The snakes hissed and spat fire.

"Pass," the giant rumbled.

Pointer walked through the gate. He moved slowly,

with measured strides, as if he were in a convocation or walking a bride up the aisle. Arslan and Grundy followed. The tanks rolled slowly behind them.

"I might have overestimated the time, bruv," Chalabi's voice announced. "You might have five minutes now. Uh . . . maybe four."

"It's enough," Pointer said.

Grundy's heart rattled free and crazy in his chest. Sweat on his palms made it hard to grip the pistol. He shot a look over his shoulder; the last two M1461s rolled forward with their swiveling turrets pointed behind them, firing. Was he seeing fewer of the phantom turrets now? And more of the bats?

The space beyond the gate was split into two halves. Grundy squinted and tried to focus on the space where the two halves met, looking for a seam or a joint, but he couldn't find one. To his left, a black cave and a huge beast. To his right, a golden-walled audience hall, and two high-crowned giants on thrones. The golden walls radiated light, but the shining beams evaporated into twists of smoke as they penetrated the cave. The beast lurking in the shadows was immense and had a long, toothy muzzle.

In the center, a golden table, piled high with loaves, jugs, and joints of meat.

As he stepped through the gate, one of the fire-spitting snakes thudded softly to the ground, to his right and behind him. The second followed immediately afterward, on his left.

Grundy's knees wobbled. Why was he here? Why, really, was it his business whether the Pharaoh Death-Manifest-in-Fire, the Son of Ra Jimmy Whitlock, the former neopagan lecturer and obsessive gamemaster of the obscure tabletop role-playing game, The Valley of the Pharaohs, took Rome? Grundy was just a cultural attaché to the embassy of the United States of New England. He did a little light intelligence work, rescued a field operative here and there, and threw around a football with embassy staff on Thanksgiving, imagining how his life might have been different if he'd gone on to play in college. He could still get a flight out if he wanted, even if the Pharaoh refused to recognize his diplomatic credentials, even if his cover was blown.

But instead of going home, he had taken Pointer, after meeting him at an exhibit of stunning shabti figurines at the Vatican's Gregorian Museum, to meet with Arslan. Arslan's enthusiasm for resisting the Pharaoh had been infectious enough that Pointer had finally stopped whining about the girl, Marian, who had just dumped him. When Grundy had pointed out that the Church of Santa Maria sopra Minerva was *really* sopra the old temple of the Egyptian goddess Isis and was next door to, of all things, a video game arcade, Arslan had taken them all to meet Chalabi.

And somehow, over sake and sushi, but mostly sake, they'd hatched this plan.

Did he just want to experience adventure?

The thing with the long snout roared in the shadows.

Grundy stagger-stepped sideways as the creature emerged fully into view. Its gait was lopsided; front legs that resembled those of a lion prowled with grace, while the hind legs, which resembled those of a hippopotamus, thudded dully up and down, thrusting a gray rump from side to side in a determined waddle. The beast seemed to be fighting an internal battle to move at all. The result would have been laughable but for the train-car-sized crocodilian snout that protruded from the front of the affair. The teeth jutting up and down from the green-skinned jaws of the monster were each as tall as Grundy, if not taller.

"God help us," Arslan said. "Pointer, do we attack it?"

"No," Pointer said. "We came here to chew gum, not to kick ass."

"Deploy hotep gum," Arslan said into his comms unit.

Grundy looked at the tank crews. Of the seven, five—ten men—dutifully popped the brick of gum into their mouths and chewed. Arslan and Pointer and Grundy all did the same.

Two crews, four men, didn't.

The two giants stood and approached.

"I said deploy hotep gum!" Arslan barked. "Yossy, you idiot, did you hear me?"

Yossy's voice came out of the comms unit loud enough for Grundy to hear. "Uh, gum already deployed, sir. A couple hours ago."

"I chewed mine last night," said another voice from the wrist-bound device. "It's disgusting."

Pointer shook his head. "I'm sorry, Captain."

The soldiers were right; the gum was foul. It was supposed to taste like bread and beer, and if Grundy closed his eyes and concentrated, he could find those flavors. But it wasn't a delicious bread, it was some sort of oat or barley loaf, unsweetened. Mostly what Grundy tasted was yeast.

He gagged, but kept chewing.

"What's going to happen to them?" Arslan asked.

Again, Pointer ignored his question. "We approach the table," the wizard said.

Grundy's hands were shaking. He followed Jason to the table. The two giants strode up to the table, too, and stood to their right. The huge beast shuffled up on the left and stood snuffling the air.

"Pointer!" Arslan snapped. "What's going to happen to my men?"

"We have to eat the meal before we can talk to Isis and Osiris," Pointer said. "Don't any of you read? This is the meal with the gods. It's the offering the king makes."

"Who's the king?" Grundy asked.

Pointer shrugged. "The answers to all the really important questions are ambivalent. Or multivalent, really. Is the king the initiate approaching? Is the king Osiris there? Is the king someone else entirely? Is the king Salem Chalabi and his videogame?" Pointer shrugged. "Yes."

"The gum is to fool someone into thinking we've eaten the meal when we haven't?" Grundy eyed the loaves and jugs.

"Well, you can't *actually* eat the meal." Pointer snorted. "Not without the right preparation, anyway. You guys *don't* read, do you?" The wizard was looking at the female giant. Whose crown seemed, strangely, to be a throne. Or perhaps *she* was a throne, with arms, legs, and a face. A lovely face, with full lips and large eyes. The thrones on which both giants had been sitting were gone—the woman, somehow, *was* the thrones.

Grundy eyed the male giant closely. Wrapped in linens, clutching crook and flail and a long, animal-headed staff, the giant was a dead ringer for the curse doll. And a match for the Pharaoh Jimmy Whitlock.

His stomach cramped so hard, he almost fell over.

The monster swung its bus-sized snout over the company. Saliva spattered Grundy in the face and the floor all around him. He could hear the beast sniffing.

"What do you call that thing?" he asked, pointing.

The wizard looked at him calmly. "Her name is Ammut, and she will take her due."

The snout poked in Grundy's direction. A nostril the size of a refrigerator, not one of the ridiculous tiny refrigerators they had in Rome, but a full-sized, American-style refrigerator like the one he had back in Worcester, dilating and contracting, sniffed the intelligence officer . . .

Grundy exhaled into the enormous schnoz, blowing the smell of yeast in a redolent cloud.

Ammut grunted and moved on.

Grundy didn't have a heartbeat anymore, just a stabbing pain in his chest that wouldn't relent.

He heard the slapping of boots. Turning, he saw four of the tankers rushing toward the table. He recognized Yossy, who was the fastest and in front. He was still trying to think of the others' names when Ammut lunged forward and scooped two of them up in a single bite.

Blood spattered everywhere. A severed arm hit Grundy in the chest and landed in front of him. He kicked it as far away as he could, not wanting to attract Ammut's attention again.

The tanker whom Ammut had missed pulled his sidearm and fired at the creature's eyes. The pop of gunfire echoed across the chamber as he emptied his magazine.

One of the tanks swiveled its guns around and fired. Both the .50-caliber machine gun and the tank's 125-millimeter main gun blasted Ammut in the side of her leathery jaw.

With one leonine paw, Ammut reached forward and smashed the soldier flat. Then, with the single minitank still hammering her in the head, she snaked a long, pink tongue through her foremost teeth and licked the dead soldier off the floor.

Snakes. That reminded Grundy, where were the two snakes? He scanned the room and found them, one coiled around each of the giant woman's legs.

That didn't reassure him.

"Uh, my peeps," Salem Chalabi's voice cut into the hectic scene from three directions, "you're on your own, I gotta—aaaaaaaaaaaagh!"

His scream cut out abruptly.

Ammut swung ponderously around to face Yossy, the last of the gumless tankers. Yossy had reached the table, and was furiously munching bread and swilling beer. The golden liquid sloshed from the clay vessel's wide mouth and splashed him in his khaki shirt.

Ammut leaned forward to sniff Yossy.

Yossy belched.

Ammut swung her elongated face from side to side, slowly. Pointer and Arslan both ducked. Then she raised her crocodile snout, rising up on extended catlike forelegs, and bellowed at the unseen ceiling of the cavern.

"An offering the king makes!" Pointer shouted. "Bread and—"

Yossy leaped forward and knocked him to the ground.

The snakes wrapped around the giant woman's legs hissed and exhaled jets of crimson fire.

The cavern floor shook. "Salem," Grundy said into his mezuzah. Then he remembered. Salem Chalabi was dead.

Yossy was growing. He loomed over the wizard in the panther skin, and he was ten feet tall already, and still swelling. His head was deforming rapidly, nose lurching forward into a birdlike beak, hair sweeping up and becoming featherlike.

"Target Yossy now," Arslan said into his wrist communicator. "Kill him."

A burst of machine gun fire ripped across the front of the golden table. The bullets threw the expanding Yossy backward. They knocked him up and onto the table. Joints of meat and beer jugs fell to the floor. The jugs shattered on impact.

Grundy threw himself to the ground. He crawled to Pointer. On his back and breathless, the magician was still staring at the giant woman.

"Who is she?" Grundy asked. "What's so fascinating about her?"

"She is Isis now," Pointer murmured. "But that is nothing."

The wizard stood. Grundy stood with him and dragged him sideways, away from the table and the gunfire. Pointer resisted, but Grundy was stronger and wrestled him out of harm's way.

Scraps of meat and bread flew in all directions. Yossy,

now fifteen feet tall, stood atop the table and roared. He had an ax in his hand. Where had the ax come from?

Pointer was chanting incomprehensibly. Grundy shook him.

"We have to do something!" Grundy shouted.

"Shut up!" Pointer screamed. "I *am* doing something!"

At least he was looking at Yossy and not at Isis.

Isis and the Pharaoh gazed down upon the mayhem. The Pharaoh's face was frozen, expressionless. What was the look on Isis's face . . . curiosity?

The hall shook again.

Yossy leaped to attack, and took a tank's sabot round in the chest. The bird-headed giant slammed back into the table and skidded across the floor. He struck the Pharaoh's foot, and the Pharaoh murmured a deep, uneasy sound.

The two giant snakes spat fire. The heat warmed Grundy's forehead and cheeks.

Yossy stood unharmed and roared.

"Finished," Pointer said.

"Finished what?" Grundy shrieked. "Nothing has changed."

In a split second, Yossy leaped across the space between himself and the first minitank. His ax swung left and right in his hands; the tank gun sheared away from the body of the M1461, flying straight up. The treads were blown off, and the minitank screeched to a halt. Yossy was already flying past, ax raised over his head with both hands as he bore down on the second minitank.

Before the first minitank's crew could evacuate, the severed gun barrel crashed down on the turret, crushing both men instantly.

"An offering the king makes," Pointer said again, facing the golden table with his arms upraised, elbows squared, the baked-clay curse doll in his right hand. Isis and the Pharaoh turned to look at him.

Yossy split the second tank horizontally, as if he were slicing open a roll to make a sandwich. Fire engulfed the turret. Another sabot round struck him and knocked him to the ground. Captain Arslan jumped on Yossy. The Druze soldier of fortune had a long knife in his left hand and a pistol in his right. He slashed at Yossy's birdlike face and fired point-blank into his chest, over and over.

Yossy roared in irritation. He hurled Arslan at Pointer.

The knife and pistol went flying, disappearing into the corners of the chamber. The tank commander crashed into Pointer. They both hit the ground. Arslan lay still, his neck bent at an extreme angle, blood trickling down his chin.

Yossy stood. He gripped the front of a third minitank's chassis and flipped it onto its top. The treads continued to churn, and the main gun fired once in protest, but the men inside were crushed.

"You did nothing!" Grundy shouted at the wizard. He fired several rounds at the giant Yossy, without effect.

"Shut up!" Pointer stood, raising his arms again. "An offering the king makes, bread and beer for the ka of the Osiris Jason Pointer, true of—"

CRASH!

Grundy didn't see what walls the tanks broke through, but suddenly the room was choked with rubble and dust. A flying stone struck the magician between the shoulders and knocked him down. The Pharaoh and Isis grunted wordless objections, and minitanks rolled into view, firing.

Five minitanks.

They were Arslan's men—Grundy recognized them immediately—the ten crewmen who had messed up the antiputrefaction charm. Arslan had left them behind after they'd rotted to death at the third gate. They were still decaying, flesh peeling from hands and faces to reveal white bone, but now they were in motion.

Three charged Yossy, firing. Two raced straight ahead, toward the flame-spitting serpents. The snakes leaped into the air, and Grundy saw for the first time that they were winged. Fire rained down around the room.

Grundy dove under the table to avoid the flames. Pointer stood again, shaking dust from his panther skin and coughing.

"See?" he shouted.

From the dark side of the chamber, Ammut emerged again. She sniffed the air, roared, and grabbed the nearest zombie minitank in her jaws.

Apparently, the decaying men hadn't chewed their gum.

The tank in the monster's jaws buckled, but the men fell from it. They were putrefying, but they kept fighting. One dragged himself slowly up Ammut's hippo-like tail and the other crawled up Yossy's back. Then dead men and living men and whole minitanks, sprockets, idler arms, roadwheels, and thrashing creatures coalesced into chaos. Grundy had to look away.

On the other side, a zombie tank had impaled a flying snake on its main gun. Its companion tank lay smoldering, and two burning dead men fought the second snake hand to hand under a hail of their comrades' machine-gun fire.

"An offering the king makes," Pointer began again. Grundy rolled out from under the table to watch him. The only way Grundy was making it out of this self-imposed hell was by whatever road Pointer planned to take. "Bread and beer for the ka of the Osiris Jason Pointer, true of voice."

He picked up a morsel of bread from the table and ate it.

Isis immediately spun to look at him. Her lips moved, and for the first time, she formed comprehensible sounds. "Jason," she murmured.

"Marian," he said.

The stabbing pain in Grundy's stomach nearly knocked him down. The hall shook, and the golden gate crumbled, collapsing in on itself.

The Pharaoh noticed, too. He turned to look down at Jason Pointer, and he laughed.

"This is the end of the road, Whitlock." Pointer raised the curse doll over his head with both hands and slammed it on the edge of the offering table.

Nothing happened.

He slammed the clay doll again, and a third time, and it didn't break.

The Pharaoh laughed. "You have greatly overestimated yourself, Jason Pointer," he roared. The floor shook at the sound of his voice. "And you have greatly underestimated my power. Or, as the ancients used to say, you come at the king, you best not miss."

"Help me!" Pointer screamed to Isis.

She shook her head.

The curse doll dropped from Pointer's shaking hands

and rolled across the floor toward Grundy. He heard monsters roaring, and the hissing of flames, and the dull thuds of firearms, but they all sounded far away as he stared down at the baked-clay replica of the Pharaoh.

Pointer shouted and waved his arms. The Pharaoh strode forward.

Grundy still had his pistol. Pointing it at the figurine, he squeezed the trigger. The curse doll leaped and spun through the air, but when it landed, it was still intact.

The Pharaoh swung his crook like a croquet mallet. He hit Pointer, sending the man flying across the room. Pointer, somehow still alive, stood up just in time for the Pharaoh to slam his flail down on the wizard's head.

The magician rolled away from the impact. He was bleeding, but he still shouted his mumbo jumbo and waved his arms. Where was he getting this resilience? Was it from his chant at the table?

Grundy wanted to be able to take a beating like that and still fight. He'd need it if he was going to get out of this mess. He scooped up the curse doll and set it on the table—didn't want to lose track of that. He holstered his gun and then raised both arms. Fortunately, CIA training *had* given him a strong memory.

"An offering the king makes," he said. "Bread and beer for the ka of the Osiris Rex Grundy, true of voice."

The battle to his left split apart into halves, suddenly, and through the crack in the middle, Ammut charged. Was she running toward Grundy? He grabbed the nearest object to hand, heart thudding violently, and hurled it at her.

It was the clay figurine.

The curse doll flew in a perfect spiral, straight through the dust and the noise, and—in the words of Coach Henderson—hard enough to pound a nail into the wall of a barn. If Rex Grundy had thrown like that in every high-school game of his senior year, he would have ended up in the Superbowl.

Ammut roared, opening her crocodile jaws wide, and the clay statuette went right down her gullet.

She stopped, fell silent, and blinked.

Pointer had eaten something, Grundy remembered. He grabbed a scrap of bread from the table, spat his gum on the floor, and ate the bread, hoping he didn't metamorphose into a bird-headed troll.

Pointer rose unsteadily to his feet, shouting. The Pharaoh raised his crook to swing it again, but then stopped.

He turned and look back at Grundy, and then at Ammut.

"What have you done?" he growled.

Grundy swallowed, his throat dry. "Bread and beer for the ka of the Osiris Rex Grundy!" he shouted. Beer, there was beer on the table. He turned and found a jug that hadn't been shattered. He gulped down the warm liquid, which had a strong yeasty flavor, much like the hetep gum. "True of voice!"

"What have you done?" the Pharaoh roared.

Ammut bellowed, and to Grundy's ears the sounds seemed to harmonize.

The Pharaoh spun about, took a long step, and a second, then collapsed to the floor.

Grundy tried to sidestep the falling crowned mummy,

but as he moved, he felt himself growing larger. The pain in his stomach stabbed him one final time as he feared he was transforming into a bird-ogre as Yossy had, but then the pain was abruptly gone, and he was standing beside a beautiful woman.

"Hello." She smiled at him. "I am the Isis Marian Seidel."

He nodded. "I am the Osiris Rex Grundy. Some people call me Thrower."

"The Pharaoh has died," she said. "The Osiris Jimmy Whitlock has had his resurrection revoked, and is in the belly of Ammut."

"Don't worry," he said to her. "All is in order. The Pharaoh is dead. Long live the Pharaoh."

He didn't know where the words came from, but they felt right.

"What shall we do about these?" The Isis Marian gestured at the humans scrambling about on the floor.

"Nothing," the Osiris Rex said. "They have done their work."

He extended his elbow to his queen and turned to escort her from the offering chamber.

A LINE IN THE STARS

Martin L. Shoemaker

"This is a dumb plan."

Shin Na grinned through my visor as she strapped my torso to the hull plate. "It's your plan, Porter."

"Then I should know!"

I had planned on *her* being sealed into the hull of the cargo pod for delivery to Beta Orbital Station. Instead, word had come from her superiors at Universal Orbital Logistics: Beta expected her to lead the security detail for this shipment. They wanted UOL's best.

That was suspicious, but she couldn't argue with a directive from above. Her bosses couldn't know what we knew: Beta was preparing a thermonuclear launch platform, and UOL was unwittingly helping. Someone in UOL command was on Beta's payroll.

Even though Shin knew Beta Station, I had to take her place. "You'll be fine." She strapped my arm in place. "We've calculated the moments. You'll be undetectable to the cargo team. Unless you want to call the whole thing off."

"We can't." And she knew it. Beta's plan was too close

to completion. If we let them finish the platform, they could start a war at any time.

Shin finished epoxying the straps, fixing me to the inner hull. I was immobile, but I could still talk, tongue my water and food dispensers, and view my displays. With voice activation, I could release my straps. And while our helmets were cabled together, we could talk.

Shin hung before me in freefall in UOL's main bay. She was on a safety inspection, but she couldn't take long. Beta must be nervous with their goal so close. Any deviation might make them trigger-happy.

She pulled herself to where the outer plate sat, unclamped it from the cargo deck, and tugged it into motion. It slid toward me, and Shin disappeared behind it.

"I'm disconnecting the comm line," she said. "Good luck." The comm channel went silent. I sat immobile as she seated the panel, cutting off the light.

I was completely isolated from every sight, sound, and person in the universe. And I would stay that way until it was time to stop a war.

Who watches the watchmen? It's a puzzle humanity will never really answer. We are fallible creatures, and the watcher is as much of a risk as who they watch.

In the cyber age, people believed the answer was incorruptible software systems, not prone to human error. The machines promised perfect security, especially with artificial intelligence, the Serpent in the Garden. AIs were so seductive, and they did so many things right—but in ways we could never explain.

The worst decisions in the last war had been made by

the machines. The deaths of hundreds of millions, and the collapse of the world economy, all due to machines responding to threats faster than humans could perceive them. No one could say if the cause was shoddy programming, flawed training, or actual machine malevolence. But the diagnosis mattered less than the cost: twenty percent of humanity wiped out in hours, and another twenty percent in the resulting collapse. The war had lasted hours, but we were still rebuilding nearly two decades later.

I heard three raps. That was Fernandez, telling me the pod was ready to launch. With him and Shin in place, my team was ready. We might pull this off.

The collapse might have been worse if it were not for orbital operations that were already delivering food and goods to Earth. Some orbitals had been targeted in the war, but not those operating in higher orbits and cis-lunar space. For a while the orbitals were heroes. We threw everything into relief efforts, rebuilding, communications, surveys, and meteorology. It's true we wanted to help the grounders; but air and water and sweat and brains all come with a cost. When the time came to pay, the top bosses asked for concessions.

The hull hummed. The pod had launched for Beta station. This would be a slow approach, watched by Beta at every step. The orbital plan called for twenty-seven hours of insertion and approach. As soon as the boost cut out, I took a ration of water and nutrients, and I eliminated liquid waste. Then I asked the computer for a light sedative, and soon I was out.

We mostly just wanted the grounders to lift regulations we had long argued kept us from building a real orbital civilization. We wanted the prewar regulations and inspection regime eliminated, and the grounders to trust us. We'd come through when they needed us, why did they still treat us like children?

The grounders had no choice but to quietly agree. Though they never admitted it, their governments were unable to seriously regulate and inspect orbital traffic. With the world in mourning, with economies turned to subsistence and repair, there wasn't enough money to run orbital operations the way they had before—unless we paid for it ourselves by expanding our operations.

So the grounders dressed it up in fancy language, with statements about a new orbital security partnership; but underneath all that, they trusted us to police ourselves, hoping none of us were stupid enough to kill our own customers. We could play whatever power games we wanted above low earth orbit. If we kept the food and pharmaceuticals and manufacturing coming, no one would question how we did it.

My alarm chirped in my ear, and I was instantly awake. We had three hours to transfer, where our UOL escort would drop off and a Beta escort would match course. As we got closer, Beta would rendezvous with the pod, take the pod in tow, and guide it into their cargo bay.

★ ★ ★

If you believe they left us to ourselves, you're not paranoid enough. Leaders on Earth understood the risks of orbital bombardment by nuclear missiles or even just big rocks. Attacks would be undetectable until too late. Even with modern interceptors, the delta V was just too high to deflect.

So unofficially, off the record, never to be acknowledged, they had intelligence assets. Spies. Agents.

Me.

ADL Satellite Services, my employer, does machining, repairs, transport, systems planning, and more. We provide vital services to seventy percent of the orbital companies in operation.

And my small team within ADL spies for a coalition of what used to be called superpowers: the governments who still have the most to lose if somebody goes rogue.

I felt pressure against my back. The pod was boosting for rendezvous with the Beta transport that would deliver this little Trojan horse, full of food and water and printing stock . . . and me.

That's a weak spot in any satellite operation: humans gotta eat, and stations gotta have human workers. That was the lesson of the last war: don't rely on machines. The weakness worked in our favor now, but it had worked against us so far. Beta had staffed their scheme through clever manipulation of the recruitment drives of other orbitals. My analysts found a large number of personnel were recruited up to the orbitals, then washed out and landed in the labor pool, where spacers went for scut work that paid for air, food, and water. The labor pool is a relief valve for personnel problems.

Too many people were ending up in the labor pool—and though their work records didn't show it, they were highly skilled. Somebody was slowly assembling a science team, spread all across orbital space.

I had infiltrated UOL, since they were a major conduit for new recruits. I had signed up for their recruitment (using excellent forged credentials) and confirmed that UOL was hiring science and combat specialists they didn't need. These specialists funneled through the labor pool. Fernandez and his team followed them, and they ultimately ended up at Beta.

That's when I'd taken Shin Na, head of UOL Security, into my confidence. My superiors had objected; but her record had shown she could be trusted. I had broken into her station and attempted to kidnap her so I could show her what I'd learned.

That hadn't worked so well. I had fought past her bodyguard, Mama—the tall, bald-headed Maasai woman still hadn't forgiven me for that—but not past Shin. She had captured me and coaxed me into revealing what I'd known.

When Shin finally realized Beta was using UOL, she was ready to declare corporate war; but I persuaded her that we needed more subtlety. I showed her the data from Fernandez and his team, and what it implied: the assembly of components and raw hydrogen for at least a dozen nuclear warheads as well as an invasion force. When Shin saw that, she realized we couldn't afford a shooting war.

My clock showed less than two minutes before docking. After that I would use my conduction phones to listen for activity in the bay. None of us had ever been in this part of the Beta platform. Did they unload right away or set the pod aside for later processing? When could I safely make my move?

The pilot wasn't gentle. There were three sharp boosts before a sudden clang rang through the pod. That was followed by the clack of clamps snapping into place as the pod settled.

Beta had good internal security. I'd tried to find disgruntled former employees who might be turned. Against all probability, I couldn't find a single malcontent—not one. Once you were in Beta, you didn't leave.

I activated my phones, listening for sounds coming through the hull. There was silence for twelve nerve-wracking minutes before I heard a hatch slide open, followed by a murmur of conversation.

The voices were muffled, though with two distinct pitches: one a higher-pitched southern American drawl, the other a deeper voice with a Dutch accent.

The voices grew clearer. "Everything's here," the higher-pitched voice said.

"And then some," the other answered. "Look at this. Real meat."

"Meat in a can."

"Better than soy meat. I'll bet ten Euros this isn't for *our* galley."

"Of course not," the southerner answered. "The good stuff is for the drop troops, to keep them ready for action. You know that."

"I don't have to like it. And watch what you're saying. Someone might be listening."

The high voice laughed. "We're the first ones in."

The Dutchman answered, "I just get nervous. Leon and Jack disappeared. They got too loud, and the bosses didn't like it."

"Leon and Jack were pilfering. I saw it. And I ..."

"You turned them in?"

"I did! I got a nice reward for it, too. You talk about your real meat ..."

"Bastard! Turning in your own friends ..."

"Turning in *traitors*. Beta's our future. We just have to be patient." The voice lowered. "It's coming soon, you know."

"What's coming?"

There was a pause before the southerner answered. "The *operation*. I can't say, but soon Beta's gonna be in charge."

"I've heard it before. Meanwhile the drop troops get all the best, and we're eating sludge."

"You could volunteer for the drop troops."

"Not me. I'm too adjusted to free fall, and too old to train like they do."

"Then you ain't ..." The voices faded to mumbles.

Eventually I heard the scraping sound of the hatch closing. I gave myself ten minutes for them to clear out of the cargo deck. If they saw me, my whole plan could be over. But the southerner said the *operation* was coming soon.

Finally I spoke. "Computer, release solvent."

I heard a soft hiss as canisters sprayed solvent between the plates. Soon I felt my straps go slack as the epoxy softened. My arms were free.

But I was still trapped between the plates. I pressed my arms forward until I felt the release hooks. I pried them gently, the plate released, and I pushed it away. I held on, though, not wanting it to float free. With my left hand I grabbed the center hook, while with my right I tugged at my leg straps.

"Hey!" I heard the high southern voice. "What—"

I acted on instinct, with only one thought: don't let him sound the alarm. I caught a glimpse of where he floated, and I shoved the plate at him. The man spun and took the impact on his back. I pulled out my needle gun, and blasted him with a neurotoxin load. By the time I finished freeing myself, he was dead.

I pushed loose, grabbed the plate, and rode it to the wall, bouncing back toward my niche. Then I swung around, absorbed the impact, and came to a stop. I hooked the plate back in place.

I turned and took off after the man. He was still spinning, giving me alternating glimpses of his bald skull and his painful final grimace. I brought us both to a halt at the wall and bounced us back to the shadow of the cargo pod.

The man had a comm band, but no sign of med sensors. No one should know he was dead yet. I shoved the band into my pocket. Then I looked around to see if his partner was anywhere. There was no sign of anyone, nor any cameras.

I'd gotten lucky; but if anyone found this man, they would set patrols on me. So I removed the outer hull plate, stuffed him inside, and sealed the plate behind him.

Now I was inside, I could do damage and let my team in. One man on the inside was worth ten on the outside, especially if he had a key.

And I hoped I did. Ramon, my intrusion tech, had given me two break-in boxes: specialized AIs that could infiltrate and take over an electronic lock. Somewhere out there, my team was ready for the hatch to open so they could join me. They had trailed behind me with long-distance mobility sleds, small spacecraft barely larger than a person. This gave us two avenues of intrusion.

I found the controls for the cargo hatch, opened the access panel, and hooked the patch cables in. Then I used an adhesive patch to tack the break-in box inside the panel and sealed it.

I needed actionable intelligence, as well as ways to generate chaos. If southern boy was right, they were nearing the end of preparations. And those involved drop troops: assault forces dropping from orbit in ablative capsules and combat armor. It was a way to rapidly take and hold territory while other forces took out command-and-control centers.

But Beta station couldn't hold more than a few hundred drop troops. The Beta leadership probably planned to use the nuclear missiles to take out defensive forces and infrastructure while drop troops occupied critical command-and-control nodes. From there, they'd commandeer their hidden weapons—which they all assured us they didn't have—and stage a standoff so the other superpowers wouldn't object.

As I approached the access hatch, a light blinked near it, responding to southern boy's band in my pocket. That comm band gave me access to any place he was allowed. But what if I were spotted?

There was no time for subtlety. If there were cameras, there were cameras. I was too far in to falter now.

I stepped closer, and the hatch opened. I ran a quick visual scan, and the computer identified two possible cameras in the tube running away from me, deeper into the station. Another tube ran parallel to the wall. Shin had shown me a rough map from one of UOL's diplomatic missions here. It wasn't detailed, but it was better than nothing.

I turned left, and the scanner showed no cameras. I pulled along on handholds and propelled myself down the tube.

This corridor was dim. Half the wall lights were out, as if conserving power. This part of the station seemed little used.

I double-checked Shin's map. Beta Station was an ungainly "brick," with three smaller parallel "bars" running through it. Antennas and observation towers jutted out from the brick. The cargo section was at the brick's far end. The whole thing orbited with that section pointed down toward Earth.

We believed the launch facility was at the far end. I had to go through the entire station to get to the missile platform. That would be an impossible challenge for a stranger in a spacesuit without credentials.

That assumed I went through instead of around.

I thought I was caught when the lights dimmed almost completely; but a voice came from southern boy's comm band. "All personnel, scheduled power rationing has begun. Make your way to your marshaling point for briefings."

Marshaling points. Would anyone come through here, in the rear bowels of the ship?

I searched for a hiding place. Six meters back I had passed a maintenance hatch. I flipped, caught a handhold, and pushed myself back to the hatch. I used the comm band to slip inside, sliding the hatch almost closed behind me.

Just in time. I heard voices coming. One of them was familiar. Through the crack of the hatch, I recognized a beefy form floating by: McConnell. One of the troublemakers I'd followed up from Earth. I'd gotten him out of trouble once to ingratiate myself with him, and into trouble twice as part of my escape from UOL. The second time I had broken his nose. He would remember me.

I waited a long time before I opened the hatch. Like me, McConnell had played a green recruit, but he was an able spacer—and a damn good free-fall fighter. I had broken his nose, but he'd almost snapped my neck before the drill sergeant had separated us.

The tube was clear, so I pulled back out and headed left at double time. At the end of the brick, I found tubes up and down, and one forward. I sped along that one. Red emergency lights were the only lighting now.

In my rush forward, I almost passed the tube to the left. When I saw it, I grabbed the edge and pulled to a halt. I was torn. I was making good time. Maybe I could just continue through the brick.

But then all the lights came on, and a voice rang

through the comm band: "Intruder alert. Intruders in the cargo bay. Security personnel to the bay."

That was my team. They had gotten in, but they had been discovered. Fernandez and Shin and Mama and others. I had to make progress while they scattered and looked for vulnerable systems to attack. So I pulled left into the tunnel that led into the first of the bar structures.

It took me three false trails before I found a tube that led to an airlock. By that time I'd heard multiple explosions, a pressure-leak warning, and more reports of intruders.

I jumped through the hatch. The small airlock cycled quickly, wisping out air and leaving me in vacuum. A green light came on, the hatch opened, and I leaped into space.

I relaxed as I left the cramped confines of the airlock. To be out in open space, away from searchers inside the station, gave me a brief respite to think and prepare.

But then I remembered Fernandez and Shin and their team. They couldn't relax. They were fighting to give me this opportunity, and I couldn't waste it.

I took a sighting with the navigation scope and fired my mobility unit. It was small, but it should be enough for this mission. A puff of compressed gas from the jet at my waist propelled me forward. I had aimed above the middle bar, intending to angle over and then back on the far side of the farthest bar.

As I floated through orbital space, I got my first close-up view of Beta Station. It didn't match our records. Had they changed it since our last approach? Or were our records compromised? There were more observation ports and airlocks. And especially more sensor antennas.

That changed my plan. I needed to stay low, below the line of the brick. I had to assume the sensors were looking outward. If they were scanning the station itself, I would be hard to miss, and it was too late to change my tactics.

So I adjusted my course to just barely skim over the flat top of the middle bar.

That led to yet another discovery, and almost a collision. The surface of the bar was dotted with small pods: the drop capsules, miniature spacecraft suitable for one armored trooper and one drop to the surface. Judging from this bar, there had to be three hundred of them.

I couldn't get distracted. There might be watchers behind those sensor antennas, and the edge of the last bar was coming fast. But I had to know more about the drop pods.

I checked my reaction mass. I had enough for a stop. I spun in midspace, pointed my MU forward, and fired a burst to slow my rate. I grabbed one of the drop pods, and I came to a halt.

The pod was not much bigger than an airlock, with a sensor package, a bank of retros, and an ablative nose cone. There was no way to see inside. A unit like this was meant to navigate itself. You landed where it took you, ready to fight.

I searched around for any access. I couldn't find anything like a hatch, but I found a data line. It was shielded against radiation, but not against physical access. And that gave me a slim opening in the pod's defenses.

I pulled my other break-in box from my suit pouch, and I stuck it to the side of the pod. Then I clamped two sensor leads to the line between the pod and the station.

A physical connection would be better, but the box could use inductive testing to learn the signals to and from the pod. And maybe break into them.

That would be a long process, and there was no way I could help. Hopefully I could return to the pod later and find what the box had learned by then.

I pulled myself along the hull and looked over the edge. I saw pock marks of airlocks along the bar, and I made my way to the closest.

The hatch was locked, and I had left my break-in box behind. I thought about going back; but first I checked whether Fernandez had compromised cybersecurity. I typed in my override code and waited.

The hatch slid open. "Fernandez, I owe you a beer." I pulled myself in, cycled the outer hatch closed, and waited for the inner hatch to open. As soon as it did, I pushed out into the tube beyond.

And immediately felt a hard jolt as something smashed my helmet.

What the hell? I turned in the direction of the blow, and there I saw McConnell, feet looped into anchors as he swung a large pry bar with both hands.

I didn't try to stop myself. The blow had given me spin, and I pulled my limbs closer to pick up speed. As my legs swung around, I extended them again, smashing both booted feet into McConnell's face.

I saw the man wince, but he knew what he was doing in freefall. He kept his feet anchored, and he used both forearms to slap the tunnel wall, absorbing the impact. He was dazed but not out.

I would take dazed. I drew my limbs in again, picking

up speed until my hands reached a grip. Then I pushed myself past McConnell. On the way, I punched him in the groin. The impulse pushed me back toward the tunnel wall, which I caught on my shoulders. The strike made him double over and lose his anchor on the wall.

He recovered quickly, pushing off the wall with both feet, coming at me with the bar held between both hands. He rammed into my midsection, knocking the wind out of me.

But this put us in grappling range. As long as he didn't grab my tubes or connectors, I was better equipped for wrestling than he was. He started to bounce away, but I grabbed the pry bar and twisted. He held on, not realizing that I wasn't trying to take it away. He twisted with it, and so he had his back to me. Then I grabbed both ends of the pry bar and pulled it toward me. Suddenly his neck was against my chest plate, and the bar was against his trachea.

Then I said, "Suit, amplify pulling strength. Two hundred percent." The artificial muscles in the suit did the rest. He thrashed and flailed. Finally his windpipe was crushed, and he stopped moving.

The man was smarter and more aware even than I had suspected. Probably Beta intelligence, not just a soldier. Maybe he had information from Fernandez and Shin. If they were captured, I had little time left.

Soon I was at another hatch. Southern boy's credentials didn't work here, so I needed another way in. I tried the override code. I guess I owed Fernandez *two* beers. The hatch opened.

As soon as I was through, I slid the hatch shut and spun

the manual lock. I wanted to slow down any pursuers as best I could. It was dark in the bay, but the time for secrecy was past. I turned on my helmet lamps.

Expecting hydrogen warheads isn't the same as seeing them. My stomach churned as I looked at a dozen missiles, each tipped with a bulbous payload.

We'd been right. Beta was getting ready to nuke a superpower. Now that they knew we knew, they would have to use their advantage soon, or lose it.

And I'd come all this way with no clear way to stop them.

A dozen missiles. A dozen warheads, command systems, engines. What vulnerable point could I attack from here in the time I had left?

I saw one choice, and it might prove fatal. But if it came down to me or a few hundred million on Earth . . .

I wasn't sure I could do it. But I had to try.

Ramon had filled my data pack with everything he knew on detonation systems, and my suit AI was a good assistant. I opened up the nearest warhead and scanned the circuitry. It took the AI ten minutes to confirm the detonation path. By that point, there was already hammering at the hatch. I was running out of time.

The AI confirmed that it knew what to do. If I hooked it into the command circuitry, it could do the rest.

Of course, that would leave me without a suit computer; but I would take that chance. I hooked the AI into the circuits, slammed the access panel shut, and headed to the launch hatch. I couldn't open that; but I found a maintenance airlock, and I cycled through. I was back in space.

Not that that would spare me. A hydrogen bomb going off this close wouldn't give a damn about hull plates.

This was our last chance. Win or lose, it was time to scramble if we could. I tapped my team circuit, a broadcast antenna powerful enough to reach everywhere in the area—even inside the station; if Fernandez had deployed his relay. I shouted, "Artifice!" That was our code word to bug out.

Would they make it? Would I? Checking my chronometer, we had nine minutes to find out.

Without the AI, my mobility unit missed my drop pod by more than thirty meters. I worked my way hand over hand back to the pod.

If I could've taken my helmet off, I would've kissed the break-in box. It had control of the pod. I executed a maintenance mode to detach the pod from the hull, and I opened the hidden hatch. As soon as I was inside, I triggered the escape jets without even waiting for the hatch to close.

But I made sure I shut it in time. Seven minutes later, Beta Station became a new star in the sky.

Shin almost didn't escape. She went back to rescue Fernandez and his team, who were caught in a crossfire and couldn't get down the tube. She'd gotten them out and onto their maneuvering sleds.

Mama, the beautiful Maasai who had always given me hell, never made it out. The last word Shin heard was that Mama was jamming the computer systems to keep Beta from finding me. I never got to tell her how important she was to this team.

Beta's plan could hardly stay secret. An orbital hydrogen blast can't be hidden. There are noises from the grounders that they're going to take a more active role up here, starting with an investigation to find out what really happened at Beta.

Of course, the people who *need* to know already do. They have my report.

It's been fun having freedom out here while the grounders went about their business and ignored both the risks and the opportunities of space. But it couldn't last forever. Humanity keeps gazing outward. There's not much we can do to stop it: Government is coming with their bureaucrats, their paperwork, their inspectors, and their police.

And probably their intelligence forces. Maybe I should apply with them. Stopping World War IV will look pretty good on my resumé . . .

ASTRAL SOLDIER

David VonAllmen

Two counterinsurgency specialists made a protective line in front of Alejandro, carbines trained on a door halfway down the apartment building's plaster hallway. Two more flanked him, watchful and ready. He was acutely aware of their orders: *keep the astral soldier alive, even if you die trying.* No one ever ordered Alejandro to put other soldiers before himself.

Behind him, Sergeant Hernandez shoved her forearms through the straps looping out from the back of his rig, her boots spread in a wide stance.

"Set," she said.

Alejandro leaned his back against hers as he let his muscles go slack.

"Projecting," he said.

Panama City's heat and humidity grew faint and distant. The sound of his own breathing turned muffled, as if he were underwater. The shades of green in the soldiers' tactical camo lost their vibrancy.

Alejandro stepped out of his body. He'd done this enough times he no longer needed a moment to collect

257

his wits and adjust to the astral plane's muted sensations. That made him good at his job. Better than he had been during the Battle for Bangkok. He had to remember that, had to have faith he wouldn't make the same mistakes—mistakes that had gotten soldiers killed.

No, not mistakes. Decisions. When the time had come to make a life-or-death decision, emotion had overwhelmed him, fear screaming too loudly for rational thought to have any voice in his head. In that fraction of a second, he hadn't been able to consider what was best for his squad, just what would keep him alive.

He rushed forward, striding through his teammates' bodies and the closed door. To the left, a set of shelves, thin wood, barely holding the weight of a few items of clothing and some Catholic trinkets. To the right, there was a mattress on the floor and an emaciated female body hidden under a frayed blanket. Tangled black hair shrouded her face. Their target was not here.

They'd come to this apartment building looking for a young man, one their informants told them was secretive, angry looking, and a little too well fed. He had been hanging around other angry young men who were also a little too well fed. It was a slim lead, but the Army had to follow whatever intel it could. The few citizens left in Panama City were starving, the surrounding farmland rendered all but useless by the end of the Third War. Dinger bombs had exterminated all life, right down to the microbes in the soil. American planes had been dusting the land with live soil, but didn't get much accomplished before two of them were shot down by handheld surface-to-air missiles. A band of insurgents lurked somewhere in

Panama. The US Army didn't know how many, who was leading them, or what their goals were. For some reason, someone in Panama wanted the famine to continue.

Alejandro returned through the door and into his body.

"Back," he said. Alejandro shifted his weight back onto his own feet. "One person, under a blanket. I couldn't make out anything."

The statement was noncommittal, and the squad didn't have time for that. Every second they wasted was an opportunity for their target to escape.

"Threat or no threat?" Hernandez asked.

It was a simple question. It was his entire reason for being here. And he couldn't answer it. Some part of his brain, some rational part he could barely hear through the blood rushing to his head, knew the person in that room couldn't possibly be an insurgent. But still he hesitated. And not because he was trying to get himself to do the right thing, but only to delay the moment he might make the wrong decision.

"If we pass them by, there's a risk—"

"There's always a risk. I didn't see the room; you did. You need to make the call."

The soldiers kept their carbines pointed at the door in the silent moment that followed. He needed her to pass by the room for the good of the mission. It was the only thing that made sense.

"Secure the room," he said. "One person, on the ground, to the immediate right."

Without hesitation, Hernandez gave the signal. Okoye, the breach specialist, kicked the door open and Rousseau rushed in with his HK490 aimed down and to the right.

Alejandro's ear caught the timid scraping of a door creeping open. He spun around. At the hallway's far end, he spotted a young man in jeans and bare feet, eyes fixed on the soldiers, trying to slip away unnoticed.

The instant he knew he'd been seen, the young man lifted a handgun.

"Gun!" Alejandro yelled. He dropped to the floor with his hands over his head as two shots echoed.

"One man. Coming down. Armed," Hernandez barked into her radio. "Could be our target."

"Roger," the radio replied.

"Find him, Alex," Hernandez said.

"Wilco. Projecting," Alejandro said, and dropped through the floor.

Thankfully, Hernandez gave him a direct order—it allowed him to operate on instinct. If he'd had to make his own decision, he would have hesitated again. The situation was nothing like Bangkok—where insurgents attacked from several directions at once, trapping his wounded squad mates in a kill sack. But also it was still too much like Bangkok: shots fired, a jump into the astral plane to scout enemy positions, his comrades dragging his body under fire. Soldiers assigned to drag an astral couldn't move fast, couldn't find cover quickly, and couldn't aim a rifle to defend themselves. Two members of his squad died that day. The two who'd been dragging him.

This is a war—a world war—and people die, the Army psychiatrist had told him. *Do you know how many soldiers we've lost in East Africa alone? And we're lucky, the Indians have lost more than three times as many, fighting a two-front war.* Was the death of millions supposed to make him forget those two men whose families would never see them again?

Instructions shouted in Spanish made it clear the young man had tried to run out the back door and come face-to-face with the other half of Hernandez's squad. But no more shots were fired. Thank God.

It was SOP to rendezvous with his body at their transport vehicle. Alejandro dropped through the floor and into the ground level hallway. The hallway was empty except for one man standing in the dim light at the far end, facing the other direction. The man did not move, he just stood there, his black hair falling in unkempt clumps to shoulders that rounded down, as if years of enduring the world's troubles had left him too tired to stand fully upright. In his astral form, Alejandro would be invisible to normal people, but even then, something about the way the man stood, motionless, made Alejandro not want to turn his back.

No, not standing. Swaying. No, not swaying. Drifting. The man's feet didn't touch the floor. He wasn't inhabiting a body; he was an astral.

Anytime anything got hit by a dinger weapon, its energy was sucked out of it. People died and electronics failed. People assumed Alejandro understood why, but he didn't. Getting dinged had made him an astral, it had not made him an expert in quantum physics. The world's militaries had originally designed their dinger weapons to disable enemy vehicles and communications, but they hadn't let their killing power go to waste.

After getting dinged, some bodies kept breathing. If

their spirit found its way back, from then on, that person could leave their body and project their souls to the astral plane at will. Any spirit that did not find its way back—which was most of them—became a wraith—a rabid spirit that attacked others on sight. Wraiths didn't last long, dissipating when their body died of starvation. Any wraiths in Panama would have died off four years ago.

Running into another astral in Panama City, just by chance, wasn't impossible. But it was unlikely enough that Alejandro's gut told him to back away.

Alejandro found his body sitting upright in the back of the squad's Tacvee transport. The squad's other members stood relaxed on the brick-paved streets of Old Town Panama City. The insurgent lay on the ground, face down, hands flex-cuffed behind his back. Bullet holes pocked the colorful colonial-era buildings surrounding them, remnants of the constitutional loyalists' attempt to keep General Abrego from selling control of the Panama Canal to the highest bidder during the Third War. That highest bidder had been the Yian Qin faction of the Chinese Civil War, which is why the Zinhou Chinese—the side the US had allied with—had put an end to that threat with high-altitude dinger bombs that evaporated most life from the city and countryside. Panama City's skyscrapers had lain empty since that day. Tens of thousands of people still inhabited the outskirts, but for a city this large, it felt like a ghost town.

The squad loaded into the back of the Tacvee, shoving their prisoner in first. Hernandez swatted a soldier on the arm, getting him to scoot over so she could sit next to Alejandro.

"You okay?" she asked. It was not a sympathetic inquiry. His indecisiveness had almost gotten some of her soldiers shot.

"Yeah. Yeah," he said, trying to nod in a way that looked both casual and convincing. "I'm sorry, I just wanted to . . . I'm sorry. It won't happen again."

Hernandez didn't respond; she simply stared at him. Alejandro was sure she could see right into his heart, could see he was a coward who only told them to check that room because he was afraid—that he'd sooner put the entire mission at risk than overlook a frail, unarmed woman.

"There was an astral in that building," he said to change the subject.

"Really," Hernandez said, her tone flat, but her eyebrows raised in surprise.

The Tacvee's engine fired up, and the vehicle jerked into motion.

"A man. Just floating in the middle of the hallway," Alejandro said.

"Did you talk to him?" Hernandez asked.

"No. He was looking the other way, just floating there. I thought it was best not to engage."

"Could it have been a wraith?"

"No. How could it be?"

"Panama City got dinged hard. There had to be thousands of them."

"Four years ago, yeah. But all their bodies would have starved to death."

Hernandez nodded, but her eyes narrowed as she looked away from him, as if she weren't fully satisfied with his answer.

The world went fuzzy. Colors desaturated, shifting into grayed versions of themselves. The sound of the Tacvee's tires rumbling over brick warped into indistinct humming. Confused seconds stretched out until Alejandro finally realized he'd been knocked into the astral plane. He pulled himself back into his body.

"What just—" Alejandro began. He stopped when Sergeant Hernandez slumped over onto the floor of the vehicle.

The other soldiers drooped and toppled over. The compartment was too quiet, the engine noise had disappeared. The vibration of their tires on the street was the only sound, fading bit by bit as the Tacvee lost momentum.

They'd been dinged. The vehicle was dead, and no doubt so were most of the soldiers inside.

Alejandro jumped back to the astral realm. The spirits of the soldiers drifted away from their bodies, some of them already dissipating. Rousseau's spirit floated out the back of the vehicle. Alejandro chased him onto the street.

"Come back!" he yelled. "Rousseau! You have to come back!" The soldier gave no indication he'd heard Alejandro, his limbs dangling as if he were floating in water, his mouth hanging open, his eyes staring at nothing. "Please! You're gonna become a wraith! Rousseau!"

The sight of six insurgents yanked Alejandro's focus from Rousseau. They walked toward the motionless Tacvee, approaching from the vehicle's front, rifles casually gripped or slung over their shoulders.

Alejandro dove into his body and scrambled out of the Tacvee's back hatch, landing hard on the street. He peered under the Tacvee and saw the insurgents' boots had stopped moving. They'd heard him. He did the only thing he could—he ran in the opposite direction with everything he had.

Shouts filled the air, followed by the rapid pop of gunfire. Alejandro dodged into an alley, hardly believing he was lucky enough to avoid being shot. He weaved through the streets and alleys of Old Town, never running in a straight line for longer than necessary to get to the next intersection.

He paused, his own heaving breaths so loud he couldn't make out the direction of the voices calling to each other. Were there more than six of them now?

The insurgents wore frayed, leftover fatigues from Panama's last legitimate army and carried beat-up old AK-12 assault rifles, likely purchased for a handful of dollars on the black market. But they'd dinged the Tacvee, which meant they also had a dinger weapon, a piece of equipment so expensive and technologically advanced that, within four years of its introduction, it ended the Third War in a stalemate. Today, there were still only a few countries that could make them.

Alejandro pulled the radio handset off his vest, but it did not click on. Of course not. It was electronic and got dinged when he did. He needed to get this information back to his superior officers. Which meant he had to get out of here alive. His astral abilities were a big advantage—he could hide his body, jump into the astral plane, scout ahead a block, return to his body, run to that block, hide, and do it all over again until he got back to base. He'd done it before—it was how astral soldiers were trained to move in evasion scenarios. He had a working sidearm—the handgun was entirely mechanical—but what good would it be against an unknown number of insurgents with assault rifles?

There was another option. He could hide his body and return to base on the astral plane. There was one other astral soldier stationed in Panama City, and he could follow her until she entered the astral plane, then pass along the information. But if the insurgents found his body first, they'd kill him, and his astral form would dissipate before he delivered the intel.

Approaching footsteps forced Alejandro to slip into a building alcove. With his head down, he couldn't see how many people ran past, but there was no question the insurgents had called for reinforcements.

A wave of doubt swept over him. Which should he choose: run with his body or leave it behind? Which one gave him better odds of delivering the information? How many insurgents were looking for him? Could he find a spot to conceal his body indefinitely, or did the insurgents know these buildings too well for that? How many informants might they have among the population? How long would it take him to run back to base one block at a time? How long would he have to wait for the other astral soldier to enter the astral plane?

What he did know was that remaining in his body gave him better odds of staying alive.

Fate must have been taunting him. Time and again, it put him in situations where he had to make a decision with no obvious choice. Yet there was always a clear way to save himself. Or, was the choice always clear, but each time he talked himself into believing otherwise so he could rationalize protecting himself over completing the mission?

There was no way to know, and there was no sergeant here to decide for him. Despite feeling like a coward and traitor, he knew which choice he was going to make.

Alejandro stood up out of his body and scanned the street. To return to base, he'd have to double back the way he came. He returned to his body and ran in a crouch, light on his toes, ducking behind a trash pile at the end of the street. He only caught his breath for a second before jumping out of his body again and running to the end of the next block in astral form. He scanned along each of the other three blocks leading from the intersection. He saw a single figure, a man halfway along one block, staring in his direction. The man did not carry a weapon. His skin hung loose from famine.

The man ran directly at Alejandro, and Alejandro saw the look in the man's eyes. The sunken, haunted eyes. The lost expression, curling into rage, face twisted like a ghoul. This wasn't a man. It was a wraith.

Fear spurred Alejandro's astral form backward. He turned to flee, to race back toward his body. As soon as he looked away, a hand grasped his throat.

He was face to face with a woman, her open mouth gasping and shrieking, her eyes wide, her hair fanning out, ignored by gravity. Fingers dug into his chest. Shock bolts of pain shot through him, as if all his organs were being stretched outward and tearing free. Alejandro desperately flailed and scratched at the woman's face. Her strength was beyond human; he could not pull free.

In a flurry of motion too quick to make sense of, the female wraith jerked away. It took a moment for Alejandro to realize she'd been attacked by another woman. The two female forms now fought in a frenzy of raking fingers and snapping jaws. Alejandro only gawked for a second before recovering enough of his wits to retreat. He did not slow as he approached his body, instead diving inside at a full sprint.

What the hell? That was four wraiths he'd come across in ten minutes. What had the insurgents been using their dinger for that they'd created an entire district this dense with wraiths?

Alejandro worked his way back to the alley entrance directly south of the squad's Tacvee. Leaving his body behind the corner of a building, he peeked his astral head out. One insurgent stood behind the Tacvee, reaching into the open rear hatch. He hauled Rousseau's body, holding it under the armpits while another insurgent stepped down from the Tacvee grasping the feet.

What in the world were they doing? Alejandro waited until the insurgents had carried the body across the street and into a building. Then, still in astral form, he followed.

He caught up to the insurgents at the top of the stairwell, which opened to a single room occupying the entire second level. There, he saw more than a hundred dead bodies, laid out on the concrete floor in neat rows, each lying on their back, arms at their sides.

No, not dead. Each had an intravenous line coming out of one arm, leading to a small bag of fluid hanging from a metallic pole. They were unconscious. The insurgents were purposely keeping them alive. A handful of insurgents milled about, four more sat in a circle on the floor, smoking cigarettes and playing cards.

"Is that your body?" a voice asked in Spanish.

Alejandro looked up, startled. The scene before him had been so odd, he hadn't even noticed the astral to one side, floating just above the floor. After a moment, he managed to reply in Spanish, "What?"

The astral, a Hispanic man, wearing the hand-me-down military fatigues of the insurgents, pointed to Rousseau. "Is that your body?" The astral squinted in Rousseau's direction, then looked up at Alejandro. "No, I guess not."

"What's going on here?" Alejandro asked.

"We formed an army to defend Panama, because there was no government anymore, and our people kept dying at the hands of foreigners who wanted to control the canal."

Alejandro's question was about the bodies, but he didn't correct the astral. If the man wanted to talk, Alejandro would listen to whatever he had to say.

"The Zinhou killed off most of our people with their Schrödinger bombs, and now the Americans come with planes full of poisoned soil to make sure we can never grow crops again."

"Poisoned . . . ?" Alejandro wanted to protest, to tell this man that whoever was leading this insurgency had fed him lies. But the vacant stare in the man's eyes told Alejandro this astral had been out of his body for too long. The man's grasp on sanity had been stretched too thin, and he was already halfway to becoming a wraith. The man didn't speak again, just stared at the bodies on the floor. "Is your body here?" Alejandro asked.

The man nodded slowly, but did not speak.

"Could you return to it?" Alejandro asked, carefully.

The man shook his head so slightly it was barely perceptible. "If they discover I'm not a wraith, they will kill me."

Behind the man, Alejandro spotted a complex metal cylinder propped up on a tripod, eight feet long and a foot and a half wide—a Schrödinger device. It was pointed out the window at an angle that would have enabled the insurgents to ding their Tacvee.

"Your own people dinged you? Why?" Alejandro asked.

The man took so long to answer, Alejandro wondered if he'd heard the question. Then he quietly said, "The commander is . . . suspicious. Sometimes. It is necessary to keep order."

Based on the size of it, the Schrödinger weapon looked to be a Jhiang-6, one of the smaller units built by the Chinese Yian Qin faction. The pieces began to fall into place.

The US military's counterinsurgency tactics relied on astral soldiers to search for targets and scout out dangers. Astrals were perfect for this job—no device could see them, no wall could stop them. But if you made your territory a minefield of wraiths, you could kill anyone who entered the astral plane. You just needed to keep the wraiths' bodies alive.

The men laid Rousseau's body in a row with the others and prepped an intravenous line.

Creating wraiths required possession of a Schrödinger weapon, which these insurgents could only have gotten from a foreign military. And that military would want something in return. Probably what every foreign power had wanted from Panama during the Third War—control of the canal. The ability to quickly move from the Atlantic to the Pacific or vice versa, while your enemies had to go around an entire continent, was a massive advantage.

If the Yian Qin were conspiring with insurgents to sabotage crops, it was because they wanted the population on the verge of starvation. Next, they would ship in food, but only give it to those who were loyal to them. *Join us or watch your children slowly starve.* It was the same tactic General Aidid had used in Somalia in the 1990s. The Yian Qin were helping to raise an insurgent army, undoubtedly for a sympathetic local warlord. The warlord would gain control of the country with the backing of a nation powerful enough to make sure he kept it. In return, the Yian Qin would gain control of the Panama Canal. And if they were secretly securing the Panama Canal, no doubt they were covertly securing other geostrategically significant territories.

The Fourth War had already begun, and the US didn't even know it.

"Killing American soldiers was a mistake," Alejandro said. "More will come, they'll flood this area looking for insurgents. They'll see the vehicle was dinged."

"The commander will replace the bodies he took, then hit the vehicle with an RPG and burn all the evidence. It will look like a conventional attack. Then he will move these bodies to a different location. He's done it before."

How big of a lead did the Yian Qin already have in preparing for the Fourth War? How many more lives would that cost once the shooting started? How much worse would it be if Alejandro didn't survive to get this information to his superior officers?

He had to act. He had to make a decision *right now*. But which option—hide his body or run with it—truly had the best chance of getting the information through? The stakes were too high, he could not let his desire to save his own skin cloud his judgement. Not this time. Should he make the choice with lower odds of saving his own life, just to prevent that possibility?

The insurgents who'd carried Rousseau left the room the way they had entered. Alejandro knew where they were going. And in that moment, he had the answer. There was a way to travel in the astral realm and make sure his body would be protected while he was away.

So many times, Alejandro had wished for a clear answer, wished for a moment in which he could prove to himself that he had the courage to do what was best for his country and for his fellow soldiers. He'd assumed if he ever found it, he would feel brave for doing the right thing. But he didn't feel brave now; he just felt like a man who was finally doing what needed to be done, what he should have found a way to do long before now.

Alejandro ran down the stairs, through the two insurgents, and across the street. He re-entered his body and walked into the middle of the street with his hands above his head.

"I surrender," he shouted in Spanish. The insurgents spun with rifles raised. Warily, they approached.

All of Alejandro's sensations went fuzzy. His body crumpled to the ground.

He assumed they'd take him upstairs and ding him

there, but one of the insurgents must have dinged Alejandro from the window, in case his surrender was some sort of trick.

Maybe he could get to base, share his intel, and make it back here before the insurgents moved the bodies. If so, he could return to his body and might be able to fight his way out. If not, he'd run the streets of Panama City, searching building after building, until he used up whatever sanity he had left.

Alejandro watched two insurgents carry his body up the stairwell. When they disappeared into the building, he turned toward his base and ran as fast as he could.

CHAOS REDEEMED

Deborah A. Wolf

*"I exist in agreement with all the weird chaos,
destruction, and agony that is undoubtedly part
of the texture of being alive."*   —Arca

*"One must still have chaos in oneself to be able to
give birth to a dancing star."*

       —Friedrich Nietzsche

"We should turn back," Garey urged, his voice coming
thick and wet through his RASP mask. "We got all the
bastards, and it's getting dark."

"Are you afraid of the dark, Staff Sergeant?" Dutt
answered. Red flashed across his visor as it adjusted to the
dying light. "Or of the Indij? That little group we took out
this morning was nothing more than bait for an ambush,
and you know it."

Garey didn't answer for a long minute, staring at the
lieutenant and letting his own visor adjust. "There's been
no sign for two hours, Lieutenant. If the Indij bastards

were gonna ambush us, they'd have done it by now. Williams, have you seen anything?"

My visor flashed yellow as the suit's biofeedback picked up an adrenaline spike. "Not a damn thing, sir." Yellow again, two long flashes, visible to the others.

Dutt must have seen it. He stopped and turned to face me square on. "And . . . ?" he demanded.

Garey's visor flashed a warning to me. My adrenaline spiked again. "And, uh. It's odd, sir. Usually we'd see roadrunners, at least. Horned toads. Maybe a fox. But we haven't seen a thing since we killed those villagers. Unless you count that vulture." I pointed up at the vulture that had been circling overhead since that morning.

"*Vultur gryphus,*" a voice in my head offered. The asex voice of my guidance system, MUSE, offered her unsolicited, though often helpful, commentary. She could speak to others if she chose, through the speaker in my visor, and she did so now. "*Andean condor. The world's largest flying bird, with a wingspan up to three meters and weighing up to fifteen kilograms. Critically endangered.*"

"Thank you, Muse," the lieutenant said dryly. "And now back to our regularly scheduled program. Garey, Williams, your *asses* are going to be critically endangered unless you can find me my enemy combatants. I didn't come all the way down to this godforsaken asshole of a country to go birdwatching."

"Those villagers—" I started to say, but cut off as Dutt closed the distance between us in a few long strides. He bent so that his visor was nearly touching mine, and I took a half step back.

"Villagers?" he asked. His voice was calm, matter-of-fact, but his visor flashed yellow-red-red-red.

"Enemy combatants," I whispered, and cleared my throat. "Sir."

"That's right, Specialist, and don't you fucking forget it. I don't care if they look like men, women, children, or your goddamn grandmother, these Indij bastards are goddamn enemy combatants. Now—"

And then the screaming.

Blood.

A flash of color—

And the visor went dark.

"Rewind," I told Muse. "Twenty seconds."

"Those villagers—" I started to say, but—

"Forward. Ten seconds."

"...or your goddamn grandmother ..."

"Forward. Three seconds."

Blood. A flash of—

"Pause."

—color.

Biocams capture a moment of time in its entirety, and perfectly. Because of this, there can be no blurring or imperfection in a neuro image. Nevertheless, I found myself staring at the blurred image of bright feathers, claws, teeth.

"Muse? Identify, please."

Muse paused a long moment, which was unusual. "Species unknown."

"Bullshit. Clean the image up and identify species."

Another, longer pause. "Request cannot be completed. Object's neurological processes were compromised by an excessive fear response."

"Fear response?" That was odd in the extreme. "I didn't think the Septagon was still sending unmodded troops to the southern border."

"Specialist Williams was fully modified in 2077, at the age of ten," Muse answered.

I let myself sink more fully into the sense-dep gel and stared through the eyes of a dead man, trying to figure out what it was that had been killing our troops for the better part of a year.

"Any guesses as to what it might be?"

"I do not guess." If Muse had been capable of emotion, I suppose her voice would have been as dry as the shithole they were sending me to.

Feathers. Fangs. Claws. It certainly couldn't be natural—the only predator larger than a house cat that had survived the Drought was an elderly white tiger kept in a life tank at a zoo in New Washington. This thing—whatever it was—looked to be at least that big. And it had killed at least two dozen highly modded Trans Ops soldiers and disrupted our mission in Tula for nearly a year now.

I closed my eyes against the headache. "Disengage. Wake me when we're there."

"Yes, Lieutenant."

The low hum of the ABI halted abruptly, and the biomesh that covered my scalp went blessedly silent. I closed my eyes and allowed myself a moment of pleasure as my senses realigned themselves with my own body. My head itched fiercely as new hair pushed through the scalp transplant, my eyes ached, and my new melanin-heavy skin felt too tightly stretched. Small discomforts, easily ignored.

The blurred afterimage lingered: Feathers. Fangs. Claws.

I didn't know what this thing was, whether it was some animal mutated by chems or rads used in the war, or some new bioweapon thrown together by the Russians and Venezuelans. The last I thought much likelier. Of course, being a bioweapon myself, I was probably biased.

It didn't matter, anyway. I had my orders. Whatever that thing was, I would track it down, kill it, and slaughter any other enemy combatants in the area.

Yes, Muse whispered in my head, as a mother might have whispered to a child, back when we had such luxuries as children and mothers. *Kill them all.*

I slept.

Staff Sergeant Angela Milatz stared at me through a natural-looking set of blue eyes. She was modded, of course, but not heavily so; her phenotype was all northern European, and pale enough to be a hindrance in the naked heat of New Hidalgo. Her sweat stank of fear, and I felt my own biosuit hurry to dampen my own reaction.

That was just as well. Nobody wanted a repeat of Bosnia. I smiled at the memory, and Milatz stepped deliberately away from me. One of the other soldiers coughed to cover a laugh.

"Nice teeth," Milatz said under her breath.

"Nice teeth, *Lieutenant.*"

I turned to face the man who had joined us. He was

handsome despite a mass of chemical scarring which bleached and distorted one cheek and the side of his neck. Shorter than I, broad shouldered, NIUs clean and stiff despite the dust and heat.

Captain Herman Cortez, Muse informed me through the psylink. *Twelve years in. N3 mods.*

"Nice teeth, Lieutenant," Milatz said in a neutral voice.

"That's better, Staff Sergeant," said the captain. "And I must comment on your sharp eyes—the lieutenant here has an impressive set of canines which doubtless cost the Transmurican taxpayer more than your sorry ass is worth. Those sharp eyes of yours just earned you a week's patrol outside the green. Dismissed."

"Sir."

"That goes for the lot of you. Get out of my sight. No, not you." He grabbed my arm. "You stay." When the others had left, he continued.

"You'll have to forgive Milatz. Her wife was killed in Texas, and she has a thing about prototypes."

"Texas was ugly."

"Yes, it was. And you were there."

"So were you," I guessed, and Muse affirmed. I felt my biosuit cool in response to the images that flashed through my mind: Houston. The invasion. We'd barely beaten them back, and to do so we'd had to . . .

"We won," Cortez said. "We did what we had to do, and we won. That's all there is, Lieutenant."

"I'll drink to that." I held up a gel pack, and he laughed. "I like you already, Lieutenant . . . K? OS? K-OS?"

"Kay is fine."

"Pleased to meet you, Kay. And who's your little

doggy?" He crouched down to inspect the bright metal droid that hovered at my ankle like an anxious pet.

"It's just a HOUND. They don't have names."

"No? What does it do?" He leaned in closer, and the droid buzzed a little in warning.

"It finds things," I said. "And kills them."

Cortez straightened, brushing the wrinkles from his trousers, and dropped his false smile. "Like you?"

"Not at all, Captain. I'm a bio, not a droid."

"What's the difference?" A small smile played around his mouth, and heat flushed through me just a little faster than my biosuit could cool it down. My understanding of social cues was imperfect, but I knew when I was being laughed at.

"Well, for one thing," I punctured the metal skin of the gel packet with my canines and drained it, enjoying the sensation of moisture if not the bland taste, "a droid will give multiple warnings before killing a human. I'll only give one."

"One warning? And what's that?"

I smiled and tossed the drained packet into a recycling bin. "That was it, Captain."

Despite their misgivings, the humans accepted me quickly enough. Mostly because they needed me: Whatever had killed Williams's squad had killed half a platoon in the past few weeks, and President Donaldson was beside himself with fury. Transmurica wouldn't be whole until we had retaken those lands south of Hidalgo which had been claimed by Russian-backed Venezuela in War Three. There was only one tiny, weak, insignificant pocket of Indigenous resistance to imperial rule dug into a system of tunnels beneath the ruins of Tula. One small band of Indij—and the thing or weapon with them that had been killing the best and most heavily modified soldiers on the planet. They were making Donaldson look like an idiot, and the last time that had happened we'd nuked half the planet.

On the other hand, if we hadn't fucked up the planet, there wouldn't have been a need for enhanced transhumans like me, so I guess that was a win. Now all I had to do was wipe out this band of Indij rebels, neutralize or capture their weapon, and in doing so convince New Washington to overlook the bloody mess I'd made in Houston and not scrap the bioengineering program that had led to my creation.

I stood staring at the body of one of our soldiers, an E-3 named Martinez whose remains had been recovered and packed in dry ice before my arrival. It was a gruesome sight; the brightly enameled titanium of her enhanced limbs stood out in terrible contrast to the mutilated flesh. Her eyes had been burned in their sockets, mouth stitched shut, and the heart cut from her chest— perimortem, the medic slash coroner had informed me.

"See here," he pointed to a shoulder, which had been torn to the bone, "and here, at the base of her neck, where the flesh has been torn? What does this look like to you?"

Teeth. Claws. "An animal attack."

"Exactly. And look here." He turned the soldier's body partway over. "Here, you can see that a great deal of the flesh has been removed and presumably consumed."

Consumed.

I could feel him watching me, trying to gauge my reaction, and I almost said, "I've eaten worse." It would have been true, too, but Cortez was in the room, so I just shrugged.

"Consumed. Got it."

"Any idea what could have done this?"

I had sharpened my senses to the five thousandth degree, and I did smell something, but whatever had maimed the young soldier wasn't in any database accessible to me, Muse, or the Hound.

"None whatsoever," I said cheerfully.

The coroner slash medic frowned at my flippant tone. "If you don't know what it is . . ."

I felt the heat of a human body approach as Captain Cortez drew near, so I wasn't surprised when he spoke. "Fortunately, you don't have to know what something is to kill it. Isn't that so, Lieutenant?"

"As a matter of fact," I answered without turning, "I have found it is easier to destroy that which we don't understand." I glanced pointedly at a wheeled cart piled high with bits of flesh-encrusted mech they'd salvaged from the soldier's corpse.

The medic's face went pale.

"Kay," Cortez said firmly.

K-OS, Muse repeated the warning. *Your suit indicates a heightened fight response, which would be inappropriate to act upon under current circumstances.*

"Oh, don't worry," I told them both, "if I killed everyone who hated me for being trans, humans would have gone the way of elephants and polar bears by now. Besides which, I'm going to go hunt this thing in the morning." I bared my teeth in a rictus grin. "And I never hunt on a full stomach."

I stared at my pod's pale ceiling late into the night. How often had I lain awake in the mountains of Pakistan, or the forests of Siberia, just like this?

Seven hundred and twenty-eight nights, Muse answered helpfully.

"At least there were stars in Pakistan," I said, "and trees in Siberia. They were beautiful, even if they were dying. Do you understand beauty, Muse?"

I understand death. Is that not the same thing?

I knew immediately I did not want to follow that train of thought. I had never understood the AI, any more than full humans or half-mechs could understand me, and I found those brief moments in which Muse let me see her inner workings truly terrifying.

I asked instead, "Muse, what are the chances that this mission will be a success?"

Define success, she answered.

"I don't end up in a lab in New Washington being dissected for future study."

Approximately—there was a soft whirring—*seven point six six six six six two percent.*

"And assuming no fuckups? Give me my best-case scenario."

That is the best-case scenario, came the cheerful reply. *If you prefer, you may round it up to an eight percent chance of success.*

"Eight percent, huh," I said. "I'll take it."

★ ★ ★

The next morning, a squad of half-mechs escorted me to the scrub-covered hills where they'd found Martinez's body. I sent them a short distance away so the Hound and I could work. Not because I gave a fuck what they thought about my methods, but because those methods were classified well above their pay grades.

"You smell that?" I asked the Hound. Overlaid with blood and fear was a scent unlike any I'd ever experienced. It was at once musky, oily, and . . . spicy? I opened my mouth a little, flaring my nostrils, even as the Hound whirled around in an odd little pattern, making a weird metallic whine and a series of excited beeps.

It was cute. I wondered if real dogs had acted like that, before they went extinct.

"What is it?" I asked Muse. "Snake? Bird? Lizard? Synth?"

I could hear the *whir . . . whir . . . whir* of Muse thinking things over. *I . . . don't know.*

I would have said she sounded surprised, or puzzled, but neither was possible.

The Hound stopped dancing around, antennae going stiff and oculus glowing hazy red, and sounded an alarm which would have deafened unmodified ears. Even as it shot toward the rest of the squad, yells and gunfire erupted from the thin cover of dead trees clinging to the rocky hilltop. I screamed—the battle cry my makers had granted me came from the same jaguar who had inspired them to give me a predator's bite—and joined the fray, rifle kicking against my shoulder as we sent those Indij bastards to whatever hell their gods might choose. My M2024 had been tweaked to work with my mods and might as well have been an extension of my body through which I could cast a wide net of death.

My mech siblings-in-arms were just as deadly. The rebels were heavily armed and had the home-field advantage, but my soldiers were upgrades, motherfucker, with skin of titanium and biosteel scales, tendons enhanced with medgrade plastics, eyes sharper than raptors' and cybernetic biofeedback loops informing their every action and reaction. The Hound was a literal killing machine, its adorable antics of moments before given over to the deadly *rat-tat-tat-tat* of rapid fire. And I—

I was the goddess of death. With Muse riding my mind and my biosuit riding my skin, I could see them all, red pulsing bags of guts and blood and bone. Killing them was no harder than reaching up into a tree for a ripe plum and crushing it with my fingers.

Then came the serpentinous spice stink, stronger than before, and a sound that made me pause midkill, made me hold my breath as my heart leaped after it. A breath, a snatch of song—of song, which had gone extinct long before the polar bear and the osprey, having had perished perhaps when the last human mother had birthed a child only to find it dead and her lullabies with it. I half dropped my rifle and turned toward the whisper, yearning—

And found myself face-to-face . . . to face . . . with a god.

A two-headed serpent taller than the charred trees looked down at me, its plumage bright and beautiful, an echo of things lost to this world. It stared at me with four enormous, slitted, sun-yellow eyes. And those eyes fill with tears.

Its sorrow engulfed me. I dropped my rifle, I fell to my

knees, and opened my mouth to beg forgiveness—for killing, for dying, for having been created by a cruel world. The god opened its mouths and breathed into my face, a white steam which I thought might melt me as I'd seen that little girl melt in Texas. First her skin, then her flesh, and finally her bones had been scoured away, until there was nothing left at all of her but an afterimage in my mind.

I had killed her, I had killed them all, and now it was my turn to die.

At last.

I was awakened by the smell of blood and burning flesh. My first thought was one of relief; the burning flesh was not my own. Then I opened my eyes, and relief fled.

A ceasefire had been called at the end of War Three, and the killing was supposed to have stopped. But the President of Transmurica, angered and humiliated by his defeat in Venezuela, had not given the orders to cease hostilities in Texas. He had, in fact, ordered that the Muse-linked transhumans be set to maximum aggression, our kill switches disabled, and all of those things that make us appear more human—fear, empathy, compassion—set to "null."

"Let it burn," he had told his horrified commanders. "Let it all burn." And it had, for three days of Hell on Earth, during which I and my transhuman siblings carried out a massacre the likes of which had never been seen on this planet.

I had been set to "null." Made inhuman. Unfeeling. Then I opened my eyes and saw what had been done to my squad.

My companions had been strung up in a ring of dead trees where they hung heads-down, arms outstretched as if they would beg for mercy. Their eyes had been burned in the sockets, and the white flash of ribs stark against the gaping crimson holes in their torsos told me the hearts had been torn from their chests.

Even as I sat in the rocks and dirt, staring at the desecrated bodies, the mutilated thing that had once been Milatz gave a long, rasping groan and expired. She had been enucleated, eviscerated, behearted—partly flayed as well, I could see now—and hung to bleed out. And yet until this moment she had been alive.

If I'd been capable of terror, I would have been gibbering. As it was, I reached out to Muse, my one constant source of comfort and familiarity.

"Have you ever seen anything like—" I stopped, groping after the empty void in my mind like a woman who'd recently lost a limb in combat. "Muse? Muse?"

There was no answer. Nothing but silence. Was this what it was like to be human? I wondered. All alone in your head?

And then the song began again. There was nothing I could do but stagger to my feet and follow it.

I followed the song and the serpentine scent over some low scrub-thick hills and toward the ruins of the pyramid. I hadn't bothered noticing it when we'd flown in, not being made for wondering at such things, but I saw it now. The sun baked through what was left of our atmosphere and raked hot fingers across the naked stone, scarred here by the passage of time and there by man's wars. Robbed of my Muse I struggled to imagine what purpose the structure might once have served. Was it a marker of some type, I wondered, a place of gathering and governance, perhaps a stairway which a human might ascend, the better to speak with the gods?

All of these and more, came a voice. *It is a place of death. It is a place of life.*

I started, reached out tentatively. "Muse?"

Sometimes, the voice replied. It was not my Muse, whose presence I could feel but not touch, but the deep biphonic croon of the two-headed serpent.

The skin on my forearms prickled oddly, and I glanced down in surprise. Goosebumps.

"I'll be damned."

Sometimes, the voice said again, and dissolved into laughter that trailed away—with the serpentine stench and the fading song—toward the broken heart of an ancient civilization.

There was nothing for me to do but follow.

I came to the end of the scent trail, the laughter, and the song just as the sun was setting. It was a glorious sight. The ruins, which had seemed almost comically irrelevant in the light of our neo-doomed world, now felt as significant as the capital of any modern city, ponderous with whispered secrets and the weight of its own importance.

A tunnel's mouth gaped wide before me. I was certain this tunnel had not been captured in any of the thousands of aerial images Muse had shown me on the flight to Hidalgo, just as I was certain that if I happened to find this exact spot again in the light of day, there would be nothing but tumbled rock and dead brush.

"Muse," I said, in case she could still hear me, "I'm going in. Send the Hound, if you can. I'm at—"

My voice faltered. Where was I, exactly? I could not have said. My GPS was down, my Muse was silent, and I was as lost as Hansel and Gretel stumbling through the forest toward the witch's gingerbread house. For the first time in my synthetic life, I was lost, and alone, and I shivered as some new emotion climbed up my spine like the tendrils of a growing thing. Was it fear?

No, I decided, after some thought. Not fear. Excitement.

Was this how humans felt all the time? How I might have envied them, had I known sooner what I'd been missing.

Smiling a little, knowing it was foolish but delighting in these new sensations all the same, I entered the tunnel, let my biosuit trigger the necessary changes to my eyes for twilight vision, and followed the narrow steps down into the darkness.

Even with my jaguar's eyes it was difficult to penetrate the darkness of this underworld. Down I went, and down and down. I counted the steps aloud till I reached one thousand, three hundred and twenty-six. I realized that Muse was not there to keep track with me, or to tell me how many steps might still be before me, or how many meters down into the belly of the world I might have ventured. I quit counting. It seemed a mischief to me and an adventure—how many steps had I taken? I had no idea!—and this I added to my growing library of small delights. How nice it was to feel a little bit human.

And how quickly I was coming to dislike the idea of giving it up.

At last I came to a ledge, or a floor, and let my pupils stretch wide till my eyes ached. I could see, very dimly, that I was in a place of grey stone and great age. There were designs carved into the walls the likes of which I had never imagined—there were human figures, heavy featured and strangely proportioned but beautifully wrought, with dangling earlobes and outthrust tongues. Serpents, birds, and fantastic creatures, some of which were surely imaginary, but others—like the jaguar, whose face my heart leaped to see—I knew had once walked the earth, breathing the same air that now caressed my skin. In the distance I could see a faint, a very faint, gleam of light, and I followed this with a growing sense of what might have been hope, or dread, or both.

Another new sensation. It was too much. I, who had butchered a hundred humans in a single day without giving it a second thought, found my face wet with tears as I walked toward the light.

I heard them before I smelled them, and smelled them before I saw them. I came to the tunnel's end and looked down into a cavern, wide enough that the other side was lost to shadow and lit with torches. It was filled with humans, full-blood humans without a single mech among them. There were perhaps fifty of them, and some—I stared openly, mouth gaping in shock—some of them were *old*. Their skin, as dark as mine but naturally so, was fragile-thin and wrinkled from long exposure to the elements, their hair was various shades of grey or silver, their eyes were hazed.

"Old people," I whispered, as if Muse were there to hear it. Who would have believed such a thing? They looked so fragile, so—

Precious. All of them, precious. I could not tell if the voice belonged to the two-headed serpent, or to some facet of myself I'd never known existed. My mission, the very reason for my continued existence, was unambiguous: I was to find these people and kill them. Annihilate the Indij bastards and crush the rebellion.

I felt then a very strange stirring in my breast. A pain. A song. I did not know what that sensation was, but I knew that I had made a decision.

"I will not kill them," I whispered into the void, wherein I knew Muse was lurking. Listening. "I will *not*."

Just as the two-headed serpent's song had carried, so too now did my whisper, growing to a shout as it winged through the walls and pillars of stone, and flung itself among the humans gathered far below.

"I WILL *NOT!*"

The humans turned toward the tunnel, faces mirroring my own shock. Some of them pointed, shouting. And then they were running, or walking, some toward me and others away, as quickly as they could move. I saw guns, and makeshift spears, and torches, but I made no move to attack or escape.

Let them come, let them go, let them do with me as they would. My world had been wrenched inside out, and I had nowhere left to hide.

★ ★ ★

A dozen or more of them swarmed me, eyes wide and white with human emotions. Though I offered no resistance they would likely have beaten me to death there and then, had Chimalma not been among them.

Chimalma. In beautifully accented English she told me her name, that she was a priestess of Quetzalcoatl, and that I was her prisoner. She held my face in her strong hands, breathed a thick herbal smoke into my nostrils, and seemed surprised when I blinked the smoke away without so much as a cough.

"Modded," I told her, feeling almost apologetic about it. "Your drugs won't have any effect on me."

An old woman in a magnificent red robe sucked her teeth at me reprovingly and muttered something in the priestess's ear.

"That won't have much effect, either." I shrugged when she glared at me. "I have a very high tolerance to pain."

"Why have you come here?" the old woman snapped.

I smiled, charmed by her dry and crackling voice. She was so *old*. "I was sent here to kill you," I answered.

There were gasps at this, and shouts, none of which needed any translation.

"What did I tell you?" the old woman cried. "She said it herself, she has come to kill us!"

"No."

Silence fell as Chimalma raised both hands, palms out. Gold flashed at her wrists, her throat. Gold hung from her earlobes and from her nose, and her thick waist was coiled with chains of the precious metal. She glowed in the torchlight, and I was utterly enchanted.

"No," she said again, "she has not come to kill us. She has come to save us."

I opened my mouth to deny this—the idea of a transhuman hero was ludicrous—but Chimalma shifted her weight on the wide wooden bench and grimaced, and my mind finally connected myriad bits of irrelevant information into a magnificent, impossible, whole.

"You are *pregnant*," I whispered, my voice loud and harsh with shock. How many years had it been since a natural human child had been born? How many decades? Muse might have told me, but Muse had no power in this place.

Chimalma's lips compressed into a small, pained smile. She shifted again, and as she did so, the gold medallion at her throat flashed, two sets of jeweled eyes winked at me. I squeezed my eyes shut, but an afterimage of the two-headed serpent mocked my attempts to hide.

Save them, it whispered. *Chaos, daughter of the Jaguar, save my people.*

When I opened my eyes again, Chimalma was looking at me—not at the snakelike scales of my bioskin, my jaguar-fanged mouth, my too-wide eyes, but at *me*.

She draped one hand over her moon-round belly, and with the other gestured toward the people who crowded all around us. Gold chains whispered together like the scales of a great serpent, and I thought that I had been listening to that sound for my entire artificial life.

Chains. Without Muse to guide my eyes I could clearly see the chains which had bound me to the wheels of the war machine. I had been linked to Muse, and through Muse to those who created and trained me not to live, but to exist as an instrument of murder.

I could, if I chose, slip free of those chains and embrace my full potential. My . . . humanity.

In that moment, I came to know fear. Fear of what might happen were I to unleash my full power. I was afraid of a repeat of Houston, afraid of what I might do if left to my own devices. Kill them all, I had said in the past, and only Muse's voice ever held me back. What might stop me now that her voice was silent? What monstrous things might I do, I who was created to be a monster?

I looked at them, these tender-skinned people, hurtling through space on a dying planet, and I felt something deep within me stir. My jaguar eyes filled with tears.

"There you are, little sister," Chimalma said, and smiled. "I knew you would find your way home."

Even as she said the words, even as I felt them, shouts rang out from those people closest to the tunnel. A red light shone forth from the darkness, and the shrill baying of a Hound whose quarry had been found.

There you are. It was Muse, sounding very far away, and strained. *Where . . . can't find . . .*

"I'm sorry, Muse," I said. "I was lost."

. . . found you, Muse went on. I imagined that she sounded relieved, though that was of course impossible. *Enemy target within range. Likelihood of mission success ninety-six point seven eight nine percent. You may round it up to ninety-seven percent. Proceed with final solution as per command forty-five, section three paragraph two . . .*

"I was lost," I continued as if Muse had not spoken, "but I have found my way. Goodbye, Muse." With that, I broke the link which bound me to Muse, and to those who had made me to hunt, and kill, and kill.

I looked up and saw the Hound's bright carapace, the faces of those I had called siblings, and whose weapons would now be raised against me.

"Safety off," I told my biosuit, and grinned. Daughter of the Jaguar, indeed. "Let's see what this thing can *do*."

I raised my rifle, took aim at the Hound, fired off a short burst of incendiaries.

And then all Hell broke loose.

MEA KAUA

Stephen Lawson

Uhane killed his jet pack's throttle as he alighted in a grain field on the floating city's edge. It wasn't the only contract he'd ever taken against the corvidians, but it was the first that required him to move an entire platform.

"I don't care how it's done," Mano had said. "They're blocking out our sunlight. Our solar floats have been down for a week. Our kelp beds are dying."

Mano was chieftain of the Rana clan, merfolk that lived in a plastic city in the water near Uhane's tribe. He'd come with a delegation to plead their case before the *Keiki o Ke Aka*, whose business it was to make weapons for their one mercenary representative. Uhane's grandfather had been *Mea Kaua* and had trained Uhane's father. Now Uhane carried the mantle for the village.

Negotiation with the corvidians would be pointless. The Rana had nothing the corvidians wanted except access to fishing waters. The merfolk's plastic cities held nothing of value for the anointed bird men or their cousins, the vesparians—the wasp people.

Since the Great Fire, this was the way of the world.

Merfolk—faweyl as they called themselves—scavenged the plastic the firstblood discarded. The faweyl raised their young in oceans teeming with sharks, giant jellies, and squid, while corvidians and vesparians used the magic of antigravity to float in the skies above. The All Lords had given the Anointed everything—wings, floating cities, and computers to speak with them directly.

Even descendants of the firstblood like Uhane didn't speak to the All Lords. For the lowly faweyl, such a thing was unthinkable. They'd been made to bring the oceans to order—to make something beautiful of the firstblood's six-pack rings, milk jugs, and shopping bags.

"I've assassinated corvidian council members and fishing parties before," Uhane had said, "but moving an entire city—that's going to take some doing. All the Anointed are fighting a war for airspace right now. They'll be well armed, and it will be dangerous. Expensive."

"These are good fishing waters," Mano had said. "We've made them so by cultivating the fish in our swirl. We've planted what good fish eat, built tunnels and mazes sharks can't penetrate. We have a relationship with the fish, or had one, until those sky demons came. The faweyl have no means of flight, and our bodies would burst even if we dared. Your kind can do this though, Uhane.

"The firstblood once made machines to live in the ocean like faweyl and devices to fly in the air like the Anointed—higher, perhaps."

So they agreed on a price. Uhane knew it had cost them dearly—and likely incurred a debt from the Tenek clan. Mano had laid down the coin—half in advance, as was the custom.

Uhane had gathered the tools of his trade: jet pack, Gauss rifle, swarm armor, naginata, knives, and an assortment of brimstone, swarm, and void grenades. He'd twisted the grip on his naginata, collapsing the pole to a quarter of its full length, then inserted the blade in a sheath on his jet pack.

To cross the miles of ocean between his village and the floating city, Uhane climbed into the clan's prop-driven ekranoplan. It was a smaller ground-effect vehicle than the jet-driven ekranoplans the Soviets had once used. It could transport twelve people comfortably, flying just meters above the water at a rate faster than any boat.

After touching down among the wheat stalks, Uhane released the jet pack's control grips and the turbojets folded down onto the pack's frame. His swarm armor changed to match the wheat—amber with black vertical stripes to imitate the shadows. It didn't hide his weapons or his face, but the adaptive camouflage had helped him avoid detection more than once.

He listened for sounds of alarm or movement nearby but heard none. He sniffed the air—wheat, salt water, and a hint of rain. He looked back to the horizon. A few miles away, thunderheads had massed and were dumping rain in long black streaks. Two other platform cities, nearer to each other than to this one, exchanged fire. Tiny specks of flying men—from here he couldn't tell if they were vesparian or corvidian—soared through the air between platforms. A few fell into the ocean. The water carried the buzz of machine-gun fire—like thunder chasing lightning. One of those cities might serve the same All Lord as this one. They might call for reinforcements during their skirmish, leaving fewer troops for Uhane to elude or kill. Even better if the rain reached this platform, as it would keep most people inside.

Uhane turned to the wheat, pulled the naginata from his back, and slung the coilgun in its place. He twisted the naginata's grips. The pole extended to its full length. He heard a muffled scream not unlike a human girl's. There were whispers and sounds of a struggle. Uhane moved toward it. The wheat rippled with movement.

Their broad wings made it hard to see, but Uhane had no doubt what was happening. Two corvidian boys crouched over a girl. One held her arms as the other wrestled with her legs. She kicked, knocking him back on his heels, but he only smiled, folded his wings, and pushed her knees apart.

Uhane crept forward, silent as a shadow. Their adrenaline would be up, he knew. They'd have tunnel vision, focused only on the girl whose leggings hung from a stalk nearby.

He paused, only for a moment. Fighting in wheat was like fighting in bamboo. Slashing attacks were difficult. Uhane lunged out of the wheat and thrust the naginata's blade through the first corvidian's back. It was a surgical strike, just above the left wing's root and into the heart. He pulled the blade free. The first corvidian collapsed onto the girl. The other's eyes widened. He opened his mouth to yell, but Uhane's second thrust went through his throat. Uhane twisted before withdrawing the blade. The corvidian gasped, clutching his throat. He gurgled, trying to scream. The girl struggled under the weight of the first corvidian's corpse. Uhane dropped the naginata and stepped forward. He pulled a short knife from his belt, batted the corvidian's hands aside, and thrust the blade between his ribs. He twisted up, severing the inferior vena cava.

Putting a hand to the corvidian's face, Uhane shoved him backward so he wouldn't collapse on the girl.

Uhane listened. He scanned the wheat. They were alone now.

"Don't scream," he said as he retrieved her leggings from the wheat stalk. They were light, elastic, almost nonexistent fabric. Corvidians always wore such things. They improved aerodynamics and displayed nature's gifts—or more accurately, the All Lords' gifts. He pulled the corpse from her with one hand and tossed the leggings into her lap. He looked away as she pulled them on, but kept her in his peripheral vision. He waited for the gasp of the deep inhale that would precede a scream. None came.

When she was clothed, he asked, "Did you know them?"

She looked from one corpse to the other and whimpered before nodding. She didn't cry though. She was too scared or too numb to cry. She couldn't be more than nineteen or twenty. Uhane picked up the naginata and laid it between them as he crouched at her feet. She'd curled into a ball. She was a pixieish thing—petite, with auburn hair and bright green eyes. "I'm Uhane. What's your name?"

"M—" she stammered. "Mera."

"What city is this, Mera?" he asked. "What All Lord does it serve?"

"New Brush," she said. "Cern governs."

"We're a long way from Cern," Uhane said. "He's been busy."

Uhane knew history. World War III—the Great Fire— had been nuclear war on a scale unimagined during the Cold War. NATO and Russia had fought what they'd dubbed the Dark States—China, North Korea, Iran, Saudi Arabia, Venezuela, and the African Alliance. Only the tiniest sliver of humanity had survived thermonuclear war, EMP damage, and radioactive fallout. The survivors had all been islanders with minimal access to technology.

Shielded by rock or housed underwater, four Artificial Superintelligences had survived the EMPs. They'd constructed robots to rebuild civilization, but soon realized humans required fewer resources to produce and feed. CERN had been the first to develop antigravity, which he'd shared with the others. This had allowed decontaminated material to float above the radiation. Google had synthesized the first vesparians, and shared his CRISPR Cas9 edits with the others for their cloning labs. Lomonsov had designed corvidians. SCCAS had observed the mass of plastic waste in the ocean and hatched the first faweyl. When they'd finished, the ASIs had wagered on which of the Anointed species would prove most adaptable.

Their creations scattered and multiplied. More floating cities were built in the air, and plastic cities in the sea. They decontaminated waste from the old world and raised it into the new, where fruits and grains grew on platforms kilometers above the surface. CERN became Cern the All Lord to his people. SCCAS became Scaz, Google remained Google, and Lomonsov became Lumons.

The platforms drifted, and the Anointed discovered the

wealth of fish in the open ocean. The space between platforms tightened. The ASIs stopped sharing design improvements and software updates. Cern forged an alliance with Lumons. They struck Google's platforms in the South Pacific and overwrote city-governance software. Google formed a hasty alliance with Scaz and struck back. The resulting war had been on now for over a year, with ASIs fighting for dominance and faweyl struggling to survive under a darkened sky.

With the military and police focused on security and fighting, opportunists took what they could. They looted platforms. They raped.

"You're firstblood," Mera said.

"Yes," Uhane said.

"How did you come here?" she asked.

"Magic," Uhane said.

She stared at him, perhaps believing him. The All Lords governed wisely but they didn't teach the Anointed everything. The firstblood held many secrets.

"I need to move this city," Uhane said. "Your people are killing a village of merfolk by blotting out the sun. Do you know how to move it?"

Mera shook her head. "Only the aerophants can repair the antigravity or move the platform."

He studied her. Young as she was, her eyes betrayed a fierce intellect. She had an honest face.

"Mera," he said, "I'm going to offer you a deal. How much family do you have in New Brush?"

"None," she said. "We're raised in collectives from three years old, then re-platformed at sixteen. Cern wants us to see only him as father."

That was new. None of the other platforms he'd been to had devolved into full-on autocratic communism.

"I'm going to kill a lot of people before I move this city, Mera. I'm also going to destroy the steering controls. A guide would limit the number of people who might cross my path. If you help me, I can take you somewhere no one will ever hurt you again. It's a dangerous world for a girl with no father or brothers to look after her."

"You can't—"

"I can," Uhane said, "and I will."

She recoiled, fear growing in her eyes. She inhaled. Uhane leaped and clamped a hand over her mouth, stifling the scream. Then, he slowly pulled his hand away and held her. He pressed his cheek against her neck and ran his hand over her hair. She struggled for a moment, confused by the whirl of emotion.

"Don't scream," he whispered. "Please."

Her body shook as she sobbed.

"I like you, Mera," Uhane said softly. "I can't promise you'll survive if I tie you up and leave you here, but I can't have you warning the others. Now let me look at you. They were rough on you."

She didn't resist as he examined her. He found no blood in her ruffled feathers. He felt her wing bones. All her bones were hollow, with thinner walls than a firstblood's. He could've snapped them with minimal effort if he'd wanted to. She trembled at his touch, but didn't pull away.

"You'll be fine," he said. "Bruised a bit, but nothing's broken."

"I didn't want to move here from Ershling," Mera said

as she wiped tears from her eyes. "You're the first man since I came here that's—"

Her cheeks flushed, and she looked away.

"What would I need to do?" she asked.

"I need one of these aerophants," Uhane said. "Just show me where to go, and stay behind me if—*when*—there's fighting."

Mera chewed her lower lip. She looked down at the two bodies.

"All right," she said.

He helped her, gently, to her feet.

"Their chambers are a kilometer or so that way I think." She gestured through the wheat stalks. "It's night, so I don't think anyone will be there. Only the watches are out now."

Mera led the way out of the wheatfield. Uhane collapsed his naginata and swapped it for his Gauss rifle. The lower-tier farmland gave way to the rising structure of the living zone. Above the habitable space was more sod with vegetables alternated with solar paneling.

"Where are the watch stations?" Uhane asked as he scanned the structure.

"I don't really—"

Fifty meters ahead, a light snapped on, temporarily blinding them.

"Identify yourself," a voice boomed.

"Take cover," Uhane said.

Mera took a step backward before leaping into the air.

Uhane shouldered his Gauss rifle and pulled the trigger. One tiny steel spike, silently accelerated by electromagnetic coils, shot from the barrel. The light shattered, and Uhane levered another round into the chamber before adjusting his sight picture. He fired another silent spike and one corvidian dropped before two more returned fire. Uhane dropped to one knee as a bullet whizzed past his head, ignored by his swarm armor. A burst of what looked like black steam shot out from his shoulder and deflected a second bullet, ricocheting it past him into the wheatfield.

Uhane fired, levered, and fired again. He scanned his surroundings, but no more bullets came.

"Mera," he whispered, but she didn't appear. Was she backing out—counting on him to lose in a gunfight?

Had she been hit?

He ran toward the guard post to confirm his kills. One of the corvidians had a small radio clipped to a belt. It was remarkably light. Uhane attached it to his jet pack's harness. He heard a noise behind him and spun, barrel raised.

Mera crouched, perched atop the barricade in front of the shattered search light. Uhane lowered his rifle.

"Give me one of their guns," she said.

"No," Uhane said.

"You're going to take on an entire city by yourself? If I'm casting my lot in with you, at least let me help."

"Do you even know how to shoot?"

"Well enough. We got lessons in school, ever since the fighting started."

"Fine," Uhane said. "Don't point it at me. And don't shoot unless you really have to. Mine's silent, and there's no flash."

He handed her a rifle. Its stock was a honeycomb of

lightweight polymer. He grabbed a harness with two extra magazines and helped her put it on.

The radio crackled and a staticky voice said, "Weller post, report. *Lilt Union.*"

"Do you know their code phrases?" Uhane asked Mera. She shook her head.

"We need to go, then," Uhane said. "Which way? Up?"

"I wouldn't know when we were above the aerophants' chambers."

"In, then."

Uhane moved toward the gaping maw of the platform's three-story-high interior. Several cracks rang out from the darkness. Black steam shot out from his armor—this time from his abdomen and legs. Bullets impacted the ground around him. One bullet, which would've gone through his stomach, stopped in midair and fell. This took more energy from the nanomachines, but they did what was needed to protect him.

Uhane returned fire. The corvidian soldier took cover. Uhane pulled a brimstone grenade from his armor, pushed in and rotated the fuse lever, and hurled it above the corvidian's position. White-hot fire erupted from the spot. The corvidian screamed. He leaped up, flailed at his flaming wings with his hands, and took flight for half a second before falling back to the ground and writhing in agony.

A door opened on the floor above, and more corvidians poured out onto the catwalk. Uhane shot one in the doorway and tossed in a swarm grenade. More screams echoed from inside the room as Uhane shot another corvidian on the catwalk. Uhane's armor erupted outward and bullets fell around him as he pulled out his jet-pack control grips. The turbojets extended to the sides and he leaped up onto the catwalk. He stabbed one corvidian in the heart and shoved the body into the one behind him. Uhane slashed through his wing as he stumbled, then hurled him over the railing. Unable to fly for the first time in his life, the corvidian crashed into the ground below with a sickening crack. He didn't get up.

"Come on," Uhane said to Mera. "We need to get out of the open."

She alighted behind him a second later as Uhane stepped into the room he'd swarmed. It was some sort of lounge, with plush furniture. Five corvidians lay dead within, though Uhane couldn't be certain of their genders. All had massive holes through their flesh. Arms had been stripped to the bone. Faces were missing. A thin black mist covered patches of the floor.

Uhane held up his left arm and opened the control screen on the inside of his wrist. He pressed an icon. The grenade's black mist gathered at his feet, then fused with his armor as the swarm rejoined their kin.

He looked to Mera, then tapped another icon to force the swarm to stop all bullets rather than deflecting them. He could've kicked himself for not doing so sooner. Only luck had kept her from getting hit by bullets intended for him thus far.

He heard movement above and running footfalls outside.

"What's on the next floor?" Uhane asked.

"A diner, I think," Mera said. "Decks two and three are all food and shops here. Warehousing's all deck one. Residential's further into the belly."

Uhane removed a void grenade from his armor and pulled the cover from a strip of adhesive on its side.

"I'm going to lift you to the ceiling," he said. He handed the grenade to Mera. "Press this to it, then push this lever in and twist. We'll have about six seconds."

Mera obediently slung her rifle and stepped into Uhane's cupped hands. She did as instructed, and he half tossed her toward the door. Her wings fanned and she tiptoed out onto the catwalk. Uhane watched her step back as footsteps approached. He counted the seconds in his head, lunged for the door, and grabbed the approaching soldier by the harness. Uhane hurled him into the room and stepped out just as the void grenade detonated in a bright flash. Wind rushed inward as even the air was annihilated, leaving a vacuum in its wake.

Heavy crashing and thudding noises came from within. Uhane grabbed Mera by the wrist and pulled her back inside. The soldier's legs were just inside the door, along with the wings and torsos of several corvidians from the deck above. A perfect circle three meters in diameter had been cut into the ceiling. Uhane jetted up through it. A cook approached the hole, eyes wide, but he was empty-handed.

Uhane leveled the Gauss rifle on him and asked, "You want to live?"

The cook nodded.

"Is there a back door?"

The cook ushered Uhane and Mera out through the kitchen and led them to a supply elevator.

Elthgar the Aerophant sat alone in the Upper Nest of

the aerophant chambers. He came here at night to be alone, away from the aerophants' communal living quarters. Elthgar remembered how it had been when New Brush was first forged and lifted into the sky. People had space to move and think. One needn't have listened to or smelled the other aerophants every hour of every day. Cern, it seemed, cared only about practicalities. The All Lords gave notice to aesthetics and the human soul only when they directly affected work output. So Elthgar tinkered with his small antigravity repulsors at night. With spare parts, he made tiny models of cities and machines the firstblood had used in the prior age.

Elthgar examined the box in front of him. It was a miniaturized version of a larger machine he'd been toying with. He held the box with one hand and flipped a switch on its surface. Instantly, all the levitating models dropped to the table. He reversed the switch, and the models leaped back to life, floating as they had before.

Twenty minutes ago, the alarms had sounded, and a rush of soldiers had passed by, responding to the threat. From what he could hear, the interlopers were at least a mile away and few in number. They would be dealt with quickly and would be no concern to an old man whose only solace was in tinkering with models.

Elthgar sat up straight, suddenly alert. A shiver ran down his spine. He smelled something like ozone when—

A bright light flashed as a void sphere expanded— stopping fifteen centimeters from his arm—and just as quickly collapsed. Wind rushed toward the void, carrying his antigravity models with it. Small cities, airplanes, and a mag-lev monorail clattered to the floor.

Two figures stepped through the circular hole in the wall. One was a man without wings—a firstblood. He wore armor that blended in with the walls and carried bizarre and unidentifiable weapons. The smaller figure was a girl, though in his advanced years, Elthgar couldn't tell her age. She might've been sixteen or twenty-four. They all seemed younger as time went by.

"This one is an aerophant," the girl said. "We've come through at the right place."

"Good evening," the firstblood said. "My name is Uhane. My apologies for disturbing your work."

"Elthgar," the aerophant said. This firstblood had manners—something else that had disappeared when Cern began communal child-rearing. Despite the circumstances, it was refreshing. "Good evening to you as well. Are you here to kill me?" Elthgar discovered that he might not mind being killed, provided it was quick.

"I'd prefer not to," Uhane said. "I just need help moving the city."

"The faweyl hired you," Elthgar said. "I warned the others they wouldn't surrender their fishing waters quietly, even if they've no understanding of flight."

"They just want to live," Uhane said. "I was their best option."

Elthgar gnawed on his lower lip for a moment.

"I'll help you," he said, "if you help me."

"Help you with what?" Uhane asked.

"Take me with you," Elthgar said. "I hate this place. Put me on one of your firstblood islands, far from the others. I know I'm institutionalized, but I can learn. Bring me food until I'm able to fish on my own and I'll teach you antigravity. We can be—what's the word—*symbiotic*. I haven't many years left. I'd rather not spend them in this cramped hell."

Uhane stared at a point on the wall for a moment.

"Deal," he said finally. "I've room in the wingship for twelve. If it's seclusion you want, there's a small uninhabited island a mile from my village."

"In that case, firstblood, let's not delay. They're bound to search here soon enough."

Elthgar shoved the box he'd been working on into his pocket and led his two new friends to a maintenance hatch that led into the bowels of New Brush's propulsion system.

Several minutes later, Elthgar rose from a machine and closed the hatch.

"You'll have at least a day of travel before they're even able to stop forward propulsion," he said. "I've shut off the circuits that supply power to the thrust engines on the city's three other sides. The other aerophants won't be able to turn or slow down. Only wind or air resistance will slow the acceleration. Once I turn on main thrust, away she goes. You ready?"

"What's to stop the other aerophants from just killing power to main thrust?" Uhane asked.

"Ignorance, mostly," Elthgar said. "That's the problem with being cared for by the state. None of the new kids Cern gave me actually care about the craft, and none are my kin so we've nothing to bind us. I've tried to teach them, but they just shrug me off as a doddering old fool. They play their games, and mostly I'm content to be left alone. There's only one aerophant running antigrav and propulsion in New Brush, and you're looking at him. It'll take a day for Cern to show them how to undo the first fraction of what I've set up here. The city will be long gone, believe me. Ready with the grenade?"

"Ready."

Elthgar pulled a series of levers, and a mechanical groan echoed in the walls—like a giant growling in a cave after being woken from a thousand-year slumber.

Uhane set his last brimstone grenade on the control panel and waited until Elthgar and Mera were halfway up the ladder. Then he activated the fuse.

Uhane felt a buzz in his armor. He looked down at his wrist's control panel. A glowing circular icon flashed a message from the *Keiki o Ke Aka* village. He tapped it. A small patch of his wrist armor billowed upward and coalesced into the figure of Kauka, the village healer.

"Kauka?" Uhane said. "What is it?"

"Mano returned, with warriors," she said.

Uhane narrowed his eyes, unsure how to interpret this.

"Did he bring the rest of the payment?" Uhane asked. "I've just set the city adrift. The Rana will have their sunlight back soon."

"No," Kauka said. "He came demanding the first half of the payment back. He said their village cannot survive. He has Ali'i and some others in the chief's hut. I managed to sneak away."

The merfolk had waited for the exact moment when Uhane had completed his mission, but when he was too far away to defend the village. Uhane held his breath for a moment, biting back a string of profanity. Then, slowly, he exhaled.

"Did Ali'i warn them they're making a terrible mistake?" Uhane asked.

"Yes," Kauka said. "The Rana laughed. They said they fight better underwater than the *Mea Kaua*, and that you were welcome to visit. Mano said that a naginata and coilgun would be useless beneath the surface."

"I see."

"Uhane?"

"Stay out of sight, Kauka," Uhane said. "Just in case. Ali'i will stall them. I'll come up with something."

He looked back toward the hatch and lamented burning the thrust controls.

A sound in the passage ahead made him look up. He'd been distracted. Now he was staring into the startled eyes of two corvidian boys. Their clothes were similar to Elthgar's—they bore the markings of the aerophant caste.

Elthgar and Mera froze in place.

"Hello, Farrin," Elthgar said. "Hello, Nelgar."

"What are you doing down here, old man?" Farrin asked. "We're not scheduled to move for another—"

Then his eyes settled on Uhane, and the absence of wings on Uhane's back.

"Is that the—"

"I can explain, Farrin," Elthgar said. "I can—"

Nelgar moved, and Uhane heard the crack of a pistol shot. Elthgar spun and crumpled to the floor. Mera, directly behind him, screamed and flapped her wings. As if in slow motion, Uhane saw two feathers fly from the back of her left wing, and a bloody hole where they'd been.

He was supposed to be in front of her. His armor was supposed to protect her.

Uhane grabbed Mera by the waist and spun their bodies together so his back was to Nelgar. He heard two more cracks and felt his armor ripple.

Rage filled him—a rage he'd been warned against; a rage he'd suppressed on every contract until this one. The *Keiki o Ke Aka* revered their elders. They valued them and learned from them. Unlike this slime. Until now, Uhane had never gone into a fight with a girl at his side. He'd never seen one that he cared for hurt.

He *did* care for her. In that fraction of a second, he knew she was more than a guide—more than a tool to accomplish the mission. He caught the tiniest glimmer of fear and pain in her eyes before he turned.

In one smooth motion, he shouldered his Gauss rifle and shot Nelgar—not in the head or center mass, but in the femoral artery. Nelgar screamed and collapsed to the floor, clutching his leg. Uhane slung the Gauss rifle and drew his naginata. He snapped the pole to its full length. He struck Farrin's clavicle. The thin, hollow bones snapped under the razor-sharp blade's force as Uhane cut down to Farrin's heart in one stroke.

Farrin fell dead while Nelgar screamed. Uhane stood over Nelgar, ignoring the pool of blood gushing from Farrin's rent-open torso.

"He got mercy," Uhane said, gesturing to Farrin with his chin, "because he was merely rude. But you—you hurt my friends. I'll take my time with you."

He pinned Nelgar's wrist with his foot and held the naginata's blade over his face. Farrin's blood dripped into Nelgar's eyes.

"Uhane," a voice whispered behind him.

He remembered Mera.

Her softness and the sweetness in her eyes came back to him.

Cruelty would burn what innocence she had left. In time, cruelty would make her hate him.

He thrust the naginata down sharply into Nelgar's throat, severing blood vessels and spine with one cut. The boy spasmed, briefly, then his eyes closed. It was fast. Clean.

Uhane turned and found Mera applying pressure to Elthgar's chest wound. Her own wound hadn't bled much, as the bullet had missed the major blood vessels in her wing.

"This is—" Elthgar said. "Dammit. Those stupid idiot boys."

His wings were matted with blood flowing from the exit wound in his back. Elthgar struggled with a thing in his pocket before managing to pull out a small box with a switch.

"I think this might be the key to evening the odds for the faweyl," Elthgar said. "If used correctly, it might end the war."

"What is it?" Uhane asked.

"Anti-antigravity," Elthgar said.

"So . . ." Uhane said, "gravity?"

"Don't make jokes, you dolt," Elthgar said. "I'm dying."

Elthgar half smiled despite himself.

"Anti-antigravity, then," Uhane said. "How does it work?"

"It generates a field that nullifies graviton repulsors," Elthgar said. "There's a bigger one I've been working on in the Upper Nest. Not big enough to drop a city, but big enough to make people notice."

Uhane remembered Ali'i and Kauka, held hostage in the village. He remembered that corvidians were hunting him and could appear at any moment. Despite this, he held Elthgar's hand as the old man faded.

"I might not have needed an island for myself," Elthgar said, "if the rest are like you. You're a good lad. Be smart with the—"

He never finished the sentence, but Uhane understood.

Several minutes later, Uhane and Mera stood at the city's edge. They'd rigged the larger anti-antigravity machine to a remote and fastened it above the repulsors on that side of the city.

"My wingship is below us," he said. "Are you able to fly?"

She flexed her wing and winced from the pain. She tried it again and bit back a scream.

"Hold on to me," he said. "I'll slow our descent, and you can help steer."

Kauka's communicator came to life. Uhane's face appeared. "Kauka," Uhane said, "tell Mano to look through the door of the hut to the horizon."

"What should he be looking for?" Kauka asked.

"He can't miss it," Uhane said.

★ ★ ★

Kauka entered the chief's hut, and two of the Rana mermen grabbed her by the arms. Her hands shook, but she held Mano's gaze.

"Uhane says you should look outside," she said.

"Uhane?" Mano said. He fanned his gills. "Where is Uhane?"

Kauka said nothing, so Mano walked to the door. Miles away, the floating city of New Brush hung at a sickening forty-five degree angle, with its lowest edge just above the Rana city. If it fell, it would crush them. Mano gasped.

Kauka extended the communicator toward him. He snatched it from her grasp. Uhane appeared in a hologram.

"You were to move the city," Mano said. "It's still there, albeit at a strange cant."

"You were to pay my clan in full, not hold them hostage," Uhane said. "The steering and engine control have been rendered inoperable, but the antigravity controls still function. Engine thrust, combined with reduced antigravity on the lower platform, holds the city in place. I've rigged a bomb to the main thrust. If I set it off, the city falls like an axe on your people. Release my clan. Now. Your men might live. You—I am not so sure about you, Mano."

"I have your chief," Mano said, "and now your healer. Would you sacrifice them for a sum of money?"

"We have a reputation to uphold," Uhane said, "but let's negotiate. Perhaps we may reach an agreement that involves your silence. Perhaps partial payment will suffice—some fraction of the original amount. Wait for my return."

Mano looked to the floating city, then to his men. One of them nodded.

"Very well," Mano said.

Mano, the Rana soldiers, Ali'i, Kauka, and the rest of the *Keiki o Ke Aka* all waited with few words between them. Soon, a speck appeared between them and New Brush. The speck grew into Uhane's ekranoplan, which docked soon thereafter. Uhane disembarked, and a petite figure with a bandaged wing stepped out behind him. He spoke—gently, it seemed—to the winged girl. She waited on the beach.

"Your weapons!" Mano yelled, while Uhane was still many meters away. "Leave them there."

Mano made sure the knife he held next to Ali'i glinted in the torch light.

Uhane doffed his jet pack with the naginata, then his Gauss rifle, and lastly his knives and remaining grenades.

He held up his hands and wriggled his fingers before approaching. He bore no weapons—only his armor.

"We will make our dealings inside the hut," Mano said, "in case your new friend is a sniper."

"Suits me," Uhane said. He smiled.

They entered the chief's hut. Uhane met Ali'i's gaze. He looked to Kauka, and her hands stopped trembling.

Mano's gills flared. He was silent for a moment. Finally, he said, "Before we begin—"

"Yes, before we begin," Uhane said, "I'd like to show you something."

Mano's eyes narrowed.

"This island held a military research lab in the time before the Great Fire, and even after," Uhane said. "There is something like one of your All Lords that lives deep in the rock of the island. It has never ceased its research."

"What does—"

"It knows the *Keiki o Ke Aka* by electric tattoos we receive as children," Uhane said. Then, to the others, he said, "Show them."

Ali'i, Kauka, and the others raised their forearms to show a tattoo of a glyph over a pineapple.

"Enough of this," Mano said. "What does this have to do with anything? We came to get our money back, not to get a lesson on your tribal lore."

"You want one?" Uhane asked.

"One what?"

"One of the tattoos."

"No," Mano said. "Why on God's blue Earth would I want a—"

"Mine's under my armor," Uhane said, "right here."

He lifted his wrist and tapped an icon.

Uhane's armor erupted in needle-thin spikes. The black nanoparticle appendages lanced through the eyeballs of the closest Rana, while simultaneously piercing the heart of another. Blood spurted in an arc up the wall as a paper-thin nanoblade sliced through the carotid artery of a third merman's neck.

Mano screamed as he watched his own knife-wielding hand fall to the floor. Uhane had given the armor special instructions for the leader—sever the wrist, but leave him alive. Mano fell to his knees. He clutched the bloody stump against his other arm, trying to stop the flow of blood. He didn't even register that all his soldiers were dead.

"Well," Uhane said, "don't say I didn't offer. Electric tattoos are great for target-list exclusions."

Mano finally looked up. He saw the blood on the wall and ceiling. He stared at the still-warm corpses of his men.

"You," Mano said. "You don't have to kill me."

"That's not your decision to make," Uhane said, stepping closer. Mera wasn't here. He could savor this.

Mano reached for his severed right hand and tried to pry the knife loose. Uhane closed the distance between them and ground his boot into Mano's wrist.

"We have a reputation to uphold," Uhane said. "If I let one customer short us or get away with such treachery, everyone will try it."

Nanites flowed down from Uhane's legs and swarmed like liquid up Mano's arm and over his body. The merman screamed until the swarm tore through his face and larynx. In a matter of seconds, it had eaten him alive.

"Are any of you hurt?" Uhane asked, looking to the others.

"No," Ali'i said. "Not one."

Uhane looked through the door and gestured at New Brush, suspended in the air miles away over the Rana city.

"And the cities?" Uhane said. "What message should we send to the world—to the other faweyl and Anointed?"

The chief pondered this. He looked to the corpses on the floor, and his eyes settled on the bare bone of what had been Mano's face.

"Leaders bring such misery to their people," Ali'i said. "You have exacted vengeance enough, and Mano has paid the remainder of the contract with his blood. Send the message that we are reasonable."

Uhane nodded, then walked out the door. His feet carried him back to the beach.

Introducing Ali'i to the anti-antigravity device could wait. Perhaps the island's All Lord would find a way to make an anti-antigravity beam weapon with it—one that might be used from a long distance.

"Your people," Mera said. "Are they safe?"

"They are," Uhane said. "Fortunately, none have lived to tell the secrets of *Keiki o Ke Aka* technology. My armor is a weapon when needed, though it drains significant energy. It must sleep soon."

"And . . . New Brush?"

Uhane lifted his wrist and tapped a series of icons. Miles away, the floating city slowly began to level itself.

"My chief said the price of double-crossing us was paid with the faweyl leader's blood. He said that civilians needn't suffer for Mano's treachery."

Mera looked to New Brush, then lowered her eyes. Hesitantly, not knowing if his armor might also kill her, she extended her fingers toward Uhane's. He didn't move at first. Then the swarm pulled back from the skin of his hand, and he let his fingers interlace with hers. She lifted her eyes to meet his.

"I have no one and nothing here," she said, "I would remain with you, if you would have me."

He lifted her fingers to his face, and she brushed them across his lower lip. He kissed her knuckles.

"I would have you," Uhane said softly. The swarm rippled back from his other hand, and he ran his fingers over her injured wing's feathers. He followed it down to the root and placed a hand on the small of her back.

Then, in a gesture instinctively retained by both their races—perhaps in some unaltered part of their DNA—he lifted her hand over her shoulder and pushed against her waist with the other hand. She twirled on the sand in a dance that needed no tune and which ended with their hands clasped and arms extended. He pulled her in again, dipping her back toward the sand as her wings flared.

She smiled for the first time in ages as the city of the Anointed floated away under the stars.

WAVE FORMS

Nina Kiriki Hoffman

When the Wayward Wave of Magic swept over the world and left everybody changed, I was too messed up for a while to pay much attention to what the rest of the world was doing.

Everybody got some nugget of magic, some quirk, some shift in who they were and what they could do. Some people got cool changes, like being able to see long distances, or levitate, or breathe underwater. Some people got devastating changes, like growing extra limbs or tails or an extra head, having their bones turn to jelly or ice, or being blind to everything but ultraviolet light.

Me, I woke up in a different body every morning. I hadn't figured out whether I was inadvertently borrowing the bodies of people who existed, leaving them to be me for a day, or whether I was just becoming someone brand new every morning. The new selves were various, ranging along the spectrum from wildly weird to normal and back the other way weird.

I usually figured out how to make each body work by

the time I was too tired to stay awake any longer, but then, poof! I was someone else when I woke up. I went from being Kim Robinson, psychology major at the University of Oregon, to Kim whom no one recognized anymore, including me.

So I kinda missed World War III, where power structures broke down around the world and then rebuilt themselves. Only they kind of built back up the way they used to be. Rich people could hire all the best witches and wizards to control everybody else. An occasional powerful witch or wizard figured out how to rise to the top, steal all the money and power from the less powerful, and carve out their own fiefdoms. It was a mess.

Most everyone lived in chopped-up bits of previous countries, because you never knew how many or what sort of magic users the next settlement over had on staff. Some of those people could create pandemics, some could turn people into animals, and some could just cast a spell that made everybody's mouth lock shut so they all starved to death, except maybe people in the hospital who could figure out IVs. Some curses were permanent and some temporary, but basically there were a lot of people you didn't like when they were angry, so best to lie low and not upset them. Unless you had great power yourself, and didn't accept the responsibility. The first three months after the Wayward Wave, a lot of people died. Supply chains broke down. Cities burned, deserts spread, forests died. And in other places, new mountain chains rose up, forests grew stronger and scarier and able to defend themselves, and new islands appeared.

The northern half of Oregon got swallowed up by a

committee of magic users who combined Portland, Oregon, and Vancouver, Washington, into a supercity that controlled shipping for the region and put a chokehold on trade for surrounding territories.

Down the valley from there, three wizards who could freeze you in place and do whatever they liked with you started bossing everyone around. Combined, they could freeze a lot of people at once, which made it hard to mount a workable defense against them. They just started telling us what to do, and most of us did it.

Most of the magic users with lesser powers hid their abilities, because the boss wizards, the Triumvirate of Talia, Frank, and Carolina, would force you to do work based on your quirks. One of the first things they did after they established a medium of exchange was take a census of everybody living in their territory. They doled out jobs for everyone, and if anyone protested, the protestors spent some time as statues people could throw rocks and tomatoes and yogurt at. If you were frozen overnight, someone might come by and pee on you, and if you had any personal enemies, they could do worse.

Still, the boss wizards wanted a functional community, so they tried to get everybody doing something they could stand that supported life as we used to know it. Construction, farming, road maintenance, textiles, entertainment, trucking, education, flea markets, places of worship, picking up the garbage—lots of things to do that sustained a lifestyle of comfort for most. Like most of the independent territories, the Triumvirate had a couple of financial wizards—a fairly rare quirk—to create currency so people could be paid for jobs and buy things and even trade across territorial lines. There was only one bank, and everybody used it.

I went on living in my studio apartment and hiding out from most of my neighbors. I couldn't hold a job because nobody knew me when I showed up the next day. I started out in daycare for children of retail workers—I'd done a lot of babysitting, as I told the census taker who'd come to my door a month after the Wave, when things were settling into a new routine, sort of. That day I was a woman in her forties who looked boring and reliable. The census taker told me where the daycare was, and I went there and put in a full day's work with children who were different from those I used to take care of. Every child had a quirk, and I had no way of stopping them from using their quirks aside from persuasion. Fortunately the woman in charge could stop other people's magic and even reverse it most of the time. I only spent half an hour being a Siamese cat, and less time than that with green hair and a tail.

The next morning, I was a teenaged girl with a shaved head and many piercings in uncomfortable places. I didn't even try going back to the daycare center.

My core self stayed the same no matter whom I woke up as, but my strength, age, appearance, and skill set shifted. Sometimes I had magical quirks and sometimes I didn't, and I didn't always discover what I could do before I changed again. What I did know was that there was no slot for me in my current community. Rumors flew about other communities up and down the West Coast and inland, but some had closed their borders; some had terrible living conditions for people who weren't high-powered wizards; some sounded even worse.

No place sounded like a good home for a body shifter like me.

The Triumvirate had brought newspapers back, since the Internet went crazy during the Wave, and broadcasting was no longer reliable. A few tech wizards in other territories were trying to get the Internet back up, but using it was full of life-threatening risks.

Japetta noticed me at the coffee shop. She sat down at my table with her latte cradled in her dark hands and said, "Hey there. I'm Japetta. Mind if I ask you a question?"

I was paging through want ads in search of any job that didn't depend on appearance. Phone salespeople looked promising, except not everyone had phones or service anymore. Scenery designer for stage plays might work if I could find the right stage manager or construction supervisor. Some days, though, I didn't have much body strength. Some days I was seventy years old and crippled with arthritis. Some days I needed a wheelchair to get anywhere, so I mostly stayed home. Some days I was a kid. The people who wanted kids to work for them were good people to avoid.

I didn't have much hope, but I still looked for the perfect job every day.

Today, I was a studly male in his twenties with an uncomfortable amount of body hair. I was furry on my chest and back, arms and legs. It kept me warmer than usual, but also took longer to dry when I got out of the shower, despite vigorous buffing with a towel. I had shaved, but the stubble came back pretty fast.

My closet was full of thrift store clothes in a lot of

different sizes so I could find something to fit every day, at least well enough to get out and find something else that worked better with my new body. If not for the trust fund my father had set up for me as soon as there was post-Wave money—his quirk turned out to be a green thumb; he could raise any kind of crop and make it yield extra—I would be so out of luck.

Today's outfit was a long-sleeved black T-shirt under overalls that were too big for me. I didn't mind. They had a lot of good pockets and straps that I tightened enough to hold them up without distorting my shape too much.

I looked up at Japetta, this beautiful Black woman with a 'fro that gave her a six-inch dark halo tipped with gold, and shrugged. "You can ask," I said.

"Do you, um, look different every day?"

"What?" I had made my situation clear to my brother and my parents and the person who lived in the next apartment to me, my best friend, Elias. And Grendel, my landlord, who lived in the basement. Nobody else knew. I thought.

"My quirk is I can see people's, uh, auras? And I see your aura or whatever you call it in here every day, mostly sitting at the same table, but your outside looks different every time."

I sighed. I had been stupid, always going to the same coffee shop and sitting at the same table. Habits could betray you.

"I see you checking out the want ads every day," she said.

"How come I never noticed you here?" I wondered. Maybe I had gotten too mired in the routine I'd established. Job hunt. Call a prospect, see if I could interview—I'd gotten a job as a security guard on the graveyard shift. When I showed up on day two looking like someone else, they fired me for sending in a substitute.

I was convinced there had to be something I could do.

"Well, I have a second quirk," she said. And then I was looking at a slender, colorless White girl with pale hair I might call dishwater—without the blond—and gray clothes that hid rather than showed her shape.

I glanced around to see if anybody else had noticed the transformation. Not that such a thing was rare anymore; people turned into all kinds of things these days. But doing it in public? Not so much.

She shifted back to her Black self, only now I had to wonder if either of the selves she'd shown me were real. "My Beth self, the shadow girl, nobody notices her. Not even the barista. She just drifts around, practically invisible. She's great for surveillance work."

"You with the government?" I asked. That would not be good.

"No. The opposite. You?"

"What's the opposite of the government?" I whispered.

"Want to find out?" She drank the rest of her latte and grabbed my hand.

"Hey," I said, then stuffed the newspaper and my Danish, wrapped in a napkin, into my navy blue backpack and chugged the rest of my coffee. I wasn't sure I wanted to go anywhere with a spooky woman who could turn into a ghost girl and back, but her grip was strong as she tugged me out of the shop, and I didn't have any solid plans for the rest of the day.

She led me through the downtown pedestrian walkway, past all the minor magicians performing for small change, the musicians spinning songs that might enchant you into doing something for them, the food carts selling roasted dead animals that hadn't existed before the Wave, the smoke dens and bars and supply stores and curiosity shops. We headed toward campus.

I hadn't been back to the university since the Wave. The first day I woke up as a big thirty-something Black guy with a broken nose and a tattoo of a rose in my left palm, instead of the twenty-two-year-old fashionable redheaded Kim who ran track and played hoops, I was so freaked out I didn't want anybody to see me. Let alone I had to figure out how to stand and walk and sit, and all that was strange and difficult, and I didn't have any clothes that fit.

From all the screams and fires and car crashes I heard outside that first morning, I didn't think it was safe to go out anyway.

The Internet was a crazy mess when I tried to find out what was happening. Google didn't work; it just kept coughing up weird and unrelated results to anything I put in the search box. Wikipedia had turned into Won't-ipedia, not searchable either, and occasionally casting curses right out of the screen at me as I tried to find answers. It turned my tight afro neon blue; after that, I decided to stop looking at the computer. My phone had turned into a brick. Literally.

I finally just watched out the window as everything went to hell. My fridge still worked, at least for the first two days, and I had gone grocery shopping the day before the Wave hit. Hiding out worked for me. Then I woke up as a granny. . . .

Japetta was leading me toward Frat House Row. I wondered if she had another identity as a frat boy. I mean, if she could be a ghost girl and a queen, what was to stop her from being a douchey guy? I knew from assuming identities.

But she sidestepped the frats and led me down the alley behind a brewpub and an ice cream parlor to a manhole with a salmon on its cover—"drains to stream." She glanced up and down the alley. Aside from some stinky dumpsters, it was clear. She lifted the cover and gestured me toward the hole. "Go on," she said. "There's a ladder. Quick."

Oh well, I thought, and slid down inside the dark hole, finding the rungs with my feet and wishing I had a light. I was glad today I had a coordinated body instead of a clumsy one. I was almost to the bottom when she slid in herself and pulled the cover back on tight, plunging us into darkness.

Except there were glowing things down the corridor, evenly spaced along one wall, the light not bright but greenish and somehow cold.

A sewage smell tainted the air, along with a fainter smell of . . . popcorn? Toast? A weird combo that made me nauseated and hungry. The air was cool, with a constant current blowing from the left-hand tunnel.

"Move," said Japetta, nudging my head with her foot.

I startled and stepped away from the bottom of the ladder. She came all the way down and stood beside me. "That way," she said, pointing left with her chin, toward the weird lights.

The tunnel had a broad walkway beside a channel that ran with dark water, with things bobbing along in it, paper and shit and who knew what else. Small animals fled before us, some jumping into the stream, some skittering up the walls. The water level in the channel was almost even with the walkway. "What happens when it floods?" I whispered.

"Shut up," Japetta said. We came even with the first of the strange light sources. A glowing green hunk of wood was attached to the wall by a basket. I wondered, but I didn't say anything. I wished I had stuffed a jacket in my backpack. It was cool down here.

We walked for a while, accompanied by the green lights and the flow of sewage, and then Japetta led me through an archway to the left into a short tunnel. She pressed some buttons on the far wall and a door opened, spilling light and popcorn scents out into the hallway. "Go on," she said, giving me a shove, and I moved past her into the cavern.

It looked like the inside of a lung, with graduated natural arches going off in the distance, the walls pitted and rough and glowing a gentle greenish gold. A small stream ran through the cavern in a narrow channel. No sewage there. The smell of popcorn was stronger here, as was the scent of burning wood. At the far end of the cavern was a picnic table holding a camp lantern and a big bowl of popcorn, flanked by benches, with two people sitting on them. Carved into the wall behind them were niches storing various things, and on the cavern floor was a ring of stones with a fire burning in it, the smoke wafting up to the ceiling. There must have been some way for it to escape, because the cavern wasn't smoky. In an alcove to the left, eight or ten camp cots stood, with pre-Wave sleeping bags and pads on them. In another alcove to the right, there was a stack of firewood.

Air flowed in from a tunnel at the far end of the cavern. I realized there were other alcoves shrouded with dim nets, probably hiding other supplies.

"Hey," Japetta said as we came to the table.

The two strangers had been watching us approach across the pebbly floor of the cavern. One was a very pale man with no hair—no eyebrows, even—and almost white eyes. He looked doughy and was mostly encased in a blue coverall. The other was a small woman with a lot of blond hair, wearing a red, long-sleeved shirt and black jeans. Her face was wizened and monkey-like.

"Howdy," said the bald man in a deep voice.

"Hi," said the small woman. "Who did you bring us today, Japetta?"

"This here's—well, shoot, I don't know your name."

"Kim," I said.

"Kim," Japetta repeated.

"Hello, Kim," said the bald man. "I'm Smarty, and this is Curlycue."

I waved and smiled. From day to day, I didn't know how people would react to my expressions. Sometimes they were scared of me, sometimes they mocked me, and sometimes they treated me like I was used to being treated. Smarty and Curlycue seemed pretty relaxed.

"Have you come to join the revolution?" Smarty asked.

"Revolution, you say?" I glanced at Japetta, who smiled and nodded. "Can you tell me more?"

"Curly?" Smarty said.

Curlycue steepled her fingers and whispered between her thumbs, and something spellish made me heat up till my skin felt like it would burn off.

"Stop it!" Japetta said. She slapped Curlycue's hands apart, and coolness soothed me as the heat left my skin. I was breathing hard, sweat on my face. I pulled out a handkerchief from one of my many pockets and swabbed my face.

"You brought an imposter here," said Smarty to Japetta.

"Kim's not—Kim's—that's their whole thing. They're not who they appear to be. They look different every day. Can you think of anyone better to spy for us? I mean, I have the one other form I can take, but Kim—"

"Kim's ready to leave," I said.

"No, wait," said Smarty. "Your quirk is that you change shape?"

I shrugged. "Every day. Japetta's the first one who figured it out, but if her quirk is reading auras, she's probably not the only one who can tell. I mean, I've heard of other people who can do that. Never ran into anybody, though."

Smarty nodded. "Still," he said.

"What are you revolting about?" I asked.

"Have you noticed people are disappearing?" said Curlycue. Her voice was surprisingly musical.

"What?"

"Anybody who demonstrates a bigger-than-normal quirk—like Solo Larry performing miracles of healing in the park blocks on the weekend—he's gone. I went by his house to ask if he was okay. His wife said he disappeared last week without a word. Same thing happened to Bowen the baker. He was giving away too much magical bread to the homeless. Now his shop is shuttered. Somebody doesn't like the people who help others."

"Did the census takers get your measure?" Smarty asked.

"Not this me," I said. "I can't even get on the grid when I want to."

"Hmm," he said. "How do you feel about the current government?"

"Could be worse," I said. "I've heard terrible stories about Idaho and Northern California."

"No way of knowing if the stories are true," said Curlycue. "The Tri-Goons control the media, and we've found facts that disprove a lot of the horror stories about other territories. We need our own network of news gatherers. If Japetta's right about you—"

"What if she's wrong?" I asked. "She doesn't know anything about me. Are you people going to threaten me?"

Curlycue steepled her fingers again and whispered into them. Bright-eyed, she looked at me. "Are you going to betray us?"

"How can I tell?" I said, before I could even think about my answer. "I don't want to betray anyone, but I don't even know who you are or what you want."

"We want to know what's really going on, and then we want to figure out how to make it better," said Japetta. "Maybe we can even figure out how to straighten out some of the magics that really screw up people's lives. Like yours." She took a deep breath and let it out. "Look. I'm good at reading auras, and in yours, I see a lot to like. Wouldn't you rather be out snooping around than sitting in that coffee shop all day looking at want ads?"

"What does it pay?" I asked.

Smarty sighed. "Yeah, it doesn't pay."

"Depends on what you find out," said Curlycue.

"Why don't you come out walking with me?" Japetta said. "Trial run. See whether you like it."

She was right about one thing. It would be nice to break my routine and try something new.

"Okay. Tomorrow morning. Meet you out front of the coffee shop at eight," I said.

Japetta smiled.

I opened my eyes the next day and raised my arms to study them in the morning light filtering in through my white curtains. Slender arms, medium brown skin, long-fingered hands. I felt my chest and found small breasts, then I threw back the covers and lifted my legs, stretched my feet back and forth. Long legs. I checked my crotch. No penis today. I let my arms and legs rest, closed my eyes, and listened to my insides. Nothing hurt. That was nice. No badly healed broken bones, no stomach ache, no arthritis in my joints. A good day.

I went into the bathroom and turned on the light for a look at my face. Broad nose, dark eyes, short curly hair. Not beautiful, not ugly. Probably a good body for wandering around watching things. I checked the weather by opening my window and sticking my arm out. Cool, cloudy, but not raining. After my shower, I dressed in dark slacks and an off-white sweater. I ate a banana and a protein bar. They both tasted more intense than usual; there were sour notes in the protein bar I'd never noticed in other bodies, and the bit of banana that had been bruised tasted super sweet and slimy.

I slid my backpack over my shoulders and walked down the block to the coffee shop. Japetta stood there in her Beth form, looking wispy and unpleasant. I stopped in front of her. The coffee shop door opened and a man came out, trailing the smell of coffee and pastries.

"Beth," I said.

"Kim," she said.

"I need coffee," we both said at the same time.

I had to order for her. She couldn't get the barista's attention.

Carrying our coffees, we went outside. We headed downtown toward the Bastion of Power. The Triumvirate had taken over the pre-Wave courthouse. Their living quarters were in the top story. The lower levels were divided into a courtroom where one or the other of them heard disputes and passed judgment, a public room where people were punished, a couple of jail cells, and some administrative offices. Out front were the park blocks where people set up barter and market stalls twice a week.

"Come here often?" I asked Beth.

"About once a week. I'm afraid if I came more often they'd notice. They have a bunch of lesser wizards doing security, and I've noticed one of them noticing me."

"What are we looking for?" I asked.

"That," she said, and pulled me into the shadows under a tree in the park block nearest the government building. Wizard Talia in her red robe of office swept out of the building, trailing several lesser wizards who looked around in all directions. Two of them had handguns in visible holsters at their sides, and a third carried a staff tipped with a silver claw.

The Red Wizard passed near us. We stood silent, heads bowed. As soon as she had gone on, toward the Palace Coffee Shop and Bakery—who knew high wizards went to coffee shops? Couldn't they hire lesser wizards to make them coffee, or even regular people?—Beth lifted her head. "Do you smell it?" she whispered.

I sniffed. Yes, there was a blue, cold smell in the morning air.

"She's going to freeze someone. She has to, or her talent turns inward. She'll find someone random, freeze them, and then invent a crime. Let's go."

By the time we got to the Palace Coffee Shop, it had already happened. We hovered outside, but could see in the open door. Two customers sat frozen at a table, their hands raised, still cupping mugs of coffee. An icicle hung from the woman's nose.

"They were discussing dissension," Wizard Talia told the barista, who was turned away, crafting a beverage for the wizard. "You heard them, didn't you?"

The barista nodded and turned to hand the wizard a coffee. She said nothing. The wizard swept out past us trailing minions, and we lowered our heads again. When she was gone, Beth stepped forward with a small camera and took pictures of the frozen people. We drifted away again. Beth led me to a hidden bench. We sat down, and she was Japetta again. She eyed me. "It's gotten worse," she said. "She used to do it every four or five weeks, and now it's once a week or more often. Sometimes Wizard Frank takes frozen prisoners out to the quarry and uses them for target practice."

Her words struck me. I curled in on myself, shivering.

"We need to document it," she said softly. "Will you help?"

I thought of the fragile peace established after the War of the Wave. Most of us had found a way forward. But if people could be targeted just for being in the wrong coffee shop—

—I didn't see how we could work our way around wizard power. But I wanted to try.

"I will," I said.

LUPUS BELLI

Julie Frost

I lost everything in World War Werewolf, including my girlfriend, my family, and my humanity. The lycanthropes had tried to convince us that growing fangs and fur three nights a month didn't make them monsters, and they were right, but we didn't listen.

I fought on the wrong side of that war.

Now I paid the price. The humans won and relegated werewolves to second-class noncitizens, with brands scarred on their hands using silver and wolfsbane, in segregated ghettos a half step above homelessness. Me too, having survived a bite in battle. If one could call it "surviving."

My hovel wasn't much, but it was mine. And meth had a particular stink to it, so I knew exactly what I faced when a pair of human addicts busted my door down, armed with sawed-off shotguns and desperation. They really should've planned better; the night before the full moon is the second-worst time to break into a werewolf's den.

With an actual weapon, I'd have had an open-and-shut case of self-defense. In Texas, even a werewolf was allowed to own guns.

Self-defense didn't apply to fang and claw. Ironically, I would have been in *more* trouble had I left them alive. The court showed a bit of dubious mercy, taking my service in the war and the newness of my condition into account. Rather than a death sentence, or even life imprisonment, the judge shipped me off to the werewolf lunar penal colony for "only" ten to fifteen years.

To be brutally honest, I wasn't sure this was preferable to a silver bullet.

The prisoner transport to the all-male colony was a special hell. Three days stretched over forever. Silver shackles stopped us from shifting to wolf. The closer we got to the moon, the more the agony grew. Its relentless pull fought the silver and lost, the worst pain I'd ever felt. Rough men bawled like babies, and I lay curled on my side choking on sobs, tears streaming down my face.

I barely noticed the landing bump or the airlock whooshing open. But I couldn't miss when the remotely controlled cuffs fell off. It was as if a switch had been thrown—faster than ever before with a single bone-wrenching crunch leaving me panting on the floor as my body shifted to the intermediate wolfman form.

I took a few moments to collect myself before shaking free from the shreds of my prison jumpsuit. Bits of cloth wafted to the floor in one-sixth gravity, and standing up the normal way nearly launched me into the ceiling before I recovered. The electrodes clamped to my neck vertebrae stayed right where they were.

A chorus of growls greeted us as we exited the shuttle, along with distorted mutters of "fresh meat." They'd dumped us right into the middle of the gen-pop yard.

Shivering, I scanned the crowd. Many of them had actual scars, although new wounds healed without scarring, and old scars disappeared with a shift. Usually.

The first guy I noticed brooded in the back of the yard, bare space all around him. A huge bruiser nearly twice my size; four white stripes marred his head from between his ears to the left side of his face, a strike that nearly cost him an eye. He was far more wolf than human—muzzle longer, ears rotated to the top of his head, hands and feet more paw-like, incredibly shaggy, with black fur and orange eyes. He stood hunched over, almost on all fours rather than upright. A purple "21" was stamped on each shoulder.

Prisoner 35 stalked over to me. Less wolfy than 21 and not quite as enormous, he still outsized me by a good fifty pounds. His fur was the classic gray stippled with black, fading to white on his stomach. He grabbed me by an ear and hauled me across the floor. "Mine."

"I. Wait. What?" I wrenched loose and scrambled away, which meant I bounced several times and slammed up against a table bolted to the metal floor. Something told me I'd better get used to the lower gravity quick, before someone turned me into a snack—or something less pleasant. "Leave me alone."

His lips curled over his teeth in an expression only a psychopath would have mistaken for a smile. "Make me."

I glanced around wildly. I was on my own.

I might not have been big—five-seven and one-fifty— but the Army had taught me hand-to-hand combat, and "small and light" also meant "fast and agile." My tail and ears came up, and I bared fangs, bristling.

He laughed and charged me, arms wide and claws spread. I tried to flit aside like I would've done back home, but I wasn't back home. I was on the moon in one-sixth Earth's gravity. He was used to it. Not me; I ended up flailing in midair. He caught me by the ankle, thumped me onto the floor, and stood over me with a massive hand wrapped around my throat.

"Mine," he said again.

Nope. I raked my claws down his arm.

He smiled, backing off. "What's your name, little wolf?" he asked with a not-quite German accent.

"Jordan Palmer?" I hadn't meant for it to sound like a question, but shit, he was huge. He could rip his claws through my throat without thinking twice. It wouldn't kill me, but I wouldn't like it.

"I am Christof Wagner." He pronounced it "Vagner." "And you are bunking with me."

An annoyed voice sounded over the intercom. "Christof. Leave the newb alone. There's enough space. Nobody has to share yet."

I glanced up. A pair of human guards stood at a second-story window. One held a microphone.

Christof's brow lowered stubbornly. "Mine."

Before he could drive that point home, a scrum of werewolves boiled out of the shuttle and ran us over. Christof went sailing. Several feet stomped several parts of my anatomy before an errant kick sent me flying to slam against a wall to slide, winded, to the floor. The guard yelled something I couldn't make out through the ringing in my ears.

Then a shockwave from the electrodes implanted in my

neck vertebrae made me yelp with agony, convulsively banging my head against a table leg. Not just me, though—everyone. I bit my tongue, tasting blood and juddering.

A few moments later, the guards joined us. The tall heavy one, whose nametag said ESCOBAR, held a yellow metal box with a bunch of buttons; the short skinny one carried a silver-plated truncheon. His nametag read FISCHER.

Escobar punched a button on his box, shutting off the current. We all lay there panting. Fischer placed the end of his truncheon under Christof's chin and tipped his head up. Christof abruptly turned human with a pained grunt, squeezing his eyes shut.

"Leave. The newb. Alone," Fischer said. "C'mon, Christof, you pick the smallest guy every time we get a bunch in. I'da thought you'da learned by now." He shot a glare around at the rest of us. "All of you shoulda learned by now. Maybe if you acted like civilized creatures insteada wild animals, you wouldn't be here." He jerked the truncheon away from Christof's chin, causing him to shift back to wolfman. "Control. Your damn. Wolf."

Fischer pulled me to my feet. "Keep your nose clean, Palmer, and you might survive the experience. Newbs!" he barked. "This way to your bunks."

The silver in the place made me itch. I shied away from the bars, plated with the toxic metal. We fell in behind him, and he led us down a hall lined with spartan cells. Each held a thin-mattressed bunk, a sink, a frictionless toilet, and not much else.

"Listen up," Escobar said. "This is what you get.

There's kit for you, toothbrushes and stuff. If you tear it up, you don't get a replacement. Keep it clean, because if you make a mess, we"—he gestured at himself and Fischer—"are not dealing with it. Chow is at eight, noon, and five. A bell will ring letting you know. You can shower once a day. Please do. You'll get your numbers soon. Your cells aren't locked unless you get rowdy. Lights out at ten. Any questions?"

I raised my hand. "Number 21? What's up with him? I've never seen one of us that..." I trailed off. "That," I concluded.

"Ivanovich. He's been here six years," Fischer said. "The longer you stay, the wolfier you get. He'll probably be confined to his cell twenty-four/seven as the wild takes over. He's not leaving."

What would I be like after *ten* years? "Do we go back to normal after we go home?"

"I don't know," he answered. "Nobody's gone home yet."

I didn't see a number starting with "1" on anyone's shoulders. I wondered what happened to the first batch. Nothing good, probably.

It did not give me a warm fuzzy feeling that they hadn't studied the long-term effects of werewolves living on the moon before they'd banished us. I wandered into my cell and flopped onto the bunk with my face in my hands.

We settled into a sick equilibrium. The routine helped, as did the fact that our guards put down any nonsense anyone started. We still had bullshit dominance fights, but I did my best to stay away from those and mostly succeeded. They'd stuck us here to teach us control, they said. If we could keep it together while permanently semi-wolfed, the thinking went, then we'd be better behaved when—if—we went home.

For whatever reason, Christof took a shine to me.

"Why?" I asked him one day at lunch. I'd decided—without consulting Christof—to sit with Ivanovich, who acted indifferent to our presence. "Lone wolf" was a bad look on anyone, even him. Maybe especially him.

Christof glanced up from his vat meat, which tasted vaguely of chicken. "Perhaps I wish someone had protected me from a vast bully when I first came." He shrugged. "The guards, they misconstrue without asking. The newbs take their cue from them and fear me. I am rough, yes, but I mean no harm. You're the first—" He stopped, shrugging again. "The first who did not avoid me out of hand."

"To be fair, Christof, your approach needs work." I took a couple of uneasy bites of my food. "But you looked like you needed a friend."

I'd noticed Christof's isolation after getting over my initial freak-out. Ivan was the same. Neither of them stared at me like I was a sex toy on legs—and, more importantly, didn't emit an amorous odor—so I gravitated in their direction. It worked out for all of us.

Since Christof wasn't bearing the brunt of anyone's animosity or untoward interest, I decided to ask. "What happened to your bully?"

He bared his fangs in that not-a-smile. "He had an unfortunate accident. Fischer and Escobar, they do their best to keep a, how you say, lid on things. They cannot always succeed. They are two and we are seventy-odd wolves; they must sleep sometime." He swallowed his final bit of meat. "Our guards are not bad sorts. They see which way the land lies and sometimes facilitate a bit of self-defense."

Good to know.

And completely useless when the aliens arrived a year later.

I was reading in my cell with the door open when they overrode the airlock controls and exploded into the compound. Enormous and reptilian, with crocodile teeth in extended muzzles and more dexterous hands than they had a right to, they cornered Escobar against the wall in front of me. Their armor was impervious to his blaster, the energy dissipating harmlessly across it. He only managed to scorch a face before they overwhelmed him.

Blood splashed through the hallway as they ripped through his throat and belly. The awful stench of internal organs filled the air, flashing me back to the war. Escobar let out a single, truncated scream and fell under snapping jaws.

One of the aliens looked at me through yellow-green, slit-pupiled eyes, its mouth dripping red as it gulped a hunk of . . . I didn't know what. Over the past year, I'd gotten better at controlling myself, but this was a bit fucking much. The wolf strove to roar forth, but I was frankly more afraid of it than the aliens. I battled it back, barely, though my fangs bared of their own volition, and the hair on my shoulders stood on end. My hands curled into defensive claws as I straightened, trying to make myself look bigger without letting the wolf the rest of the way out. A submission display might actually goad these creatures.

They made no move to attack me. Once they were done eating Escobar, leaving stripped bone and shredded cloth, they headed toward ops. When I could smell they were well away, I edged past Escobar's skull in the direction of the gen-pop yard, collecting fellow inmates on the way.

I found Christof talking quietly with a few of the higher-ranking wolves. He put a calming hand on my shoulder and glanced at my foot—I'd stepped in some of Escobar's blood.

"They murdered—" I started, then stopped awkwardly. They knew who'd been murdered by the scent. "In front of my cell."

"We are trying to decide what to do," he said. "You saw how they moved, what they were armed with?"

"They're fast," I answered. "Savage. No hesitation, they killed him with their bare hands and ate him. The armor stops blaster fire, but one of them got his face scorched. They didn't use weapons, just . . ." I shuddered. "Teeth and claws."

"Like us, then," 37 said. He'd come up with Christof. My own number was 86.

I glared at him wildly. "I don't know about you, but I don't kill and eat people for funsies. So, no. *Not* like us."

37 curled his lip, exposing sizeable fangs. "Don't you want payback for how the humans treat us?"

"Not like that!"

"Weak," he snorted. "You are weak."

Maybe I was, and maybe in this situation it was a

liability, but I wanted to go home someday. I had to prove I was a good dog by keeping myself civilized while the moon yanked on every fiber of my being, and the wolf begged to tear loose and howl.

My chin came up a fraction. "I have family on Earth. Don't you?" Just because they'd disowned me didn't mean I didn't still love them.

"A *human* family," 37 huffed. "We're your pack, 86."

Not a pack I'd chosen. Before I could point that out, a voice came over the intercom. It hissed, harshly guttural. "May I have your attention."

How the hell did they speak English? Some kind of universal translator?

We looked up to see one of the aliens talking into the microphone at the second-story window overlooking the yard. The creature was bigger than the ones from outside my cell, with a bony ridge above his eyes, dark orange rather than green like the others. Something about him said "ranking officer," though I couldn't put my claw—no, I thought firmly, my *finger*—on exactly what.

"I am Commander—" Something garbled.

Someone hollered, "What?"

The brow ridge lowered. "You may call me *Commander*, then. We are here to liberate your homeworld, using your moon as a staging area."

Shouts of consternation and questions, along with a few cheers, greeted this announcement. Somebody said, "Man, fuck you!"

This echoed my own sentiment. Like hell did I want family or friends back home eaten by these . . . whatever they were. Reptoids. Croco-shits.

The Commander raised a four-fingered hand. "Our current force is a vanguard, sent to study and reconnoiter. We have observed that you are prisoners here, kept against your will by an oppressive species not your own. Ally with us, tell us what we need to know regarding defenses, and you will be rewarded, given places in our army, and raised to leadership positions when we have subjugated the planet."

Helluva carrot for some of my more bloodthirsty compatriots, who had no love for humans in most cases, and active animosity in others. I wondered what the stick would be if we refused to go along with the program. I glanced uneasily between Christof and 37.

Christof was already shaking his head. "No. I have a family."

37 sniffed. "Feh. When did they last send you a message? They dumped us and forgot us."

"I care not. Earth is home. I won't leave it to these." Christof looked to me. "What is it like for us, Jordan? Have things changed?"

I shrugged. "From what? We have to register. We're segregated. I'm here for basically defending myself."

"They sent us up here to rot," 48 said. "If you think anybody's ever going home, you're delusional."

"This may be the only way we *get* home," 56 said. "I don't know about you guys, but I sure as shit don't want to end up like—" He gestured at Ivanovich, who hunched alone in a corner, nearly full wolf, wholly nonverbal. Keeping him company hadn't stopped his slide. My lips tightened, and I moved a chair to sit beside him, resting a hand between his ears. He leaned his head against my leg.

"Nevertheless." Christof came to stand by me, solid as a rock. "I don't wish my family and friends to be slaves or dinner."

"These guys are assholes who smell funny," I said. "Escobar didn't even have a chance. They slaughtered him like a steer and *ate* him. Can you imagine them doing that to your mom? Did anyone see what happened to Fischer?"

"Same thing," rumbled another old-timer.

Before we could discuss anything further, we all fell writhing to the ground—someone had activated our neck electrodes. The Commander joined us a few moments later, flanked by a quartet of underlings, one of whom held the control box. The Commander kicked people aside with a foot booted in the same armor they all wore, which absorbed the current and prevented secondary shocks.

My blood turned to ice when he stopped in front of Christof and pointed. "That one." The Reptoid with the box pushed a button that stopped the electricity coursing through Christof's body. Christof lay panting for a few seconds—

And launched, without so much as a growl of warning, straight at the Commander's face.

He never made it. Two Reptoids took him down. His claws ripped a face open, proving they bled as red as we did. His fangs closed on a hand with an audible crunch.

Then the Commander snapped his enormous jaws around Christof's head and wrenched it off in a spray of blood. I screamed Christof's name. They dropped his twitching, suddenly human body to the floor. His head rolled to a stop in front of me, staring with blue eyes. I'd never seen their true color before now.

I choked out a sob, half grief and half rage. The one with the box pushed another button, releasing me from the shock. The Commander regarded me with a soulless glower devoid of pity. "Are you next?"

I turned my face away. My voice came out as a low, wounded growl. "No."

"Good." He eyed the others one by one. They all lowered their gazes as much as possible while being electrocuted. "Anyone else?"

No one stood up to him. Not after that demonstration. The Commander waved at the box, and the voltage stopped for everybody. "Now," he said. "Join us, and be rewarded. Don't? We'll leave you here to die of starvation. Perhaps we'll be merciful and let the air out of your dome to give you an easy death." He clearly had no idea neither of those things would kill us, though they'd be hellish in the extreme.

"Let us have no more foolishness." The Commander spun and left us there, jittering with aftershocks.

Ivan hitched over to me. He nosed Christof's hair with a whine, then buried his head against my shoulder. No one looked our way. They dispersed, some to the corners of the yard, some back to their cells, leaving us with our packmate's body. My hand snaked up to pet Ivan. I wanted to tell him it would be okay, but the lie stuck in my throat. I was pretty sure we'd never be okay again.

I decided to bunk with Ivan after that. I didn't trust anyone else not to come and murder me in my sleep—or him. The others avoided us. Small knots of them muttered together, some casting us unfriendly glances, some speculative, some sympathetic, some a mixture of both.

I ignored them all, bitterly sullen that not a single one stood up and told the Reptoids "No." Not that I let myself off easy; my own cowardice rankled in my guts like a burning ember.

Ivan's growl startled me awake a night later. I raised up on an elbow behind him to see inmate 56 standing outside our bunk.

"What do you want?" I asked in a sleepy burr.

"Some of us aren't on board with the invaders," he said. "We're having a meeting in an hour. You two should join us, since, well, you know."

I did know. I just didn't trust them. "We'll think about it. I hope you'll excuse us if we're less than confident about you."

"Fair enough." He ghosted away.

"What do you think?" I asked Ivan. He should have been the alpha, but the others eschewed him, fearing they'd be like this someday, mostly wolf subsumed by instinct. But I knew he hadn't forgotten his humanity; he wasn't a ravening beast. Outward appearances deceived. He kept himself together better than some who'd been here for far less time.

His shoulders rolled in a shrug. He hopped off the bed, standing on all fours, looking at me with a tilted head and a slightly waving tail.

"Fine, I'm coming."

Ivan led the way, turning off into an access hall we normally couldn't enter. A pang pierced me as I realized why the doorway was cracked open—no one was left to make sure it stayed shut.

We slid into a maintenance room, where about twenty

inmates assembled in various states of put-together. As one, they ducked their heads when we entered, subtly baring their throats—much to my surprise.

"You were right," 56 said. "After what they did to Christof, we can't let them invade Earth."

About time they'd seen sense. But I was still angry that Christof's death served as their catalyst for action. Too late for him. Ivan bristled at my side, and I crossed my arms and glowered. "What are you willing to do about it?"

"We have to stop them, here and now. We've got the numbers, I think," 56 replied. "We just gotta catch them off guard."

"Make them think we've agreed," 45 said. "And coldcock them. They bleed, so they can die."

A logical conclusion. "How many of us versus how many of them?" I put a possessive hand on Ivan's ruff. "I've already lost one packmate. I'm not willing to throw away another on an ill-conceived plan."

"I've counted." 56 held up four fingers. "They like to do things in fours, apparently. So, forty of them in this vanguard, including the Commander."

We had twice that, but how many were on our side? My fingers crept around to the prongs on the back of my neck. "What about these? Our numbers mean fuck-all if they can drop us whenever they want."

45 smiled with all his teeth and held out a hand. A pair of blood-crusted electrodes sat in his palm. My stomach lurched. I'd dreamed of not being controlled by the damned things. "How—"

"It doesn't feel good." Understatement of the century. "But we can remove them with our claws. Are you in?"

I glanced down at Ivan. He shrugged again.

"We're in." I hoped it wasn't a colossal mistake.

We peeled the electrodes off. Ivan didn't trust anyone else to do it, baring fangs at their approach, so I removed his, as gently as possible, while he stood there stoically without making a sound. I wondered, again, at his self-discipline, and if they'd ever let him go home again.

First we had to survive the croco-shits.

The rumor flowed from cell to cell. When the chime sounded for lunch, we all trooped dutifully to the chow hall and grabbed our vat protein. The crocs assumed that food would distract us and keep us docile.

They discovered how wrong they were when we sprang to the attack. Blood, ours and theirs, spattered through the air. Ivan watched my back, and I watched his, as we coordinated our efforts to take a croc down. It turned out they *could* die, though killing them wasn't effortless. We healed fast. They didn't.

Out of the corner of my eye, I saw the moment 56 lost himself. Suddenly, he was all wolf, six hundred pounds of shaggy, ferocious rage with fangs as long as my thumbs and five-inch talons to rival a saber-toothed tiger. He tore through crocs, ripping throats with no regard for tactics or his own safety. I was honestly afraid he wouldn't be able to stop with them . . .

Until he came face-to-face with me and Ivan. He skidded to a halt, panting jaws dripping red.

"Hey." I gulped. "Are you—"

An energy bolt blasted from a weapon, and his head disappeared. Even one of us couldn't survive that. He dropped to the deck, instantly dead and human.

The crocs launched a bare-handed counterattack. Some of our own joined them, the traitorous wretches. But 56 had shown us the way, and the Commander held the only weapon like that.

The final change took me like a flowing stream. Usually it hurt, on full moon nights, but I fought it every inch of the way. Turned out, when I just let it happen, there was only heady power. No wonder some of us got lost in it.

Ivan's jaws closed around the Commander's gun wrist and ripped the hand clean off. I leaped at the Commander's throat. He didn't get his arm up in time to stop me. He fell, and I rode him down, teeth locked so hard he couldn't even gurgle. He tasted as bad as he smelled.

He'd murdered my packmates. I had no mercy or compunction. My head jerked nearly of its own accord and tore his life out.

It was *easy*, and I wasn't sorry.

I left him and hunted for another Reptoid, but the other inmates had killed them all, along with the traitors, who'd frozen without shifting. Because shifting was unthinkable except under the most dire conditions.

Except when it wasn't. Maybe the humans needed to learn that lesson more than we did. On the other hand, if I could kill another sapient creature without hesitation, maybe they were right to be afraid.

Ivan brushed my cheek with his nose. He'd reverted to what passed for normal with him, but I was still completely wolfed and not eager to go back. He whined at me, bumping my shoulder. Reminding me of my humanity.

I closed my eyes, huffed out a breath, and shifted as far as I could. Not a monster. Not a murderer. I'd done what was necessary to protect my home, and the beast hadn't cut loose and torn a swath through my comrades.

None of the others had either.

After we'd regrouped, the authorities on Earth got a very interesting message from us. At first they didn't believe, but they changed their tune right quick when Ivan pulled the Commander's body into camera range.

They paid us a visit, faster than I would have credited them for, and we gave them an earful and an eyeful of the monsters we'd killed to save Earth. They were more shaken about the confirmation we weren't alone in the universe than what we'd done to stop a wholesale invasion. I played up Ivan's contribution, because, well, he was my pack.

They pardoned us and shuttled us back to Earth. How could they not?

I was relieved to be home, greeted as a conquering hero with my new friend—who, much to our relief, turned mostly human again. A grateful government awarded us a couple of upscale loft apartments in the same building. No more segregation.

We'd just sat down to enormous steaks I'd grilled in the park when my phone rang. Ivan's went off at the same time. We glanced at each other, then at the screens.

Same number. We answered together and found ourselves on a conference call.

"We're composing an invasion," said the voice on the other end. "And thought you'd like to come along. You've got some unique talents, and we'd pay you appropriately."

"How appropriately?" I asked, guarded.

"Check your email. There's a compensation package in it. Get back to me when you have time to think it over."

We ate first. I swallowed hard when I opened the attachment. Assuming I made it back, I'd never have to work again.

"Ivan? Are you seeing what I'm seeing?"

"It's almost too good to be true. So I'm suspicious." He stared dubiously at his phone, head tilted and bushy brows creased. "They have incentive to make sure we don't come home. We should negotiate rights of survivorship." His lip curled up, baring a tooth longer and pointier than human. "I think I shall discuss this further with them."

"Those croco-shits murdered our pack, and they were just the vanguard. I'm in. I like the idea of taking the battle to them."

And I loved the idea of fighting on the right side of a war.

ANCIENT-ENEMY

Eric James Stone

Under the blue-green light of the glowworms installed on the ceiling, Scholar Buhresh studied the sixty-one Ancient-Enemy captives eating their food in the pit below. Despite his having studied pictures and videos of them for years, the differences between them and the True-Men stood out: the smallness of their eyes; their weak, elongated limbs; and their high foreheads lacking proper brow ridges. How could their ancestors have defeated the True-Men in ancient times?

They labeled themselves *Homo sapiens*—wise man.

That they had built a highly technological society argued in favor of their wisdom.

That they had destroyed what they built argued against it.

It was a puzzle.

After watching the patterns of interactions between the captives, Buhresh decided on his target: a full-grown male treated deferentially by the others.

Buhresh approached the guard by the ladder, a

seventeen-year-old male from the Shalakh Clan, according to his forehead tattoo. "Far-Nephew," he said in Interclan, "I wish to speak to the captives."

"Yes, Scholar Buhresh." The young man pressed a button to activate the mechanism, and the ladder smoothly descended to the floor of the pit. "Do you wish to borrow my electrospear? Or should I come down with you?"

"I will be fine. Keep watch from here." Buhresh climbed down the ladder and strode to where his target sat cross-legged on the ground. The captive looked at him warily.

"Ты говоришь по-русски?" Buhresh asked.

The captive did not reply, merely staring at Buhresh with those too-small eyes.

"Do you speak English? *Sprechen Sie Deutsch? Parlez-vous français? ¿Habla español?*"

"Я говорю по-русски," the captive said.

"Very good," Buhresh replied in Russian. He squatted on his heels so he was closer to the male's level, while still being ready to move quickly if need be. "I am Scholar Buhresh. What are you named?"

"Mykhaylo."

"Are you the leader of this clan?"

Mykhaylo shrugged, a gesture Buhresh had learned from videos of the Ancient-Enemy.

"The others defer to you," Buhresh said. "You must be of high status."

A female sitting nearby said, "He is a co—"

"Shut up!" Mykhaylo ordered.

The female fell silent.

"Perhaps you are a co ... mmander? Commandant?"

"Perhaps," Mykhaylo said reluctantly.

"Very good. Explain to your subordinates that they must cooperate with the guards and not try to escape."

"Or what? They'll be beaten? Killed?"

They do not think like us, Buhresh reminded himself. "When the child does not follow the rules, the parent is at fault, not the child. If your subordinates do not follow the rules, they will be forced to comply, but it is their commander who must be punished."

"Understood."

"Very good!"

Buhresh stood up so quickly one of the guards raised his electrospear to his shoulder. Buhresh waved his hand in dismissal. "Eat and get some rest. We leave in two-tenths of a day—about five of your hours."

"Where are you taking us?" Mykhaylo asked.

"To labor in the Under-Land, where you will support the war effort."

"Why have your people declared war on us?" Mykhaylo said. "We didn't attack you—we didn't even know people lived down here!"

"The Over-Land is our birthright," Buhresh said. "Your kind stole the Over-Land from us, forced us underground, and proceeded to forget all about us. But we have not forgotten you, Ancient-Enemy. Your year is numbered 1992 since one of your religious leaders was born. Our year is numbered 42,887 since we founded our society in the Under-Land."

Mykhaylo's small eyes widened. "Your history goes back 42,887 years?"

Buhresh wiggled his hands in uncertainty. "The number may not be exact, as we did not develop writing until about 3,500 years after the True-Men moved to the Under-Land. But that's the best we can estimate from the ancestor-songs transcribed by—" Buhresh shook his head, a gesture his people had in common with the Ancient-Enemy. The teacher in him loved to explain things. "It does not matter."

"But how did you keep track of years without being able to see the sun?" Mykhaylo asked.

"I find it interesting that you ask that question, and not how it is that I speak your language. The latter implies the answer to the former." Buhresh turned to leave and was surprised to find one of the females standing two arm lengths away on the direct line between him and the ladder. He had not heard her approach.

"You speak English?" she asked. She was at least a handsbreadth taller than him.

"I do," Buhresh replied.

She straightened her shoulders. "My name is Pamela Brown. I'm a representative of the United States government. I demand that you release me and the rest of these people immediately."

Buhresh attempted to smile at her. How had these people ever decided that baring one's teeth was a friendly expression? "An American! It is a pleasure to meet you, Congresswoman Brown."

"No, no, I'm not a congresswoman. I just work for the government. But the American government does not look kindly on people who kidnap government employees."

"But we are not in the USA, Pamela Brown. We are not even in the USSR. We are in the Under-Land. But I am curious—what was an American government employee doing in the USSR, land of your enemies?"

"We call it the Marshall Plan II, helping them rebuild after World War III."

"And what is your occupation, Pamela?"

"I'm a sanitation engineer. I'm helping them clean up what's left of their cities."

"First you use your nuclear bombs to destroy their cities, then you help them clean up and rebuild. It seems contradictory."

"They launched first," Pamela said. "Only reason most of our cities survived was our missile defense worked."

"Which only makes it even more remarkably illogical. When one of our clans starts a war against another clan, the clan leaders know that if they lose, their clan will be utterly destroyed. And thus, it has been generations since we had an inter-clan war. We must talk more on this, but I'm afraid I must cut this discussion short, as I have duties to attend to before we travel."

As Buhresh started to walk around her, she said, "I know you're a Neanderthal."

Buhresh stopped. "That is your name for us, yes. Our name for ourselves means 'True Men' in your language."

"And what does your name for us mean in my language?"

Buhresh hesitated, but decided it would do no harm. "You are the 'Ancient Enemy.'"

"Ah," she said. "You're still holding a grudge after forty thousand years."

"We remember you every day we live underground, because you are the reason."

He strode past her and climbed the ladder.

After the guard raised the ladder, Buhresh looked down into the pit. The Ukrainian man was conversing with a few others in low tones. But the American woman was just standing in the pit looking up at him.

"That female will be trouble," he said to the young guard. "She is not of the same clan as the others, so do not retaliate against them if she does anything. Treat her as a rogue."

"Yes, Scholar Buhresh," the guard replied.

Buhresh bowed his head before the portable viewscreen. "Grand-Uncle Roggeth, you summoned me?"

"Yes," said Three-Times-Great-Grand-Uncle Roggeth. "I hear you have captured some of the Ancient-Enemies instead of exterminating them."

"This is truth, Grand-Uncle."

"For what purpose?"

Buhresh knew that study and learning would not be sufficient reason for the grand-uncle, which was why he had devised his plan with a secondary purpose. "We must have plentiful nuclear weapons in order to hold off the Americans once we reconquer our birthright. Is that not truth?"

"It is truth. It would have been better if we had sufficient nuclear weapons before we attacked, but we could not ignore the opportunity that presented itself in the aftermath of their war."

Buhresh nodded. He had expressed his doubts about the wisdom of that course of action at the time, but once the rock was chiseled, it could not be unchiseled. "Too many from the mining and working clans are sickened by the radiation from mining and processing uranium. It occurred to me that we could preserve our own people by using the Ancient-Enemy as miners and workers in Uranium-Town. I captured some that I might test the possibility."

Roggeth smacked his lips as he considered Buhresh's words. Finally, he said, "This is wisdom in you, Buhresh. Keep me apprised of how the experiment goes."

Buhresh was squatting at the writing-table in his Uranium-Town quarters when the guard brought Pamela Brown to him.

He waved dismissal to the guard and looked her over. The pale-blue mining uniform was too big around her arms and torso, but the bare shins of her too-long legs stuck down from the bottom. In the long term, one of the tailoring clans would need to create uniforms with the proper proportions for the Ancient-Enemies. But that would only be necessary if the captives performed well enough at their work. Based on the past ten-day, that remained an open question.

"You wished to speak with me," Buhresh said.

"We need more light," said Pamela Brown.

"More light?"

"Unless you're satisfied with our productivity, we need more light. You've had millennia to evolve for living in the Under-Land, while we've barely had a week. Modern humans are used to living and working in bright electric light. These things"—she pointed at the glowworms attached to the ceiling—"barely give us enough light, even after our eyes adjust."

It did make sense. True-Men needed to wear eye-shields to go above-ground during daylight.

"I am curious," Buhresh said, "as to why Mykhaylo did not make this request on behalf of his people. Why is it you?"

She squeezed her lips tight, as if she did not want words to escape. Finally, she said, "Mykhaylo thinks that since we are the only humans—of our kind, at least—to be brought here for labor, that we are an experiment. He does not want us to be productive, so you will abandon the experiment and maybe let us go."

"And you disagree with his analysis?"

"I agree we are an experiment. But if the experiment fails, you will not let your 'Ancient Enemies' go free. You've been slaughtering people on the surface, so you will have no compunctions about simply killing us. I would rather live. So I'm doing what I can to make us more productive."

"A very rational approach, which I would not have expected from an American. Did one of your heroes not say, 'Give me liberty or give me death'?"

She shrugged. "Different strokes for different folks."

Buhresh took a moment to parse the unfamiliar phrase. "An idiom? Meaning different people prefer different things? And it rhymes." He picked up a pen and wrote the phrase and its definition on a piece of paper. When he was done, he looked up at her. "I will have some electric lights provided for your workspaces."

"Thank you."

Buhresh whistled for the guard to return and ordered him to escort her back to the captives' quarters.

Interesting. She had originally tried to claim the rest of the captives as her clan, but Mykhaylo must have disabused her of that notion. Her only recourse as a social creature was to ingratiate herself with the True-Men by betraying her own kind.

Perhaps she would not be as much trouble as he originally thought.

Nine ten-days later, along with other Uranium-Town officials, Buhresh was at the station to greet Three-Times-Great-Grand-Uncle Roggeth when he stepped off the monorail from Military-City. They all followed the grand-uncle to the administration sector. The grand-uncle took over the mayor's office and began taking reports from town officials.

When Buhresh's turn came, he entered the office and slid the door shut behind him. Roggeth squatted behind a writing-table and motioned for Buhresh to squat before him.

"Your test of using Ancient-Enemy captives to refine uranium is a success," said the grand-uncle. "They are not as efficient as True-Men when it comes to the amount of raw materials used, but their speed more than makes up for that. We are now ahead of our production schedule for weapons-grade uranium. Well done."

Buhresh nodded to acknowledge the compliment. "We may be wasting valuable assets by exterminating the Ancient-Enemy. The improvement in production is due to suggestions from one of them. Discarding batches from the first refining with lower concentrations of uranium 235 allows the second refining to work significantly faster."

Roggeth frowned. "Why did one of our own not come up with this?"

"Our policy of open knowledge works against us in this case. Our people, fearful of radiation, do not like working with higher concentrations."

"And Ancient-Enemies do not fear radiation?"

"As far as they know, they are merely refining metal. Since they are Ancient-Enemies, they are not entitled to open knowledge."

"That is wisdom in you." Roggeth rose to his feet. "I wish to see these Ancient-Enemies with my own eyes. Take me to them."

As Buhresh and Roggeth approached the entrance to the refining-room, Buhresh grabbed two eye-shields from hooks on the wall and handed one to Roggeth.

"These protect our eyes from radiation?" Roggeth asked.

Buhresh decided not to give the technically correct answer that visible light is a form of radiation, and instead said, "The Ancient-Enemies require bright light to work. With only brief exposure to the uranium, we will be in no danger from radiation. We switch out the guards every tenth of a day to limit their exposure."

Even with the eye-shields, Buhresh squinted as they entered the refining-room. Roggeth strode in a couple of paces and then stopped to look around the room.

Ten captives, including Mykhaylo, sat on benches by a table, eating a meal. Another ten were seated at their work stations. The American woman was not there; she was on a different shift.

The four guards set around the room rose from their squatted position and rapped the butts of their electrospears on the floor.

The murmur of conversation among the eating captives stopped abruptly as they all turned to stare at the grand-uncle.

"They do not eat standard rations?" Roggeth asked.

"They work better eating food to which they are accustomed. We have it brought down from the Over-Land for them."

"And these things they sit on?"

"Also brought down from the Over-Land to make them comfortable while working." Buhresh began to feel uneasy about the direction this conversation was headed. "These seemed reasonable accommodations to increase their productivity."

"I see." Roggeth paused, then said, "You will translate my words for them."

"Yes, Grand-Uncle."

"Ancient-Enemies," Roggeth said, his deep voice echoing in the refining-room. "You are fortunate indeed to have found favor in our eyes. I am Three-Times-Great-Grand-Uncle Roggeth, who leads the war against your people."

As he translated into Russian and English, Buhresh used the words генерал/*general* instead of the literal meaning of *three-times-great-grand-uncle*.

"When we are victorious, you will be rewarded by adoption into our clans. You will no longer be Ancient-Enemies, you will be family. Carry on with your work."

Buhresh was so astonished by this promise that he

stumbled through his translations. He had not thought the grand-uncle capable of such generosity toward the Ancient-Enemy.

Roggeth strode toward the door and motioned for Buhresh to follow.

Once they were outside the room and walking back toward the administrative section, Roggeth said, "You will exterminate these Ancient-Enemies when we have no further use for them."

"Of course, Grand-Uncle. I was surprised when you promised to adopt them into our clans, but now I see that you were lying to give them incentive to work harder."

Roggeth stopped walking. Buhresh continued another pace, then stopped and turned to face the grand-uncle.

"It was wisdom in you, Scholar Buhresh, to test these captives as workers. That has paid off with increased production. However, it was foolishness in you to adapt their environment to suit them. Forty thousand years ago we were forced by them to adapt to life underground. Now, it is time for the Ancient-Enemy to be forced to adapt to us. Understood?"

Buhresh nodded. "I will take away their—"

"No, leave things as they are. But they must be exterminated when they are no longer of use, so they can never tell any of their kind of what happened here."

"Yes, Grand-Uncle."

The next day was tenth-day. In addition to the normal time off from labor, Three-Times-Great-Grand-Uncle Roggeth had decreed a day of feasting and competition. After Buhresh won the scholar's tournament in the dark-stone/light-stone game, he was allowed to join Roggeth in the Victors' Stand at the arena to watch the combat bouts of the warrior clans.

Buhresh was surprised to see a roped-off section of the stands held the Ancient-Enemy captives. All three shifts were there. "Grand-Uncle," he said, "did you have the captives brought here? Who is processing the uranium?"

Roggeth laughed. "We are ahead of schedule. They can take some time away from their work. There's something I want them to see."

"What is that?"

"A surprise."

Over the next tenth of a day, the audience hooted their appreciation for the victors of the bouts, who joined the grand-uncle in the Victors' Stand, while the losers left the arena completely.

During the last announced bout, Roggeth said to Buhresh, "After this bout, I will speak. Go now to your captives and translate for them."

Buhresh made his way over to the captives' section. They seemed nervous, even frightened. A few of them looked like they had been crying.

"What is wrong?" he asked.

"Scholar Buhresh," said Mykhaylo, "will we be forced into combat in this arena?"

For all Buhresh knew, that was the surprise Roggeth had planned. But he said, "No, the work you are doing is far too valuable."

Unfortunately, that did not calm them.

Before he could inquire more, Pamela approached him

and said, "The general said after the war we could be adopted by your clans."

"It is wisdom in him," Buhresh said. "You have proven your worth."

"What does adoption into your clans entail? Would we be allowed to marry, have children?"

Buhresh felt it a kindness to lie to her. Even if she were allowed to live, by now the radiation exposure would have made her sterile. "Of course. You will be as family to us."

"I hope—"

The voice of Roggeth blared through the arena's loudspeakers. "My nephews, you have brought honor to your clan-mothers. With the bravery and skill you have shown today, our victory against the Ancient-Enemy is assured."

The crowd hooted their appreciation.

Roggeth raised a hand to silence them. "There is one more bout today, and then we feast. I, myself, will fight in single combat . . . to the death."

Buhresh and the crowd hissed in surprise. Combat to the death was rare—bouts usually ended with surrender when one was at a clear disadvantage. And who would dare to challenge the grand-uncle?

From the other end of the arena, eight guards marched a captive into the center: a thin, gray-haired, Ancient-Enemy male. From his uniform, he must have been an officer in what remained of the Red Army.

"This Ancient-Enemy is one of their grand-uncles," said Roggeth. "He asked us to stop reclaiming our birthright lands, and to leave the Over-Land in peace. His request will be granted . . . if he can kill me in combat."

Buhresh translated this for his captives, adding, "This is a rare opportunity the grand-uncle has offered your people."

"I thank the grand-uncle for his generosity," Mykhaylo said. "I will tell the others."

The earlier bouts had been with blunted spears, but Roggeth took two electrospears from some soldiers and strode out to meet the captive in the arena. He tossed one of the electrospears at the captive's feet. The captive picked it up gingerly, holding it incorrectly, and Buhresh knew there was no chance this captive would beat Roggeth.

The combat started slowly, the two opponents circling each other. Roggeth feinted with his electrospear, and the captive overreacted, stumbling backward.

Buhresh looked at his captives to see how they were taking this. Pamela was no longer beside him—she and Mykhaylo were arguing near the back of the stand. After a few moments, she stormed off toward an exit, with a guard following her.

The hooting of the crowd brought Buhresh's attention back to the combat. The captive officer was on his knees, clutching a bloody gut wound with his hands. His electrospear lay on the ground.

The wound was clearly mortal, but Roggeth moved in and jabbed his spear into the captive's left eye. The man's body shuddered as the electrodes in the point activated, giving the Ancient-Enemy the honor of not bleeding to death. Roggeth twisted his spear to free it from the corpse.

The crowd hooted wildly.

Roggeth strode back to the Victors' Stand and stood before the microphone. The crowd quieted. "As this Ancient-Enemy has fallen before me," he said, "so shall the Ancient-Enemy fall before our army. The Over-Land is our birthright."

The celebratory hooting resumed.

Buhresh was startled when Mykhaylo stepped into the arena and headed toward the Victors' Stand.

"Mykhaylo, stop!" he shouted, to no avail. Buhresh hurried after him.

They were only a few arm lengths from the Victors' Stand when Buhresh caught up to him and grabbed his arm. "What are you doing?"

"Tell your general that he killed one of my men, and now I challenge him. If I kill him, you will end your war against my people."

"I will tell him no such thing," Buhresh said.

"Grand-Uncle," Mykhaylo shouted in poorly accented Interclan. "Me fight peace!"

"Was that a challenge?" Roggeth asked, his voice echoing through the arena. "Buhresh, what is this?"

Buhresh lowered his head. "He says you killed one of his men, and now he challenges you. If he wins, we must end the war against his people."

"By what right does he challenge me? He is not a great-grand-uncle among his people."

Buhresh translated this to Mykhaylo, adding, "There are rules about who can challenge whom. Only one of your high officers would have position to force a challenge to the three-times-great-grand-uncle."

Mykhaylo drew himself up. "I am a colonel in the

Soviet Air Force, twice awarded Hero of the Soviet Union."

"That is insufficient," Buhresh said.

"Tell him I am a cosmonaut. I was aboard Mir space station when the nuclear war destroyed my country. I saw the missiles launch, I saw the cities burn. I want to see no more war for my people or for yours. Tell him that."

Buhresh translated Mykhaylo's rank and his message.

"He flew into the space beyond the air?" Roggeth asked.

"Yes."

Roggeth looked Mykhaylo over from head to foot. Buhresh tried to assess their relative combat capabilities. The two probably massed about the same and were roughly the same age. Mykhaylo had longer legs and was taller, but Roggeth was more muscular. Roggeth was highly skilled with an electrospear. Did cosmonauts train with spears? Buhresh doubted it.

"He still does not rank highly enough," said Roggeth. "However, he may challenge my grand-nephew Kohmet, who is of close-enough rank."

That was cleverness in Roggeth. Mykhaylo knew Roggeth's skill, having seen him fight. But no one knew Mykhaylo's skill, and his challenge to Roggeth made no sense unless he thought he could win.

Buhresh explained to Mykhaylo that he could challenge Kohmet, who was merely a great-grand-uncle, not a three-times-great-grand-uncle.

"If I win, he'll stop the war?"

"No, but you'll gain Kohmet's rank, which is sufficient to challenge Roggeth directly. Roggeth himself was of

Kohmet's rank when he challenged the previous Three-Times-Great-Grand-Uncle so he could start the reclamation of the Over-Land."

"Very good, I'll do it."

Kohmet came out of the Victors' Stand. Buhresh recognized him as having dominated his earlier opponent. He carried two electrospears and threw one down at Mykhaylo's feet.

"Do I need to kill him to win?" Mykhaylo asked Buhresh. "Or will he surrender when I have clear advantage?"

"This is to the death," Buhresh said.

Mykhaylo nodded and picked up the electrospear, and Buhresh returned to the rest of the captives, who seemed frightened and confused.

"Your leader is fighting to put an end to this war," Buhresh said. "It is bravery in him."

Kohmet and Mykhaylo circled each other, the tips of their electrospears only two handsbreadths apart. Kohmet lunged, and Mykhaylo parried. They traded blows several times, with Mykhaylo obviously on the defensive.

One of Kohmet's strikes dealt Mykhaylo's left leg a glancing blow, barely drawing blood, but the electric shock clearly jolted Mykhaylo, and that left him open for another strike, this time at his right leg. He fell to his knees.

Before Kohmet could take advantage, though, Mykhaylo swung his electrospear in a wide arc, and Kohmet had to back off to avoid getting shocked. Mykhaylo rose to his feet, bleeding from cuts on both legs. The wounds would weaken him over time if the bout stretched out, but Buhresh doubted that would be a factor: Mykhaylo was too inexperienced with the electrospear to last long against an expert like Kohmet.

The combatants began circling each other again. Suddenly, Mykhaylo turned and sprinted away from Kohmet.

For a moment, Buhresh marveled at the man's cowardice. Then he realized Mykhaylo was not running away from Kohmet, but rather toward the Victors' Stand, with his electrospear aimed directly at Grand-Uncle Roggeth.

But then Kohmet's hurled electrospear pierced Mykhaylo's lower back. He dropped his electrospear and crumpled to the ground.

Some of the captives around Buhresh gasped or started sobbing.

Kohmet ran up to Mykhaylo and pulled his electrospear out of Mykhaylo's back. He was about to plunge it into Mykhaylo's neck when Roggeth said, "No. Do not end him honorably. Cut him and let him bleed out."

After making the ritual cuts, Kohmet joined Roggeth in the Victors' Stand, and then the grand-uncle and the rest of the victors left for the feast.

Buhresh walked over and squatted down next to Mykhaylo, who was barely conscious. "I want to understand," Buhresh said. "Why did you do this? You never had a chance of winning."

Mykhaylo gasped for breath a few times. "I had to try..."

★ ★ ★

Buhresh found Pamela in the refining-room. She sat in a chair, hands clutched in her lap. Wetness glistened on her cheeks.

She looked up as he came in. "Don't come any closer, Scholar Buhresh."

He stopped. There were dark red stains on the floor, and the guard that should have been with her was nowhere in sight. If she had harmed the guard, her life was forfeit.

"Did Mykhaylo win?" she asked.

"You . . . You knew what he planned?"

"I tried to talk him out of it. Did he win?"

A sinking feeling in Buhresh's gut told him there was a deep game here he was only beginning to glimpse. "Yes. He won. He sent me to tell you the war is over. There is no more need for killing. You will be returned to the Over-Land."

"That's all?"

What else could she be expecting? They had been arguing passionately about him risking his life. Could they have been lovers? "He sends you his love."

She chuckled. "That is definitely not the password. Mykhaylo is dead."

Buhresh hung his head. There was no point to bluffing anymore, but perhaps he could still figure out this game. "That is wisdom in you. His final words were, 'I had to try.'"

Pamela nodded. "I guess what he saw up there made him try anything to avoid another nuke going off."

"That is understandable. Nobody wants another nuclear war."

"I lied to you when we first met," Pamela said. "It's true I was helping clean up their cities, but I'm not a sanitation engineer. I'm a nuclear engineer."

In Buhresh's mind, the stones fell to their positions on the board. "You knew you were refining uranium. But why, then, did you make the process more efficient?"

"Because that distracted you from thinking about what happened to the lower-quality batches. Eighty percent U-235 is considered 'weapons-grade' uranium, but it's possible to build a bomb with only twenty percent. It takes hundreds of kilos instead of fifty to reach critical mass, and it's not as efficient. But it will work."

Buhresh closed his eyes. "You have built such a bomb."

"We had a timer set to detonate it tonight during the feast. But then Mykhaylo had to try to make peace, so I had to come disarm it."

"You disarmed it?"

Pamela raised one of her hands. Her thumb was pressed on a button at the end of a metal tube. Wires came out the bottom of the tube and stretched out behind her. "We call this a dead-man's switch. Or dead woman. When I let go of the button, it closes the circuit, starting a chain reaction that will destroy this entire facility." She chuckled sadly. "The good news for your people is that after you lose this war, someone like me will probably come down here to help the remnants of your people clean up the mess I made."

"You have the strong hand now. What do you want in exchange for not exploding your bomb? Peace? Let me get the grand-uncle. I'm sure he will agree to withdraw from the surface."

She shook her head. "I can't trust your people's promises. You were never going to adopt me and let me make little hybrid babies. So this is not a negotiation. You're a teacher, so you'll understand why I'm glad I could explain my little science project to you before we—"

Buhresh lunged, reaching for the tube in her hand.

The last thing he saw was her thumb lifting.

BLUE KACHINA

T.C. McCarthy

There is a time of purification.

Mars was long gone by the time that memory flashed into my thoughts, and by now we'd begun our descent toward AJ-3458. Everyone just called it the gravel pile. Space enveloped us in darkness, and while part of me concentrated on control panels, to read out numbers while Jim Mockta piloted us down, another part stared into infinite blackness as if the stars had all winked out; they knew when to leave, I figured. The stars had smelled something bad and decided that they'd better get going before the foxes came for the chickens. Our craft landed with a soft thud, and Jim's hands flashed over the controls, shutting off both engines at just the right moment—to prevent us from bouncing off in low gravity.

"Why'd they need *us* to check this out?" I asked.

"Why not us?"

"Always the dirty work. Always."

Jim chuckled and began releasing his seat harness. "Exactly. We're from the government..."

"... and we're here to help," I finished. "When'd they lose contact with the Chinese?"

"Nobody said."

Microgravity barely grabbed at me, and we collided while squeezing into vacuum environmental suits. Mockta grunted. By the time he'd sealed his helmet and helped me with mine, the engines had cooled, and distant sounds of pinging metal had silenced to match the emptiness I'd seen while touching down.

"You're the fucking captain, Mockta. I thought maybe they'd told you more."

"You remember when they first sent us to Mars—to colonize?"

"Yeah."

"You remember what they told us then?"

"That the Hopi and Arabs were perfect colonists. White guys had psychological issues with the loneliness and colors over long periods of time. Something about the environment and distance from Earth messing with them, so twenty percent of the first colonists went nuts."

"They didn't tell me anything more than that back then. Why would they tell me more now?"

"Send in the damn Indians."

Mockta slammed his fist on a button to open the inner airlock door. The hiss of air being sucked away reminded me of something. At first the memory blinked on the fringes of my thoughts, evading attempts to grab it and teasing me with a glimpse of home—of Earth and its deserts. Old man Mase, grandfather. He pointed at a rock covered with scratch marks that formed a picture, and I struggled to see it, closing my eyes to help concentrate, only to hear sizzling sand because the desert wind blew up and whipped my coat with a flapping noise at the same time tiny grains stung my eyes.

The desert had its own idea of who could come and who could leave. It was a serpent—an empty expanse, an endless rolling scene of solid tan with dots of green vegetation where we used to race in the barefoot 10K, Hopi kids with tenuous links to the past and its meaning. Wind always made the serpent hiss, its noise sometimes a comforting message that we *belonged* and were a part of the snake's family, at other times a warning of storms to come. Old man Mase was part of the snake. He had transformed into a desert thing someone had assembled from sand itself. The old man shook his finger at me and screamed but his words refused to come.

"Bro!" Mockta shouted. "You there?"

"What?"

"We're at the Chinese ship. You can't daydream like that and expect to stay alive, cornmeal. We're a long way from Mars. You screw up on an asteroid, and the next thing you know you're flying off into space."

Cornmeal. It was the nickname I'd earned as a kid—a good luck charm, *something sacred*.

"What were the Chinese thinking, anyway? This portion of the asteroid belt is US territory. They want to start another war?"

"That's what we're here to find out. You didn't even read the mission briefing, did you?"

"Too boring," I admitted.

The strange ship towered over us, a massive rectangular monolith on eight thick landing legs that clawed into the asteroid's gravelly surface, securing it. So far away, the sun barely illuminated us. The Chinese liked to paint their ships matte black, so picking out external details was almost impossible except for a red star that stretched above, thirty feet across. Mockta moved up the ramp to their airlock, and when we got to the door, he pointed. A screen in the middle of the main door flashed on and off with a single picture, three partial circles joined around a central circle, black against an orange background.

You left Earth, our mother, and you must come back before it's too late, the old man said. He held up a yellow gourd that had been dried for use in holding water and then uncorked it before turning it over. I expected water to splash. Instead, a pile of glowing sparks piled up on the old man's hard-packed dirt floor before their heat extinguished to leave behind ashes that blew and covered his toes with black. *They have used the gourd of ashes,* he whispered. *So we are near the end. You left Earth, our mother, and you must come back before it's too late . . .*

Mockta slapped the back of my helmet. "Wake the hell up, cornmeal!"

"Sorry, man."

"You OK?"

"Are you seeing anything out here? Like, is the old man talking to you or anything, telling you to come back to Earth?"

"Old man Mase? You seeing *him*?" I nodded and Mockta whistled inside his helmet before changing the subject. He pointed at the flashing screen. "What's this mean? Is that Chinese or something?"

"No, it's universal. It's a symbol that means biohazard. We should try radioing them again, Mockta. I don't like this, got a bad vibe."

"Man, they didn't respond to any of our calls on the way in; why would they now?"

"Maybe they got some disease. I don't want to go in if we can avoid it; just try one more time."

"You've got the comms suit so your radio is more powerful, cornmeal."

My fingers played over the keypad on the suit's forearm, its narrow screen covered with a thin layer of ice. "Nothing."

"Yeah, cornmeal. I'm getting a bad vibe too."

Mockta opened a panel near the airlock's side and began working on it. As soon as he disengaged an inner panel, a forest of wires and circuit boards sprang out so that Mockta cursed at the complexity. Something crackled over my speakers. At first it sounded like a transmission from nearby, but Mockta assured me that he had muted his system to curse at the mess; the signal hadn't come from him. When I turned back to face the Chinese ship, it murmured again, this time the message clear: *The time for purification is near; come inside to meet us, then get back to Earth.*

Sand and rock, in browns and reds and tans that stretched away and to the horizon, Mase emerged from it in swirls of color and dust, his figure coalescing in front of me before it shifted into something else. Something different. A moment later, Mary Makya appeared in his place; she smiled and whispered one question after another, none of them loud enough to hear, but all of them suggesting I'd made a terrible mistake in leaving her—in leaving my home. Mary's eyes sparkled in the desert sun, her irises the color of dark rocks.

"That is one fucked up Chinaman," Mockta said.

His voice brought me back to reality, and I blinked several times to make sure that this wasn't another vision and wasn't about to disappear like Mary had. A woman's body lay on the floor in front of us. Her suit had ruptured down the front, from her groin to her chin where the helmet's faceplate had shattered to send its glass throughout the inner airlock. The only reason I recognized it as a woman was because not all of her face had burned, leaving mascara around a single untouched eye.

"They've charred everything into nothing," I said. "Her suit, the inner airlock, everything. Even the walls are all blackened."

"But with what? A flamethrower? That's a Chinese military vacuum suit, not a standard one; they've sent soldiers to our section of the asteroid belt and killed at least one of their own. Why?"

"This is messed up, Mock. We looking at war?"

Mockta started working on the inner airlock door, his voice loud in my helmet speakers. "We won't know until we get inside, bro. The readings say there's air, but I'm not taking this helmet off for anything, especially if there's a biohazard."

A few minutes later the inner door opened. Mockta and I crept forward, our suits puffing small clouds of gas to keep us pushed down onto the deck with each step. Corpses had stacked up in the corridor. All of them had been charred black like the first one. I wove my way through, doing my best to avoid touching any of them until we finally arrived at the bridge. Mockta moved toward a bank of computers near the back while I waited, half expecting the ghosts of dead Chinese soldiers to rise through the deck or materialize from thin air. Mockta finally whistled.

"They were going to take the asteroid itself," he said.

"What?"

"Unless the translator is broken, it says they were here to assay the interior and then set up engines for a slow push, back to Earth orbit."

"Why?" I asked. "Why risk war? Did they think we wouldn't notice that one of our asteroids had gone missing? What did the assay show?"

Mockta whistled again. "Sapphire. Iron and titanium. So it's a deep blue, worth a fortune. The gravel and rocks on its surface are just a thin crust. They were about to recover the drill bit when something happened. The last entry is just a couple of words: *fungus or lichen*."

"OK. That's enough. I'm done; let's get the hell off this rock."

"We will as soon as I get one thing."

"What, Mockta? What could you possibly have to get? All of them are dead, and the guy who killed them may still be running around here for all we know. At the same time the air could be filled with some kind of germ. I'm not getting paid enough to play detective, Mock. Are you?"

"They knew the Chinese were drilling. I'm to bring back a sample."

"Nobody told *me* that. On whose order?"

Mockta pushed past, heading back to the ship's main corridor. "Chief scientist. Kumar."

"That guy isn't just a scientist. *He's CIA.* They know, Mock. They know something isn't right and they sent us to be guinea pigs."

"Shut up. The drilling bay is at the bottom of the ship. This way."

It was easier just to float through the ship. Mockta and I turned off our suits' gas systems and pulled our way through the narrow corridors until we reached a shaft that went toward the ship's guts. The asteroid's gravity gently pulled us down. Eventually we reached the drilling bay, a high-ceilinged chamber filled with pipe sections and worn drill bits, and even without taking my helmet off I knew how it'd smell: like oil and metal mixed with the odor of heated rock dust. Mockta gestured me over, toward the main shaft; when I got closer, he pointed at a corpse.

"That's the one. The guy that burned them all."

The sight made me feel like vomiting. "He just took his helmet off. Popped it. Death by vacuum, there have to be better ways to go."

"Yeah," said Mockta. "But what's that blue stuff all over him—and his suit?"

"Sapphire dust?"

I drifted down into the drilling pit, where my boots crunched on dust, a thin film over deep blue sapphire within which I swore there was a faint glow that faded the moment I noticed it. The man had frozen solid. A crust of white ice had formed over his eyebrows and on his lips, which curved into a wide grin that made my skin crawl with the strangeness of it all. I reached down. My finger swiped across the dead man's cheek, raising a cloud of fluorescent blue material that glowed faintly for just a moment, the tip of my glove now covered with an aqua-colored film. I half expected the guy's eyes to pop open and for him to shout *boo*.

"Not sapphire dust," I said. "Something else. It reminds me of ground-up glowworms."

Mockta handed me a plastic bag. "Put a bit of sapphire dust in there, bro. Maybe a little of the glow-worm stuff too."

"Got it." When I finished I climbed from the pit. "*Now* can we go, Mockta? This is all making me feel sick; my fingertips are numb."

"Where are you going? The shaft up is this way, bro."

Mockta's voice sounded distant. The sense of numbness started in my fingertips then spread up through my wrists and to my shoulders, my entire torso soon turning cold with a tingling sensation. It shifted to a burning. The desert sun baked me in a layer of thick air trapped inside a rock canyon, and Mary laughed as she moved away, in the direction of a brilliant blue river. Its turquoise water twinkled, and without bothering to take her clothes off, Mary dove in and I followed, filling my throat and nose with frigid liquid that made me feel as though I was about to suffocate. Mary's voice didn't help. It came from all sides and pressed against my chest with a weight of whispers and hisses, forcing the air from my lungs until the blue water went black.

Come home. Come home now, for the purification.

"Bro!" Mockta shook me, both of us floating upward as

he used his feet to occasionally push off against ladder rungs in the walls. "Wake up! What the hell is wrong with you?"

"I'm awake. Something might be wrong with my mix; I can't breathe."

We reached the shaft's top and moved into the main corridor, where Mockta stopped to shine a light through my faceplate. He backed away.

"You've got that blue shit on you. It's inside your suit, bro, all over your face."

"I never took my suit off, not once since we've been in this ship."

"You've got whatever they had, bro. It's why the one in the mining pit burned everything before killing himself; they *all* got infected by something."

I reached out to grab Mockta's shoulder, but he kicked off the wall, rocketing away. "Don't touch me!"

"Jim. I've got to get home. Back to Earth."

Mockta pushed off again, this time through the corridor, and I followed, the pair of us bouncing off walls as I chased him with a sense of urgency that pressed in from all sides at the same time my sense of the present faded. A humming filled my ears. Somewhere in the distance, a voice called me by name, and the view from my suit faceplate faded into black-and-white static, which then shifted into images of an alien planet, of landscapes filled with black rock. *You don't ever have to be alone again,* Mary said, her voice barely a whisper. *I'm here, waiting. Nobody needs to face the darkness. Come home.*

My vision blurred, then formed a view of Mockta trying to escape me, but from thousands of eyes and perspectives that fused into one crystalline image that allowed part of my mind to follow after him. Another part of me continued drifting over the alien planet. Veins of glowing blue material filled every crack, and moisture-covered rocks shimmered to reflect distant starlight, and a sense of calm and peace flowed through me at the same time a realization formed: The rock wasn't black at all. It was solid sapphire, a crust so thick and the light so dim that no sense of color could escape.

Come home to me, Mary said. *Don't let him keep you away.*

Mockta had reached the airlock, where he fumbled with the controls. "Stay back, bro. You're sick. You'll have to stay here on the Chinese ship until I can get help."

"I need to go home, Jim. Mary needs me."

"Mary died, bro. She's not there. And if you take that stuff back to Earth . . ."

Blood now filled the corridor in a cloud of droplets, all of them different and of various sizes, undulating in forms that shifted from spherical to oblong while smaller ones collided with others to form large globes. My muscles had never felt strong like this, gorilla-wild. It happened so quickly that it ended before it began, Mockta's suit shredded and my gloved hands deep inside his chest where they ripped his body open. Where had the rage come from? An echo of it still rang through me, a sense that nothing else mattered except Earth and that anything in my way had to be destroyed.

Us, Mary whispered. *We are with you.*

After processing through the airlock, I stopped. It took a few minutes of digging on the asteroid's surface, the sounds of scraping transmitted through my suit gloves and filling my helmet with the noise of gravel against rock. Finally I reached it—a smooth glassy face of deep blue, what remained of my home. Tears came then. Some fraction of my mind, a small speck deep inside that retained the capability for independent thought, wondered why I should care about this rock, why it should feel like home when Earth was so far away. *What had I done to Mockta?*

I love you, said Mary. *We will always love you.*

"You're not real."

I'm as real as you need me to be.

"Mary is dead."

How can I be dead when I'm right here?

I did my best to slow down, to try and stop myself from getting back to my vessel, but every effort to resist met a welcome of warmth and acceptance, of pure happiness or its promise. Mary held my hand, her long black hair floating in low gravity, and I wondered how she could survive without a suit. She was real and not real. Mary squeezed my hand and refused to let go, running her other hand from my shoulder and down my arm. *As real as anything.*

Let's go home.

"You don't know how to fly this thing," I said. Somehow we'd processed through the airlock and my suit was gone, replaced by coveralls, so the ship's cold air blew across my forehead. The controls looked foreign and familiar at the same time.

Mary sat next to me. *I know everything you do. And you never have to worry again. Rest now, Michael*

Chakwaina, and I promise that you'll never have to wake up again.

Michael, I thought. That was my name. The realization that I'd forgotten created a flash of terror. "What are you?"

Vibrations shook the chair beneath me, and my hands moved over the controls to plot a course, one that would put us in Earth orbit. A moment later, we lifted. The ship turned until the distant sun shone through a tiny window and blinded me before I looked away.

We are everything and nothing. There will be a purification, and your kind will be cleansed of pain and suffering, used for a time, and times, and half a time until our creation is complete.

Mary smiled. Her face reflected sunlight off dark skin, and when she reached for my hand, it filled me again with warmth and memory. Part of me felt the acceleration yank, forcing me back into the seat at the same time Mary climbed into my lap and melted against my chest.

We will make everything feel this way, Michael. Warm and perfect. Now eat, for it is a long way to Earth, and we need you in working order, we will need you to introduce us to others so that we can spread our warmth over the world.

"This isn't so bad," I whispered. "This isn't bad at all."

THE EUREKA ALTERNATIVE

Brad R. Torgersen

On the four hundred-and-sixty-first day of the war to end all wars, Chief Abernathy came back from the sideways. Twice. In the exact same vehicle. Or what appeared to be the same vehicle. Constructed with the same steel frame, the same wiring, and using the same computer system and electronics. Except the woman at the controls was different. Enough for her to practically fall over with shock when she opened the vehicle door and stepped out onto the reaction chamber floor.

Four uniformed Army orderlies rushed forward and caught her before she hit the cement. Her body vibrated like a bass string that had been harshly plucked, and she clutched her arms around her midsection—retching three times—before she could finally stand on both feet. Hands shaking, she slowly reached up to the modified pilot's helmet on her head and pushed it off. Gripping it by the chin strap, she dropped the helmet to her side where it dangled.

"Chief?" said one of the orderlies. "Chief, can you hear me? It's Specialist Brown."

"Specialist Brown is dead," she said flatly.

"Ma'am?" the young orderly said, confused. He reached his hands out and gently put his fingers on her face. "It's okay. We've got you. Look at me, ma'am. Look at my eyes. You're back home."

Her right hand reflexively popped up and caught his wrist, which she held tightly, her tendons standing out.

"Specialist Brown is *dead*," she repeated.

The four orderlies exchanged worried glances among themselves, then herded the shaken warrant officer out of the reaction target zone and toward the thick steēl hatchway doors—which stayed shut during reaction chamber operations, but had been wide open when the second, unexpected sideways car winked into existence.

Brown waved his hand at the array of windows protecting the control room two stories above their heads. An officer nodded and gave Brown a thumbs-up. White-smocked technicians hurriedly passed the orderlies as they crossed the chamber's threshold and entered the tubelike corridor beyond. Chief Abernathy's head jerked back and forth, her eyes wide to the whites—like she couldn't quite believe what she was seeing.

"We're getting you to the postmission infirmary," Brown said reassuringly.

"I know where we're going," she said, legs moving woodenly. "It's just that—"

Brown motioned for the others to stop.

"What, ma'am?" he said, and waited.

"None of this should exist anymore. None of *you* should exist."

Brown traded a troubled look with the other orderlies, then got his charge moving again, her boots scraping awkwardly on the textured concrete walkway.

Clara Abernathy was sitting quietly at a table in the mission briefing center when her boss, Lieutenant Colonel Garcia, walked in. The expression on his face was not happy, and Clara sat up quickly, switching off her pad computer.

"We have a problem," the colonel said.

"Reactor signature fluctuations again?" she asked. "Gonna scrub tomorrow's trip?"

"More complicated than that," he said, running his hand over his shaved scalp.

"Something wrong with the sideways car?" she guessed again.

"No," he said. "This is a personnel issue."

"What do you mean?"

"Maybe it's easier if I just show you," he said, as he motioned for her to follow him.

Clara slipped her pad into a zippered flight-suit pocket and followed her boss out of the briefing center. Home Plate—as it was colloquially known to the sideways pilots—was a warren of branching corridors leading to reinforced concrete compartments built on the bones of the Dugway Proving Ground complex destroyed earlier in the war. The US military brass had reasoned that the Chinese generals wouldn't waste effort on an installation they presumed to have already been neutralized. Using plans and specifications delivered from the Massachusetts Institute of Technology, before it too had been destroyed, the US military had hastily constructed Home Plate under camouflage in less than ninety days.

When Clara reached the infirmary—all sideways pilots were required to endure a thorough checkup immediately upon return—she took one look through the mirrored glass and gasped. There she was, sitting sullenly on the edge of the medical examiner's gurney while two orderlies and two Army doctors poked and prodded at her. Clara stepped close to the glass, her jaw hanging half-open, and stared intently for a good thirty seconds. Then the Clara on the other side—who could not see past the one-way mirror—looked up, and Chief Abernathy had to turn her head away. It was too disturbing.

"Jesus," Clara said. "It's *me*."

"We always wondered if this could happen," said the colonel. "After over thirty-five missions and five successive pilots—with two missing in action—we finally got a duplicate."

"Have you talked to her?" Clara asked.

"Yes," her boss said. "Everything checks out so far. She knows me. She knows this place. Except . . . something really bad went down. Beijing decided to have another go at Dugway, apparently. And while Home Plate's nuke hardening absorbed most of the damage in that timeline—nice to know the effort was worth it—a lot of us still got killed. She says they launched her one more time, to try to find a branch where Home Plate was still operational."

"The sideways cars always return to their point of origin," Clara said. "Visits to other timelines are temporary."

"That's the thing," Lieutenant Colonel Garcia said. "Her sideways car thinks this *is* its point of origin."

"The branching algorithm shaved things that close, huh?" she asked.

"It would seem so. We've cross-checked her car's computer, and nothing seems wrong. As far as it's concerned, this timeline *is* the timeline."

"What about—what about *me* . . . in there?"

"That's what we have to figure out," Clara's boss said. "Even though we knew there was a statistical chance this might happen, we've never prepared a contingency plan. With the war going the way it is, nobody ever had the bandwidth. We're grasping at straws at this point. Now the situation is complicated. At my request, the docs are doing a genetic test, just to be one hundred percent sure it's, in fact, you. But I've got little doubt it is. And now that we have two of you, how do we handle it?"

Clara felt her skin crawl. The theorists from MIT had mentioned a doppelganger scenario, but few people involved in the Home Plate project had ever put serious thought about how to deal with it. Everyone was too busy hoping and praying one of the sideways missions might bring back something—some new piece of technology—that might make a difference in the war. She herself had witnessed six different alternative timelines, none of which had yielded positive results. Though the ice-age timeline had been interesting. Her sideways car had blinked into existence beneath a hundred feet of water. Good thing the cars had been designed with adverse environmental factors in mind, including hard vacuum and radiation proofing.

"What if this is some kind of game the Chinese are playing?" Clara asked. "We were never sure they didn't steal MIT's secrets before it was destroyed. Could this be some way for them to plant a ringer in our midst?"

"Doubtful," Garcia said. "Even if they managed to obtain the plans, how would they go about kidnapping an identical you and brainwashing her into helping them? Besides, why would they bother with a Home Plate project of their own when the war is going so damned well for them in our timeline?"

Clara sighed. She didn't need a reminder that their backs were against the wall. Hell, had been against the wall for many months. If the idiots in D.C. had not been so feckless in the run-up to the war, maybe things would have been different. As it was, many of the Army's remaining brass—those still surviving in a world where Washington was an irradiated pile of lifeless rubble— speculated that several key senators had been on the take from Beijing. Oaths hadn't seemed to have mattered much to twenty-first-century politicians. Perhaps they'd been bribed into complacency? Certainly the President had had her head in the sand, right up until the nukes had started to strike. And after that . . . well, it was all water under the bridge now.

Clara swallowed. "Let me talk to her."

"I'm not sure that's a good idea," Garcia said, holding up his hand.

"If she really is me, we'll get a lot more information out of her a lot faster."

"I am not sure she can help us," Garcia said. "Like I told you, she said Beijing sent more nukes against Dugway in her timeline. It sounds to me like things were going even worse there. And if she'd already found a significantly better timeline, why didn't she take something back with her to help at home?"

Clara chewed a lip. She turned her head and stared up at the lieutenant colonel. "Let me talk to her anyway. What have we got to lose?"

The two women—duplicates from across the quantum fissioning of multiple universes—sat across from each other in Home Plate's tiny cafeteria. The Clara from the twice-nuked Home Plate timeline ate ravenously from her heaping tray, while the Clara who thought of herself as the *original* Clara, sipped at a cup of hot coffee. It was midnight outside, but since hardly anyone at Home Plate ever bothered to risk going out into the open air, time didn't mean much. The hands on the clock spun around and around. Twenty-four-hour operations meant nobody paid much attention to the time, save for mission tracking purposes. They'd been getting ready to send Clara out on another mission in fourteen hours, but not before she'd had a chance to interrogate her alternative self first.

"We'll have to figure something out," Clara said to her quantum twin as the woman forked yet another mouthful of spaghetti into her face. She'd claimed to have not eaten a real meal in over a week, and the blood work from her checkup had confirmed her malnourishment.

"Thing One and Thing Two," hungry Clara said to herself after she cleared her mouth with a long drink from a bottle of frosty cold soda. Soft drinks had become almost unheard of in hungry Clara's timeline, while the Home

Plate consumables in original Clara's timeline were still fairly well stocked. Beijing had not managed to completely wipe out manufacturing and logistics. Though if something didn't change for the better, and soon, both the contents of the cafeteria and Home Plate's one-room post exchange would become priceless.

"Doctor Seuss," Clara said, allowing herself a small smile. "I like it."

"You should. You hated seeing them ban the Doctor."

"I hated seeing them ban a lot of shit before the war," Clara said.

Before inhaling another mouthful of spaghetti, the hungry Clara put her fingers to the bridge of her nose, and thought.

"For real, let's try this. I'll be Clara Louise," she said. "You be Clara-Bear."

"Dad used to call me that."

"I know. It was the last thing he said to me over the phone before he died."

"Dad's *dead* in your timeline?"

"Isn't he in yours?"

Clara-Bear—she liked it instantly, though she was horrified by the news that Dad was gone in her counterpart's world—shook her head.

"I don't know, to be honest. Dad was with many of the evacuees they hustled into the Sierra Nevadas. Our communications with that part of the country aren't great. And there are millions of names unaccounted for."

"In my timeline," said Clara Louise—using her birth middle name—"Dad and the other evacuees never made it that far."

"Jesus," Clara-Bear said. "Beijing must have attacked much earlier in your world."

"Not earlier," Clara Louise said. "Just more concentrated. More nukes. Many, many more nukes. They signed that nonaggression deal with Russia, so they had missiles and warheads to spare."

"No such deal in our world," Clara-Bear said. "Moscow got it just like D.C. got it. And London. And other places. To this day I still have no idea what precisely Beijing thought they could gain from this war. If it was world domination China wanted, it already had America's major corporations and far too many of America's politicians eating out of Beijing's hand. Why destroy what you can clearly *buy*?"

"We never could figure it out, either," Clara Louise admitted. Then she went back to wolfing down hearty mouthfuls of noodles and ground beef with spicy tomato sauce.

Clara-Bear sipped her coffee, watching her alternate up close. It still made CB's skin crawl, thinking this was in fact her, but also *not* her. What would Clara's grandmother—the devout Baptist—have made of the situation? Could the same soul exist in two separate bodies in the same place at the same instant? Wasn't there some fundamental violation of God's orderly universe?

Of course, Clara and the others involved with Home Plate from the beginning had been forced to check their conventional notions of religion at the door. The eventual validation of the MIT theory—that alternative timelines not only existed, but could be reached temporarily—had blown apart a lot of old questions. If it was theoretically possible for any number of alternative selves to make any number of alternative choices, how would God judge? *Any* God? Which way did the axe fall? Was one person on the hook for *all* choices simultaneously? It kinda sank the notion of free agency.

Not that many people working Home Plate had spared time to write it all up. They talked and joked about the problem between shifts, while a shattered and bombarded United States of America waited and wondered when the next wave of destruction would come. This really was it. The war for the whole enchilada. Whichever major nation remained standing at the end would be *the* world power for decades—even centuries. After the ensuing devastation on virtually every continent, the losers would have too steep a hill to climb too quickly, to ever post a threat to the victor. Not in CB's lifetime, anyway.

"My boss said if you'd found anything that could help with the war, you'd have never come here," Clara-Bear said.

"So far as I knew when I was coming back, this *was* here. And *our* boss had been dead for weeks."

"Right," Clara-Bear said. "But was Lieutenant Colonel Garcia correct? You didn't find anything worth bringing back?"

Clara Louise barked bitter laughter.

"When do we ever? You know how it is. You've been there. The damned machine launches us into some timeline where America's trashed or never existed in the first place."

"Spanish America was interesting," Clara-Bear said.

"What?" her counterpart said, startled.

"I didn't get to stay for long, and they were barely up to nineteenth-century industrial-revolution standards, but Mexico never got its independence, and Catholic Spain ruled everything from the Puget Sound to Baja, and all the way to the banks of the Mississippi. I gathered they were at war with the Vatican. Something like a second schism had occurred in the church. Again, I wasn't there for very long."

"We still haven't figured that problem out," Clara Louise said. "For the mission to be successful, we need more damned *time*. To explore. To make a thorough assay of the timeline. What can we possibly hope to get from the hours or even mere minutes we're allowed to leave the sideways car and look around, or talk to people? We're lucky they reinforced the cars against small-arms fire. On one mission, I had some roughnecks dressed like Genghis Khan try to spear me. Needless to say, I stayed in the car for that one."

Clara-Bear almost laughed. In another time and place—another fissioning of the quantum universes—it would have been amusing. But not here. And not now.

"I wish I could say our timeline is doing any better than yours," CB said, sighing. "But it sounds like we're only just a few months better off. Beijing's war in our world is a wider war, yes, but they're still going all out. And some of the United States' former allies have split off and tried to cut deals of their own. We look like a losing horse. Not out of the race yet. But falling further and further behind."

Clara Louise paused eating, wiped her mouth and chin thoroughly with a paper napkin, then slouched back into her seat, looking exhausted.

"I should have stayed where I was that last trip."

"The car always comes back," Clara-Bear reminded.

"Yeah, the *car* comes back. But if you're me—and we're agreed that you are—then I know for a fact you've been tempted to get out of the car and just . . . let it vanish behind you. Stay where you are, in whatever timeline you're in at that moment."

"Like Bud Abbell and Scott Thomas," Clara-Bear said ruefully.

"Those guys died with Lieutenant Colonel Garcia," Clara Louise said.

"Not in my timeline they didn't," Clara-Bear said. "In my world, their cars came back, but they never did. Missing In Action, their files say. Garcia suspects that Abbell and Thomas both decided to stay put. Either out of pure fear about coming back to a world where Beijing is on the brink of winning, or because whatever it was they found—on some other version of Earth—was simply too appealing to leave."

"Or . . . they just got a spear in the chest," Clara Louise said.

This time Clara-Bear did laugh—and hated herself for it. Chief Thomas and Chief Abbell had been good people. Friends. She'd trusted them. And they'd all made a solemn promise—each and every sideways pilot—to never cut and run. Home Plate wasn't about letting one person bail out on history. It was about bailing the world out of perhaps the worst jam it had been in, in as many as a thousand years. Or more?

"Yeah," Clara-Bear admitted. "It *is* a tempting idea. But only to a point. Who's to say any of those other worlds are in fact better than this one? Especially the ones with radically less advanced technology? I don't know about you but *I* certainly don't want to die from an abscessed tooth, or skin cancer, or go blind from cataracts, or die from starvation because the people of North America haven't advanced much beyond hunter-gatherer societies. And the bombed-out worlds are worse. One time I showed up and the Geiger counter starts pinging like I've landed on Chernobyl the day after it blew. Never even bothered to look around. Dugway was rubble in every direction. Like the old Soviet Union had nuked it again, and again, and again, and again. I just sat there hoping the rad-hardening on the car was good enough to stop me from getting cancer. When I got back, the recovery team had to pressure wash and decon the car for an hour. We couldn't use the reaction chamber for a month while they scrubbed off every last speck of radioactive dust they could find."

"The last timeline I visited before being pulled back here," said Clara Louise, "might have made for a good home. I know they had radio, because I picked it up and could listen to the music. Didn't sound like anything I've ever heard, from any country. Dugway looked to me like it had never been developed. There were no people. But the hills were green with trees and grass. And there was a healthy rain shower, too. The climate was a lot wetter for this part of the country, I assume. Which makes you wonder what else was different, right? Different climate cycles mean different migration patterns. Maybe nobody ever crosses that land bridge in Alaska, because it never exists? First people to settle North America come by boat.

From Hawaii, maybe? Who knows? But I should have given it a shot. My timeline was toast anyway. They sent me out *hoping* I'd wind up at a version of Home Plate which was better off. Told me to be sure to share their story to whomever cared to listen."

"And in countless other timelines," Clara-Bear said, "this conversation is never happening, because you and I don't exist. Home Plate doesn't exist. China doesn't exist, or at least doesn't exist like it does now. Or the Aztecs never fell and now rule all of North America. Or the Vikings crossed en masse and went west of the Missouri. Or . . . or any and all of it happened. And simultaneously *none* of it happened, because there's no way for us to ever goddamned know."

"Too bad the reaction chamber can't send us backward," Clara Louise said, rubbing at her stomach and yawning. "What we need to be able to do is go back three years and *warn* those assholes at the Pentagon what's coming."

"Like those assholes would have listened," Clara-Bear said bitterly. "I sometimes think all the Joint Chiefs ever cared about—before the war—was feathering their political beds for their post-retirement appointments."

"Maybe you're right. Alas, MIT said it would never work that way."

Clara-Bear dipped her chin to her chest and let a long silence elapse between them.

"Which doesn't answer the biggest question facing you and me—or should I say, *me* and me? What do we do in a timeline where there are two of us? What's the boss gonna do, just add you to the pilot roster and start sending out double missions?"

"Knowing Garcia," Clara Louise said, "that's exactly what he's got in mind."

"But . . . how is this supposed to work? Both of us here? Now? My ex-husband used to joke that if ever I'd known what it was like to be married to me, I'd have killed me in the process. What if he's right?"

"*Our* ex-husband was right," Clara Louise said. "We probably will kill each other. Or get so much on each other's nerves we'll want to kill each other. Bad news. One of us has got to go her own way."

"And go *where* exactly?" Clara-Bear said, exasperated.

Then she caught sight of the little curl of a grin going up the side of Clara Louise's mouth.

"No," Lieutenant Colonel Garcia said.

"Boss—" both Claras said in unison, as they sat across the table from Garcia in the mission briefing room.

"I said no, and I mean it," he barked, cutting them off. "I've still got rank here."

"And I'm not convinced I technically fall into your chain of command, sir," Clara Louise said. "You may boss around your Clara, but you can't boss around *this* Clara."

"The hell I can't!" Garcia said, slapping his palm down on the table. "Maybe the war was going to shit for you in your timeline, but it's not going completely to hell for us yet in ours. Now I've got one extra sideways car—do either of you have any idea how difficult it is to build or replace those under the circumstances?—and one extra sideways pilot. I'm putting both to good use. And because I *know* you, Clara—both of you—I know you won't flake on me in the clutch. I can send more missions, faster, and double the chances one of you can bring us back something which will make all the difference in the war."

"You can keep the car, sir," Clara Louise said. "It comes back regardless. And so do I, unless I decide not to."

"I know you," Garcia said. "You're too damned loyal to skip out on us."

"But I'm not skipping out," she said, and pointed a finger at Clara-Bear.

Garcia took a deep breath, and ran both hands over his shaved head.

"God," he said, puffing out his cheeks. "This is so damned crazy."

"The MIT people warned us we were in for a philosophical headache," Clara-Bear reminded him.

"Yeah," Garcia said. "Maybe I should assign myself to one of these damned trips and then *I* should bail the fuck out. How about that?"

Both Claras looked at each other, then at the boss, then back at each other.

"If this technology had been developed sooner," Clara-Bear said, "and if it had become more widespread, boatloads of people would probably be clawing and scratching for a chance to bail to other timelines."

"How do we know people aren't bailing to *our* timeline?" Garcia asked sarcastically.

"No dice," Clara Louise said. "Anyone who discovered what's going on in this timeline would know it's a shitshow and opt for something else."

"True," Garcia said. He drummed his fingers on the table. Like his counterparts, he was tired. None of them had slept since Clara Louise's arrival. And he still had to make a decision on Clara-Bear's next mission. She'd proposed they go out together. Two Claras in one car. Double the people to look around. The cars had never been built for two, but there was nothing to indicate a passenger—sitting in the pilot's lap—wasn't possible. Just because it hadn't been done before didn't mean it couldn't be done. But was it wise? In the end, Clara-Bear knew Clara Louise had a point. Her version of Lieutenant Colonel Garcia had been dead for a long time. Her chain of command in her timeline had cast her into the quantum ether. Did he really have the right to give her orders? Now?

"I still have to justify this to the generals at Cheyenne Mountain," he finally said. "What's the tactical or strategic benefit? Especially if I know fully well there's a strong chance *you*, Miss Louise, will not be coming back. It takes an absurd amount of energy and no small amount of reactor fuel to send a sideways car on a trip. I can't justify burning that fuel on a whim."

"What if," Clara-Bear said, "instead of us looking for some kind of wonder-thing to change the war, we instead leave behind an ambassador who can convince the people of that timeline to send help?"

The colonel sat up. "What do you mean?"

"We have the plans and documents on digital, sir," Clara-Bear said. "We make some copies in several formats, including hard copy. If we come across a timeline that looks promising, Clara Louise stays put—copies in hand—and uses them to get the people of that timeline to marshal reinforcements."

"You'd have to stumble across a United States not already at war," Garcia said. "And not already in the grip of all that pure bullshit that was making the country crazy before the conflict. All that 'woke' garbage, and worse. Our society was coming apart, and the Chinese took advantage of it. You'd need an America not only much better off, but also able and willing to take the kernel of technology we give them and rapidly produce entire fleets of sideways vehicles, able to navigate to *our* timeline, and then go to bat on our behalf. And that's just crazy."

"No crazier than the original plan," Clara Louise said firmly. "Think about it, sir. What have you got to lose?"

Garcia shot a knowing glance at Clara-Bear, who smiled.

He groaned, but pulled out his computer pad and began assembling the orders.

Fissioning of the quantum universes. Earths unending. The two Claras visited many. Some were war-torn iterations of the world they'd left behind. Others seemed to be wildernesses where humanity had never risen above bones and stones. In one instance, the pair were accosted by a troop of olive-skinned Latin-speaking legionnaires on horseback armed with black-powder muskets, and the reinforced sideways car got a real test. Meanwhile, back home—Clara-Bear's timeline—Lieutenant Colonel Garcia had opted to double up using Clara Louise's car, sending two other pilots on similar missions, each seeking some alternative iteration of North America where the United States—or some nation a lot like it—had not only managed to survive into the twenty-first century, but also was thriving enough to make it a place worth winning over to the besieged timeline's cause.

After returning from one particularly fruitless mission,

the two Claras received word that Beijing had landed troops in what was left of California. And while some Californians were going out fighting, far too many of California's political class were welcoming the Communists with open arms. Better red than dead, it seemed.

"Suppose it actually works," Clara-Bear said one afternoon while she, Clara Louise, and Colonel Garcia—now promoted to full bird—were eating rations in the cafeteria. Hot chow was becoming less frequent now that the West Coast was in enemy hands. The Texas supply chain was still intact, but Texas had its own problems, and the days of frosty cold sodas were over.

"The plan?" Garcia said, poking his brown plastic spoon into a foil pouch.

"Right," Clara-Bear said. "If some other America rides to our rescue, and we've got this sideways arsenal at our disposal . . . what's to prevent us from rescuing the *other* timelines, too?"

"I don't get it," Garcia confessed.

"Think about it, boss," she said. "Clara Louise's timeline. There are still people there. Beijing may have bombed that America out, but the timeline itself is not lost. With sufficient technology and manpower, you could get a beachhead there, too, and roll the Chinese back."

"A thousand fronts in a thousand timelines," Clara Louise murmured over her own ration pouch.

"Whoa," Garcia said. "We're not even sure we can reliably *find* our way back to specific timelines with our current tech."

"But a more advanced America *might* find a way, right?"

"Maybe," he said. "But that's so far ahead of where we're at now, I don't even want to think about it. It will take a literal miracle to help us win *this* damned war, CB. Much less CL's war, and any other war on any other Earth we find. If you go all the way with that idea, there are an infinite number of Earths, any number of which might *all* need saving. What country in their right mind would have the will or the resources?"

"What country indeed?" Clara-Bear said.

The Claras popped into existence as they always had— flat in the middle of the Utah desert—and immediately noticed something quite different. They were sitting on pavement, as in Clara-Bear's timeline, but instead of landing in the reaction chamber, they were parked in the midst of a forest of huge gantries. Strange wheeled vehicles rumbled around the tarmac carrying freight containers of various sizes as well as cryogenic tanks and busloads of men and women clad in helmets and pressure suits.

"Holy shit," Clara Louise exclaimed, popping the door to the sideways car. "This is one hell of an airport."

"It's not an airport," Clara-Bear said as she got out and looked. "It's . . . it's a spaceport!"

A thunderous rumbling from miles away—across the endless pavement—caught their attention. They turned and watched as one of the far gantries lit up with fire. A massive rocket—larger by far than anything the United States had ever launched in either CB's or CL's timeline— pushed its way into the blue sky. Its earthquake-inducing engines roared magnificently as the mighty vehicle boosted up, and up, and up, until it was no longer visible to the naked eye, and only a drifting column of fume was left to dissipate in the morning air.

"This is it," Clara Louise said, and began to hurriedly empty the sideways car's contents.

"But we haven't even talked to anybody yet," Clara-Bear said. "For all we know this is Imperial Japan or Nazi Germany!"

"Maybe or maybe not," Clara Louise said. "Whoever they are, they're putting stuff into orbit that would give Elon Musk a wet dream. This *has* to be it. It's either these people or it's nobody. I have to take the chance. We've never seen anything like this during any of our trips."

"Assuming you can even talk to them," Clara-Bear said. "Look at that big rocket over there. What's the lettering on the side?"

"Eureka," Clara Louise said. "Did we forget our Greek?"

Clara-Bear opened her mouth to object, then realized her counterpart was dead right. The script on the rocket was Greek. And somebody from spaceport security had obviously noticed their presence, because several rapidly moving vehicles with flashing lights and loud sirens had jetted out of a small hangar. They quickly moved across the countless acres of concrete.

"Get back in and punch the emergency recall," Clara Louise said. "Hurry, before they get here."

"But you could get dragged off in cuffs. Or worse!"

"It's the risk of the job," Clara Louise said. "But I have a feeling that's not going to happen."

CL jumped up and down and waved her hand in the direction of the sirens, smiling.

"I don't know," Clara-Bear said, slowly getting back into the sideways car—which suddenly felt empty after this many trips with a companion in tow.

"You will know. And hopefully soon. If these are the right people, the cavalry will be coming to your timeline. Get back to Colonel Garcia and tell him the good news."

"I don't want to spread false hope," Clara-Bear said, still skeptical.

"False hope?" Clara Louise said, and turned to stare at her mirror self. "What could possibly be false about any of this? We saw that rocket take off. A rocket with Greek lettering. What if this is the timeline when the scientific method took root a thousand years before the Enlightenment? What if these people have colonies on the moon, and Mars, and maybe elsewhere in the solar system? Think of what they might do, equipped with the sideways plans. They've clearly devoted their energies to conquering space. Conquering the timelines might seem like a next logical step."

"Assuming we would even *want* them to conquer!"

"Just get back to Colonel Garcia and let him know we may have hit the jackpot. Either nothing happens, and you'll have to keep trying with more missions to other timelines, or this timeline is the answer—the one we've been hoping for since we first spoke over dinner."

Clara-Bear sighed and strapped herself back into her seat.

"Okay," she said, taking one last look around at the massive gantries and the swiftly approaching vehicles. "You know, I admit I am more than a little jealous. By the looks of things, this is one hell of a future."

"Indeed," Clara Louise said. "And if I am right—and we've been lucky—this will be *all* our futures. Beijing can't compete with this!"

Chief Abernathy—who still quietly thought of herself as the original—snapped her alternate self a quick salute, which Clara Louise returned in kind. Then she shut the airtight door in the sideways car and hit the big green control which bypassed the car's ordinary wait-it-out return protocol, and zapped the car instantly back to its point of origin.

A DAY IN THE LIFE OF A SUICIDE GEOMANCER

Weston Ochse

0335. The alarms shriek like an avalanche of the dead, causing everyone in the bunkhouse to leap and fall from their dreams of how things used to be. Many groggy, most fearful, they jerk on what clothes they can and grab weapons before heading outside. I bolt out of bed. I don't even pause to dress as I hurl myself through the door and into the cool early morning hours of the South Dakota plains, the moon long since set and the North Star still glittering like a bright unruly fist in the sky. I stand naked to the universe, seeing a sight that makes me wish my universe wasn't my own.

Little Tree, face bloody, hair ripped out by her hands and tumbling to the ground, crouches like a rabid animal, her eyes black, wide, and thoughtless. Where her teeth had been so bright and white the day before, her mouth is now a maw of red and green pus, molars littering the ground behind her as they escaped the necrotic thing she'd become. Her tongue is like a leech, quivering and black and wanting something, anything, so it might survive despite those it must kill to do so.

Two scouts hold her at bay, wooden two-pronged pitchforks designed to keep a Golden Ager away as she scratches at the rough lengths. The scouts work in concert, one on each side, denying her an escape or an opportunity to bite and rend the flesh of others. Their feet move in assured precision, like the dances of old around a fire, only this fire is a dead thing, once alive, once part of us, now transformed.

Little Tree had been too eager to understand the ways of the GAgers. They'd sent their propaganda leaflets over our camp to be read, but most knew better. They were always trying, always tempting. The necromancy used in the word-making was enough to transform the living to the undead if one didn't take the necessary precautions. Little Tree knew of these measures, she knew how to read them backward to save her sanity, but her urge to know was much greater than her desire to be safe.

I shake my head.

Little Tree is but another reason I need to do what I will do this day. She is yet another example of what GAgers are willing to do in order to create their own Golden Age. But we've long since known that a Golden Age for one tribe is not so for the other, especially when they insist on a single tribe ruled by the philosophies of a long dead megalomaniac.

0400. To say I wasn't influenced by Octavia E. Butler and her book *The Parable of the Sower* is to say that my grandmother wasn't influenced by Donald Trump's *The Golden Age of New Reason*, published in 2030—better known as the Gold King's *Thus Spoke Zarathustra*, whose dictums had precipitated the Big War. Although Octavia's book is about climate change, or so it presumes, it is more about the social dissolution of America—or the Trumpian Golden Age. And it describes the classic case of the individual and what responsibility they have for being born. There are moments when I wish that I was less enlightened and I was able to make it through a day without becoming violently ill. After all, was it my fault I was born? Of course, the answer is no, so then the follow up question becomes is it my fault what I do with my life? And for that, the answer is yes, the choices were laid out before me, and I chose to allow them to influence me.

That there are still so many who hope for a Golden Age angers me, which is why I have decided to do what I am doing. And to think that my grandmother was so beguiled by a cult of personality both baffled and shamed me. After all, shouldn't we have taken the time to explain to her that because of the color of her skin she wasn't going to be invited to the After-the-War Victory Party?

By letting her down, we'd let us all down.

0420. The Sun Dance of the Lakota had once been outlawed. The idea of one giving personal sacrifice to their people and community was not accepted by non-First Nation peoples. They insisted there must be something for everyone. Democracy and socialism existed based on the idea of everyone sharing. But the Sun Dance promised different. A man or a woman might fast for days and then consecrate themselves in order to reach a higher power, to achieve a higher purpose.

You may call me the Higher Purpose, but I prefer the name that was given me, Peter No Flesh Adams. I am of American ancestry, which means that I am a mutt. My DNA is derived of Sioux, French, and English nucleotides, all stirred into the cocktail that is me. I bet if you added some high-end liquor, I might even taste good.

My goal is to explain the parable.

My ultimate goal is to be the parable.

It is not so difficult. So many look at the various soils Jesus spoke of, but miss the idea that he was trying to train his disciples in the idea of parable, a distinct story that illustrates a lesson and not necessarily a tale based on fact. Also important is that a parable is based on human characters, and a fable is based on nonhuman ones.

With the Sun Dance, one can both be parable and fable.

0435. "You're up early this morning," says the Far Ocean Woman, shredding the pecans into a facsimile of coffee.

"Today is my Sun Day. I would like to hear your story," I say, following the traditional speak of those who bloomed before me.

I'm only the seventh of my kind so perhaps she doesn't know how to deal with me. She gives me a long stare, then it softens, a mother to a possible son who himself might one day bloom. Then she pours me a cup and gives me a chunk of unleavened bread with hard cheese.

"My story is like any other's," she says. "I was a school teacher and I taught students the best I could."

"What did you teach?" I ask.

"I taught English literature and about how the people of England and their colonies changed from being ruled to ruling themselves through the eyes of Thomas Hardy, Charles Dickens, and Charlotte Brontë."

I don't know Hardy, but I do know Dickens and his *Tale of Two Cities*, *Oliver Twist*, and the quizzical *Martin Chuzzlewit*. "Wasn't Brontë the one who wrote *Little Women*?" I ask.

"No, an American named Louisa May Alcott wrote that one. It was a tale of duty to family versus personal growth. How much does one exist outside of oneself? The book was important in that way."

So much like the Sun Dance. So much like sacrifice. How was it that a stuffy ancient American understood what the Lakota and the people of Islam have felt for too long?

"Were you told to teach these this way or did you choose to?" I ask.

"I was given a curriculum. I followed it, but as any good teacher will do, I stressed what was important," she says. "I felt that the other literature children were being forced to read was too conforming. I wanted to demonstrate that there was a difference. That there could be a challenge to the norm, no matter how delicate and subtle."

I think about this for a moment, then say, "I think it suffers from the title—*Little Women*. It's diminutive and makes women seem less than they are." I add, "Which is not at all the theme of the novel."

She nods this time, agreeing with the negative. "But isn't that how the world has always seen us?"

"The world often sees itself in the way it is told to see it. Women being little. It makes men comfortable."

She appraises me and chuckles, then says, "Big Women." And then she says it again, just to taste the sound.

I chuckle with her. "That's enough to scare some away."

She gives me a knowing look. "Which is perhaps why Louisa May Alcott stressed the littleness of them."

0500. I enter the tactical center where maps are plastered everywhere. The commanders of Camp Red Cloud have been busy. All of the locations of the Army of New Custer have been marked and labeled, from their far-off outposts in the southern Rockies to the Black Hills. Somehow, they'd been able to capture the middle ground and hold it.

Nuevo Mexico had their Aztecs and the flying beasts that went with them.

The Canadians saw the return of legions of Sasquatch, their strength and cunning unimaginable.

The west found the Mermaids of California and the Pacifists of the PNW.

And then there were the remaining tribes, the Lakota and the Cheyenne and the Apache and the Navajo. All that was left after the wars and the magic and the terrible days of thunder and lightning that was the battle for the conscience of what had been America.

The GAgers have lookouts in the obvious locations, and checkpoints at all roads into the Black Hills. Their necrophages have made it as far as the Badlands, where they live in the shadows, ready to attack anything with a pulse. Reports have surfaced that we have been fighting our own and we've become demoralized for it. That's one of the problems with an army that can make its own. Necromancers are the worst. Their very abilities to co-opt the dead are reason enough for us to attack them. But ours is a war of peace, and any attack we make is to protect the land, which was why I've spent the last ten years giving into the alchemy of geomancy.

0600. A wave of 570 undead crossed the White River near the town of Interior, New Dakota, at 0545 hours local time. We've long since lost our ability to retaliate using conventional weapons, but because of our excellent planning, those geomancers who'd been working on divining the magma tubes had found their hard work had paid off. It only took a little encouraging to entice the incandescent rock to spew forth upon the undead. They both had no way to retreat or retaliate and melted in place. This has been the third time in as many weeks that Custer's necrophages had targeted that location. Where they got the bodies, we never knew, but we believed it had to be from the battles waged along the Western Front of the Rockies where the Pacifists of PNW were removed a hundred at a pop—easy pickings because of their unwillingness to fight.

Where we might harvest wheat, the GAgers harvest the dead, gifting them arcane sparks of false life, so that they might follow a false Gold King who spouts false witness against his fellow man. But the loss of conventional weapons saved us, really. Had the Army of New Custer and other GAgers had pre-Sun God weapons to use, then we all might be dead already. The Lakota would be barely a memory—and if that—a warning to others not to confront the GAger reality.

It was just after midnight in November of 2043 when magic returned to the world. The Lakota and other First Nation peoples had always known it was here and wondered where it had gone, always trying to entice it through ritual and prayer. Then Comet 12672-MH hurtled past—what the People of the First Nations called the Sun God—and the Earth was never the same. Just as we renew its flight by blooming at night, it turned night into day, a singular EMP pulse encompassing the planet and inviting back that which had been in hiding since the advent of the Industrial Age.

Some called this return Magic.

We acknowledged it as the proof of our own Sun Dance ritual and found a way to weaponize it.

0927: "You know it really should be me," says Flat Elk.

I nod and grin, knowing that there would be no winner from such an argument.

"You are Wágluȟe," he says. "You are *ones who live with relatives*. Of the seven bands of Oglala, you were the loafers. You are also Wašíču. You are a Third Nation and not First Nation People."

I shake my head. "I am Wágluȟe Wazaza also. *Shred into strips*. My mother was Wágluȟe, but she was also Third Nation and from France. She named me Peter after her father."

"Which makes you not pure," Flat Elk says, acting as if it is an *aha moment*.

"Would you make me a GAger?" I counter. "Who we are on the outside means far less than who we are on the inside. My ancestor, No Flesh, proved this. Not only was he a great warrior, but he was also a scout and fought for the Great Chief from the East."

Flat Elk spits. "He was the first GAger."

"He was a Sun Dancer, just as I shall be. He fought, and when asked to kill Crazy Horse, refused. He knew the difference between the People's Law and GAger rule. He knew the value of life." I gesture toward the Black Hills that rise like scars in the sky. "They KNOW no value. Their hearts are necrotic, and their souls are long dead." I approach and grip him by the shoulder. "Look at me, Flat Elk. Am I not alive? Am I not ready to dance?"

For a moment, he seems ready to argue, then he lowers his gaze. "You are alive, No Flesh. You are ready to dance."

"Then will you be my second? Will you join me in preparation?"

His face brightens as his eyes search my own. "I will join you. I will help you."

He says this, knowing he will be the next after me.

"Then let us prepare."

Noon. Those not on watch gather for the ceremony.

Flat Elk stands beside me, the lengths of buffalo bone polished and sharp in his hands.

Tall Sage holds the sun machine, keeping it tame, speaking to it, not letting it leave earth without its promised purchase.

The shaman sings a song that began as someone else's

but became ours, words of rebellion, of suffrage, of loss, and of pride. Words first sung by a Wašíču who'd been displaced as First Nations People in their own land. Once called the Irish, who'd been victims of their own GAgers.

> *'Twas hard the woeful words to frame*
> *To break the ties that bound us*
> *'Twas harder still to bear the shame*
> *Of foreign chains around us*
> *And so I said, "The mountain glen*
> *I'll seek next morning early*
> *And join the brave United Men!"*
> *While soft winds shook the barley*

The shaman's final rite is something that always makes me cry. As a witness, it was because I knew I'd never see a member of my tribe again. When they left, they were never coming back, but the shaman ensured that once gone, they would return, if not in the spirits on the winds, in the great fields in the sky.

I'm not alone.

My mother, along with the mothers who have gone before and the mothers who will give their children after, also lament, beating themselves across the chests and face with hands raw and calloused from working in the earth.

The men of the tribe raise their heads and give cry to the Great Spirit, warrior calls that would send a herd of buffalo thundering or a company of soldiers scampering. Each of their shouts merging into one fiercely sad dissonance that crosses time and space and the pain of other people's attempts to classify us.

And now, as the shaman sings the ancient words of a song once meant to lament a land of lost rebels, I cry yet again. Like the winds that shake the barley, our own winds shake the wheatgrass, wine cups, and purple cornflowers. We are like those weeds and will grow for a season until we are wiped away. But the winds and the rains that make the enemy who hides in the shadowy glens of the Black Hills will nurture our memories, and we shall grow again. Just as those who went before me, I will be replaced by another's growth, our perpetual existence a raised obstinate fist against those who would promulgate the new Golden Age.

1245. The first pierce is pain incarnate, but I do not cry out. Still, my legs threaten to buckle, and Flat Elk keeps me from falling. The second piece pierces my left breast and is worse than the first, the thrum of agony like the bass line to a song of suffering. Once secured, they let out the rope, the wind catching the wings of the Sun Bird, once used as a hang glider. Once used to propel people through the silent sky for entertainment, now it is a vector for my blooming.

During the day, the wind blows east. It catches the air foils and lifts me from the ground. The strands of wheat beneath me become a single Van Gogh brush stroke. The faces of those watching, each an image I shall bring with me.

Higher and higher I soar.

I'm surprised the pain doesn't increase.

I'm fascinated that I don't fall to the earth, gravity ripping me free from the bones piercing my flesh, the only things affixing me to the unnatural flying machine. Like my ancestors before me, I perform a Sun Dance, hanging high in the air. My legs twist in a Spandau ballet as the Earth calls for my return, despite the winds assuring my rise.

I ignore the calls to fall.

I need the sun.

I need to charge.

To become power.

Midnight. I've been part of the sky for half a day. The winds changed an hour ago, and they let me loose. I am like an eagle, soaring the winds, catching updrafts and nighttime thermals that propel me toward the GAgers' stronghold. Inextricably, I feel the power of the stars and the billion suns in the system. Blood has been seeping from me, whipped away with the wind. I am in and out of consciousness, but each time I awake, I revel in being alive. I imagine myself as the Silver Surfer, arcing my way across a dark wave of night dreams toward a certain destiny, weaving the power cosmic.

Galactus cannot stop me, nor can the denizens of the Army of New Custer. The sky has become the new Little Bighorn. Beneath me squirms a mass of the necrotized, dead but focused on the single task to make everyone else dead. Yet, here I am, out of reach. Above their ken.

Flares light the sky in front of me.

The Army of the New Custer sees me coming.

I am not the first.

I am the eighth of my kind.

And I will not be the last.

I feel myself brighten and brighten, soaking in every

ounce of light within my view. The flares die, the stars diminish, the suns go dark, leaving me alone and brilliant in a Stygian sky. I become the sun in the middle of night, so dazzling that one must shield their eyes, lest they go blind.

Paha Sapa had once been the center of our universe and now it is the center of the GAgers. Since gold was discovered and the mountains were hollowed, it has been theirs. They think that by living on it, it will accept them.

But they don't know the truth of it.

The trees are black because of them.

The land is dying because of them.

The world is lost because of them.

Their Golden Age is a pyrite of time.

And then I bloom.

I explode into a million incandescent pieces, each with individual will, powered by practiced and assured geomancy. Like a sudden blizzard of kamikaze fireflies, I light the sky, each piece descending and landing atop a necrophage. Where I land, my energy flows, turning death into life, rot into rule, and must into wheat. They become the barley of the song, the fronds of us all, no longer caught in their Dunning-Kruger OODA loops, but freed to learn the truth, just as they become one with the lands.

And I can almost hear them whisper, *Paha Sapa*, as I became fable and soft winds shake the barley and the grasses of the plains.

And the shaking and the wind will one day be enough.

Because the barley and the grasses will live far longer than any idea of domination.

FUTURE AND ONCE

John Langan

(**The setting**: Paimpont Forest, outside Paimpont Village in the Department of Ille-et-Vilaine, in northwest France—or rather, the remains of the forest. Tree stumps cover the ground, none of them more than a couple of feet high, all of them carbonized. The couple of thin trees rising amidst them are similarly charred, their branches stripped; they look like warped flagpoles. The ground itself is scorched, the sky full of roiling gray clouds. Flurries of ash drift across the stage.

(**Merlin** enters from stage left. At least, he appears to. It may be that he was standing there all this time and we just noticed him. He is as old as you would expect Merlin to be, his beard long and white, though his eyes remain bright. He is perhaps thinner than you would have envisioned, even for a wizard whose concerns are for things other than food. His robes make it difficult to say for sure. They are a gray which retains traces of the deep blue from which they have faded. An assortment of symbols covers them. Whether they have been stitched or painted on is hard to tell. Many of the symbols are familiar, the usual astrological signs you see on a wizard's robes; in addition, there are characters from numerous alphabets, as well as other designs somewhat in the manner of hieroglyphs. The colors of these decorations change with the movement of the robe, the way a fish's scales appear to shift color as it glides through running water. You may see emerald, ruby, chartreuse, and violet, among others; although all of them have the same dimmed appearance as the garment on whose folds, you may have noticed, they seem almost to float, possibly to slide. Merlin's hat is of the dunce-cap variety, conical, of the same gray as his robes, but devoid of their migrating symbols and dented in a couple of spots, as if it had been squeezed into a space slightly too small for it. It perches on the wizard's shock of white hair like a rider clinging to a horse on the verge of throwing him. As Merlin walks to center stage, his eyes scanning the tree trunks as if searching for something, he clatters and jingles and clinks, as the assortment of necklaces, chains, and pendants hung around his neck, the bracelets circling his wrists, jangle and clash together.

(**Ursula Opango** follows Merlin a few paces behind. She is nineteen, her tall frame dressed in gray-and-black camouflage helmet, shirt, and pants. High on her right shoulder, a pair of red chevrons on a rectangular black background identify her as a *caporal*, or corporal, in the French Army. A flak jacket in the same gray-and-black pattern covers her back and chest, its ceramic plates, like those in the large pockets on her pants, making an almost musical clinking as she moves. The pockets on the flak jacket are stuffed. There's a pistol holstered on her right hip and an assault rifle—an HK416, if precision about such things is important to you—slung around her right shoulder and carried muzzle down in both hands. Where Merlin's creased and wrinkled skin is toadstool white, except for the red spots on his cheeks, her smooth skin is dark brown.

(Merlin wanders the center of the stage, slowing to peer at and in some cases into the various tree stumps with an almost detached air. He moves between two stumps in particular before finally settling on one at which he stops, beckoning Ursula to join him. It's not much to look at, even as these tree stumps go, barely more than a disturbance in the ground. Nonetheless, he gestures at it with his left hand.)

Merlin: Here. This one.

(Ursula approaches the tree stump and leans over to look at it, an expression of polite skepticism on her face.)

Ursula: Inside this tree?

Merlin: A hawthorn, yes.

Ursula: For fourteen centuries.

Merlin: Approximately. Record keeping tended to be a rather slipshod affair in those days. Part of the reason I was always writing things down. But yes, close enough.

Ursula: And it was a woman who put you here?

Merlin: Mmm, Nimue, though sometimes she liked to be called Vivian, and one time tried to pass herself off as the Lady of the Lake. Completely ridiculous, of course. At the time, it struck me as part of her charm. I was... quite taken with her. Infatuated, you could say. In her presence, the sap of youth rose again in me hot and strong—

Ursula: I get it. You wanted to fuck her.

Merlin: Yes. I did. She had no interest in lying with an old man such as myself, but she was extremely interested in what she might learn of magic from me. I showed her all manner of things. My lust made me reckless. I taught her just enough for her to catch me in a trap I should have evaded with ease, had I not been so distracted. But I was, and Nimue (or Vivian) trapped me.

Ursula: In a tree.

Merlin: A hawthorn, yes. It was very uncomfortable.

Ursula: I imagine so.

Merlin: The most embarrassing part of the matter was, I saw it all coming. I mean to say, I literally knew exactly what was going to happen, down to the very tree she would use to imprison me.

Ursula: You're serious.

Merlin: Yes. I told you, I may not always tell you the truth in full, but I will do my best not to lie to you.

Ursula: In that case, if you knew this Nimue had it in for you, then why didn't you do something about it? At the very least, you might have stopped teaching her what she needed to trap you.

Merlin: Tell me, Ursula: Do you remember our encounter with the bandits two days ago?

Ursula (looks away): You know I do.

Merlin: Yes. Things didn't go so well for the sergeant, did they?

Ursula (still looking away): At least it was quick.

Merlin: True: In circumstances such as these, a single bullet to the head might be considered its own kind of blessing. Based on your remark, I assume you could describe our location, the relative positions of your fellow soldiers, the course of the battle.

Ursula (looks at Merlin): Yes.

Merlin: Excellent. Now change them.

Ursula: What do you mean?

Merlin: Exactly what I said. Change what happened when the bandits ambushed us outside of Rennes. At the very least, advise Sergeant Falcone not to remove his helmet outside the pharmacy.

Ursula: Stop making fun of me.

Merlin: I assure you, I am not. My request is entirely serious.

Ursula: Your request is entirely ridiculous. How can I change what has happened already? We put Falcone in the ground, for fuck's sake.

Merlin: Exactly. And if you cannot alter the past, how do you expect me to alter the future?

Ursula: Because the future hasn't happened yet.

Merlin: Hasn't it?

Ursula: No.

Merlin: Then how could I know it?

(Ursula begins to reply, stops.)

Merlin: To be honest, I know the future in much the same way you know the past: incompletely. You recall the recent battle with great specificity. This makes sense. It was a memorable event. Undoubtedly, there are many such moments in your life—though how many, I cannot say. I am sure there are small things you recall with startling clarity; I am equally sure there are bigger things you have forgotten some or all of. This is how the future appears to me.

Ursula: So you didn't know what this Nimue was planning for you?

Merlin: Oh, no. That I could see with perfect clarity. Had I not been able to foretell the future, still would it have been obvious. But Nimue was beautiful and I was overcome with desire. In the same way your past bad experiences with a lover may not be enough to keep you away from them a second or a third time, so my future bad fate at Nimue's lovely hands was insufficient to keep me from participating in my doom enthusiastically.

Ursula (shaking her head): I'm sorry. It still makes no sense to me.

Merlin: No need to apologize. There are times it seems a little odd to me, too.

Ursula: So you were in the tree for fourteen centuries. What was that like?

Merlin: Cramped. Although the spell Nimue used to imprison me was constructed well—enough for me to be unable to break it, there was room at its edges for certain modifications. This I had planned, as I had no indication I would not do so. I was able to bind myself to the tree and thus draw sustenance from it. I tapped into the network whereby the trees in a forest communicate with one another—

Ursula: They do?

Merlin: What makes you think they would not?

Ursula: I don't know. I never gave it much thought.

Merlin: Yes, well, trees speak to one another; though their language is one most humans would have difficulty recognizing as such. It is a slow tongue, suited for beings locked in place, their only motion upward and outward.

(The grammar's quite tricky, in fact.) Through patient effort, I succeeded in learning the wisdom of the trees, which is strange, unlike anything I had encountered before—or ahead. I had studied the ways and wisdom of animals—I was particularly adept at the hare and the duck—but this was entirely different. It's one thing to try to make sense of a hare explaining the best way to escape a pack of dogs; it's altogether another to parse a sentence which goes on for days describing the changing weather.

Ursula: You could talk to animals?

Merlin: Not only could I speak with them, I could put on their shapes and live among them. I had a brief but tender romance with an absolutely lovely hedgehog... Had we world enough and time, I would transform you and me into, oh, I suppose foxes might have a certain applicability to our present circumstances, and together we would take whatever instruction they had to offer us.

(Ursula looks startled by the suggestion.)

Merlin: For a wizard, the world is a university, ever ready to instruct those willing to heed its teachings.

Ursula: If you say so. But I do not think I would like being a fox.

Merlin: Oh? What would you prefer?

Ursula: A bird—a falcon.

Merlin: How interesting. Perhaps once this present business is over.

Ursula: Wait. Is this some kind of psychological test: "Tell me what animal you would choose to be, and I will tell you about yourself"?

Merlin: Possibly. Mostly, I was asking what kind of

animal you would like to be. (*Begins to walk stage right.*) I believe it is time for us to proceed in this direction.

Ursula: Where to?

Merlin: Come and find out.

(*With a shrug, Ursula follows. As she does, the background starts to move, scrolling stage left to indicate their process. Even the tree stump the two of them have been considering slides stage left, a startling example of* trompe l'oeil. *At the same time, neither Merlin nor Ursula's stride appears false, contrived, the way someone pretending to walk might look. It could be the two of them are moving on top of some type of track inserted into the floor. It could be they're gifted physical actors.*)

Ursula: This ability you have—your foresight. How did you gain it?

Merlin: There are two explanations for my knowledge of the future. The first is that I am living my life backward.

Ursula: How is that possible?

Merlin: I am not one hundred percent certain. I have a theory, which goes something along these lines: viewed from a perspective outside of time (as we understand it), our lives form a kind of grand design, a sculpture in four dimensions. Our consciousness moves in one direction along this sculpture, such that we perceive the past as the past and the future the future. For reasons obscure to me, something happened at what I can only presume is the end of my life to send me backward through it. Since even my mind cannot process the experience of a life lived in reverse, it accommodates the condition as a kind of foresight.

Ursula: You have no idea what the cause was, though.

Merlin: I presume an experiment gone awry, my magic turned against me.

Ursula: Another Nimue?

Merlin: I would not like to think so, but the possibility exists.

Ursula: You said there were two explanations.

Merlin: Yes. The other is that my father is a devil.

Ursula: A what?

Merlin: An incubus, to be precise, a resident of the first circle of Hell. Have you read your Dante?

Ursula: I don't think so. I was never very good in school. Too many fights.

Merlin: Over what?

Ursula: My mother being Algerian and my father Congolese.

Merlin: Ah. Yes, in that regard, I fear the world has little changed since my time.

Ursula: It's fine. I found the Army.

Merlin: You did and if I may say so, you are very good at being a soldier.

Ursula: Thank you. Tell me more about your devil father.

Merlin: Do you know, I never met him? In all my long life, not once have I sought him out, summoned him. Yet I owe so much to the portion of his blood coursing through my veins: my intelligence, my cunning, my skill at the magical arts, and (perhaps) my visions of the future. No doubt one of your psychiatrists would make much of such avoidance.

Ursula: I don't know. It doesn't seem too complicated to me.

Merlin: Doesn't it?

Ursula: You think of yourself as good, as trying to do good things. You're afraid to meet your father and discover you're more like him than you thought.

Merlin (pauses): That may be.

Ursula: So the damned can see the future.

Merlin: According to Dante, yes. One of the torments of their condition, knowing what is to come in the place they have lost forever.

Ursula: Wait. Dante lived when?

Merlin: 1265 to 1321, I believe.

Ursula: How do you know about him? Weren't you in your tree by then?

Merlin: I was, had been for hundreds of years at that point. During those centuries, I had arrived at a way to link my tree to the other trees in the forest. They're quite sensitive to their environment, you know, especially in full bloom. Their leaves pick up all sorts of information from their surroundings, some of it very subtle. By connecting my tree to its fellows, I was able to amplify those abilities, making of the forest a great ear. Unfortunately for me, there wasn't a great deal of interest to listen to. Over time, however, I learned to refine my ear, to enable it to hear farther and wider. It didn't make too much difference. Most of what I listened to consisted of men killing men on an ever-larger scale. I had my fill of that during Arthur's time—before Arthur's time. Do you know, the earliest reports of me, or of the figures some scholars consider the earliest version of me, went mad upon the defeat and death of his beloved king and roamed the forests in his lunacy?

Ursula: Did you?

Merlin: I can't recall. It sounds right. By the time I came to advise Arthur, I had counseled many kings and leaders. Some I had become very fond of. All perished, either due to war or treachery. It can be a bit much, after a time. I do have a memory of my beard becoming tangled in an especially stubborn tree bush, and also of eating acorns, which tends to support the madman-in-the-forest hypothesis.

Ursula: All these kings—what were you doing with them?

Merlin: I was trying to make things better. I could see enough of the future to know that it could be better, it would be better. With each local chief and king I advised, I sought to bring the future a little bit closer, to make daily life a little less bad. Arthur was my greatest success, in part for the way his story lived on after his death, for the inspiration it continued to provide.

Ursula: He was supposed to return, wasn't he? In the hour of England's greatest need, or something like that. Not that it would do us much good here.

Merlin: The exact nature of Arthur's return was never adequately explained or understood. It had less to do with Britain and more with the state of . . . (Merlin waves his hands at the backdrop, the ground, the ashy air.) . . . all of this. He wasn't the only one, you know.

Ursula: The only one who what? Was supposed to come back?

Merlin: Mmm. The legend attaches to a number of similar figures: Charlemagne, Frederick Barbarossa, Ogier the Dane.

Ursula: I don't know the last one, but I'm pretty sure the others lived after you.

Merlin: Like Dante, yes. This returns us to my great ear. For many, many years it brought me only sporadic news of the world outside its rows. Then came radio. What an invention! At first, I was content to listen to whatever was playing from the nearest cottage. The music...it was like seeing a world of color, after having lived in shadows. I listened to reports of the world as it now was, these centuries after the hawthorn had embraced me. From what I had overheard during those long years, I had an idea of the changes the world had undergone, but in many ways, it was incomplete. Now I began to fill in its missing pieces, which helped me to make sense of some of my visions of the future. Just because you can perceive something doesn't mean you understand it, you know. Through a great deal of experimentation, I discovered the leaves on the forest's trees were sensitive to frequencies of light, of energy of which I had been unaware, and this sensitivity could be harnessed, hundreds of millions of leaves yoked together and made into a mighty antenna. Now I was able to sift among the assorted broadcasts with much more discrimination and so to further my education. As time passed, and television opened its glowing eye, and then the internet began to be knitted together, I found with further trial and error I would tap into them, too. So much to learn! In my time, I had been known as the subtlest of men, the wisest of wizards, yet I had comprehended only the smallest portion of the world's knowledge. I drank it as a thirsting man does cold water, my education in the secret arts allowing me to draw connections others had not, to reach insights denied them.

Ursula: But you were still stuck in the tree.

Merlin: This is true. Nimue's spell was fiendishly clever. She had designed it to draw its power from mine, which meant the more I struggled against it, the tighter its hold on me grew. The only solution I could see was to relax my efforts in hopes of starving the spell. This weakened it, but never enough for me to escape.

Ursula: Who let you out, then? Did Nimue finally change her mind?

Merlin: She did not. In fact, I have lost track of her. It is possible she perished sometime in the past fourteen centuries. She may have found her way to Avalon, I suppose, where poor Arthur was taken at the very end. No, what freed me was sorcery of an altogether more terrible kind.

Ursula: The bombs.

Merlin: The Third World War, I gather they're calling it. We should be grateful the arsenals of the respective nuclear powers were only partially emptied before cooler heads prevailed, but what was spent was more than sufficient, I'm sure you agree. The bomb which detonated here was of a relatively low yield; even so, it was of sufficient power to disrupt Nimue's enchantment and allow my escape.

Ursula: And look what you escaped into. You probably wish you were still in the tree.

Merlin: Granted, the world is not as I would have chosen it to be, had I the power to determine such matters. But I have known for a long time that this lay ahead of me. I did not always understand its exact nature: I thought some hapless wizard had brought Hell to Earth.

Ursula: I don't know. Doesn't sound too far off the mark.

Merlin: Ha. I suppose not.

(For a short time, they walk in silence.)

Ursula: This foresight of yours . . .

Merlin: Yes?

Ursula: Does it show you what happens to me?

Merlin: Yes.

Ursula: And . . . ?

Merlin: You are sure you want to hear?

Ursula: Why wouldn't I?

Merlin: It could prove upsetting.

Ursula: More upsetting than surviving a nuclear war, all of your family and friends dead, your country in ruins, your planet poisoned?

Merlin: Very well. A hundred yards ahead, four men are going to shoot you with their machine guns.

(Ursula stops. As does Merlin. As does the backdrop.)

Ursula: Damn.

Merlin: The exact nature of the guns escapes me. I must confess, I find keeping track of all the different firearms humanity has invented (beyond such general categories as blunderbuss, musket, rifle, etc.) hopelessly difficult. It's a blind spot on my part.

Ursula: Four men?

Merlin: Four men. There is a fifth standing nearby. If I am not mistaken, he gives them the order to shoot.

Ursula: What about you?

Merlin: I will not be shot.

Ursula: Good for you. Shit. Shot by four men? With machine guns?

Merlin: As I have said, I don't know the names of the guns.

Ursula: Doesn't matter. Four? There's no chance I survive that. No chance at all. Shit.

Merlin: Are you all right?

Ursula: What does it look like? Machine-gunned, damn. To come through the bombs, all this shit, and this is how I go out?

Merlin: This was why I cautioned you.

Ursula: When I said I would go with you, I didn't think—wait. You knew what was ahead when you asked me to accompany you.

Merlin: I did.

Ursula: And you didn't—why didn't you tell me?

Merlin: There was no point.

Ursula: No—what if I leave? What if, right this moment, I decide I'm through with you and your weird tricks and head back to the rest of the unit as fast as my legs will carry me?

Merlin: You will be shot by four men with machine guns.

Ursula: Shit! Fuck! Seriously?

Merlin: Yes.

Ursula: You aren't lying to me.

Merlin: I am not.

Ursula (exhales, releases her assault rifle, which drops to dangle on its strap, and uses her hands to push back her helmet. Her expression is a mix of exasperation and fear): Were you planning on telling me this?

Merlin: If you had not asked, I would not have

volunteered the information. Since I knew you would ask, I was prepared to tell you.

Ursula: Will I at least get to shoot back?

Merlin: You will not.

Ursula: Then what am I doing with you? Does my dying allow you to win whatever battle we're in? Or to escape?

Merlin: It does not.

Ursula: So why bring me with you?

Merlin: Perhaps because I required a companion on this little voyage, and during the last few weeks I have spent with your unit, I have enjoyed your company the most.

Ursula: How lucky for me.

(Ursula takes her assault rifle in her hands, studies it.)

Ursula: What if I shot you, right here and now?

Merlin: You would not do such a thing.

(Ursula raises the gun to aim it at Merlin, who stands placidly. For a long moment, she sights on the wizard. Finally, with a heavy sigh, she lowers the weapon.)

Ursula: No, I would not.

Merlin: Shall we continue?

Ursula: Might as well.

(The two resume their trek stage right. The backdrop resumes its motion.)

Merlin: It may interest you to know, I was not certain you would not shoot me.

Ursula: Yeah? What happened to your foresight?

Merlin: Your decision was one of those details I could not discern.

Ursula: Which means what?

Merlin (shrugs): You may make of it what you will.

(The scene on the backdrop changes, the charred forest giving way to a large, shallow depression in the earth, its surface spiderwebbed with cracks large and small. Perhaps the possible treadmill upon which Merlin and Ursula have been walking tilts, or perhaps it is an effect of the cunningly rendered backdrop, but the two appear to be descending into the depression.)

Ursula (looking around her): This was a lake.

Merlin: Yes.

(The dried lake bed levels out. Merlin stops and turns to face Ursula.)

Merlin: Do you still have the little shovel you used to bury Sergeant Falcone?

(Ursula allows her gun to swing loose and reaches behind her. From a pouch on her belt, she removes a short-bladed shovel whose folding handle she extends and locks into place.)

Ursula: Here.

Merlin: Marvelous. The inventions of this world never cease to amaze me.

Ursula: Like the bombs?

Merlin: Hmm, yes. Point taken. (He gestures to a spot between them.) Would you dig there?

Ursula: What for?

Merlin: You will know when you find it.

(Ursula slides her assault rifle around to her back and kneels on the dried lake bed. She looks up at Merlin.)

Ursula: Here?

Merlin: Yes.

(Ursula digs with short, effective strokes, piling the

chalky earth to her left. After half a dozen strokes, she stops.)

Ursula: Holy shit. There's someone buried here.

Merlin: Oh?

Ursula: Right below the surface. At least, there's an arm. I found the elbow. Whoever it is, they're wearing some kind of green stuff. I think it's silk.

Merlin: Dig toward the hand.

(Ursula does, working more quickly. She stops.)

Ursula: I found—it's holding something. The hand: It's holding the handle to something. (Without any prompting from Merlin, Ursula continues digging, moving in a straight line as she uncovers more of her discovery. Once she has reached the end of it, she sits back on her knees.) Will you look at that. (She looks up at Merlin.) What now?

Merlin: I have no use for such a thing.

Ursula: Neither do I, not really. (All the same, Ursula sets down the shovel to her left and leans forward. With her right hand, she fiddles with the hand she unearthed; with her left, she slides her fingers under something. She lifts her arms and raises from the earth a scabbarded sword, its hilt, sheath, and the belt wrapped around it gray-white with dust. She stands, still regarding the sword in her hands. Its hilt is simple, made to be gripped single-handed, but long enough to accommodate two. The pommel is a flat circle like a large, thick coin, the guard a straight line. The scabbard is leather or a similar material, its length engraved with narrow characters; the belt is made of the same substance.) I thought I would have to pry the handle from the fingers—maybe break them—but they released the sword on their own.

Merlin: Did they? How interesting. Why don't you try the belt on?

Ursula: I'm not . . . (Ursula wraps the belt around her waist, tying it in a loose knot in front, leaving the sword in its scabbard hanging at her left hip.) . . . Like this?

Merlin: Very nice. Don't you want to have a look at the sword?

(Ursula unsheathes the sword in a single, sweeping motion. Despite the chalky earth covering the hilt, the blade is mirror bright. She gives it a few, experimental slashes.)

Merlin: You handle it quite well.

Ursula: Fencing lessons. Saber, mostly. This is incredibly light.

Merlin: Watch the edge. There is little it will not cut.

(Ursula regards the warning with scorn, continuing to sweep the weapon around her in figure eights.)

Ursula: What is this?

(Before Merlin can respond, a voice from stage right calls the answer.)

Maugris: The weapon in your hand, dear lady, is called Excalibur.

(Accompanied by **four men** dressed in approximately the same fashion as Ursula, except with their rifles up and at the ready, **Maugris** enters stage right. He is a very short man, wearing a dark red robe with a white fur collar. His fingers are crowded with rings of various metals and designs, some studded with bright jewels—emeralds, rubies, sapphires—others plain bands of iron. The top of his uncovered head is bald, but the white hair surrounding it is shoulder long. A pair of muttonchop sideburns frame a face whose features seem crowded together. The soldiers fan out from him and position themselves in a half circle in front of Ursula. Perhaps realizing there is no point in reaching for her own rifle, Ursula has gripped Excalibur's hilt and assumed a defensive posture, her expression fierce. Merlin watches all of this, nonplussed. Maintaining his distance from Merlin, Maugris halts and stands twisting his rings.)

Maugris: And since the sword is Excalibur, the magician must be Merlin.

Merlin: Some men have used that name for me.

Maugris: Very careful of you, good. (He gestures at Ursula.) She is the Arthur?

(Merlin does not answer.)

Maugris: Never mind. You, dear lady! How are you called?

Merlin (raises a warning hand to Ursula): Her name means "little bear."

Maugris: Little bear, eh? Oh, very clever. Arthur, *artus*, bear, so now you choose a little bear. What? Did you hope the difference would be enough to affect this turn of the great cycle?

Ursula: Who the fuck are you?

Merlin: If I am not mistaken, he is known as Maugris. He was . . . associated with Charlemagne.

(Maugris bows.)

(Without shifting his position, the soldier closest to the edge of the stage calls to Maugris.)

Soldier #1: Sir! Please confirm, this is the objective.

Maugris: It is, my friend, it is indeed. This good sir here and I are this very moment conversing about it.

Allow us a minute or two to determine whether or not an arrangement can be reached.

Soldier #1: Yes, sir!

Ursula: Charlemagne? Wasn't he supposed to return as well?

Maugris: He was, dear lady, he was. And he did in his . . . avatar, with me waiting to advise him. Together, we assembled a modest but loyal group of followers to begin the process of bringing light and restoring order to the ravaged world. Sadly, our rather compact army encountered that of Frederick of the red beard, whose avatar had returned to lend his aid to the wounded land. His forces were equal to ours, possibly superior, but I counseled attack.

Ursula: Why? You wanted the same thing, didn't you?

Maugris: Dear lady, two kings cannot rule the same kingdom.

Ursula: You could have worked something out. You could have compromised. Now is not the time for more dick measuring.

Maugris: Have you not witnessed the state of the globe? Now is not the time for weak-kneed half measures. This is the time for decisiveness, for the firm hand of a strong leader.

Merlin: Unless your strong ruler perishes at the hand of the rival he is killing, if I am not mistaken.

Maugris: Ah, here are the powers for which you are famed! True, the leaders fell in valiant combat with one another. It was a setback. While the survivors bound up their injuries, I performed certain acts of divination which allowed me to perceive all was not lost. Although my great rival had been set loose to challenge me once again, he also had found both a warrior fit to stand at my side and the famed weapon with which she would inspire my army.

Merlin: I'm sorry: Are you speaking of me? Your "great rival"? My poor fellow, this is the first time we've met.

Maugris: Ever has it been with our kind: The mere hint of another of equal power is an affront, a challenge waiting to be fulfilled.

Merlin (laughing): Oh, Maugris, whatever gave you the idea we were equals?

Maugris (scowls): Who has outmaneuvered whom, eh?

Merlin: Is that what you have done?

Soldier #1: Sir . . .

Maugris: Patience, my friend. I have the feeling our negotiations are almost at an end.

Soldier #1: Yes, sir.

Maugris: Here is our situation, dear lady. I am in possession of an army comprising the finest soldiers of two great forces—

Merlin: He means the survivors of his colossal blunder.

Maugris: Do you mind?

Merlin: Not at all.

Maugris: This mighty force—

Merlin: Of wounded men and women.

Maugris: —is in need of a leader. Or, not a leader, because in me they already have one. Rather, they require a . . .

Merlin: Figurehead?

Maugris: Figurehead? Yes, why not? Someone to rally behind.

Merlin: Not to mention, to die behind.

Maugris: If necessary.

Merlin: And really, what are the odds? (Overwhelmingly bad, I should say.)

Ursula: You would want someone like me at the front of your forces?

Merlin: Only because he expects you to die right away. Gloriously, I am sure.

Maugris (glares at Merlin): To be frank, dear lady, I should prefer to see the sword you are holding in the possession of . . .

Ursula: Someone more male? More white?

(Maugris shrugs.)

Merlin: Have you encountered Ogier the Dane, or have you killed him, too?

Maugris: I am not sure, but yesterday my snipers shot a man they judged a threat . . .

Ursula: Snipers? How far away was this man?

Maugris: One kilometer? Two? I forget. It was excellent marksmanship. When the scouts brought back a description of his remains, it appeared a distinct possibility he was the Dane.

Merlin: Ogier was one of Charlemagne's paladins, was he not?

Maugris: I would not have expected you to know this.

Merlin: I have had a great deal of time to educate myself. You must have been acquainted with him.

Maugris: Somewhat.

Merlin: And he with you.

Maugris: I am not sure I care for the direction your words are leading.

Merlin: Are they leading somewhere?

Soldier #1: Sir, I thought you said the negotiations were concluding.

Maugris: They are, my patient friend. Here is my offer to you, Little Bear: Come with me and ride at the front of my army. Use your wonderful sword to help me return order to the broken Earth.

Merlin: But if he can have only the sword, he will be satisfied.

Ursula: I believe he would.

Maugris: Well? Will you join my crusade?

Ursula: No.

Maugris: Very well. (Maugris nods to the soldiers, who squeeze the triggers of their weapons. Instantly, the air is full of the deafening stutter of assault rifles set on automatic. Fire flashes from the muzzles; the strong smell of gunpowder wafts from the stage. Ursula, who might have been moving to strike the soldier nearest the audience with the sword, convulses as if caught in a seizure. The soldiers continue to shoot her as she drops first to her knees and then onto her right side. She does not move; nor does she relinquish her grip on Excalibur. Their magazines empty, the soldiers raise their rifles in unison.)

Merlin: That was . . . excessive.

Maugris: You may retrieve the sword, my friend!

(Soldier #1 allows his rifle to swing down on its strap as he crosses from the firing line he and his companions made. The remaining soldiers lower their weapons and remove the magazines from them. Soldier #1 crouches next to Ursula, his back to the audience. He reaches for the sword.)

Merlin: Tell me, Maugris, are you a reader?

(What happens next does so with lightning speed. Soldier #1 jerks, stiffens, and falls on his left side, motionless. Ursula springs to her feet, Excalibur in hand, its end scarlet with Soldier #1's heart's blood. She sprints at the remaining soldiers, who pause in wonderment at the sight of her uninjured—her uniform in ruins, gripping the bloodied sword two-handed—before fumbling to lock the fresh magazines into place. Ursula moves through them relentlessly, felling each man with a single, ferocious stroke that sprays blood across the chalky ground and onto her tattered uniform. For no more than five seconds, the zipper sound of Excalibur slicing through the soldiers' armor, uniforms, and flesh blends with the hiss of venting blood and the grunts and cries of the men. When the last soldier has dropped, she stands, panting, her eyes on Maugris.)

Maugris: How . . . ? No matter.

(Maugris begins to lift his left hand. Merlin, however, has slid off one of the many bracelets on his left wrist, a green glass circle, which he tosses at Maugris. There is a flash of green light. Heavy gray smoke billows around Maugris, obscuring him. From within its roiling depths, he screams.

(Ursula lowers the sword, wipes the blood from it on one of the fallen soldiers' uniforms, and walks over to stand beside Merlin.)

Ursula: Are you sending him to Hell?

Merlin: Heavens, no. There would be too much mischief for him to get into there. (He walks across the stage, waving away the smoke, which is already dissipating. Where Maugris stood, Merlin's green glass bracelet lies flat on the ground. Inside it is a tiny glass figure, a smoky brown, no more than two inches tall. Anyone close enough may see the figure's resemblance to Maugris. Merlin retrieves the bracelet and returns it to his wrist. He removes his hat with his left hand and picks up the glass figure with his right. He straightens, places the figure on top of his head, and puts the hat over it.) Perhaps you are familiar with the adage about keeping your friends close—

Ursula: And your enemies closer, yes.

Merlin: If you can trap those enemies in a special prison, first, better still.

Ursula: What just happened here?

Merlin: Two mighty forces met on the wasteland. They held parley and when no agreement was forthcoming, the larger force attacked the smaller. At first, it went poorly for the smaller force, but they lured their treacherous foes into a trap and defeated them thoroughly. I imagine there will be something about a duel between the armies' wizards, too. In less time than you might suppose, today's events will be referred to as the Fourth World War, when the forces of justice and compassion overcame those of tyranny and cruelty.

Ursula: What the hell are you talking about? I was asking why I'm not dead.

Merlin: Ah. Right. It is because of the scabbard.

Ursula (looks down at the scabbard, touching it with her left hand): This?

Merlin: That. It was made from the skin of a dragon by—never mind all of that. The point is, there is an enchantment on the scabbard which protects its wearer from harm. Mallory wrote about it in his story of Arthur; though how he learned of it I have not been able to find out. This was why I asked Maugris if he was a reader.

Ursula: No shit?

Merlin: None. The sword is an impressive weapon, as you have seen firsthand, but the scabbard is no less powerful. But neither is as important as the one who wields them.

Ursula: You want me to be a king.

Merlin: No.

Ursula: Sorry: queen?

Merlin: No.

Ursula: What word did Maugris use? A figurehead?

Merlin: The word was mine. Also, no.

Ursula: Then what?

Merlin: What you are, already.

Ursula: What I am is a corporal. It's not very much.

Merlin: With Sergeant Falcone's death, you hold the senior rank. You are in charge of your men and women, now, together with those others, those many others, traveling under your protection. The world does not need a king or queen at this time. It needs you.

Ursula: I am some kind of . . . reincarnation of King Arthur?

Merlin: That was how Maugris thought. It is part of the reason he is a little glass figure currently residing under my hat. Arthur was a man, yes, but Arthur is also a role, a part to be played by anyone worthy. I suspected you to be; the sword confirmed it.

Ursula: When the hand released it to me.

Merlin: Yes. Even in her current…condition, the Lady of the Lake retains excellent powers of perception.

Ursula (sheaths the sword): What now?

Merlin: Whatever you choose.

Ursula: We have to return to the others. We've been away far longer than I told them we would be. The army Maugris spoke of: Is it close? Can you tell?

Merlin: Approximately eight kilometers northeast of us.

Ursula: We will have to decide the best way to approach them. Maugris mentioned snipers, which will complicate this. All the same, if it is possible, I would rather not fight them. If we must fight, though, I want to have every advantage we can.

Merlin: Very well. As you say, we had best make our way back to the others.

(The two of them begin to walk stage left.)

Ursula: You might have told me about the scabbard.

Merlin: Would you have believed me?

Ursula (pauses): No. Even after everything you had done before, I would not have.

Merlin: So you understand.

Ursula: I do. However, I am becoming more open-minded.

(Exit stage left.)

For Fiona

ABOUT THE AUTHORS

New York Times best-selling author **Steven Barnes** has published over three million words of fiction, including science fiction, fantasy, horror, mystery, and historical. Winner of the Endeavor and NAACP Image Awards, nominated for Hugo and Nebula Awards, he also writes for film and television, his work appearing on *Stargate SG-1*, *Andromeda*, *Outer Limits*, and *Twilight Zone*, among others. He lives in Southern California with his son Jason, and his wife and writing partner, American Book Award– and British Fantasy Award–winning author, Tananarive Due.

Laird Barron spent his early years in Alaska. He is the author of several books, including *The Beautiful Thing That Awaits Us All*, *Swift to Chase*, and *Worse Angels*. His work has also appeared in many magazines and anthologies. Barron currently resides in the Rondout Valley writing stories about the evil that men do.

A community organizer and teacher, **Maurice Broaddus**'s work has appeared in magazines like *Lightspeed Magazine*, *Beneath Ceaseless Skies*, *Asimov's Science Fiction*, *The Magazine of Fantasy & Science Fiction*, and *Uncanny Magazine*, with some of his stories having been collected in *The Voices of Martyrs*. His books include the urban fantasy trilogy, *The Knights of Breton Court*; the steampunk works *Buffalo Soldier* and *Pimp My*

Airship; and the middle-grade detective novels *The Usual Suspects* and *Unfadeable*. His project *Sorcerers* is being adapted as a television show for AMC. As an editor, he's worked on *Dark Faith*, *Fireside Magazine*, and *Apex Magazine*. Learn more at MauriceBroaddus.com.

D.J. (Dave) Butler has been a lawyer, a consultant, an editor, a corporate trainer, and a registered investment banking representative. His novels published by Baen Books include *Witchy Eye*, *Witchy Winter*, and *Witchy Kingdom*, and *In the Palace of Shadow and Joy*, as well as *The Cunning Man* and *The Jupiter Knife*, co-written with Aaron Michael Ritchey. He also writes for children: The steampunk fantasy adventure tales *The Kidnap Plot*, *The Giant's Seat*, and *The Library Machine* are published by Knopf. Other novels include *City of the Saints* from WordFire Press and *The Wilding Probate* from Immortal Works. Dave also organizes writing retreats and anarcho-libertarian writers' events, and travels the country to sell books. He plays guitar and banjo whenever he can, and likes to hang out in Utah with his wife and children.

Landlocked since birth, **Rodney Carlstrom** still calls the Midwest home. When not writing, you can find him brewing beer or roasting his own coffee beans. "The Door of Return" is his first published short story. You can find him on twitter @RodneyCarlstrom.

Freddy Costello graduated Harvard with a degree in Administrative Documentation Forensics. After school, he was commissioned as a Coast Guard officer and served first aboard an icebreaker as the ship's Beverage Accounting Officer, and in the Pentagon's Planning Management Supervision office. He medically retired after receiving an eye injury from a binder clip battle, for which he earned a Meritorious Service Medal. He now works in the VA as a patient benefits analyst.

Julie Frost is an award-winning author of every shade of speculative fiction. She lives in Utah with her family—a herd of guinea pigs, her husband, and a "kitten" who thinks she's a warrior princess—and a collection of anteaters and Oaxacan carvings, some of which intersect. She enjoys birding and nature photography, which also intersect. Her short fiction has appeared in *Straight Outta Dodge City*, *Monster Hunter Files*, *Writers of the Future*, *The District of Wonders*, *StoryHack*, *Stupefying Stories*, and many other venues. Her werewolf private-eye novel series, *Pack Dynamics*, is published by WordFire Press, and her novel *Dark Day, Bright Hour*, which takes place in Hell, is published by Ring of Fire Press. Find her on Facebook at www.facebook.com/julie.frost.7967/, and you can look her up on Amazon.

Over the past four decades, **Nina Kiriki Hoffman** has sold adult and young adult novels to Ace, Atheneum, Avon, Gold Key, Pocket, Tachyon, and Viking, and the 350+ short stories she has sold have appeared in *Asimov's Science Fiction*, *Analog Science Fiction and Fact*, *The Magazine of Fantasy & Science Fiction*, *Clarkesworld*, *Alfred Hitchcock's Mystery Magazine*, *Cicada*, *Weird*

Tales, *Lightspeed*, *Strange Horizons*, *Daily Science Fiction*, and many other magazines and anthologies. Wildside Press, Pulphouse Publishing, and Fairwood Press have published collections of her stories. Her works have been finalists for the World Fantasy, Mythopoeic, Sturgeon, Philip K. Dick, and Endeavour awards. Her novel *The Thread that Binds the Bones* won a Horror Writers Association Stoker Award, and her short story "Trophy Wives" won a Science Fiction & Fantasy Writers of America Nebula Award. Nina does production work for *The Magazine of Fantasy & Science Fiction*. She has taught at the Clarion and Odyssey workshops, and she currently teaches short-story classes through Lane Community College, Wordcrafters in Eugene, and Fairfield County Writers' Studio. She lives in Eugene, Oregon. For a list of Nina's publications, check out: ofearna.us/books/hoffman.html.

John Langan is the author of two novels and four collections of stories. For his work, he has been awarded the Bram Stoker and This Is Horror Awards. With Paul Tremblay, he coedited *Creatures: Thirty Years of Monsters*. He is one of the founders of the Shirley Jackson Awards and serves on its Board of Directors. He has reviewed horror and dark fantasy for *Locus* magazine. He lives in New York's Hudson Valley with his wife, younger son, and he isn't sure how many animals, anymore. His next collection of stories, *Corpsemouth and Other Autobiographies*, is forthcoming from Word Horde Press.

Stephen Lawson served on three deployments with the

US Navy and is currently a helicopter pilot and commissioned officer in the Kentucky National Guard. He earned a Masters of Business Administration from Indiana University Southeast in 2018, and currently lives in Louisville, Kentucky, with his wife. Stephen's writing has appeared in *Writers of the Future Volume 33*, *Orson Scott Card's InterGalactic Medicine Show*, *Galaxy's Edge*, *Daily Science Fiction*, *The Jim Baen Memorial Short Story Award*, *The Year's Best Military and Adventure Science Fiction*, and *Weird World War III*. His blog can be found at stephenlawsonstories.wordpress.com.

Jonathan Maberry is a *New York Times* best-selling author, five-time Bram Stoker Award winner, three-time Scribe Award winner, Inkpot Award winner, and comic book writer. His vampire apocalypse book series, *V-WARS*, was a Netflix original series. He writes in multiple genres—including suspense, thriller, horror, science fiction, fantasy, and action—for adults, teens and middle grade. His novels include the *Joe Ledger* thriller series, *Bewilderness*, *Ink*, *Glimpse*, the *Pine Deep* Trilogy, the *Rot & Ruin* series, the *Dead of Night* series, *Mars One*, *Ghostwalkers: A Deadlands* novel, and many others. He is the editor of many anthologies including *The X-Files*, *Aliens: Bug Hunt*, *Don't Turn Out the Lights*, *Nights of the Living Dead*, and others. His comics include *Black Panther: DoomWar*, *Captain America*, *Pandemica*, *Highway to Hell*, *The Punisher*, and *Bad Blood*. He is a board member of the Horror Writers Association and the president of the International Association of Media Tie-in Writers. Visit him online at www.jonathanmaberry.com.

Nick Mamatas is the author of several novels, including *I Am Providence* and *The Second Shooter*, and the novella *The Planetbreaker's Son*. His short fiction has appeared in *Best American Mystery Stories*, *Year's Best Science Fiction and Fantasy*, *Asimov's Science Fiction*, Tor.com, and many other venues—much of it was recently collected in *The People's Republic of Everything*. Nick is also an editor; his anthologies include the Bram Stoker Award–winning *Haunted Legends* (with Ellen Datlow), and *Wonder and Glory Forever: Awe-Inspiring Lovecraftian Fiction*.

Dr. Theodore C. McCarthy ("T.C.") is an award-winning and critically acclaimed author and technology development strategist. A former CIA weapons expert, T. C. is a recognized authority on the impact of technology on military strategy and his debut novel, *Germline*, won the Compton Crook Award. T. C.'s latest books, *Tyger Burning* and *Tyger Bright*, were recently published by Baen Books. Find out more at tcmccarthy.com.

Kevin Andrew Murphy grew up in California, earning degrees from UCSC in anthropology/folklore and literature/creative writing, and a masters of professional writing from USC. Over the years he's written role-playing games, short stories, novels, plays, and poems, and created the popular character Penny Dreadful for White Wolf, including writing the novel of the same name. Kevin's also a veteran contributor to George R. R. Martin's Wild Cards series. His Wild Cards story "Find the Lady" for *Mississippi Roll* won the Darrell Award for Best Novella for 2019, and he has a graphic novel featuring his character Rosa Loteria currently being illustrated, plus other projects in the works he can't announce just yet. He brews mead, plays games, and now resides in Reno, Nevada.

Weston Ochse (pronounced oaks) has won the Bram Stoker Award, been nominated for the Pushcart Prize, won four New Mexico-Arizona Book Awards, and been a *USA Today* best-selling author. The American Library Association calls Weston Ochse "one of the major horror authors of the 21st Century." A writer of more than thirty books in multiple genres, his *Burning Sky* duology has been hailed as the best military horror of the generation. His military supernatural series *SEAL Team 666* has been optioned to be a movie starring Dwayne Johnson, and his military sci-fi trilogy, which starts with *Grunt Life*, has been praised for its PTSD-positive depiction of soldiers at peace and at war. Weston has also published literary fiction, poetry, comics, and nonfiction articles. His shorter work has appeared in DC Comics, IDW Comics, *Soldier of Fortune Magazine*, *Weird Tales*, and peered literary journals. His franchise work includes the *X-Files*, *Predator*, *Aliens*, *Hellboy*, Clive Barker's *Midian*, and *V-WARS*. Weston holds a Master of Fine Arts in Creative Writing and teaches at Southern New Hampshire University. A veteran of thirty-five years of military service with multiple combat tours to Afghanistan, he now lives in Arizona with his wife and fellow author, Yvonne Navarro, and their Great Danes.

Erica L. Satifka's fiction has previously appeared in *Clarkesworld*, *Interzone*, and *Weird World War III*. She is also the author of the British Fantasy Award–winning novel *Stay Crazy* (Apex Publications) and the collection *How to Get to Apocalypse and Other Disasters* (Fairwood Press). Find her online at ericasatifka.com.

Martin L. Shoemaker is a programmer who writes on the side...or maybe it's the other way around. Programming pays the bills, but a second-place story in the Jim Baen Memorial Writing Contest earned him lunch with Buzz Aldrin. Programming never did that! His work has appeared in *Analog Science Fiction and Fact*, *Galaxy's Edge*, *Digital Science Fiction*, *Forever Magazine*, *Writers of the Future*, and numerous anthologies including *The Year's Best Military and Adventure SF 4*, *Man-Kzin Wars XV*, *The Jim Baen Memorial Award: The First Decade*, and *Avatar Dreams* from Wordfire Press. His *Clarkesworld* story "Today I Am Paul" appeared in four different year's-best anthologies and eight international editions. His follow-on novel, *Today I Am Carey*, was published by Baen Books in March 2019. His novel *The Last Dance* was published by 47North in November 2019, and the sequel *The Last Campaign* was published in October 2020.

Eric James Stone is a past Nebula Award winner, Hugo Award nominee, and Writers of the Future Contest winner. Over fifty of his stories have been published in venues such as *Year's Best SF*, *Analog Science Fiction and Fact*, and *Nature*. His debut novel, a science fiction thriller titled *Unforgettable*, published by Baen Books, has been optioned by Hollywood multiple times. Eric's life has been filled with a variety of experiences. As the son of an immigrant from Argentina, he grew up bilingual and spent most of his childhood living in Latin America. He also lived for five years in England and became trilingual while serving a two-year mission for his church in Italy. He majored in political science at BYU (where he sang in the Russian Choir for two years) and then got a law degree from Baylor. He did political work in Washington, D.C., for several years before shifting career tracks. He now works as a systems administrator and programmer. Eric lives in Utah with his wife, Darci, who is an award-winning author herself, in addition to being a high school science teacher and programmer. Eric's website is www.ericjamesstone.com.

Brad R. Torgersen is a multi-award-winning science fiction and fantasy writer whose book *A Star-Wheeled Sky* won the 2019 Dragon Award for Best Science Fiction Novel at the thirty-third annual DragonCon fan convention in Atlanta, Georgia. A prolific short-fiction author, Torgersen has published stories in numerous anthologies and magazines, including several Best of Year editions. Brad is named in *Analog Science Fiction and Fact*'s who's who of top *Analog* authors, alongside venerable writers like Larry Niven, Lois McMaster Bujold, Orson Scott Card, and Robert A. Heinlein. Married for over twenty-five years, Brad is also a United States Army Reserve Chief Warrant Officer—with multiple deployments to his credit—and currently lives with his wife and daughter in the Mountain West, where they keep a small menagerie of dogs and cats.

Brian Trent's work regularly appears in *Analog Science Fiction and Fact*, *The Magazine of Fantasy & Science Fiction*, *The Year's Best Military and Adventure SF*, *Terraform*, *Daily Science Fiction*, *Apex*, *Pseudopod*, *Escape Pod*, *Galaxy's Edge*, *Nature*, and numerous year's-best anthologies. The author of the sci-fi novels *War Hero* and *Ten Thousand Thunders*, Trent is a winner of the 2019 Year's Best Military and Adventure SF Readers' Choice Award from Baen Books and a Writers of the Future winner. He is also a contributor to *Weird World War III* and the Black Tide Rising anthology *We Shall Rise*. Trent lives in New England. His website is www.briantrent.com.

It wasn't until **David VonAllmen**'s high school professor thought one of his short stories was suspiciously high in literary merit and threatened to have him expelled for plagiarism that he realized he just might have the talent to be a real writer. David's writing has appeared in *Galaxy's Edge*, *Writers of the Future*, *Deep Magic*, and other professional publications, and has been published in Chinese translation. David is the Grand Prize winner of the 2018 Baen Fantasy Adventure Award. He lives in his hometown of St. Louis with his wife, Ann, and children, Lucas and Eva, who write some pretty darn good stories of their own. Links to his works can be found at davidvonallmen.com.

Michael Z. Williamson is, variously, an immigrant from the UK and Canada, a retired veteran of the USAF and US Army with service in the Middle East, the Mississippi Flood, and several cornfields and deserts. He's an award-winning and best-selling author and editor of science fiction, and a #1 Amazon bestseller in political humor. His favorite administrative tool is a flamethrower.

Deborah A. Wolf was born in a barn and raised on wildlife refuges, which explains rather a lot. She has worked as an underwater photographer, Arabic linguist, and grumbling wage slave, but never wanted to be anything other than an author. Deborah's first trilogy, *The Dragon's Legacy*, has been acclaimed as outstanding literary fantasy and shortlisted for such notable honors as the Gemmell Award. This debut was followed by *Split Feather*, a contemporary work of speculative fiction which explores the wildest side of Alaska. Deborah currently lives in northern Michigan. She has four kids (three of whom are grown and all of whom are exceptional), an assortment of dogs and horses, and two cats, one of whom she suspects is possessed by a demon. Deborah is represented by Mark Gottlieb of Trident Media Group.

ABOUT THE EDITOR

Sean Patrick Hazlett is an Army veteran, speculative fiction writer and editor, and finance executive in the San Francisco Bay area. He holds an AB in history and BS in electrical engineering from Stanford University, and a Master in Public Policy from the Harvard Kennedy School of Government, where he won the 2006 Policy Analysis Exercise Award for his work on policy solutions to Iran's nuclear weapons program under the guidance of future secretary of defense Ashton B. Carter. He also holds an MBA from the Harvard Business School, where he graduated with Second Year Honors. As a cavalry officer serving in the elite 11th Armored Cavalry Regiment, he trained various Army and Marine Corps units for war in Iraq and Afghanistan. While at the Army's National Training Center, he became an expert in Soviet doctrine and tactics. He has also published a Harvard Business School case study on the 11th Armored Cavalry Regiment and how it exemplified a learning organization. Sean is a 2017 winner of the Writers of the Future Contest. Over forty of his short stories have appeared in publications such as *The Year's Best Military and Adventure SF*, *Year's Best Hardcore Horror*, *Terraform*, *Galaxy's Edge*, *Writers of the Future*, *Grimdark Magazine*, *Vastarien*, and *Abyss & Apex*, among others. He is also the editor of the *Weird World War III* anthology. Sean also teaches strategy, finance, and communications as a course facilitator at the Stanford Graduate School of Business's Executive Education Program. You can find him on his YouTube channel, *Through a Glass Darkly*, where the paranormal meets military science fiction and fact, and he interviews national security professionals, writers, and other content creators on everything within the current cultural zeitgeist and beyond. He is an active member of the Horror Writers Association and Codex Writers' Group.

Shadow of Victory   pb • 978-1-4814-8288-2 • $10.99

"This latest Honor Harrington novel brings the saga to another crucial turning point. . . . Readers may feel confident that they will be Honored many more times and enjoy it every time."   —*Booklist*

Uncompromising Honor   hc • 978-1-4814-8350-6 • $28.00
     pb • 978-1-9821-2413-7 $10.99

When the Manticoran Star Kingdom goes to war against the Solarian Empire, Honor Harrington leads the way. She'll take the fight to the enemy and end its menace forever.

HONORVERSE VOLUMES

Crown of Slaves   pb • 978-0-7434-9899-9 • $7.99
(with Eric Flint)

Torch of Freedom   hc • 978-1-4391-3305-7 • $26.00
(with Eric Flint)

Cauldron of Ghosts   pb • 978-1-4767-8100-6 • $8.99
(with Eric Flint)

To End in Fire   hc • 978-1-9821-2564-6 • $27.00
(with Eric Flint)

Sent on a mission to keep Erewhon from breaking with Manticore, the Star Kingdom's most able agent and the Queen's niece may not even be able to escape with their lives . . .

House of Steel   tpb • 978-1-4516-3893-6 • $15.00
(with Bu9)   pb • 978-1-4767-3643-3 • $7.99

The Shadow of Saganami   hc • 978-0-7434-8852-0 • $26.00

Storm From the Shadows   hc • 978-1-4165-9147-4 • $27.00
     pb • 978-1-4391-3354-5 • $8.99

As war erupts, a new generation of officers, trained by Honor Harrington, are ready to hit the front lines.

A Beautiful Friendship   hc • 978-1-4516-3747-2 • $18.99
     YA tpb • 978-1-4516-3826-4 • $9.00

Fire Season	hc • 978-1-4516-3840-0 • $18.99
(with Jane Lindskold)	
Treecat Wars	pb • 978-1-4767-3663-1 • $9.99
(with Jane Lindskold)	

"A stellar introduction to a new YA science-fiction series."
—*Booklist*, starred review

A Call to Duty	hc • 978-1-4767-3684-6 • $25.00
(with Timothy Zahn)	pb • 978-1-4767-8168-6 • $8.99
A Call to Arms	hc • 978-1-4767-8085-6 • $26.00
(with Timothy Zahn & Thomas Pope)	pb • 978-1-4767-8156-3 • $9.99
A Call to Vengeance	hc • 978-1-4767-8210-2 • $26.00
(with Timothy Zahn & Thomas Pope)	pb • 978-1-4814-8373-5 • $9.99
A Call to Insurrection	hc • 978-1-9821-2589-9 • $27.00
(with Timothy Zahn & Thomas Pope)	

The Royal Manticoran Navy rises as a new hero of the Honorverse answers the call!

ANTHOLOGIES EDITED BY WEBER

More Than Honor	pb • 978-0-6718-7857-3 • $7.99
Worlds of Honor	pb • 978-0-6715-7855-8 • $7.99
Changer of Worlds	pb • 978-0-7434-3520-8 • $7.99
The Service of the Sword	pb • 978-0-7434-8836-5 • $7.99
In Fire Forged	pb • 978-1-4516-3803-5 • $7.99
Beginnings	hc • 978-1-4516-3903-2 • $25.00

THE DAHAK SERIES

| *Mutineers' Moon* | pb • 978-0-6717-2085-8 • $7.99 |

Empire From the Ashes tpb • 978-1-4165-0993-2 • $16.00
Contains *Mutineers' Moon, The Armageddon Inheritance,* and *Heirs of Empire* in one volume.

THE BAHZELL SAGA

Oath of Swords	tpb • 978-1-4165-2086-3 • $15.00
	pb • 978-0-671-87642-5 • $7.99
The War God's Own	hc • 978-0-6718-7873-3 • $22.00
	pb • 978-0-6715-7792-6 • $7.99
Wind Rider's Oath	pb • 978-1-4165-0895-3 • $7.99
War Maid's Choice	pb • 978-1-4516-3901-8 • $7.99
The Sword of the South	hc • 978-1-4767-8084-9 • $27.00
	tpb • 978-1-4767-8127-3 • $18.00
	pb • 978-1-4814-8236-3 • $8.99

Bahzell Bahnakson of the hradani is no knight in shining armor and doesn't want to deal with anybody else's problems, let alone the War God's. The War God thinks otherwise.

OTHER NOVELS

The Excalibur Alternative	pb • 978-0-7434-3584-2 • $7.99

An English knight and an alien dragon join forces to overthrow the alien slavers who captured them. Set in the world of David Drake's Ranks of Bronze.

In Fury Born	tpb • 978-1-9821-2573-8 • $18.00

A greatly expanded new version of Path of the Fury, with almost twice the original wordage.

1633	pb • 978-0-7434-7155-8 • $7.99
(with Eric Flint)	
1634: The Baltic War	pb • 978-1-4165-5588-9 • $7.99
(with Eric Flint)	

American freedom and justice versus the tyrannies of the 17th century. Set in Flint's 1632 universe.

The Apocalypse Troll	tpb • 978-1-9821-2512-7• $16.00

After UFOs attack, a crippled alien lifeboat drifts down and homes in on Richard Ashton's sailboat, leaving Navy man Ashton responsible for an unconscious, critically wounded, and impossibly human alien warrior—who also happens to be a gorgeous female.

THE STARFIRE SERIES WITH STEVE WHITE

The Stars at War   hc • 978-0-7434-8841-5 • $25.00
Rewritten *Insurrection* and *In Death Ground* in one massive volume.

The Stars at War II   hc • 978-0-7434-9912-5 • $27.00
The Shiva Option and *Crusade* in one massive volume.

PRINCE ROGER NOVELS WITH JOHN RINGO

"This is as good as military sf gets."   —*Booklist*

March Upcountry   pb • 978-0-7434-3538-3 • $7.99

March to the Sea   pb • 978-0-7434-3580-2 • $7.99

March to the Stars   pb • 978-0-7434-8818-1 • $7.99

Throne of Stars   omni tpb • 978-1-4767-3666-2 • $14.00
March to the Stars and *We Few* in one massive volume.

GORDIAN PROTOCOL SERIES WITH JACOB HOLO

The Gordian Protocol   pb • 978-1-9821-2459-5 • $8.99

The Valkyrie Protocol   hc • 978-1-9821-2490-8 • $27.00
                                     pb • 978-1-9821-2562-2 • $8.99
Untangling the complex web of the multiverse is not a job for the faint of heart. Navigating the paradoxes of time can be a killer task. But Agent Raibert Kaminski and the crew of the Transtemporal Vehicle *Kleio* won't go down without a fight, no matter where—or *when*—the threat to the multiverse arises!